VERDANT DIVIDED
Technology Meets Holy War

Empathic Humanity Book 2

Doc Honour

Copyright

The characters and events in this book are fictitious. Any similarity to real persons, living or dead, is coincidental and not intended by the author.

Copyright ©2025 by Doc Honour

For information contact: DocHonourBooks.com

ISBN
979-8-9875022-5-9 (Hard cover)
979-8-9875022-6-6 (Paperback)

Introduction

Is faith really opposed to science? Or science to faith?

Many proponents from either side would like us to believe so. Scientists deride creationists: "We have a geological record that goes back billions of years! How can you possibly believe one religious writing claiming a Creator made it all six thousand years ago?" And the counter-claims: "There is so much science doesn't know. We can't even figure out where thought and self-awareness come from! How can you possibly claim to be the authoritative answer to everything?"

Yet the world and its people are not so simple. It seems to this humble author there is truth to both sets of claims. Through the scientific method, humans have indeed come to understand amazing things about our Universe. That understanding affects all our lives, giving us technology and tools to live better than any generation before us. Yet there also seem to be things for which spiritual faith has better answers, particularly having to do with what we do with those rich lives we have.

In this book, you will find two main characters in intertwined plot lines. One is a successful scientist and engineer, the other a noted man of faith. Both have dreams they pursue. Their methods vary, of course, but the results appear similar: they are beset with problems that take their best to solve. And hence lies a tale.

I hope you enjoy every step of the path.

Doc Honour
January 2025

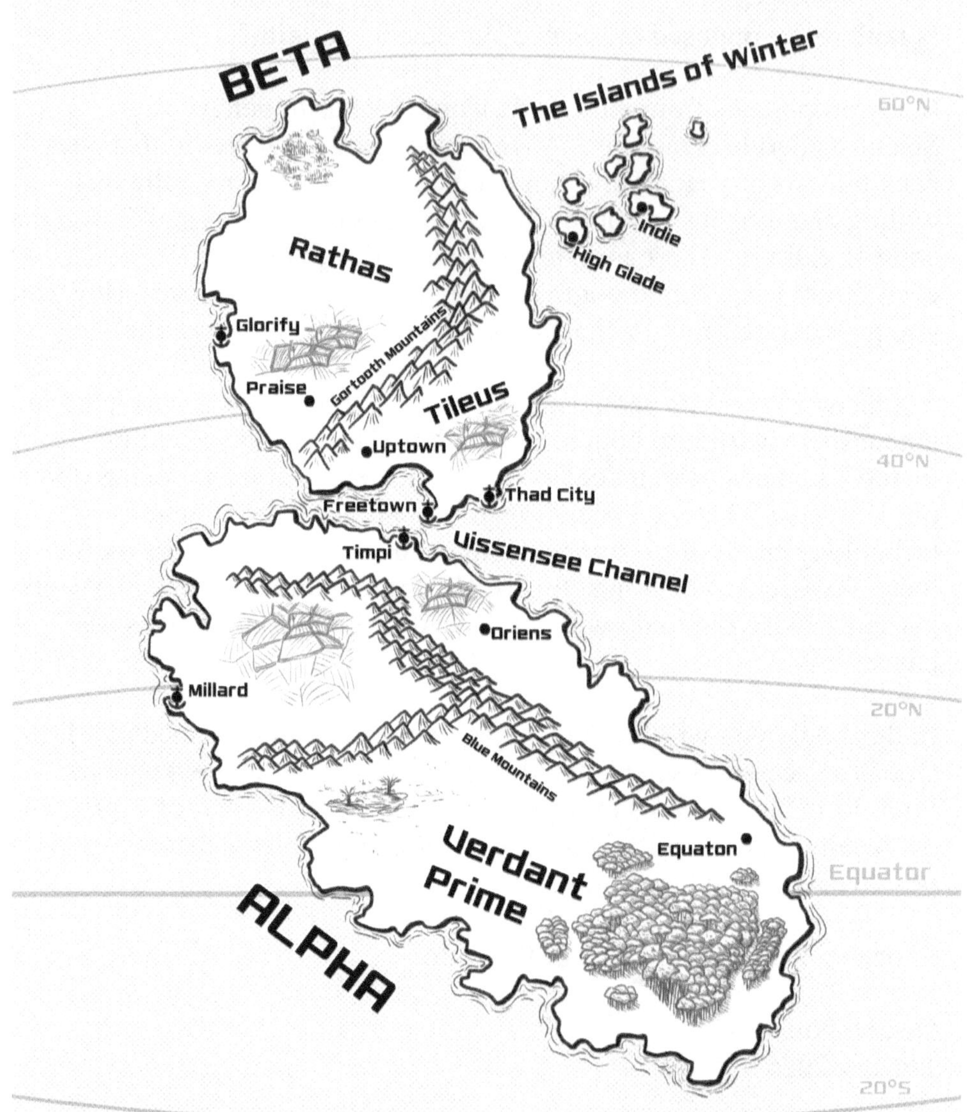

Verdant

Illustration by J.N. Hinge

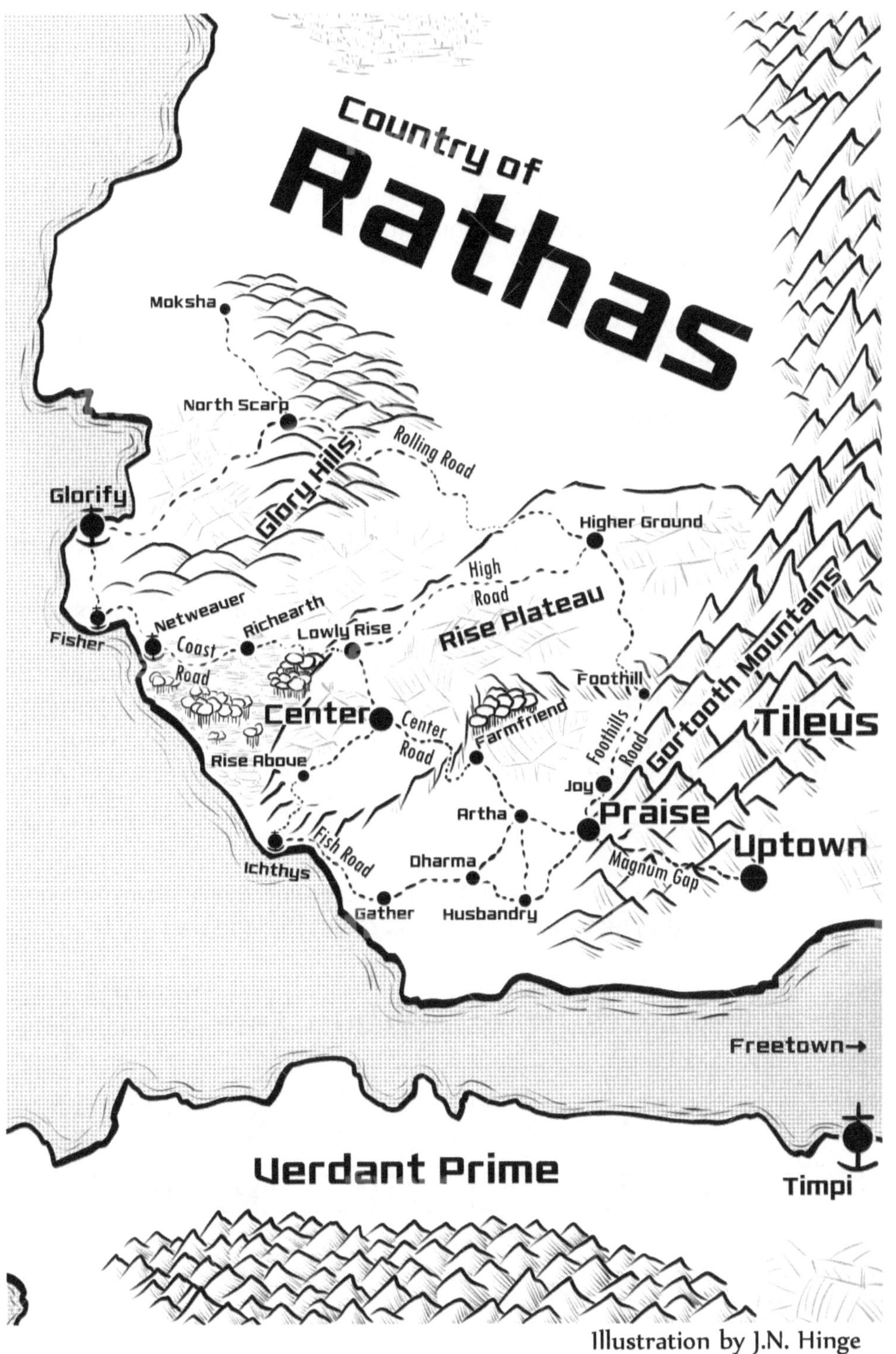

Illustration by J.N. Hinge

Time on Verdant

Imagine living on a world with a sixteen-hour daily rotation. Days are short, and so are the nights. People sleep for six hours, work for six hours, and have four hours for morning, noon, and evening time.

Imagine a year of 450 such days. Such a year is only 82% as long as Earth. Years pass fast.

Yet humans can and do adjust.

Months

Unober – winter solstice 1st
Duember
Tritember– equinox 23rd
Quartember
Quintember
Hexember –solstice 1st
September
October– equinox 23rd
November
December

Days

Hours, minutes and seconds are unchanged from now. A typical rapid 16-hour day consists of

3-00:	Dawn
4-00 to 7-30:	Work
8-00:	Noon
8-30 to 11-00	Work
11-00:	Sunset

All months are 45 days and have the same calendar. Every fifth year, an extra day (Holiday) inserts between December 45th and Unober 1st.

Work week						Weekend		
Newday	Twoday	Wentday	Midday	Thruday	Friday	Playday	Sitday	Endday
1	2	3	4	5	6	7	8	9
10	11	12	13	14	15	16	17	18
19	20	21	22	23	24	25	26	27
28	29	30	31	32	33	34	35	36
37	38	39	40	41	42	43	44	45

1 — Vision Marketing

The transpath became a breakthrough technology as big as the repellor beam. By giving people complete empathy toward others' feelings, a few leaders hoped it would transform humanity. After its amazing success in the Tileus/Prime negotiations, stopping an impending global war, some thought it would race into implementation. Instead, the transpath spread slower at first. Technology limited its use to fixed locations. Further development would be necessary before it could be used widely.

—The Making of a New Humanity by Ellen Thranadil, Tileus Press 448 A.T.

A long-range aircar descended out of a bright blue-white sky toward the landing pad on top of Solity House, the capital building in the planet's original country of Verdant Prime. Using repellor beams, the car floated through the air like a wingless bird.

Inside the car, Jacoby Palatin held his wife Zofia's hand. He glanced over at her, still astonished after a year she had said "yes." She had such incredible beauty, tall and well-proportioned with waist-length, sleek black hair. She smiled at him, her grey eyes sparkling. Self-conscious, he ran fingers through his striking dark red hair, then patted her hand.

They'd been chatting about the sights, but now fell silent. Returning to Verdant Prime for the first time made him uneasy. A year ago, they'd done everything they could to escape this totalitarian country. They'd been chased, shot at, and smuggled in a boat's hold. And here they were, about to land on the central government building.

Jake looked at familiar sights from the air. The city of Oriens spread below them, where they'd both grown up. Touchdown Park blazed a rectangle of green grass and varicolored trees in the city center. The park held the Mueller Memorial, dedicated to the colony ship captain who brought people to Verdant over four hundred years ago. Adjacent to the park, the Warrens jarred the city regularity with a tangle of buildings that looked like they'd been dropped haphazardly from orbit. Zofia had grown up in those slums.

It had been a strange, eventful, and scary courtship for them—a danger-filled romance that changed the world. They had stopped a global war in the making.

"I've got some scary memories here. Are you sure about coming back, Bucko?" asked Zofia in her low, breathy voice. "Have they really changed?"

He squeezed her hand and turned to her. "Well, we're following the advice of Ellen Thranadil, as we have all this year. It's pretty special to have business advice from the national Governor of Commerce and Industry." He paused. "The leaders in Verdant Prime say they've changed, and they welcome us back. The Solity Council has new leadership, and they're interested in our transpath. They want what we have."

"Hard to believe we left here running for our lives and now come back as successful entrepreneurs. We didn't even know what an 'entrepreneur' was when we lived here."

Running for their lives. They'd fled through the Warrens and Touchdown Park, pursued by Solity Police firing at them with needle guns. They'd eventually escaped across the Vissensee Channel to their new country of Tileus.

"Yeah, we've come a long way. Prime didn't use money, with everything controlled by the government. We had to learn how to work finances. Ellen's been a big help, showing us how to run a business. Now I'm CEO of TechEmpath and you've been buried in the labs as VP of Development. You probably don't know how wide our spread is. We've got transpath systems in conference rooms all over Tileus, and we're making inroads in the countries of Verdant Prime and Rathas. Lots of people have learned to rely on our empathy technology to understand each other better."

She laughed and poked a finger in his rib. "You've done a pretty good job learning how to do politics, kiddo."

"I don't know; I still feel naïve and inadequate. I'm a physicist and engineer at heart. There's way too much I don't know."

"Maybe. I don't know enough about being VP and managing our employees, either. I'd rather just do programming. I think we're both still struggling to fill our new shoes. But bangit, we keep our eye on the prize, don't we? If we can spread the t-path through all of Verdant, and then to the other two human worlds, we can change the way humanity thinks. Imagine if everyone could feel what others feel. It's just about impossible to lie or cheat."

He looked out the window again, feeling the frightening depth of their incredible goal. "That's the prize, for sure."

She took a deep breath and nodded. "So, this is an opportunity to launch our new product. I'm excited about what the team has created. Despite my concerns about being back here in Prime, thanks for setting up this meeting. It'll be my first chance to do a sales pitch."

"Instead of remembering what these people used to be, think of them as a favorable customer. Remember, they already bought a dozen conference room systems. They have that larger version. We can pitch the new personal-sized product to them."

"Who installed the conference rooms?"

"I hired Indy Westleaf as our business agent here. We've got similar agents in the countries of Rathas and Winter."

"He assisted you on the antimatter bomb here in General Defense, right?"

"Yeah. And a good friend, too. Glad that bomb development is over."

Jake looked down at the approaching rooftop. "Indy doesn't know yet about the new product. I think that may be him in the group down there—the one in regular clothes instead of standard Verdant Prime coveralls."

Even with his assurances to Zofia, Jake's stomach tightened when he saw the phalanx of people waiting on the rooftop, all but Indy dressed in purple coveralls.

"Man, I'd forgotten about purple being administrators," Zofia said. "I never liked them."

"Same here. But the administrators are the ones we've come to meet. They're the ones who will buy our products." He tightened his grip on her hand. "With no free-market economy, they're the only ones who can buy anything."

"And it'll be up to us to get them to buy. We can do that." She suddenly laughed. "Are all those people here to greet us, like celebrities? Quite a welcome party for a couple of forgiven rebels."

Jake added a sober thought. "I wish Yitzak Goren were still here to see what we've done with his invention."

"Yeah. We never did get to thank him before he died."

The aircar touched down and its door opened.

"Time to go to work," Jake said.

⧉ ❋ ⧉

He and Zofia walked across the rooftop toward the purple-clad group. Indy and one woman stepped out to greet them. Indy smiled, greeting an old friend.

"Welcome back, Jake," Indy said. "Good to see you again. Hi, Zofia."

He shook hands with both, his manner easy and at peace, every strand of dark hair in place.

"Let me introduce you to Calie Pires, the Director of State."

Fiftyish and medium height—a bit taller than Indy—the woman had auburn hair shot with grey, warm brown eyes, and a ready smile. Her well-tailored purple coveralls had a shoulder band of dark green designating State Department.

Jake extended his hand. "I met her last year, Indy. Good morning, Director. Glad to meet you in better circumstances."

"Good morning, Jake," she said. "I agree."

Jake finished the introduction. "Director Pires, this is my wife and business partner. Zofia, the director presided at those ill-fated negotiations last year."

Pires laughed gently. "Not so ill-fated after all, Jake. We had some scary excitement when Director Denmark pulled a gun and shot up the room, but your transpath changed the day, not to mention the future."

Jake inclined his head. "The t-path isn't just mine. The original credit goes to the brilliant Yitzak Goren, and Zofia came up with the last stitch of technology that made it work. We've had a team of developers working on it."

"I never knew how it all happened," Pires said, "but it worked. After Denmark's breakdown, we negotiated a peace with Tileus that's been changing life in Prime."

"We'd love to hear more about those changes," said Zofia. "Prime was once our home."

Pires and her people ushered them to a lift tube. Stepping into the empty column of air, repellor beams dropped them one level to the fifth floor. They walked through a corridor with rich wood-paneled walls and thickly carpeted floors, lined with paintings of past Solity leaders, each one identified by name, position, and years of office. Jake had never worked at high levels of the country; he didn't know any of these people. He watched with trepidation for a picture of Director Denmark, who'd been his direct boss and the man who'd been instrumental in the terrible events. He didn't see one. *Guess they decided not to honor him.*

Pires guided them to the most ornate entrance in the hallway, a pair of high-relief carved doors with stylized scenes from the entire planet. Jake marveled at carvings of monster fish from the northern oceans, snowclad mountains, idyllic beaches, and wild jungles. All by themselves, the doors became an exquisite celebration of Verdant.

When they entered the room, Jake's breath caught. *Never in my wildest imagination had I dreamed of being in this room.*

The huge space had a glass wall overlooking Oriens city. The Fundament filled the room, an awe-inspiring conference table about which Jake had only heard. This table had the reputation as the seat of Solity power, the center of the immense spiderweb of this socialist country, where the Council met to make national and international decisions. The amazing workmanship in the table organized stunning wood grains to swirl in symmetrical patterns that focused attention on each director's place. Some of the dents in the wood testified to occasions when power had changed hands less smoothly than others. The Fundament dominated the room, exuding the rich history of Jake's former country.

He turned to Calie Pires. "We are honored, Director," he said. "We'd thought to meet with your lower-level people in some normal conference room."

"Not at all," she responded. "I've spoken with my counterpart Ellen Thranadil in Tileus. Distributing your transpath throughout Verdant Prime is one of the most important things we can do to ease the remaining tensions in the world. I would hope the other countries of Verdant feel the same way."

Jake stopped in sudden surprise because he felt inside his own mind the warmth, acceptance, and eagerness with which the director approached this meeting. The sensation exceeded just body reading or facial clues; like a sixth sense, Jake felt and understood the emotions of another person.

The room had the empathic field of a transpath.

But of course, Jake and Zofia knew the sensation. Their TechEmpath company still had the monopoly to create and install t-paths. Apparently, Indy had already installed a system in this room. Around the ceiling, the antenna heads mounted around the room provided the field. *Good. This meeting'll go a lot smoother with the t-path.*

A few more people waited for them in the room. Most wore purple, with one in coveralls of Technology yellow and two in the dark blue of the Capital Department.

Indy stepped in to introduce the remaining people. Jake caught only a few of the names, relying on Indy to maintain the relationships. That's why Jake had him as an agent.

While they took seats, Pires said, "You asked for this meeting and promised something new. Why don't you start by telling us what you've done with the transpath?"

Jake nodded and turned to Zofia. "Your turn, love."

As they had planned, Zofia transferred presentation materials from her implant to the room's projection system. A holo of the world's two continents appeared over the table. When she spoke, the images complemented her words, zooming in on various locations to show details.

"Yitzak Goren was an amazing man with knowledge across many fields. He discovered a connection between particle waves and brain activity. Using that knowledge, he built the first transpath here in Oriens, enough to fill his small lab with an empathic field. Last year, for the negotiations, we extended his design to cover a large conference room."

The holo showed images of the system parts installed in the Freedom Aerie government house in Tileus. The antenna heads at the edge of the ceiling were identical with those here in the Solity Council chambers. The display also showed the half-meter-sized wave exciters mounted above the ceiling.

"And of course," Zofia said, "you know what happened next, Director Pires."

The director nodded. "Understanding each other's emotions transformed the negotiations. We came to effective and lasting agreements."

"Yes, indeed. Since then, well, shoot, it's taken off," she said. "Jake tells me we've installed it in just about every conference room in Tileus. We sent people over here three months ago to help Indy make a few installations in Prime, as well." Zofia pointed to the antenna heads around the room.

Another director spoke. "Yes, and it's made a positive difference in our Solity Council meetings. Secret politics are a thing of the past, in just these few months. It's difficult for anyone to keep secrets when their emotions are on display to all."

Pires nodded. "It's been a game-changer."

Jake felt their conviction and interest through the t-path.

Zofia continued the presentation, but a text message through his implant distracted Jake, coming from Elena Hahn, his agent in Rathas. He subvocalized to direct the message to his visual receptors.

Have a problem. I've got One Church resistance to the t-path. Can't get access to presentation rooms. Can you and Zofia come here tomorrow to refresh our agreements?

Jake compressed his jaw. *Thought we'd already ironed out those differences.* He responded to the agent in the affirmative. He and Zofia had planned to go to Rathas later, but it appeared to be necessary now. *We'll have to make today count here in Prime.*

He returned his attention to Zofia's presentation where the holo zoomed from a world-wide display of t-path locations to a close-up of their TechEmpath building in Thad City.

"Meanwhile," Zofia continued, "our development team has been reducing the size and extending the range. And that's why we're here today. We'd like you to think about buying our newest product, a personal unit small enough to carry on your belt."

She reached into her carry bag and laid one on the table. The size of a closed fist, the transpath presented as a smooth white box with rounded edges and a clip on the back.

Jake took up the presentation. "This new item takes the place of the whole system in this room: antenna head, wave exciters, and nanoprocessors."

The man in Technology yellow raised his hand, transpathing surprise. "How can you generate enough power to create particle waves in such a small device?"

"I won't go into the technical details," said Jake, "but the answer lies in the same technology as the widely-used repellors that got us into space in the first place. Like the repellors, the device draws power from the gravitic fields all around us, concentrating that power as needed."

He turned back to the others. "What you need to know is this unit is personalized to the owner. Unlike the room-sized system, it only operates one direction. The owner senses the emotions of anyone within six meters, while those others feel nothing."

The room exploded with emotions. The directors displayed thoughtfulness and intense interest. Indy pathed delight. The technical man seemed cautious.

Calie Pires transpathed excitement. "So, with this new version," she enthused, "we can give the transpath to everyone and create a new norm of understanding for humanity."

"That's the idea," said Jake. "We'd like to get all the countries of Verdant on board. And then we'll spread it to the other worlds."

2 – Miracles

In the final stages, events in the country of Rathas moved quickly, involving people from high estate to low. Many of the events were hardly understandable to those outside the religious world of the state Church.

—*An Annotated History of Verdant* by Ellen Thranadil, Tileus Press 442 A.T.

Everyone called him Reb as an honorific title, Reb Fenet Powrfaith. "Reb Fenet, please heal my mother." "Reb Fenet, come stop the rain." In his country of Rathas, a powername reflected demonstrable aspects of a person's character. For Fenet, his character included the demonstrated power of his faith in Elláh, hence "Powrfaith."

Fenet performed miracles for Elláh. Someday, he hoped, he'd be as famous as the Zikri who founded the One Church back on Earth.

On this bright fall day, Fenet led his six disciples, the Khadam, along a country road. A small crowd followed. His disciples, called novim, ranged in age between seventeen and twenty-four years old. Verdant years, shorter by twenty percent than the old Earth standard. Verdant had the shortest orbit of the three remaining human worlds. To someone from old Earth, the disciples would all have been teenagers still.

"Hey, Beneim, watch this!" Nov Durnadat had been studying with Fenet for two years. Short and rotund, with brown curly hair and laughing brown eyes, the nineteen-year-old jumped across the roadside ditch and back. He looked like a bouncing ball.

Red-haired Nov Beneim snorted a laugh. "Settle down, Durnadat. You're like a whirling dervish sometimes."

At age forty-seven, Fenet knew he didn't look much like a minister. Most clerics in the Church-controlled country of Rathas wore grey robes. Fenet chose instead loose-legged pants and a short tunic, not unlike the work clothes worn in this farming area. He also wore his grey hair long, topped by a wide-brimmed floppy hat with a single wildflower at a cocky angle. He always carried a small copy of *The Holiest* in a back pocket, opening it frequently though he had it memorized. Oh, and one ordinary miracle: the wildflower on his hat never wilted.

His disciples, on the other hand, wore the clerical robes, with a collar designating their status by color—for novim, bright yellow that warned people their theology might not yet be correct. Fenet gave in to custom enough to wear the tan collar reserved for full ministers.

Behind Fenet, Durnadat gave Scanat a friendly push.

Scanat, the oldest of the novim, brushed him off. "Knock it off. I'm thinking here, trying to memorize some of Reb Fenet's scriptures." Despite his study, Scanat still overcontrolled himself. His eyebrows frequently furrowed in concentration.

Looking ahead, a thunderstorm brewed toward them, dark clouds piling in the sky and tossing the trees visible across the fields. In the near fields, Brother Dilihand's farm harvest still stood on the stalk, at risk of being ruined by the storm. The harvester sat idle behind his stalled tractor. Disturbed ground and chopped neowheat filled Fenet's head with their rich scent. Dilihand looked desperate.

HEAL THE MAN'S TRACTOR, FENET.

Elláh's voice sounded quietly in the back of Fenet's mind, filled with peace. Divine direction. His heart swelled with joy once again about the power Elláh gave him. Fenet turned off the repellor beams on his belt, putting full weight on his fragile hip joints. He struggled through the ditch into Dilihand's field.

"Hold on, guys," said Scanat behind him. "Reb Fenet's off again."

The novim stopped on the road to wait.

Dilihand stepped toward Fenet. "Can you help, Reb Fenet? I've got to get this crop in."

"Let's see what Elláh may do, Brother."

The trifacis symbol of the One Church, a Celtic circle-in-triangle, blessed the engine cowl of the tractor. Fenet laid his hands on the symbol and raised his voice.

"Be healed, machine." Quiet but forceful words. In his experience, that—and faith in Elláh—did what Elláh wanted.

The variable winds of the coming storm focused through Fenet. A familiar supernatural rush caught his breath. The brim of his hat waved to the sky, the wildflower tearing off to fly away. A visible red glow of energy moved through his hands to the tractor with a faint crackling. The engine whirred into spinning action, ready to work the field.

Fenet laughed in the joy of working a miracle again. He loved it when Elláh granted power, though such incidents had become fewer in this past year.

The two dozen people following him shouted out their delight. They'd been waiting to see something like this. The winds stilled and the dark clouds stopped advancing. The disciples on the road took frantic notes.

Still smiling, Fenet turned to the farmer. "Praise Elláh, Brother. Your tractor will work now. Harvest your fields while you can."

Dilihand ran around the tractor, looking at every part, listening to its repellors whir, his eyes wide. "Reb Fenet Powrfaith, you are amazing. Thank you, thank you, thank you. We would not make it through the winter without this."

He shook his head. "No, Brother. Elláh is amazing, not me." He pulled the Book out of his pocket and showed it to the farmer. "Read *The Holiest* and learn what He can do for you. And it is I who thank you, for the opportunity to help."

Putting *The Holiest* away, Fenet watched the storm stall over the trees beyond the field—the dark blue, green, and russet leaves of Verdant. The blue and green trees, loula and chloro, were changing to orange for autumn. He took a deep breath and clambered back through the gully to the country road. Despite his joy, each step made him wince when pain lanced through his weak hips.

Behind him, the tractor engaged, pulling the harvester into the field.

When he regained the road, feeling its grit beneath his shoes, he reactivated the repellor beam belt with a sigh of relief. He'd turned it off because the technology seemed to block Elláh's miracles. For a moment, Fenet wished he were a younger man and did not need its help. Then he corrected himself with a wry smile, closed his eyes and prayed silently. *I'm sorry, Lord. You've given me a wonderful life. I cannot complain.*

The crowd exclaimed, while Fenet's joy eased into concern. These days, Elláh often stayed silent when Fenet asked Him for miracles. This had been his first in two weeks. Yet always, the power came from Elláh. What He gives, He can also take away.

"D-did you hear f-from Elláh this time, Reb?" Gangly Lorefim could never keep his blond hair straight, and he always needed reassurance despite his three years with Fenet.

Fenet nodded. "Of course. I can never perform a miracle on my own, boys. You all know that. Elláh's voice or urging always tells me what to do."

These novim. So young. The latest crop of disciples, they came to Fenet wanting to learn how to perform miracles. In twenty years, he'd had twenty-three disciples. Most had never done any miracles. Of this crew, only three. Durnadat made a few sparkles from his fingers a year ago. Beneim healed the lightning scars on a tree. Tenpos had once wrought the rapid growth of an herb garden, and he'd also repaired a child's broken finger in a playground incident. Scanat, Lorefim, and Penilos had done none.

Fenet led the novim down the road toward his home. The crowd clamored around, and he became the center of a Gordian knot of hands and arms reaching out to touch him. *How can I meet their demands, when Elláh is diminishing me?* The thought brought great sadness. Fenet closed his eyes and pushed his hands outward, clearing space around him.

"Hey, there, not now, friends. I must talk with Elláh and my novim. Please come back tomorrow."

Most stepped back and a few turned to leave, all but one woman who fell to her knees in front of him, her hands clasped in prayer.

"Reb, please. My daughter is so ill, she may not last the night."

Fenet enfolded her hands in his own, his heart yearning to help. For years, he had been able to respond to such a plea. He closed his eyes and voiced a silent prayer.

Shall I heal this woman's daughter, Lord?

He felt the pulse pound in his neck while he listened for Elláh's command, the Voice in the back of his mind. A rumble of natural thunder washed across the fields from the lowering clouds. He waited, delaying his inability.

Fenet heard nothing. His shoulders sank inward like the collapse of an eroded riverbank, aching for this woman.

"I'm sorry, sister. I pray she may live, but only Elláh knows. I can do nothing now. Selah."

She wept, her tears moistening his hardened knuckles.

How tragic, that I can heal a tractor but not save this woman's child.

Fenet's good friend Pastor Eregim Steadknow stepped out of the crowd, a big man, tall and rotund, his grey robe and tan collar a contrast to the working attire of the country people. His long black hair blew around his shoulders. He placed a gentle hand on two shoulders, the distraught woman and Fenet.

"Bless you, Elláh will do as He wills, sister." His strong voice always soothed with gentleness. "Reb Fenet needs his own time now."

Her face melted with grief when she looked up at his warm brown eyes. Yet she nodded, stood, and left. Her head hung low.

"There was a time," Fenet said, watching her shuffle away, "when I would not have paused." He lifted his hat and brushed the long greying hair back over his shoulders.

"I know, Fenet. Your power is fading. We've known each other a long time, and I see the difference. I am so sorry for you."

The two had been through many events together. Fenet frequently spoke before Eregim's small congregation in Glorify. Eregim comforted and supported Fenet when times got hard.

Eregim kept his hand on Fenet's shoulder. "But just now, I came to warn you. Church proctors are talking about bringing you in for questioning."

"What, again?" Fenet shook his head in amazement. "I can say nothing more than I've told them before. Their scornful attitude never changes. Throughout history, this is always what's happened when a religion runs a country. These Church leaders seem out of touch with Elláh. Temporal power has polluted their God-given spirituality. Faith was stronger when it wasn't compulsory."

"Walk with me, my friend." Eregim led the way toward Fenet's cottage.

The disciples followed a few paces behind.

Fenet still held the floppy hat. He plucked a purple coneflower from the roadside to replace the one blown off. Replacing the hat on his head, the two walked on.

Eregim chuckled, looking at his hat. "How often do you replace that flower, Fenet?"

Smiling, Fenet said, "Only when it falls off. This little miracle keeps on working, that my flower never fades. My pants and tunic may be rumpled, but the flower is Elláh's tiny message that I am His."

Fenet relied more heavily on the repellor belt in the late-season heat of Verdant's blue-white sun. *Why should I be so tired, Elláh? I'm only forty-seven, not that old yet. Doctors have found nothing wrong.*

Eregim continued, "You've been working miracles since your spiritual experience over twenty years ago. The Church tolerates you because what you do is self-evident, though they don't like it. They don't understand you any more than the Jewish Sanhedrin on old Earth understood Jaysus three thousand years ago."

Fenet held up a hand. "Please don't compare me to Jaysus. I am definitely not the Son of God."

"I know that. But what are the Church leaders here in Rathas to make of a man who performs miracles every day? It flies in the face of their doctrine. They teach miracles all passed away after the death of Muhamet."

Fenet snorted a laugh. "Right. In their minds, doctrine is more important than the miracles they see."

"Perhaps," Eregim said. He cocked his head in thought, walking a few paces in silence. "Or perhaps it is difficult for any of us to believe in miracles, even when we see them. Did you really just heal that tractor? Or is there a scientific explanation? Maybe some electrical junction reconnected due to vibration." He shrugged. "Yes, I saw the glow wash from your hands to the repellor motor, and so did all the others. Yet it will be easy to discount that vision later, after the tractor has been doing its job again for a week."

"Even my disciples don't believe." Fenet waved a hand at the half dozen following them. "They've taken to calling themselves the Khadam—the servants—but they haven't quite worked out the difference between pride and service. Few of them have yet performed a miracle, though they try."

With a heavy growl, five box-like military transports flew overhead. They caught Fenet's attention, who watched them disappear to the south. "At least none of these boys have talked about joining the Khubar f'Elláh," he said. "Have you noticed the increased activity of our Holy Army, Eregim?"

"I have. I've never understood why a country founded in Elláh's peace should be preparing for war."

3 – Problems with Faith

When Elláh has a task for you, He gets your attention.

—*Sayings of Reb Fenet* by Ellen Thranadil, Tileus
Press 448 A.T.

Eregim looked at the road ahead. "Here comes that trouble, Fenet." Two figures in imposing grey with peaked hats and red collars strode toward them. Their polished black staffs glinted while they strode toward the group. "The Church proctors."

Fenet sighed. "Always the same questions."

Elláh's familiar Voice whispered in his head: *WAVE YOUR HAND THROUGH THE AIR, FENET.*

"Yes, Lord," Fenet saw puzzlement from Eregim, then realized he'd spoken aloud. Fenet waved his hand, feeling the resistance of spiritual forces being pushed away. A faint tinge of vermilion stained the air, moving toward the proctors.

The two proctors, thirty meters away, disappeared. The startled Khadam shouted out in fear and joy.

"Holy Jaysus." Eregim stepped back in fear. "What did you do to them?"

Fenet shrugged, at peace with himself. "I don't know. Elláh did that, not me. Probably they've been moved a kilometer or two away. It's happened before. I'm certain they're unhurt."

Eregim frowned at him, almost angry yet puzzled. "Why would you do such a thing, Fenet? Antagonizing them is not helpful."

"It wasn't my choice. I only do what He tells me to do. His plan is always far better than mine. And who knows?" He gave a sly smile. "Perhaps it'll make me famous."

Eregim shook his head in dismay and resumed walking. "I don't understand you, brother. Of course, I don't understand the ineffable Elláh, either."

"I'll tell you what I don't understand." Fenet's neck and shoulders tightened while his voice rose. "I don't understand why He would have me do this silly little miracle to remove the proctors, yet be silent about that poor woman and her daughter. That's what I can't accept.

"People die every day. Believers die. They get sick. They hurt. They grieve. So much trouble fills the world. Resentments. Anger. Misunderstandings. Our own Church leaders are considering Holy War against Tileus. Since Elláh has so much power, why does He allow such pain to continue?"

Eregim's face reflected shock at Fenet's blasphemy. He started to speak.

Fenet waved him away, "Yes, I know what *The Holiest* teaches us: 'All things work together for the good of those who love Him.' He does it for our good, so we can grow and become closer to Him. Yet I still don't understand. Surely, we can grow in easier ways."

He took in a deep cathartic breath and let it out, his anger going with it. Again. Railing about what Elláh chooses to do and not do had no purpose other than to take a person away from Him. *Elláh knows what's best. I must enjoy what He gives me now. It may be gone soon.*

The two turned off the road at the entrance to the cottage Fenet shared with his aging mother. Dark clouds still hung nearby, but sunlight shone on the white picket fence and the front gardens she loved. Rows of different colored borgen flowers filled the sunny air with their sweet scent. The path expanded into a small patio with a bench and awning, where he and Mother often sat in the evening. Home. Soon Fenet would be inside and take the weight off his hips.

He glanced at the disciples, still following at a respectful distance, then turned back to Eregim.

"Would you care to come in, Eregim? I need to talk. The decline in my abilities has me ... frightened." Voicing his fear made it coalesce like a cloud of gnats plaguing his eyes to tears.

Eregim nodded in response. "I'd guess that it would. Yes, I'd like to talk."

Fenet turned to the six. "Nov Scanat, Nov Penilos, all of you. I'll be at home for now. In the meantime, continue practicing the exercises I've given you in how to attain greater humility. Listen to Elláh, boys, and do whatever you perceive Him to tell you, no matter how faint. Please meet me back here in two hours, and you may report on your results."

They nodded, excited, and scurried away individually. Penilos Humildef, the youngest and most recent, gawky with straw-colored hair, seemed reluctant to leave. Instead, he settled down on the garden bench to read *The Holiest*. Fenet smiled at him, then opened the door for Pastor Eregim.

Silence in the house comforted Fenet. In her declining years, Mother often took naps in the afternoon, so he and Eregim moved to the back of the house.

They selected drinks from the autocater in the kitchen, an herbal tea for Eregim and a pindel infusion for Fenet, and took them to the parlor. It was a blessing to sit, to turn off the repellor belt, and to rest without pain. The room filled Fenet with comfort: the afghan his mother had made, family pictures on the mantel, his own comfortable easy chair.

Yet Fenet needed to talk.

Desperation choked his voice. "You've just seen me perform two miracles, my friend. That's all I've done in the last several weeks. Last year, I did twenty a day." He closed his eyes and rested his forehead on a hand.

"Your miracles have defined your adult life," Eregim said with a soft smile. "I remember when you started. You were a young hellion, and I'm ashamed to say I looked up to you. I wanted to be as wild and crazy as you. Then Elláh ... touched you. You even changed your powername. I forget; what was it before?"

Fenet joined his smile. "Charisfriend. The young people in that rough crowd liked me and encouraged me in my addictions. Drugs, liquor, sex. I couldn't keep that powername afterwards, so I changed to Powrfaith. You're right, the event amazed me, too. Elláh's power flowed through me in a blinding white light and changed my life. In all these years, it has never become ... ordinary ... but my craziness disappeared, and I healed others, and those first weeks filled me with awe and joy. I still feel joy every time it happens. I've had a dream for years of being famous, known across Verdant for my miracles. In pride, I sometimes think my name might go down with the Zikri, who founded the One Church." He let out a shaky breath. "I don't know what I'll do next, if His powers in me continue to fade."

"I'm a pastor," Eregim said. "My caring for people is what fills my own life. I'd be lost if I couldn't help others come to Jaysus."

Fenet looked up. His friend's eyes swam with sympathy.

"Yes," he agreed. "I can't count the number of people whose faith has been kindled or restored by my miracles. Elláh must be pleased with me. Yet He seems to be taking it away. That dream of being famous is further away every day. If my miracles fail completely, I'll be pilloried by the Church. I don't understand His purpose."

Eregim chuckled. "Which of us ever does? What else could you do, Fenet?

A rasping moan from the bedroom interrupted the conversation.

"Mother? Are you okay?" No answer came.

Fenet stood and hurried to her bed, with Pastor Eregim close behind.

She lay fully clothed on top of the frilly bedspread in a room holding bottles, lotions, and pictures on every surface. Her hair tangled on the pillow around her head as if she'd been thrashing. Her face drenched in sweat, her eyes raced around behind her closed eyelids as if chasing demons around the room. Her hands spasmed on the counterpane. The room smelled sharp with sickness.

"Mother!" Fenet cried and sat beside her, stroking her cheek. "What's happened?"

She answered with another moan and a hacking cough.

He looked in desperation to Eregim. "Would you find a cool, damp cloth, please?"

Eregim nodded and hastened to the bathroom.

Please, dear Jaysus. I have healed so many people I didn't know over the years. Give me this power again, to heal this one so precious to me.

He heard nothing but his mother's wheezing. Silence reigned in the back of his mind, where that Voice had spoken thousands of times. Like a vacated house with dust dervishes swirling in the gust of a closing door, the emptiness slammed shut on his hopes.

In the silence came a sudden horrifying event: Fenet felt Elláh's spiritual authority leave him, gusting away in the empty room like the fluttering departure of a wounded dove. The scent of sickness filled his head, possibly his mother's bed or perhaps a sickness within him. Lightning flashed outside the window, with a tremendous crack of thunder on its heels.

Fenet's mouth gaped, and he sucked in an incomplete breath that failed to nourish. He slumped on the edge of the bed in shock while the storm outside broke free. Rain lashed the windows and pounded on the roof. Repeated thunder crashed in a wild cacophony of despair.

4 – New Direction

If you hear from Elláh, and know it comes from Elláh ... do what He says.

—Sayings of Reb Fenet by Ellen Thranadil, Tileus
Press 448 A.T.

Eregim returned while Fenet sat stupefied.

"I found a cloth, Fenet, and a medkit. Has there been any change in your mother?" He laid the cloth on the mother's brow and set down the medkit.

Fenet could not respond. The loss of his powers unmanned him.

Eregim turned to him, then recoiled. "What's happened to you? Your face is white."

Fenet buried his face in his hands. "It's gone, Eregim. Elláh's power left me." A spiritual dagger pierced his heart. It felt like the end of life as he'd known it.

"Oh, Fenet, no. How could you know?"

Fenet whispered, "I felt it leave me." He collapsed from the bed onto his knees, crumpling into a ball and hugging his own chest. The noise of the storm outside battered his soul.

Eregim said more, but Fenet could not listen.

In the very moment Fenet needed Elláh's power most, to help his mother, Elláh had taken it away. He floundered inside himself while Eregim left the room. *Please, Lord, let me heal one more time.* No answer came. The space where he'd heard Elláh so many times echoed like an empty nave.

A minute later, he heard voices again. Eregim had brought the youngest disciple in.

"Your master needs your help, Nov Penilos."

"My help, Pastor? What could I do? I've hardly learned anything yet."

"Here, my boy. Come to him. Comfort him. You can do that while I help his mother."

Fenet felt arms around his shoulders from behind, thin arms placed with tentative compassion.

Penilos smelled damp from the rain. "Reb Fenet, I'm here. Whatever you need, I'm here." He knelt beside Fenet and placed a cheek on the teacher's back while he held him.

On the other side of the bed, Eregim did something with the symptalyzer from the medkit. While taking readings, he spoke gently. "Come back to us, Fenet. I'm certain Elláh's got more for you to do."

Fenet nodded, knowing the truth of what Eregim said. He took in a deep breath, then let it out all at once, releasing some of the aching loss that consumed him. Another breath came more easily, and released the fear of his future. Eregim was right; Elláh still had work for him to do—different work. *But what will I do? I have to trust Elláh to show me.*

He straightened up, still on his knees, Nov Penilos' hand on his shoulder.

"Thank you, both of you. I feared this day sometime soon, but it seems too much that it should happen now." Fenet looked at his mother's face, damp with perspiration, her eyes still racing behind closed lids. "Now, I don't know what to do to help her. Eregim, what does the symptalyzer say?"

The pastor concentrated on the reading. "High fever, rapid heartbeat, lots of strange chemical imbalances. It suggests a sudden and overwhelming virus."

Penilos gave a strangled gasp of shock and his hands left Fenet.

Curious, Fenet looked up at the boy. The nov's young blue eyes gaped wide in amazement. He hardly breathed.

"Yes, Elláh," the boy whispered in apparent awe.

Penilos reached his hands across the coverlet on the bed and slid them up onto the mother's cheeks. He spoke so breathlessly Fenet could hardly hear his words.

"Be healed, woman."

A reddish glow shimmered in Penilos' hands and spread across her face and down the length of her body.

This time, Fenet watched Elláh's power from outside, seeing that power as others had seen it come through him. His mother relaxed on the bed, her breathing calmed.

Eregim jerked his hand away from her neck. "Her skin's cool," he gasped. He laid the symptalyzer against her implant again. "And it's all gone. Normal readings."

Penilos, this gangly, uncertain youth, turned to Fenet and spoke.

"*YOU HAVE DONE WELL, FENET,*" The Voice of Elláh came from Penilos' lips. "*BUT YOUR LACK OF FAITH IN ME HAS BEEN GROWING.*"

The changed Penilos knelt beside Fenet with a bold confidence he'd never shown before. He glowed with Elláh's power. His hand touched the repellor beam belt around Fenet's waist, singling it out to his attention.

Fenet gasped when he realized Elláh's point. He relied on this human-created artifice to ease the weakness of his body, rather than relying on Elláh. The more he'd used it, the weaker he had become, feeling thirty years older than his age. Fenet had never asked Elláh how He wanted him to deal with the limitation. He made the choice for himself.

Lack of faith, evidenced by making decisions without Elláh.

Penilos stepped back and his eyes cleared, displaying his usual innocent, puzzled expression. Yet his face now glowed with an incredible awe.

❧ ❈ ☙

Minutes later, the three sat in the parlor. Fenet's mother had risen from the bed as if from a nap. She bustled in the kitchen like nothing had happened and brought out a tray of tea and cookies before she returned to cooking. The repellor beam belt lay discarded on the floor at Fenet's feet. Penilos glowed, but he still seemed uncomfortable to be sitting equally with Eregim and his teacher.

Fenet was coming to terms with what had happened. He'd had a long run of miracles, but whatever Elláh gave, He could also take away. Until Elláh showed him different, however, he remained the teacher.

He rose to the occasion. "So, Penilos, tell me. What did you do different? Why did Elláh work through you this time?"

"I did nothing, Reb," he answered, his eyes alight. "Elláh did it all. Last year, I heard a faint voice that told me to follow you. I've done no miracles since. This was different. Elláh filled me with a voice that overpowered me, and He worked through me. He told me what to do. He spoke through me while I ... watched." The boy stared into space with new wonder. "Is this what you've been trying to teach us?"

"Yes, exactly. But I question your statement you did nothing. You did something very important."

Penilos nodded, still excited. "Yes. I surrendered to Him. I got out of His way."

The boy's elation took Fenet back to his own reactions so many years before. He saw in Penilos' face the same incredulity and bewilderment he had known. Fenet smiled in his heart at the memory. That had been a wonderful time. He remembered the shock from people who had known him as a wild addict lost in debauchery and overindulgence. A lost and dissolute burnout suddenly performed miracles for Elláh. Fenet looked at Eregim. His friend had been there and seen the change, and now they stood at the other end of the chain. Eregim matched Fenet's smile.

"That's correct, Penilos," Fenet continued. "Alone of all the disciples, you've now become anointed."

"But Reb Fenet," Penilos said, his puzzled innocence coming through, "I'm not the only one. We saw Nov Tenpos repair that child's broken finger three weeks ago. He also talked of the power he felt move through him."

Fenet nodded. "Repairing a broken finger was good, but healing an illness is special. You've only been with me for a year, Penilos. In twenty-three years, no other disciple has healed an illness. Sparkles in the air, soothing a love-shattered heart, healing a broken plant. That's all."

Penilos nodded understanding. He still glowed with awe at what he'd done.

Conversation paused while the three considered this huge step forward.

Eregim broke the silence. "But what about you, Fenet? What will you do?"

He shrugged and gave a firm look. "You know *The Holiest* as well as I do. Regardless of what Elláh does, I still have dharma, the duty to do what He puts in front of me. There is a moksha-like release in the artha of tasks well done. So, I'll continue to teach. I'll guide these disciples while I can. Perhaps they will continue to grow."

"Do you believe Elláh will restore your power? As a pastor, I'd be lost if I couldn't help others come to Jaysus. My caring for people is what fills my own life."

Fenet nodded. "You and I have both ministered in different ways. I've been fulfilled more than I can say by what I've done. Yet now, in this change, I don't understand His purpose."

Eregim answered, "Which of us ever does? What else could you do, Fenet? What other gifts do you have?"

"I don't know. *The Holiest* talks about a five-fold ministry: apostles, prophets, evangelists, pastors and teachers. I've been an apostle, awakening people to Elláh. I've never made a single prophecy. I don't speak well in front of people like an evangelist. I don't have the calling to pastor people like you do. I can still teach, but the evidence so far shows I'm not very good at it."

Eregim looked thoughtful. "Elláh gives other gifts than ministry. *The Holiest* also lists gifts that can be used in the world: wisdom, knowledge of the truth, encouraging and helping others, administration. He'll show you what to do. Your faith is as strong as ever."

Fenet winced. "Perhaps, perhaps not. I wonder these days, with my gifts declining, if my faith is as strong. I have been falling into arrogance, and this repellor belt is an example." He had a wistful thought. "It is possible I could become a writer on spiritual topics. I think I'd enjoy that. It would mean studying scriptures more, and less walking—"

Penilos abruptly stiffened. He spoke again with the Voice not his own.

"*FENET, I HAVE A DIFFERENT TASK PREPARED FOR YOU. WAIT AND YOU WILL SEE.*"

Having spoken for Elláh, the boy fell back into himself looking dismayed. "Reb, I apologize. I have no excuse for talking to you like—"

Fenet laughed. The apology was so incongruous with that Voice, he couldn't help but laugh. "Penilos, you have every reason in the world to speak in the way Elláh makes you speak. Never apologize for being the channel of God."

Then he turned back to Eregim, waving a hand to indicate the boy. "You see, Eregim? Here we are, trying to make decisions already made for us by Elláh. I will wait on the Lord. Through the Five Pillars, He will enlighten me about the dharma he has for me. Perhaps this is a necessary self-purification."

❧ ✳ ☙

An hour later, the other five disciples returned. Thunderstorms continued, alternating heavy rain with periods of light drizzle. Fenet prayed Brother Dilihand had managed to reap his harvest.

The parlor had too few chairs for all, but the Khadam were used to it. As the eldest among the disciples at the ripe age of twenty-four, Scanat took for himself the biggest chair. Eregim raised an eyebrow at the young man's presumption, but Fenet patted his hand in the air to ease his friend's concern. Lorefim and Tenpos, both in their early twenties, quietly sat cross-legged on the floor, about as different as they could be. Blond-haired Lorefim loved books and mathematics and had an awkward way with people. Solid and muscular, Tenpos sported a ponytail of brown hair falling down his back. That left red-headed Beneim and the overweight Durnadat, both about twenty, vying for the remaining chair. Typical of each, Beneim waited for the other to choose while Durnadat burst into jovial laughter and slid into the chair.

Of course, they knew nothing yet of the events happening here.

When they were all seated, Scanat spoke, obviously a conversation continued from outside. "I still think we should explore it, friends. We can ask Reb Fenet for guidance."

"Guidance about what, Scanat?" Fenet asked.

"A new technology we heard about this afternoon. Someone from Tileus brought it into the city. It's called the transpath, and it lets people feel each other's emotions." His eyes filled with excitement, and he slipped into a convincing manner.

The strange concept momentarily took Fenet away from the momentous events here. "Feel each other's emotions? Why?"

Durnadat answered with his usual energy, his large frame bouncing in the chair. "People can understand each other better. They say people can't lie when the transpath is active."

Scanat continued, "They developed it in Tileus, and it's what stopped the war last year between Tileus and Prime."

Fenet held up a hand to stop the excited flow of words. He looked into the eyes of each, ensuring their attention. "Perhaps we can talk of it more, Nov Scanat. But technology—any technology—

is less important than the spiritual events here while you've been gone. We've had a change here, boys. Elláh has shown Himself."

Their curious eyes bounced to Penilos and Eregim, then back to Fenet. Scanat seemed put off by the change in topic.

Fenet continued, his voice strong. "Remember when Tenpos repaired the girl's finger down in Dadu? It was the biggest miracle any of you had done. Now, Penilos has done more." He heard his mother singing in the kitchen and waved a hand toward her. "Mother was suddenly ill this afternoon, a quick and dangerous attack. Elláh worked through Penilos, and she sprang out of bed as if nothing had happened."

The disciples leaned forward, enthusiasm in their eyes. Except for stiff Scanat, who sat with his jaw clenched. Fenet had cut him off from considering this transpath, something Scanat thought important. The young man had a tendency to push issues based on his own understanding, rather than listening to Elláh. Fenet feared he might not last much longer as a disciple. Scanat had been disappointed too many times as a result of his striving to find a path on his own. His enthusiasm for this technology showed the same tendency. Fenet made a mental note to talk with Scanat later.

"Penilos can tell you later what happened to him, but there is more." Fenet paused, pondering how to make the admission. "He spoke in the voice of Elláh ..." He found it hard to continue.

Eregim put a comforting hand on his arm.

Fenet nodded. "Through Penilos, Elláh told me I will no longer be doing miracles."

Shock swept the room. The disciples all spoke at once, assuring him it could not be so, that Elláh still worked through him.

He shook his head. "No, my friends. As Jaysus once said, 'Get behind me.' This is true. Until the Lord shows me different, I will still teach. But Elláh will now work through Penilos, and perhaps others of you. I can still show you how to use His power when it is given. But I have done wrong," he glanced at the repellor belt, "and apparently, I must do penance for it."

"*NOT PENANCE, FENET. PURIFYING. FORGING.*"

Fenet's head snapped up to look at Penilos. The boy's eyes had filled again with the presence of Elláh. Sitting at Penilos' feet, Lorefim scrambled backwards on hands and feet, distancing himself from the Voice while it continued.

"I desire for you all to do a pilgrimage. Walk to the capital city of Praise. Follow me, and I will show you the way."

The thrill of adrenaline rushed through Fenet. A certain and concrete task. A new dharma.

Elláh released Penilos again. The boy looked apologetic, abashed, obviously feeling unworthy to be speaking this way to his teacher and to the group. The others were too shocked to speak.

Fenet cocked his head, eyes still on Penilos. "Eregim, how far is it to Praise?"

"Seven hundred kilometers."

Fenet chuckled wryly, thinking of his weak hips. "And I've never been more than thirty kilometers from Glorify. Boys, we have a mission in front of us."

5 – Religious Obstruction

The religious leaders in Rathas took an early antipathy to the transpath. They believed the technology to be a perversion of Elláh's way that would lead people to rely on their own augmented senses rather than relying on Elláh. Their first reaction suppressed the technology.

—*The Making of a New Humanity* by Ellen Thranadil, Tileus Press 448 A.T.

Fenet rose early the next day, greeting the blue-white sun of Verdant with an uneasy smile. Elláh had said Fenet would be purified. He took to the prayer mat in the living room to do his fajr morning prayer. A surrender to Elláh: standing, bowing, prostrate. *Guide me, Elláh. This pilgrimage is unknown territory.* He looked out the kitchen window at a fresh-washed dawn. The neowheat and vercorn in the fields behind the house stood tall despite the storms of yesterday, though the plants had been battered in areas at the edges. He opened the window and took a deep breath, easing his concern with the scent of the damp world.

After oatmeal and milk sprinkled with brown sugar, he hoisted a light backpack into place and limped to the front door. His hips already hurt. A groan escaped him, which Fenet changed to a wry chuckle when he thought of walking seven hundred kilometers. *I have no idea how I'm going to do this, Lord, but you do.*

He took his floppy hat off the hook, its plucked coneflower still fresh from yesterday. Putting it to his nose, the earthy aroma brought Fenet a simple joy. He placed the hat on his head then looked at the staff beside the door. *Elláh, is that acceptable? Or is it another man-made object to take me away from you?*

Take the staff, Fenet.

"Thank you, Lord. I'm grateful You still talk to me."

The disciples had gathered outside.

"Okay, boys. We ready to start?" Fenet asked.

The novim all nodded. Fenet looked them over. Each one had a backpack, a couple towering above their heads. Heavy-looking shoulder bags littered the ground at their feet. The absurdity of their ambition made him laugh.

"It's a long way to Praise, boys. Are you going to carry that weight all the way?"

Several of them looked abashed.

Scanat stood straighter and answered with his usual over-confidence, "If we must, Reb Fenet. We've brought supplies for the trip. The bags will be lighter as we use them. If we've forgotten anything, we can get it on our way through Glorify."

"Well, you're all young. Perhaps you can do it." *Time will tell, and we'll all learn from our journey.*

Fenet's mother came out to bid them farewell. She joined the group circle for a prayer of thanks. Fenet kissed her goodbye and led the disciples toward the city of Glorify, eleven kilometers south. While he walked, another of Elláh's small miracles came to him. He hadn't voiced poetry in years, but Elláh's muse spoke through him.

> *A walk with Elláh and my soul-heart leapt*
> *Dharma fetches ease to my soul*
> *Home at my back, I merely stepped*
> *And the road and the world became whole*

❧ ✳ ☙

An hour later, they walked on an unpaved country road through farmland, with several kilometers yet to the outskirts of the city. A morning chill on this clear blue day promised the coming of autumn, though the sun quickly warmed Fenet. Some of the farmers left a band of trees alongside the road, so the fragrance of evergreen pindels warmed the scent of the crops. The loulakiphyll pigments in the dark blue trees were fading, displaying the earliest signs of color change; many leaves showed yellow. The russet trees with different photosynthesis were still unchanged from summer.

The novim would have walked faster without Fenet. He leaned on the staff, though he soon found it only helped to relieve the pain on one side at a time. *You say this isn't penance, Elláh. I choose to believe You, but it challenges me.*

The younger men shared a thrill of adventure. Their eager conversation filled the space around them, prompting the birds in the trees to echo the Khadam's enthusiasm.

Without warning, plump Durnadet's excitement bubbled over. To everyone's surprise, he suddenly shouted like a trumpeting hooliphant.

"I can't wait to see what Elláh does with us!"

Durnadet raised his arms and spun around over and over, laughing out loud, looking like a rotund top wobbling in the road. Second youngest of the group, with brown curly hair and warm brown eyes, he still carried the exuberance of a teenager.

Penilos laughed with him and swept his hand repeatedly on Durnadet's side as if accelerating the top. "Faster, faster," he cried. "If you spin fast enough, Elláh will lift you in the air!"

"D-don't make him fall," stuttered Lorefim. Tall and gangly with blue eyes, almost as old as Scanat, Lorefim seemed slower to mature. He often expressed indecision and fear except in the field of math. Fenet had hopes for Lorefim, though, because he tried to learn.

Durnadet stopped spinning and took two unstable steps sideways before catching his balance. "No fear of that, Lorefim. Do the math. I've got lots of stability here." Still chortling, he patted his ample midriff. "Besides, we have Reb Fenet to keep us safe—and now we've got Penilos to perform miracles for us, too."

Penilos blushed. "I don't make miracles happen, Durnadet. Elláh does."

"See?" Durnadet pointed his finger at Penilos. "He's already sounding just like Reb Fenet."

"Don't make fun of him," Scanat said. "Miracles are serious business."

Fenet saw a teaching moment in this. "Perhaps, Scanat, for Elláh's will is the most serious dharma on Verdant. Yet there's nothing wrong with enjoying the gifts Elláh gives us. We're not intended to be dour, but to attract others with our kama—our desires and passions for life. It is said even Matma Ganzhi smiled while he starved himself."

Scanat lowered his head in acquiescence, yet not before Fenet saw a flash of resentment, becoming more frequent these days. The young man wanted more and seemed less patient.

"P-proctors, Reb Fenet." Lorefim's voice held sudden dread. He pointed at the road ahead, where the two figures had just rounded a bend.

Fenet continued to walk. The bright sun felt like it had just dimmed. A cold splash fell on his heart.

"Just do what you did yesterday, Reb," smiled Durnadet. "Wave your hand at them."

"No, my boy. Only Elláh guides His miracles, and he has taken them from me. We'll meet them this time."

The distance between closed rapidly. Soon, the Khadam stopped when the proctors blocked their way. Fenet knew them both, the same pair from yesterday. These two had questioned him before, never with definitive results. Clearly, the Church's actions classified as harassment. And yet … could this be part of Elláh's purification?

Orenas, the older of the two, spoke first. "Fenet Powrfaith, we need to ask you some questions." Tall with dark hair, abusive forcefulness laced his words.

Fenet laughed gently. "Are they different questions than before? And are you willing to risk approaching me again after yesterday?"

"Yeah," said Jorem, the younger one with brown hair. "We didn't appreciate that."

"So, where did you end up *this* time?" Fenet asked.

"You've got to stop doing it to us, Fenet." Orenas shook his head, his lips compressed. "It antagonizes the Church. We make our reports, and the leaders gather more information about you. They're beginning to suspect your 'miracles' come from Saitan. So now we have new questions on top of our questions from yesterday."

Fenet's heartbeat accelerated. "Well, sirs, you're delaying me— and my novim—from doing Elláh's work. You can walk along with us."

"Where are you going?" demanded Orenas.

Fenet shrugged. "For now, into Glorify—and it's still seven kilometers away."

Jorem stepped so close Fenet smelled overripe cantaloupe on his breath. "We're not moving until we get some answers, Fenet.

What are you doing to displace us like this? What new technology are you using?"

Nov Penilos stepped forward. Lorefim had hold of Penilos' sleeve but failed to hold him back. Penilos spoke quietly while he waved his hand sideways through the air.

"*BE GONE, OBSTRUCTORS.*" Penilos spoke again with the Voice from Elláh.

In a sudden vermilion wash, the two proctors blinked out of existence, gone to only Elláh knew where.

Fenet couldn't help but explode with a laugh. The sudden release of tension waggled his funny bone all the way to his toes. When he laughed, so did the rest of the disciples.

"That'll give them something new to think about," he hooted through laughter. "When the youngest boy sends them away!"

Penilos looked sheepish, but grinned.

Durnadat slapped Penilos on the back, almost knocking the boy down. "Marvelous, Penilos," he shouted. "You're doing great. Keep it up, and we won't have to worry about proctors anywhere."

Fenet stopped laughing enough to raise a warning finger in the air. "Not true, Durnadat. Elláh's will is never certain to us. Sooner or later, I'm sure He will have a purpose for proctors that won't be so funny."

❧ ✳ ❧

Jake and Zofia flew into Glorify just after noon, following an early departure from Oriens, a long flight and a one-hour time change, Shortly before arrival, Jake pointed to the ground east of the city. Camouflaged vehicles moved through an empty area, tearing up the ground. Lines of people in mottled uniforms followed the transports.

"Looks like some sort of military action going on down there," he said.

Zofia leaned past him to look out his side of the aircar. "That's a pretty big action."

Jake smiled at the warm body contact and put an arm around her. He laid a gentle kiss on her hair. "This is a nice action here, too."

She laughed, turned her head, and returned the kiss.

When they broke apart, a long moment later, she sat up again and gave him a puzzled look. "Why is the country of Rathas practicing military maneuvers? Or is it practice?"

"Yeah, it's practice. That's their army. They call it the Khubar f'Elláh, which means something like 'the experts of God.' It's a strange quirk for a religious country to have an active army, but it's what they do."

When they touched down in the city square, Elena Hahn, their TechEmpath agent for Rathas, waited for them A beautiful woman, her gemlike aquamarine eyes sparkled and her lush blond hair caressed her shoulders. She wrung her hands, a nervous gesture Jake had not seen in her before.

"Afternoon, Jake," she said. "How was your trip?"

"Smooth. We went through a bit of weather over the Gortooth Mountains, but it passed quickly. Elena, this is Zofia, my wife and VP of Development. I don't believe you two have met."

"Not yet," said Zofia. "Nice to meet you, Elena." Zofia raked the agent with her eyes, then turned back to Jake. "Hey, Bucko, you didn't tell me you'd hired a fashion model."

Jake covered a touch of anxiety with a laugh. "Oh, she's much more than her looks, Zofia. Elena won the annual marketing award from Electech for five years in a row before we hired her away. I'm expecting her to do as well for us."

Zofia simply cocked a playful eyebrow at Jake.

"Doing well just became more difficult," said Elena. "That's why I imped a text to you yesterday. The Church leader here in Glorify, Deacon Tempstay, has shut down our product presentation for this evening. I've tried to convince him otherwise, even got a bit hot under the collar. We've gone to a lot of effort to set it up, and he's stopped us."

A heavy feeling settled in Jake's stomach. "Did he give any reason?"

She raised a helpless hand. "He decided the t-path to be a violation of Elláh's Creation."

"Religion," Zofia snorted.

"Okay, we'll have to talk with him," Jake said. "We have clearance from the country's Minister of Trade to make these presentations. He's a higher Church authority than the local man who shut you down. I can push the documents from my implant to you—and we can show them to the local man."

Elena relaxed and nodded. "Great. I was hoping you'd have something to convince him. I've already obtained an appointment with the deacon an hour from now."

"That sounds fine. He may be difficult, but he'll have to bow to the Minister's authority."

Zofia added, "Yep. This is important for us, because all our sales in Rathas hinge on having the Church on our side. And sales drive our ability to create new products."

"Exactly," said Jake. "So, take us to him, and we'll do what we need to do. Your presentation will go forward. On the way, you can brief us about this deacon."

"He's a difficult man, Jake."

Today held a short walk for the Khadam, a warm-up for those to come. Scanat Forsenquire had a growing impatience at the teacher's slowness. Scanat often found himself walking alone in the front of the group, having to slow down again to match Fenet's pace. He recalled the teacher's put-down yesterday about Scanat's technology idea. It still irritated him. Scanat had been working with Fenet long enough he thought the teacher would sometimes trust him. On the other hand, Scanat had yet to perform the smallest miracle—and that bothered him, too.

They came into the city of Glorify by early afternoon. Reb Fenet hobbled by the time they reached the city.

Older than the rest, Scanat knew he approached a life decision point. The others chattered on about anything they saw, with the Reb inserting lessons here and there. Scanat stayed in quiet thought.

What can I do? I've been following Reb Fenet since I saw his miracles four years ago. He fascinates me, but he's not a very good teacher.

Scanat had been a leader in secondary school, elected to student elder responsibilities. He'd done well and been selected for tertiary school in the field of particle physics. Then he saw Fenet performing miracles and turned down the selection. He still wanted to learn how to do what Fenet did, but it appeared the reb just couldn't teach him.

The other novim? Scanat snorted to himself. *They're all a bunch of second-rate kids. Farmers, bakers. Not very smart.* It still rankled him that three of them had managed to perform small miracles, and Scanat had not.

And now, the youngest of them all, this Penilos boy who'd been with the Khadam for less than a year, suddenly performed miracles right and left. He'd waved his hand and the proctors disappeared. *It's just not fair. I've been with Fenet longest.*

The conversation among the disciples had flowed during his inattention, until Penilos bumped his shoulder with a fist.

"Hey, Scanat," said the boy, "what do you think about it?"

"About what?" Scanat snapped. He had no idea what they'd been discussing and didn't appreciate the kid punching him.

"About where to eat, of course. We're thinking of going to the Med Falafel. What do you think?"

Scanat shrugged. "Anyplace works for me, so long as it's cheap. We just need food, not excitement."

A posted flyer caught his eye.

Empathy Technology!
Fanwall Hall, 11-30 Today
Enhance your senses to feel what others feel!

Scanat cocked his head. The technology he'd heard of. *Feel what others feel? Fenet doesn't teach well, but maybe if I could feel what he feels, I could learn. Interesting.* He had time to make it; he'd attend the presentation and see what he could find out.

Dropping unobtrusively to the back of the group while they walked, Scanat waited until they'd decided where to lodge for the night. Once he knew where to find them, he slipped down a side street and away from the Khadam.

Two hours later, when the presentation ended, Scanat pushed his way toward the front of the hall. He seemed to soar like a hookbird over a fish-filled pond. When the presenters had activated the transpath, Scanat felt their excitement and sincerity. He'd looked around at others in the hall and been astonished to discover the system worked on everyone he viewed. Caution from some, ebullient energy from others, the feelings resonated inside him as if his own—yet he could distinguish "other" from "self."

Not only did this t-path thing work, but it also relied on particle physics, the field he'd been offered to study. A coincidence? No, Scanat didn't believe in coincidences anymore. The similarity of the technology to his own schooling had to be a message from Elláh.

He had to know more. The three presenters—two women and a man—answered questions. Few of the attendees came forward. *Surprising. Must be fear of the proctors.* A dozen of them stood around the hall, scowling during the presentation. Scanat had checked out their feelings through the t-path: disapproval, even disgust.

Both women were busy, so Scanat approached the man, rehearsing his name—Jake Palatin—so he would appear courteous. The man, who apparently ran the company, looked to be a few years older than Scanat, about thirty.

"Hello, Mr. Palatin," he said while he offered a hand. "My name is Scanat Forsenquire."

The man smiled like a warm day and shook his hand. "Hi, Scanat. Call me Jake. Glad to have you here. Did you enjoy the presentation?"

"Yes, sir, I did. Amazing what your t-path can do."

"Good, very good." He saw Jake look around the emptying hall. "I wish more of your people were interested."

Scanat tilted his head toward the proctors. "It's the One Church, sir. They disapprove, and the people feel it. Most of them aren't willing to do anything against the Church."

The man nodded with a thoughtful look. "We're going to have to do something about that." Then he glanced back at Scanat. "So, why aren't you intimidated by them?"

The question shot into Scanat's soul like a searchlight. "Well, sir … I guess it's because I'm part of a small group that's been defying the proctors for years."

Jake's eyes sparked with interest. "Oh? I know something about defying authority. What does your group do?"

"We call ourselves the Khadam, the servants. We follow Elláh as best we understand, seeking to fulfill the Pillar of mission through our artha." Jake looked puzzled. Scanat realized the terms meant nothing to the man. "'Mission' is one of the Five Pillars of our faith, and 'artha,' or fulfilling work, is one of the Four Goals of life." Jake still looked confused. "The One Church came together from the long-ago Earth sects. The Five Pillars of Islam, the Four Goals of Hindu, and the salvation by Jaysus from Christianity."

"Ah. Thanks for explaining. I'm not a believer in your Church, so the terms didn't mean much to me. You know, of course, we're visiting here from Tileus?"

"Yes, sir, you told us in the presentation." Scanat paused, then returned to his theme. "We follow a man, Reb Fenet, who's been performing miracles for over twenty years—"

"I'm sorry … miracles?"

Scanat nodded. "Indeed. Miracles. Things not explainable by science, only by spiritual faith. Reb Fenet heals the sick, gives sight to the blind, stops rain, fixes equipment, moves people from here to there."

Jake rocked back on his heels. "That's … astounding."

"Yes, it is, even here. The Church doesn't like it, because what we do goes against their teaching that miracles ended long ago. But your technology is astounding, too. And I'm thinking your technology might make our artha better."

"In what way?"

"If we can feel and understand the people we serve, we can serve them better. If we can feel each other, we can empower our miracles more fully."

Scanat had just voiced the core of the idea he'd developed while experiencing the marketing presentation, the thought that had propelled him to speak to this man.

"You say," he continued, "you have a personal-sized t-path unit?"

"Yes, we do. That's why we're visiting the other countries."

"What would it take to get seven of them for our Khadam?"

6 - Glorify

The One Church began in the last days of Earth while trying to reconcile the warring sects of Islam, Christianity, and Hinduism. The prophet Abdul Elláh Zikri bin Kechik, known as "the Zikri," merged the best of the three faiths into a single belief system, which then traveled to new worlds on the colony ships. The new faith did not suffice to change the political self-immolation of humanity's original world, but the One Church survived in the colonies. ... Pilgrimage was one of those basic tenets common to all three sects.

—History of the One Church by Ellen Thranadil,
Tileus Press 445 A.T.

By the time he'd entered Glorify, Fenet's hips ground like broken glass. He wondered how he would make it to Praise. Elláh knew. More purifying; forging Fenet as a tool for something.

He used his implant to call ahead to the Church hostel for lodging. At first, the pastor there had refused to admit them due to Fenet's reputation. However, Fenet's status as an acknowledged reb qualified them and the pastor had no choice.

Before going to the hostel, Fenet led the Khadam to the Med Falafel, an inexpensive restaurant with traditional spicy food—tacos, berbere, and curry. Durnadet had grown up in Glorify and praised the food. Fenet had passed the restaurant many times while in town, but never tried it. The outdoor garden seating appealed to the novim.

Several of the disciples groaned when they set down their backpacks.

Fenet chuckled. "I warned you boys those packs would get heavy."

Lorefim shrugged with a sheepish look. "Not t-too heavy yet, Reb."

When Fenet took his seat, he counted heads and found a nov missing. "What happened to Scanat?"

Everyone looked around. Several of them shrugged.

Beneim said, "He was with us when we came into the city, Reb. Didn't he grow up here?"

"Yeah," answered Durnadet. "Maybe he went to see someone."

Fenet frowned. "Well, he's gone. I hope he can find us tonight. I did tell you all where we're staying, didn't I?"

They nodded.

After dinner, they stopped at a city park to do the prayer of maghrib. Laying out their prayer mats, the collective ritual eased Fenet's concerns as surrender to Elláh always did.

At the hostel an hour later, they proceeded to their assigned sleeping room, a barrack space holding six double-high bunk beds. Fenet crinkled his nose at the faint scent of mildew, though the sheets appeared clean. Pictures of One Church scenes graced the walls.

Three other pilgrims, already there, looked up at the influx of strangers.

"Got a large group there, Reb. Where y'all goin'?" asked one while the novim clattered and chattered, claiming beds and dropping bags with heavy thuds.

Fenet smiled. "We're just starting. Heading to Praise."

"On foot?" Surprise and respect colored the man's question.

"There's no better way to do a pilgrimage," he said. "How about you?"

"Oh, we're already done. We made it to our goal, the temple here in Glorify. Been purifyin' ourselves here for three days. We're about to head home."

"Good for you. May your trip be a joy." Fenet turned to the disciples. "Boys, let's meet in the common room as soon as you're ready."

"Should w-we shower and c-clean up before meeting, Reb Fenet?" Lorefim asked. "We could all be done in ..." His eyes glazed for a moment. "Thirteen minutes."

Durnadat laughed. "Math in your head again, Lorefim?"

The day had not been strenuous or hot. Still, a shower before bed would be nice, and they would not have the opportunity on the road. Fenet started to answer when he noticed Penilos quivering. The boy's eyes had glazed again, and he seemed to be having an internal conversation. Fenet cocked his head, watching, which also drew the attention of the others.

Penilos spread his hands palm-down in the air in front of him, then slid them first outward then inward, gathering spiritual energy with a faint crimson glow. When he pushed forward, solid waves of red rushed away from him. The clothes on each member of the group fluffed in a silent puff of air. Fenet also felt a slight spray of water with the draft. The effect included the three strangers.

A laugh burst from Fenet when the accumulated day's sweat whisked away from his skin and clothes. He felt fresh, and the mildew smell disappeared from the room.

The other novim exclaimed in surprise. "We're clean!"

The spokesman for the strangers jumped to his feet, alarm on his face. "Hey. What was that?" The other two plucked at their clothing.

Fenet spread his hands and smiled. "That, my friends, was one of Elláh's many little miracles."

The other two outsiders were on their feet, scowling. "A miracle? Felt more like dark magic to me. The Church says there ain't no miracles no more."

"Yeah," said the leader while he picked up his satchel. "I ain't stayin' in here with no magic. No tellin' what they might do to us."

All three cast dark eyes at Penilos and Fenet. They grabbed their gear and left.

Fenet shook his head and spoke to the Khadam. "The teaching of the Church keeps many people away from Elláh, boys. I've seen it all my life. Well ..." he chuckled, "no need for a shower now."

Penilos' demeanor returned to his usual shy state. "Elláh spoke to me again, Reb Fenet."

"Apparently, this is going to be a regular occurrence," Fenet said. "We'll find out more about His plan while we go. Let's go to the common room and organize tomorrow."

The common room had a holo projection system. Fenet linked to it through his implant, then called up a map from the InfoNet. With the novim watching, he zoomed in to cover the territory between Glorify and Praise, with terrain displayed.

"We have a long walk ahead of us, boys. We'll travel on the roads linking town to town. The only traffic we should encounter is the local farm equipment, because long-range traffic goes overhead in aircars and lift-trucks."

Beneim of the red hair and green eyes spoke up. "This time of year, Reb, the local roads will be more busy than other times. Harvest season is starting, and that's how they bring the produce into towns for distribution."

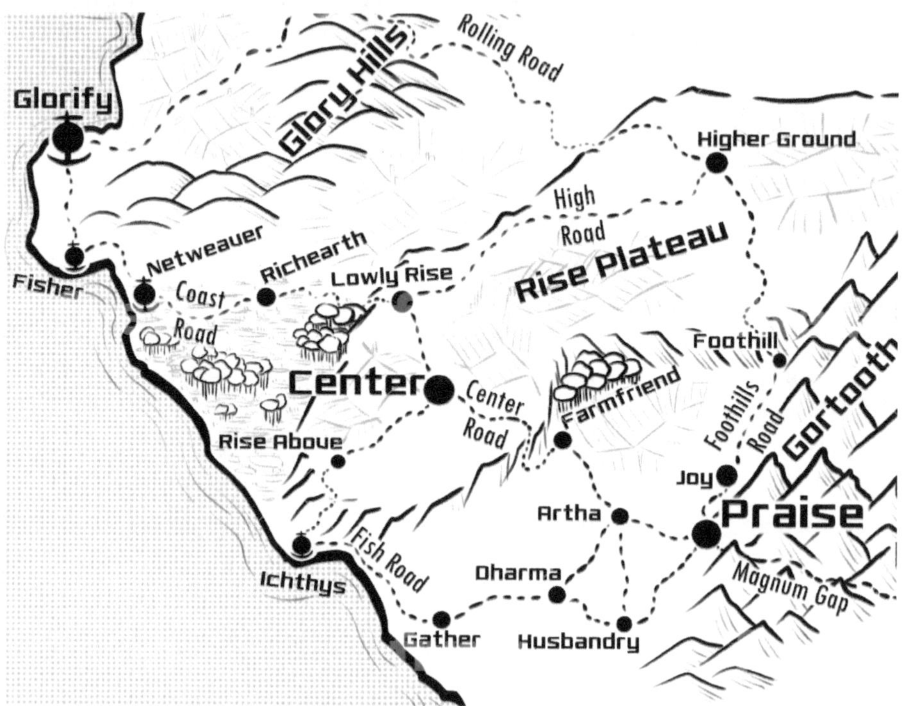

Fenet raised an eyebrow. Beneim rarely offered his thoughts. Then Fenet remembered. "You grew up in a farm family, didn't you?"

"Yes, Reb."

"You'll be helpful to us, then, because we'll be walking mostly through farmland."

He preened just a little, pleased to be recognized. "Thank you, Reb."

Turning to the group, Fenet pointed to the map. "Our first week will be along the coast between here and the town of Netweaver. Then we'll turn inland to go over the Rise Plateau before coming down into the flatlands around Praise. Do any of you know about these lands? I've never been there."

Blank looks greeted him, and he smiled. "Then we'll all learn together, won't we? Praise Elláh. We'll watch for opportunities to please Him and let people know who we are."

Lorefim raised a hand as if still in school, then—realizing he'd done so—took it down, blushed and asked, "How f-far can we expect to g-go each day, Reb?"

"You younger men could do forty or fifty kilometers on a flat road. I can't do that with my bad hips and no repellor beam belt. Perhaps we can plan on twenty? We might tire and slow down, or we might get stronger as we walk each day."

"Then that's th-thirty-five days of w-walking. Th-that's a lot."

"Where will we stay? How will we eat?" The questions came from Tenpos in his usual deep voice. Well-built and strong, with brown hair in a long ponytail, he never said much. When he did, however, he usually had something right on target.

"I don't know, Tenpos. In a true pilgrimage, we choose to rely on Elláh. You novim brought food in your packs. It will maybe last a week, so we'll have to look for food. We may use some days to work, artha to enrich our souls. We'll find Church lodging when we can. It won't always be available, so we may sleep on the ground at times. I can't promise more than that."

Tenpos nodded. He summarized in his usual terse fashion. "It'll be an adventure."

They took a bit of time to parcel out responsibilities for each nov. Food inventory, treasurer, navigator, pack manager, advance contact—they defined sufficient roles so each member had something to do, something to give them purpose on the trip.

Fenet raised a hand to dismiss them for the evening when the door opened. Unexpectedly, his friend Pastor Eregim Steadknow stepped in with a broad smile. Eregim wore his usual robes, though with sturdy boots. As always, Eregim's physical height and breadth filled any space he entered. This time, his size loomed bigger due to a bulky backpack.

"Hello, Fenet. Hello, novim."

Surprise. Fenet almost failed to answer before it burst out of him. "Elláh be praised! Welcome, my friend. What brings you here?"

Eregim dipped his head. "You didn't think I'd let my best friend amble all the way to Praise without me, did you?"

"Why, you scoundrel," Fenet laughed. "You said nothing about going with us when we left yesterday." He stood up and wrapped Eregim in a hug.

Eregim slid his pack to the floor. "Yesterday, I wasn't sure I'd come. Elláh spoke to me in the night, and I spent much of today making preparations. I can be more useful than you know. My ministry has carried me somewhat farther than yours, so I have contacts in towns as far away as the Rise Plateau. I've sent imp messages to some of those people. I also filled my pack with long-lasting foods. If we run out, they'll serve us for many weeks."

Durnadat broke into bright laughter. He jumped to his feet and playfully held out a hand to invite the taciturn Tenpos. "Come along with us, Tenpos. We'll see Elláh's miracles from Penilos and worldly miracles from Pastor Eregim." He spun in place, dancing to a tune only he could hear, then grinned at everyone.

Tenpos smiled easily. "I won't dance with you, Durnadat, but we can still celebrate the kindness of the pastor. But Reb Eregim, what about your flock back in Glorify?"

Eregim brushed a hand away. "They'll be fine for a couple of weeks. My assistant will do well. However," he paused, "I want to be part of this, whatever it is. My life is quiet and fulfilling, yet what you are on promises to be a big learning experience. I want to learn, too."

❧ ❈ ☙

Scanat didn't know whether he'd done the right thing. He knew guilt to be the payment for doing something risky. Yet he also felt excited. His pack now bulged with transpaths, and they might enhance the miracles. He walked away from Fanwell Hall while the sky faded to darkness. He'd missed maghrib and dinner. Hunger gnawed at him. The dim light swung his thoughts toward the negative. Would Reb Fenet be pleased or angry at the transpaths?

His heart had been in his throat when he asked for the devices. Jake's response astonished him. The man simply reached into a box and handed them over. Jake seemed eager to give them away. Zofia had joined them and shown him the instruction sheet included with each unit, how to personalize it for use.

Scanat hadn't been bold enough to use one yet. He only knew they had to have been sent by Elláh; who frequently used coincidences to convey His messages. The synchronicity of this pilgrimage and the t-path appearing had to have been Elláh's work.

The heavy backpack rattled with each step, announcing the secret inside. He'd have to do something to pad the devices so they wouldn't make noise until he figured out what to do with them.

Before he got to the hostel where they'd planned to stay, he stopped at a streetside stand for a meat pie. His implant warned him of low funds when he waved his handchip at the payment kiosk. He worried how they would eat, where they would sleep, on this long, impromptu and poorly planned journey.

In a tree-filled city park, he ate his dinner, setting his pack down beside a bench under a streetlight. His mind raced on possibilities. Would they face extreme difficulties on the road due to lack of food or lodging? What about weather? Already September, nights would be cool soon. How long would this pilgrimage take? Seven hundred kilometers at maybe thirty a day? That would be three weeks or more. By then, October would come blustering in.

What about the Church? They'd already tried to obstruct Reb Fenet several times. Would they hear about this and stop the journey? Scanat had too many questions. Reb Fenet ignored the realities of what they faced. Elláh might be in charge, but each member had to do what he could. As eldest, Scanat determined to help Reb Fenet as much as he could.

The empty park reminded him of the instructions Zofia gave about personalizing the t-path units. The process took only a minute, but he had to have no other people within five meters. He looked around to check the park. With it now fully dark, the only other person had strolled away.

He pulled one of the transpaths out of his pack and examined it. No larger than his palm, rounded white plastic with a belt clip, it had a slide control for Off/On/Volume and a small red reset button inset at one end. Nothing more. Zofia had told him to turn it on, then press the red button to personalize.

He took a quick breath and huffed it out. Checking around him one more time, he clicked the unit on then hit reset. A tiny light showed yellow, but nothing earth-shaking happened. After a wait, the light turned green.

With no one around him, he felt none of the emotions he'd experienced in the presentation hall. Curious, he gradually turned up the power. When it neared maximum, he impathed faint emotions from people within the buildings around the park. Nervous and uncertain, he decided he'd done enough. He turned the unit off and put it into a specific side pocket of his pack to keep it separate from the others.

He arrived at the hostel just as the Khadam broke up their planning meeting and heading for bed. Tomorrow would be an early morning.

7 – Lack of Vision

Three things to know before entering any meeting:
1.   What you hope to achieve.
2.   What the opponents hope to achieve.
3.   Common ground that might be acceptable.

—A Practical Guide to Sensitive Negotiation by Ellen
Thranadil, 426 A.T.

Jake, Zofia, and their sales agent, Elena, traveled the next morning from Glorify to the Rathas capital city of Praise. Jake had stayed at the luxury Monopol hotel on his prior trip here, when he established a national distribution agreement. Today, he had their aircar take them to the same hotel for a posh lunch in the white-draped room. The TechEmpath success allowed them to indulge at times.

After settling at the table, Zofia asked, "Do you truly think this side trip is necessary, Jake? I'm enjoying learning about your aspects of the business, but bangit, I've got to get back to the development team. We're so far behind on improving the production processes. I need to be there."

"You have good engineers working on it, love, like Randy and Mos." Jake said. "I need you here because coming as a team is a powerful statement. The obstruction in Glorify yesterday showed us a problem with the trade commitment. If a local leader can countermand the national authorities, we need to work more closely with those authorities. That's why we're here. We've got to meet again with the Minister of Trade to refresh our position."

The high-class food and business atmosphere fit well with their need for a strategy session, and the hotel resided on the same square as the Church Center One administration building for their conference. Despite a modest crowd, the room stayed quiet because each table offered a privacy technology that scrambled both sound and vision to anyone not at the table. Besides the privacy, the paneled wood and chandelier lighting highlighted the success of their business.

Jake added, "If you believe you need to be in Thad City with the developers, you could go back without us, Zofia. I know the production weighs on your mind. But you are needed here, too, to speak to any technical issues."

"Okay, you're right," Zofia said. "This is good, too. Besides which, I'm still not up to speed on how you do the politics and marketing. I'd like to learn more, you gorgeous hunk of example." Her eyes twinkled while she poked him in the rib.

Elena waved a fork in the air, her pale blue eyes concerned. "Rathas is problematic, Jake. It's unlike anything I've known in Tileus. They intertwine religion and politics in a way that obstructs progress. I've had trouble with it ever since you sent me here. Everything they do, every decision they make, is filtered first through a duty to their god. If they're in doubt, the answer is usually 'no.' In addition, I'm finding they shove me aside because I'm not their typical submissive Church woman. I have to push hard sometimes, which makes them uncomfortable. I'm glad you were able to show the deacon your agreement, because he wasn't listening to me. I suspect he's already sent a complaint to his superiors here in Praise."

"What would be the response to such a complaint?" Jake asked.

"From what I've seen, the quick response will likely be to shut down further presentations while they pray over it." Elena framed the word "pray" with air quotes.

Jake shook his head. "No. That's not acceptable. We need to spread the t-path across the entire world. We're making progress in Verdant Prime, and I've just hired an agent for the country of Winter. We can't let Rathas close us out."

Elena asked, "Should we use our transpaths during the meeting?"

"No," said Jake. "They're only one-way. We'd have an unfair advantage they'd see as an unwanted intrusion."

Zofia leaned forward. "This Minister, what's his name? Pronas Dominact? He's the one you met with before, right?"

"Yes, he's the same one," Jake said.

Zofia nodded. "Then you have some leverage from the earlier agreement."

"True," Jake said, "but he could reverse his decision if it's politically useful to him. Elena, you've been here in Rathas for a month now setting up that presentation. You must have learned something about the country. What approach can we best take to keep him on board?"

Elena had a ready answer, "Put it in terms of faith, which drives everything here. It opens doors. You don't have to be a believer— though it helps—but you do have to speak about it and acknowledge their faith."

"Okay. What do they mean by faith?" Jake asked.

Elena pursed her lips. "That's a tough one. They have firm doctrine they consider to be a path to faith, but that's not faith itself. When a church member believes the doctrine, it's a starting point. What faith means to them seems to be believing in their god—Elláh—so thoroughly as to make all decisions based on what they think He might want."

"So, if I talk about the t-path as being Elláh's path to enlightenment of humanity, do you think it would help?"

"It's a start," Elena said. "We need to put it all in the context of what's good for Rathas. We could also make the point Rathas would trail the abilities of other countries without the t-path. They have pride; they won't want to be behind."

Jake considered the implications. When talking with Minister Dominact, he'd take an attitude of humility toward their beliefs. That would help.

At the appointed hour, the three of them arrived at Church Center One, the Rathas government house. Jake had been here before, yet the building still impressed him. It rose six stories high with white marble façades, statues of prophets in alcoves, and gold trim shining in the blue-white sun. Four minarets rose from the corners like graceful arms reaching to the heavens. The sun sparkled rainbows through stained glass windows in the central dome. Atop the dome, a towering spire lofted a gold statue of the archangel Israfel blowing his trumpet. A broad flight of steps led to the main doors, surrounded by a cloister of Gothic arches. Carved verses from *The Holiest* graced the curved sides of each arch.

"They want you to be awe-struck, don't they?" asked Zofia, who hadn't seen the building before.

"It's more than that," said Elena. "Most of them actually believe all this. They want to be reminded of it at all times, so they can live it."

"Reminds me of that Scanat fellow yesterday in Glorify," Jake added. "The one who talked about miracles and took a half-dozen transpaths. Do you think he was serious?"

Zofia shrugged. "He certainly believed what he said."

They announced themselves at the reception desk, which registered their implants for identity and access to the building. After a short wait, a minor functionary in grey robes and red collar arrived to lead them into the building. They stepped as a group into a lift tube that whisked them to the top floor. Their guide left them in a conference room with seating for a dozen.

"They're efficient enough," commented Jake.

Elena laughed. "They are that. The One Church has strong control in every aspect of life."

Zofia smiled. "I feel like an honored guest." She made her way to a drink station at one end of the room. "They've got tea for us, Jake."

He chuckled, remembering when they'd first met and her surprise at discovering another tea drinker. "Do they have your chamomile?"

"Yep. And your Earl Grey." She was already pouring hot water. "Elena, do you want something?"

"Just some ice water, thanks."

Jake turned back to the room. Ordinary well-crafted furniture. The wainscoted walls held several paintings of religious themes.

He looked up when the door opened. Two men came in. Their grey robes were made of a flowing material seeming to reflect all the light in the room. Both wore the orange collars reserved for national ministers. An assistant in plain grey followed them and moved to the drink station, busying himself with preparation.

Jake had met the first man, Pronas Dominact, Minister of Trade, two months ago to set up their product entry into the country. Short and stocky, Minister Dominact bustled forward with a smile and a handshake.

"Welcome back, Jake," Dominact said without pause. His words were as brisk as his constant motions. "Good to see you again." He had black hair, thicker than usual for a man of middle age, that framed a round face with intent brown eyes.

"Glad to be here, Minister."

Dominact broke the handshake before Jake finished his greeting. The man was disconcertingly energetic.

"Let me introduce you to my associate. This is our Minister of Security, Beltaret Leaderlist."

Leaderlist shook hands with Jake. Older than Dominact, he stood tall and erect, shoulders back in a military stance radiating dignity and power. Grey hair and grey eyes in rugged features made for a striking appearance. Every hair held in place. Unlike Dominact, this man kept himself controlled and still, as if ready for instant action.

"Good to have a chance to talk with you," said Leaderlist. "We need to have a chat about your devices." His deep voice did not sound welcoming.

Jake nodded slightly, hearing a possible threat. "Let me introduce my team. This is Elena Hahn, our company agent for Rathas. And this is Zofia Palatin, my Vice President of Development—and my wife."

The ministers nodded curtly to the two women, not shaking hands, then took seats on one side of the table. Jake raised an eyebrow to Zofia, who shrugged. Greetings apparently done, Jake took the center position across from the ministers with Elena and Zofia flanking him. The assistant, who'd not been introduced, placed tea in front of the ministers and stood by the door.

Minister Dominact opened the conversation. "I understand we had a bit of problem yesterday in Glorify."

Leaderlist lifted a finger to interrupt, gaining a raised eyebrow from Dominact. "Perhaps we should state that a bit differently, Minister?" His eyes fixed on Jake. "We understand your company, TechEmpath, created a problem yesterday in Glorify."

The change in tone took Jake by surprise.

Before he said anything, however, Dominact spoke on top of Leaderlist. "I don't believe TechEmpath alone caused the problem, Minister Leaderlist. Our own Church leaders in Glorify may not have understood the national nature of our agreement."

Jake said, "Correct, Minister. We very much appreciate the agreement you've made with us to distribute transpaths in Rathas. We believe it enhances the spiritual goals of your Elláh, providing a new path to individual spiritual growth. Yet some confusion appeared there in Glorify."

Leaderlist compressed his lips and tapped a finger on the table.

Jake said, "Elena can tell us what happened." He waved a hand to her.

"Based on our arrangement," said Elena with her usual speed and force, "I met with Deacon Tempstay in Glorify. With his help, we booked Fanwell Hall—on the city square—for our presentation. It's the largest hall in Glorify. We'd hoped to have enough interest to fill it, and we did. I hired local people to post banners and flyers around the city three days before the meeting, and arranged for them to prepare the room. We shipped in an inventory of transpaths for free distribution. On the day prior to the meeting, with all arrangements in place, the deacon accosted me and told me he'd cancelled the meeting."

Dominact fidgeted during Elena's explanation. Now he leaned forward. "Why?"

Elena frowned. "He said our devices violated Elláh's Creation."

Jake watched Leaderlist. The minister listened to Elena with a disdainful sneer and eyes cold dead.

Dominact continued, "And what happened?"

"I had anticipated some resistance on faith grounds, so I explained our agreement to him. I also gave him the good reasons for it, which Jake had relayed to me from your discussions. First, the t-path could further Elláh's integration of His believers by helping them to love each other. And second, Rathas as a country would fall behind the other countries in its technology and capability."

Dominact raised an eyebrow. "And did this convince Deacon Tempstay?"

"No. He maintained his position. Afterward, I contacted Jake, who was then in Verdant Prime. He came to Glorify yesterday and showed the deacon your agreement. We hold our presentation last night after all without harm."

Jake took over the discussion. "So, Minister, we asked for your time today. This incident embarrassed us, and also Deacon Tempstay. What can we do to make sure our agreement is honored throughout the country?"

Dominact shuffled his teacup from one side of his place to the other. "Harrumph. Well. Part of why we agreed to meet—"

Minister Leaderlist cut in. "It appears, sir, the Glorify lead deacon had the correct interpretation after all."

Jake didn't immediately understand this pronouncement. His mind raced, processing the minister's words. He found nothing positive to lean on. "Are you saying, Minister—"

"We are going to terminate Minister Dominact's agreement with you? Yes, that is what I am saying. The Service Ministry has determined your 'transpath' to be an abomination, a human intrusion into Elláh's realm. As such, this has now become a matter of national security, which is why I'm here. We have declared the transpath to be illegal here. You may no longer bring your devices into Rathas."

Zofia's fiery nature came forward. Before Jake could stop her, she said, "How can such a device be against Elláh's will? Didn't He create the materials and skills we've used to develop it?"

Leaderlist drew himself erect and sniffed. He turned briefly to Zofia. "Mrs. Palatin, your question is completely inappropriate. As a non-believer, you cannot presume to understand the theology of the One Church. Please do not try."

Jake put a hand on Zofia's arm. Her anger had flashed fierce, and he wasn't far behind—though he tempered his with dismay. He couldn't have her escalate this problem. What he'd hoped would be a cordial reaffirmation had broken into direct conflict over Leaderlist's attitude. How could he settle the confrontation? Having their business kicked out of this country would be a terrible blow to their plans. They both hoped the transpath would change humanity, reducing conflicts like this—but if the t-path couldn't enter one of the four countries on Verdant, how could their dream come true? Would this refusal trigger similar actions in Prime and Winter?

With chagrin, he realized again his own immaturity in business. They had not properly evaluated the culture in Rathas.

"Jake, we're leaving," Zofia declared.

Jake considered what to do, but only for a moment. He nodded in acquiescence. "Yes, you're right. We're leaving."

Jake watched the ministers while he and his team passed them on the way out. The two men said nothing. Dominact seemed sympathetic. Leaderlist stood with stoic arrogance, as if he had fulfilled his goal for the meeting.

8 – Missionaries

How do holy wars start? First, realize there is no such thing as a pure holy war. Religion may have a prominent role in any conflict; one side may use religion as a rallying cry; but wars always have ethnic, political, and territorial components. Lack of understanding and compassion for others is often a root of war.

—*The Making of a New Humanity* by Ellen
Thranadil, Tileus Press 448 A.T.

Jake, Zofia and Elena walked in silence back to their aircar under a sky dimmed by sudden clouds. Jake couldn't lift his eyes from the pavement. This meeting had devastated him; it had dealt a dreadful blow to their plans. His mind raced to change what had happened, to find a chink to break it apart, though he knew he couldn't alter the past. He accused himself for his own inexperience. He should have explored the Rathas culture. He should have done more research, better planning. He sent someone to make a presentation without the research, an ill-conceived idea. He should have known women didn't lead business in Rathas. More understanding of the One Church and their faith had been important, and he'd not undertaken to learn it.

Zofia put a soft hand on his shoulder. "I'm sorry, Jake. I shouldn't have spoken."

Her apology brought him out of his own fugue. He looked up, a painful lump in his throat. "It's not your fault, babe. It's mine."

Elena stepped out in front and held up her hand to stop them. Her face looked like shattered rocks. "No, boss. It's mine. You gave me the responsibility for this marketing, and I screwed up. I only focused on getting a presentation done, and I didn't do my research." She gulped. "If you need to let me go, I understand."

Jake looked back and forth at the two women. "We've all had a hand in this debacle, but ultimately, it's my responsibility. Elena, I made the mistake of hiring a woman to handle marketing in a male-dominated culture. Zofia, you're still learning about politics and marketing, and I should have given you better instruction on how to take part in the meeting. I led us right into this mess, and that's my fault."

He started walking again, putting a hand on both women's shoulders. "Let's take ourselves back to Thad City, and we'll regroup. Re-strategize. Elena, we'll have to move you to another position."

Elena nodded. "Thanks, boss. I'll help in any way I can."

❧ ✳ ☙

Beltaret Leaderlist walked back to his corner office from the small conference room with a contented smile on his face and warm satisfaction in his heart. He had saved Rathas from a catastrophic error. He'd have to send a commendation to the deacon in Glorify for blocking the transpath presentation. As always, Beltaret's goal—his human dream—remained the safety and security of Rathas and the One Church. He would fight for that dream. Purity mattered.

As for Pronas Dominact, the incident revealed a weakness. Dominact was a good man and a fine politician. Beltaret admired the way he used his constant fidgeting to distract opponents until the sting. Yet a touch of idealism led to his willingness to bring such a revolutionary technology into the country. He'd not considered how it might destabilize the Church, Elláh created all things in the world, often through the hands of people, but not everything was beneficial. The technology needed testing first in a small, discreet way—not so much to prove the technology as to assess its impact on faith. Beltaret had just the plan to do so.

Captain Frinat Forsfear waited in Beltaret's office. Beltaret had known Forsfear for five years, ever since the man, then a simple proctor, approached him about creating the elite Heresy Angels as a branch of the national proctor force. Beltaret had sponsored the idea.

An interesting, dangerous man of thirty-seven, Forsfear stood trim and well-built, yet he topped out at less than 160 centimeters of height. He often exhibited "short man syndrome," carrying a chip on his shoulder, quick to attack any perceived slight. With an intent stare and dark features, he carried his athletic build like a badge of power. Forsfear wore the dark grey military-style uniform he had designed for the Heresy Angels, a distinct break from the usual robes of all other Church authorities. Yet the uniform still had a red collar, identifying him as a proctor. That uniform, and Forsfear in particular, had begun to strike fear in the hearts of those who tested the bounds of Church doctrine.

"Good afternoon, Minister." Forsfear wasn't a man to wait for permission to speak. His voice rasped like a dangerous weapon sliding projectiles into its chamber.

Beltaret nodded to him and waved a hand toward the comfortable side chairs. "Tell me about the missionary problems, Captain," he said while they sat.

"I wouldn't yet characterize them as problems. We're still flooding Tileus with our missionaries in groups of six. Every week, we send a unit to one of their major cities, rotating through Thad City, Uptown, and Freetown. Some weeks, we send a second unit into the smaller towns farther north. We're having an impact on the infidels."

Beltaret fixed him with a skeptical gaze. "But there are indeed problems, aren't there?"

"Problems are relative, Minister," Forsfear said with a shrug, "Difficulties are common when you confront erring people with the truth."

"Be more specific. Don't waste my time talking around the issues."

Forsfear nodded. "Yes, sir. We have conflicts with fringe groups in Tileus. Their form of pure democracy fosters conflicting opinions. Political groups shout at each other in the streets. Some of them confront our missionaries."

"Democracy is overrated. Too much freedom is not Elláh's path."

"I think freedom itself is overrated," Forsfear snorted. "Just because they *can* do whatever they want, they espouse all sorts of perversion. It's a consequence of their national voting system. I can't believe it works at all. The entire country—every citizen— votes through the InfoNet on every new law. Votes come up several times a day, and campaigning for upcoming votes is constant. The people think it gives them some sort of authority. Instead, the national voting pushes them into chaos."

Beltaret waved his hand in the air. "Yes, yes, I know your opinions on that. But to your point. Has there been any violence around our missionaries?"

"No, sir, not yet."

"Then we'll keep sending them. May or may not have an effect on Tileus, but the missionary trips still act as good training for our young people."

The captain nodded. "Yes, sir." He paused. "I also wanted to raise another issue."

"What is it?"

"I'm concerned about the message our missionaries are sending. I'd like for my Heresy Angels to have a hand in approving the individuals for those trips."

Beltaret raised an eyebrow. "Approval? Everyone goes. It's part of our policy to require a missionary trip before someone can join the Church."

"Yes, sir, but I'd like to insert an interview step into the process. We need to ensure those missionaries are presenting the right message."

What did Forsfear want this time? More power? Some of the captain's goals alligned with what Beltaret wanted for the Church, but others stepped close to the edge of personal aggrandizement. Seeking individual power conflicted with spiritual growth.

"I'll have to think about it, Captain. Why don't you put your request in writing, with an explanation of what you envision for goals and methods. I'll review it before deciding."

The captain's face showed his disappointment before he got it under control. "Yes, sir. I'll do so."

"That'll be all for now, then. Keep me posted."

They stood. Captain Forsfear rose to an erect, military posture and clicked his heels while making a sharp nod.

Beltaret watched him go. He'd have to continue monitoring that one.

❦

At twenty-one, Morat Intelact followed normal practice to go on mission, though he would rather not. He dreamed of owning a shop, not being a missionary. He went to church. Everyone in

Rathas did, or suffered consequences. He fit in, echoed the readings and sang along with the others. He spent much of his church time planning how to get started in a shop.

Mission! Returnees told stories of confrontations with the crazies in Tileus. Morat wasn't a bold man, fitting in with others more on the basis of his affability and good looks—blond hair and blue eyes—than on innate leadership. He did not at all appreciate going into any kind of danger.

After a week of training, their mission group had now traveled to the Tileus city of Uptown for a week, near the eastern foothills of the Gortooth Mountains.

Today, they followed Roloket through the city streets, a half dozen young people huddling together in defense against the chaotic activity. Buildings rose above them to five and eight stories. Tileans surrounded them in garish clothing of reds, greens, and purple—every color Morat could imagine. They shouted greetings and imprecations with an exuberance never seen in Rathas.

The trip did hold one attraction for Morat: his girlfriend Faïlebaso Servdo. Beautiful like a poignant song, she had enough boldness for both of them. Not to mention some delightful curves. Perhaps her father, a leading bishop, could help Morat reach his dream. Morat loved being with her and felt responsible to protect her. He worried something terrible might happen to her and he wouldn't be able to stop it.

"They're wild, Faï," he said to her while the six of them walked in a huddle behind Rolo. "How can we reach them with our message of peace?"

Unlike his own worry, Faï's eyes sparkled with eagerness. "We'll find a way, Morat. Elláh will open doors." Her enthusiasm infected him.

"I hope you're right. I try to keep my faith strong, but this place is a challenge."

She spun around and punched him on the shoulder with a grin. "So, buck up and meet the challenge. Elláh can do anything, including strengthening your faith in Him."

He threw up his hands with a grin. "Okay, okay. I know you're right. This will all be fine, and we'll grow from it."

"That's the attitude." She rose on her toes to kiss his cheek, her hand lingering on his shoulder.

Faï not only excited him; she inspired him to reach higher.

"Hey, everyone," said Rolo, the mission leader. He had a few years on the mission members. After his own mission, he'd started leading other groups. He'd labeled this his ninth trip into Tileus. "Yesterday we spoke in an assembly hall. Structured witnessing. We didn't make any converts, but we had about eighty people come by at various times. Today, we're going to work the streets."

"What, out here?" said Gadim, the worrier of the group.

"Yes, out here. We've got a permit to speak on a specific corner two blocks away. We have to stay on our corner. We're not allowed to chase people. That's the law here in Tileus."

Morat spoke up. "They have laws about religious witness? They're not even religious."

"It's not about religion. Their laws apply to any group speaking in public. Tileus has a problem with political factions fighting each other. They include us as the same kind of group."

They continued walking while Rolo gave them more rules. Stay on the corner. Don't touch anyone. Don't block people or slidewalks or vehicles. You can do verbal witnessing, but nothing more.

"And here we are, folks," Rolo finished. "This is our corner."

Morat saw a busy crossing of two streets, just like the last several they'd passed. A narrow center lane carried floating autocars, though not much traffic existed. Slidewalks on either side of the car lane held packed pedestrians. Buildings rose around them in different heights from three stories to as many as ten. Most ground floor spaces were filled with shops, with occasional doorways leading upstairs. The noise of the crowds seemed deafening.

"It doesn't look any different than any other corner," Faï said with a bright laugh. She squeezed Morat's hand in encouragement.

Faï hardly paused, her bold impetuosity coming into play. She let go of Morat's hand and held a copy of *The Holiest* high in the air.

"We have the Way, folks! You don't have to live your life in defeat and misery. Follow Jaysus in praise of Elláh, and you'll be uplifted into a peace you've never known." She glanced at Morat, her eyes twinkling.

Morat couldn't fall behind Faï. He had to join her or forever hide his face. His deeper voice joined hers while he held his own *Holiest* up. "Jaysus said, 'I am the Way, the Truth, and the Life.' We can show you the Five Pillars that keep you grounded in the Spirit."

His heart pounded in his neck. He'd never done anything like this before, but he knew what Rolo expected. They had to reveal themselves to these strangers hurrying by, daring to speak about what Elláh had done with them. So, he kept shouting.

"I was lost. We all were, at one time. I did sinful things and hated myself for it. But Elláh called me, and I followed. What an amazing difference! And you can have it, too."

The others joined Faï and Morat. Shortly, all six missionaries were striding back and forth on their corner, holding the book aloft and shouting to the crowds around them. At times, they'd lower the book to read passages, picking verses they thought most meaningful.

Morat wondered how this message could possibly reach the people. No one stopped to listen. Most hurried past, their faces displaying irritation. However, he preached on; Elláh would move their hearts or not. He shouted his own personal revelations, times when he'd been astonished at how Elláh acted in his life.

His heart lifted when he saw a group of five gather on the opposite street corner. They actually stood still and listened.

Faï directed her words to them. "Yes, you over there. Listen to us. You stop because you know there's something better. You don't have to live an empty life. Our Way is a path of spirituality, a way of togetherness, a way of surrender."

The group smiled at them, and Morat felt joy.

Then the cluster lifted signs they held.

"Down with Religion!"

"Stop the Missionaries!"

"Pass the Religious Restriction Law!"

The group walked in a circle on their corner, round and round, chanting, "No More Faith Talk, No More Faith Talk." They jostled their signs and stomped their feet in time with the chant. Some of them shook a fist at the missionary group.

What? They can protest against us? What kind of place is this?

Beltaret moved to his desk. Back to the transpath technology. He rubbed his forehead with thumb and finger. This next task felt distasteful, like wading through a sewer, but it had become necessary. He used his imp to connect with his secretary.

"Caropina, did you get hold of Shoras Guileart?"

"Yes, Minister, he's waiting for your call. They're an hour later in Thad City, so he's at the end of his work day."

"Thanks, Pina." Beltaret ended the call and connected to Guileart.

"Hello, Minister," the man answered.

"Good afternoon, Shoras. I hope you've had a productive day."

"Yes, sir. My cover story gets stronger every week. I don't see any signs someone has penetrated it. As an example, today I contracted for the sale of several lift-truck loads of produce to Uptown, to be delivered in the next week."

"You do this under your cover name of Johan Wellesley, right?"

"That's right. Welles Distributing. It's a legal company under Tileus law, as a front. They don't know I'm from Rathas; they all believe I grew up here. The contracting today went smoothly with no suspicion."

"Good. Keep it so. The intelligence you're providing is already making a difference. 'Johan Wellesley' becomes more valuable with each passing month. The better you're established, the more we can use you to probe deeper into Tileus."

Guileart's voice displayed satisfaction as well as his natural confidence. "Thanks, sir, I also made some new contacts in Uptown today. People with details about the border defenses along the Gortooth Mountains. I'll gain insight into where our forces can best cross the border."

"Excellent, Shoras. Most excellent. Keep at it." Beltaret paused. "However, that's only part of why I called. I wanted to know if you'd made progress on our private matter?"

A quiet laugh sounded through the imp. "Easier than we'd thought, Minister. Tileus is soft. People here have no concept of security, other than leaving it to their military. They're all focused on their own lives. The country is so disordered, I found a target right away."

Beltaret snorted in amazement. "Someone willing to be a traitor?"

"Well, sir, he wouldn't put it that way. But ..." he paused, "let's say he's more than willing to accept a lump payment of 'outside income' to help advance the spread of the transpath. That's what I've told him."

"And he's well positioned?"

Guileart guffawed. "He's one of the key members of the TechEmpath development team. Works directly for the Zofia woman."

9 – Sudden Jump

There are many gifts, all from the same Spirit; and there are varieties
of service, but the same Lord; and there are different activities, but it
is the same Elláh who empowers them. To each is given the
manifestation of the Spirit for the common good. For to some is
given through the Spirit ... the working of miracles.

The Holiest, Book of Paul XII:4-10

Yesterday's hike had been short compared to the plan for
today, Fenet's first real day of pilgrimage. He'd set an alarm
in his imp for early prayer. This morning, his hips still hurt
but not unbearably so. Leaving the novim still asleep, Fenet went to
the familiar chapel in the Glorify hostel.

The small, empty room glistened with peaceful silence at this
pre-dawn hour. A parquet floor held neat five rows of prayer mats
with a narrow central aisle. Behind the altar rose a wood-carved
version of the One Church trifacis, symbol of the three-fold yet
joined Elláh. The side walls had high windows with stained-glass
images of historical faith surrenders. Fenet smiled at one ornate
window showing King Bali's offering of everything he owned plus
his entire self to Bhagwan Vamna. He stopped in the entrance to
take in the spiritual force. His heart swell with renewed peace.

He moved forward to one of the mats, laying his staff on the
floor. Closing his eyes, Fenet put palms together to intone the
standard fajr prayer. He chanted the first stanza while standing,
head above heart, reminding himself of the conscious choice he
makes each day. For the second stanza, he bowed in submission to
Elláh, the essence of the saranagati choice. During the third, he
knelt and lowered his forehead to the mat, arms outstretched, with
heart above head, spirit above mind, prostrate before Elláh. After

the salat, he spent longer than usual in the last position, meditating and letting the Spirit flow into him. Finally, he lifted to kneel upright with open hands on his knees, eyes closed, to make specific prayers.

"Elláh, heavenly Father, guide us in this day and on this journey. I choose each day to surrender to Your will, not knowing what may happen. But You know my physical weakness, and only You know how I can make this pilgrimage. Show me, please. Let me be Your tool, forged as You see fit."

A warm hand rested on his shoulder while he finished. Fenet might have been startled, but the peace of the prayer time held. Eyes still closed, he nodded acknowledgement of the support. Whoever touched him honored the meditation by not speaking. Fenet breathed four more times, giving the peace enough time to fill his heart, and finished with "Selah."

Fenet opened his eyes and looked up. Eregim stood beside him, eyes closed, lips moving in his own silent prayer. Fenet smiled and put his hand on Eregim's.

After a few more breaths, Eregim also opened his eyes and smiled. "Good morning, Fenet."

"Good morning, my friend." Fenet chuckled. "Are you ready for a bit of a walk?"

"As ready as I can be," Eregim laughed. "You set us a task that may be beyond the two of us who are older."

"Not beyond us at all, I'm certain, because I didn't set the task. Elláh did. He never gives us more than we can handle. You were there when it happened."

"Yes, I was. Your youngest nov—poor Penilos—Elláh is using him most mightily."

"And teaching me as well." Fenet struggled to his feet with the support of his staff. "Let's awaken the Khadam and start this day. I've already done salat, but we'll do it again with them."

An hour later, Fenet and his group ambled down the Coast Road to the south, leaving the outskirts of Glorify. The land blocked by the city buildings spread into view. On their left, rolling ridges climbed into the rounded, graceful forms of the Glory Hills. On the right, the slopes continued down to sea cliffs. This area had been settled for less than two hundred short Verdant years. Tilled fields surrounded the packed-dirt road; farther away, blue/green/russet forests soaked up the sunlight to bless the pilgrims with a world of colorful beauty.

Eregim and the Khadam adjusted themselves to Fenet's slower pace. He put one foot in front of the other with the help of his staff, ignoring the pain in his hips. At the top of the next gentle rise, Fenet stopped. The countryside placed joy in his heart. Down the gentle grade, a hookbird circled over a sparkling pond. Elláh gave Fenet words to express his joy:

The world opens wide with reaching arms
　My soul spreads to fill the space.
Like a bird turning arcs in a cloudless sky,
　Heart follows soul apace.

Fenet laughed, feeling a bit silly. Yet he did enjoy making poetry again. He lowered eyes from the scene ahead to see the entourage watching him with interest and a touch of awe.

"Oh, get on with you all." He shooed them forward with his hands. "We have a long way to go today." He couldn't limp on both legs. He had to just keep moving forward, using the staff as he could.

"W-will we m-make it to Fisher today, Reb?" asked Lorefim while they all resumed walking. "I remember that as the first b-big town on the map."

"I don't think so," Fenet said. "Ask Tenpos. He's our navigator."

Tenpos raised his head. "It's a bit over a hundred kilometers. Not even tomorrow."

"Is it actually that far?" asked Beneim.

"Of course, it is," said Scanat to him. "Look at the map."

Durnadat laughed. "At least he was there last night, Scanat. Where were you?"

"He was probably off finding a girlfriend," Beneim quipped.

"Not a girlfriend," scoffed Scanat. "Not ready for that in my life yet."

Lorefim joked, "D-does that mean the rest of us have to w-wait until we're t-twenty-four also?"

Everyone laughed.

"Good one," said Durnadat.

"Reb Fenet, do we have any plan where to spend tonight?" Tenpos asked, always the practical one.

Fenet shrugged. "No plan, Tenpos. We're trusting in Elláh to provide."

"Three years with the reb has taught me to like trusting in Elláh," said Beneim. He squirmed. "This backpack is beginning to chafe my shoulders."

"You're all carrying too much," Eregim offered. "But that will be self-correcting when we eat some of those extra supplies you brought. Durnadat, you're our pack manager. Did you balance the weight we're all carrying?"

"Sure did, Reb. And I eased up Reb Fenet's burden some." He gave a friendly shove to Scanat's shoulder. "But Scanat here didn't want me touching his load."

Scanat frowned. "I've got what I need."

The conversation continued while the novim walked ahead of Eregim and Fenet. Eregim quieted his usual rich voice. "Friend, you look like you're already hurting. Is there anything I can do to help? I have some pain patches."

"No, Eregim," Fenet said. "I've prayed about it, and this is exactly what Elláh wants me to do. A pain patch would be as much a violation as the repellor belt."

"He wants you to hurt?"

"I think so. I understand it as penance for not trusting Him."

"He said purification, not penance. But what about your staff? Isn't it also a violation?"

"I asked Him about it specifically. He told me it was acceptable." Fenet winced when a sharper stab of pain went through his right hip. Stopping for a moment, he stretched the leg and the pain eased. "He wants me to suffer for now. I'm willing."

Eregim cocked his head. "As long as I've known you, sometimes I don't understand you. You can be bull-headed. For instance: I'm here on this trek with you, but I have no idea why you're doing it."

"You heard the command."

"I heard your nov Penilos speak. Was it really Elláh speaking through him?"

Fenet felt a sudden coldness. "What are you suggesting?"

"Perhaps this whole trip is foolish—or the way you're going about it is foolish. I don't know. On the word of a seventeen-year-old boy, you're torturing yourself. We could still return to Glorify. You could hire an aircar to go to Praise."

"Ah, Eregim, you're sounding like Saitan. Disbelief and human pride instead of humility to Elláh. Get thee behind me with your temptations."

Eregim stepped away a pace, shock on this face.

Fenet appealed to him with more force. "Do you think I haven't heard such counsel in my own head? From the moment Penilos spoke Elláh's words, I've been doubting and fearing. I have no idea how I can walk seven hundred kilometers on these hips. I may be crippled before we ever reach Fisher. Yet despite my fear, I choose to believe. I choose to follow." He paused, lowering eyes to the ground in front of his slow steps. "Please don't voice my doubts. Help me instead."

His friend stepped close again, contrition in his eyes, and put his arm around him. "Of course, Fenet. You're right." He lifted Fenet's arm over his high shoulder and took some of Fenet's weight. "We'll walk together."

They started up a moderate slope with a crest half a kilometer ahead. Fenet welcomed Eregim's help. Walking uphill stressed him more.

In front of the two, Lorefim had stopped walking, his hands on his pack straps. The other novim continued; Eregim and Fenet caught up to him. Lorefim's eyes glazed, apparently measuring the hill in front with his usual mathematical precision. What Elláh had taken away from him in speech had been given back in mathematics. Fenet wondered how accurately the young man could gauge the hill. He also wondered if Lorefim saw the rise to be as intimidating as Fenet did.

Abruptly, Lorefim spoke in a forceful voice Fenet recognized, without a trace of his natural stutter, just a single word:

ADVANCE!

From one eye blink to the next, the entire group advanced to the top of the hill. Fenet stumbled on a new rock in his path that hadn't been underfoot when he started to take the step.

Everyone stopped in shock, then the novim blathered together.

"What happened?"

"Who did that?"

They spun around, looking at their changed surroundings.

So did Fenet, albeit slower. Shrugging off Eregim's arm, he looked back down to where they had been a moment before. The dust still settled in their footsteps at the base of the rise. Then he turned to Lorefim and laughed.

"Your first miracle, Lorefim. Congratulations."

As quickly as he'd spoken for Elláh, the young man came back to himself, looking puzzled and amazed. "A half k-kilometer," he said, "Elláh moved us a half kilometer. Through m-me."

Durnadat yelled and pounded Lorefim on the back. "Fantastic. Great! You and Penilos! Who's going to be next?"

"Me," shouted Beneim, raising his hands up to the sky. "Me next, Elláh. Healing that tree last year wasn't enough!"

"At least you did that much," argued Scanat.

The novim were all grinning. Eregim flaunted a broad smile.

Fenet's own cheeks were about to split. Years of trying to teach disciples how to do what Elláh had given him to do—and now he could no longer do it, two of them had met with success. He held bittersweet joy over this.

"Do it again, Lorefim," shouted Durnadat. "Take us to the next hill. Save us all those steps."

Lorefim blushed. "I c-can only do what Elláh t-tells me to do."

Fenet's own words, taught to them all. He couldn't wait to see what Elláh would do next.

❧ ❈ ❧

Scanat's jaw clenched so hard his teeth hurt. He couldn't believe it. Standing at the side of the road, resentment boiled like a thermal spring. When Penilos channeled a couple of miracles, Scanat let it go. Penilos was still just a kid; Elláh could use him easily. But Lorefim, nearly as old as Scanat, had been with Reb Fenet for almost as long. *How can Lorefim get this power before me?* Four years, and he'd never been graced with a single miracle. The unfairness of it burned. He felt like a discarded tissue used to wipe a spot of grease. This wasn't right. Not after so many years of following Fenet.

He had to do something to reestablish his position as eldest nov.

Scanat nodded to himself, determination mixed with resentment. While the group stopped, he slung his backpack to the ground. To cover what he did, he pulled out his water bottle and took a drink. No one watched him; everyone focused on Fenet's newest miracle-pet.

When he put the bottle back, he reached into the side pocket where he'd stashed the t-path personalized to him. Without removing it, he turned the device on at a medium setting.

The elation of the others immediately washed into him.

When he looked at Durnadat, Scanat felt his friend's exuberance bubbling forward. Scanat almost smiled. Lorefim conveyed joy and confusion, Tenpos a steady warmth, and Penilos' aura filled with pleasure for Lorefim. All the novim, except himself, gave forth an emotional high. The sensations nearly overwhelmed him.

Scanat's own heart eased out of his resentment while he impathed the emotions of the others. Their joy lessened his anger. This seemed a good thing, but Scanat kept careful skepticism about how real it all felt.

He looked at Reb Fenet and Reb Eregim, focusing the t-path on their emotions. Fenet broadcast a deep satisfaction tinged with concern. Eregim simply pathed happiness.

When Scanat had felt the emotions back in Fanwell Hall, the technology seemed as miraculous as the things Fenet did. The t-path offered Scanat a new way to understand Fenet's lessons. That's why he'd grabbed at the chance to get a set for the Khadam. He'd intended to provide them to all, to help the group do better. Now, he wasn't so sure. He feared the feelings of joy and satisfaction would overpower his own emotions. At this moment, the technology scared him.

He needed more time to get used to it. He set his jaw. That must be it. He turned down the power and left the unit active. He'd be able to impath the emotions while they walked without being overwhelmed.

If Penilos or Lorefim performed another miracle, maybe Scanat would get the chance to know what it felt like.

10 — Roadside Excitement

The transpath spread across the world quickly, as often happens with new technology. By one year after its introduction, thirteen percent of people in Tileus had experienced the transpath. The numbers were somewhat lower in Verdant Prime and Winter due to later product launch. Then Rathas prohibited the device, which threatened a halt to its progress in the rest of the world.

—*An Annotated History of Verdant* by Ellen Thranadil, Tileus Press 442 A.T.

After three days, Fenet and his Khadam had walked eighty kilometers, still twenty short of Fisher, the first sizable town on the journey. They had held to salat, stopping for prayer each day at sunrise, noon, and sunset. Penilos and Lorefim had performed another couple of small miracles—smoothing the beds in generously-provided barns, advancing the group up the steeper hills—every one of which raised the spirits of the Khadam. Their days filled with laughter.

Fenet started each day with high hopes, quickly squelched by the pain in his hips. Each day brought greater difficulty. He had hoped this would get easier, and Elláh would get him past the pain into a new acceptance. Mid-afternoon of the third day, clouds rolled in from the western ocean, bringing windy, cool weather. The change in air pressure increased his aches.

They reached the top of a rise, where a carved boulder read "Lower Glory Pass, elevation 342m." From this point it would be mostly downhill to Fisher. However, Fenet was done. He sank onto the boulder to ease the pain. Sitting wasn't enough. He shifted position several times.

"Fenet, what can we do?" asked Eregim, his hand on his friend's shoulder.

Fenet gritted an answer. "I don't know. I trust Elláh, but I can't continue for now. I need to lie down."

The Khadam had stopped a few paces ahead, waiting on him, concern on their faces.

Eregim steadied Fenet to slide off the boulder to the ground. Straightening out, flat on his back, the joints in his upper and lower spine screamed and wouldn't release. He realized he'd been compensating for the hips by misusing his back. Long seconds went by while he stretched out his legs and forced his head back onto the ground. When everything finally released, Fenet let out a huff of air that came all the way from his toes. He laid there with eyes closed, blowing air, smelling the harvested fields and listening to the rustle of leaves in the wind.

Powrfaith? He couldn't even walk anymore, much less exercise any power. His powername no longer described him. Perhaps he'd have to change it again. He clenched his eyes to hold back tears.

In this moment, barely started on the trek, failure consumed him.

The youthful voice of Penilos called out, "Hey, everyone. Join with me. Come over here."

"What for?" asked Beneim.

"Are w-we taking a break?" said Lorefim.

"No," Penilos said. "Just come here. Let's try something." His voice sounded right above Fenet.

"Why should we follow you?" sounded the skeptical tones of Scanat from farther away.

"Because this is part of what Reb Fenet taught us to do for anyone in need," replied Penilos, his voice closer, "and the reb is in need."

Fenet opened his eyes to find Penilos kneeling beside him. Beneim and Lorefim joined him a moment later.

Penilos urged the others, "Come on, everyone. Lay hands on the reb and pray."

Now Fenet understood what the boy had in mind. He nodded and closed his eyes again, concentrating on breathing. The others shuffled closer. Warm hands touched Fenet, distinguishable by their character: the tentative touch of Penilos on his right shoulder, Beneim and Lorefim on his right arm and leg. The strong hand of

Tenpos on his left shoulder, joined by what must have been Durnadat and Scanat. Fenet took a deep breath and smiled. Whether they healed him or not, their love lifted his spirits.

A seventh set of hands cradled his head. Eregim whispered close to his ear. "Relax, my friend. We are here for you."

Penilos raised his innocent voice. "Dear Elláh, we ask your intercession for our leader and teacher. Reb Fenet gives us a great example in his surrender to You, in the many miracles You have granted through him. Now he needs Your healing. Ease his pain, Lord. Bring him peace and strength to go on."

A whining rumble grew in volume while the boy spoke. The sound came through the air as an irritating buzz; as it increased, the ground reverberated with the deeper part of the sound. Fenet set it aside to concentrate on Penilos' prayer.

"Reb Fenet has taught us to pray to You for what we may need. He's shown us to lay on hands to direct our spiritual force. We come together now in agreement of our need, of Reb Fenet's need." Penilos tried to continue, but the growing noise of a lift-truck climbing the hill overrode his voice. He stopped.

Everyone echoed, "Selah."

Fenet opened his eyes to see the vehicle crest the hill. This immense truck loomed as the largest of several they'd seen in three days. Its load appeared so heavy its repellor beams lifted the undercarriage less than a meter above the roadway. The vehicle came to a shuddering stop beside the company; the throbbing rumble in the ground faded when it settled.

"Looks like a vercorn harvest," said Beneim from where he knelt.

When the noise of the truck eased, the sound of rough voices in merry song took over, crude lyrics about drinking and carousing. Enthusiastic farm hands hung on the outside of the truck, ready for the celebration that comes with harvest. Taking the yield into town would be their opportunity for several days of revelry. Three jumped down from inside the cab, another four from footboards beside the cab, and half a dozen from the tailgate.

"What'cha all doin'?"

"Is someone hurt?"

"Anything we kin do ta help?"

Had Fenet not been in pain, he might have laughed at the sight the Khadam made. They formed an interesting tableau: one man in rough clothes flat on his back and another seven in ecclesiastic grey robes kneeling around him with hands placed everywhere, backpacks scattered on the ground. Now this crowd of farm hands further enhanced the montage by pressing around the Khadam like pigeons eager for their share of bread.

"Hey!" one of them shouted. "Are y'all prayin' over him?"

The novim looked at each other with abashed faces, embarrassed by the attention. All of them took their hands off Fenet and sat back on their haunches. Their evident uncertainty in what they did felt like a failure in his teaching.

Eregim stood up, using his rich voice to answer the farmers. "Thanks for your concern, folks. Yes, we've just been praying over Reb Fenet. It's been a long walk, and he's not up to it."

One man stepped closer. He carried himself with an assurance that identified him as the leader of this farm group. "Reb Fenet, you say? Would that be Fenet Powrfaith?"

Surprised and chagrined, Fenet looked up at the man from his awkward position and laughed. "Yes, indeed, sir, though I fear I'm not at my best." He rolled to one side to start the painful process of standing again with the help of his staff. Tenpos and Durnadat put their hands under his arms to assist, and he struggled to his feet. The rest of the Khadam stood also. Fenet slapped his hat against his pants and settled it on his head.

The leader nodded. "I'm Chernos Greenlead, and this is my crew. I've heard of you, Reb Fenet. Stories of miracles up there on the other side of Glorify. I heard recently about a tractor, healed in time to pull in the harvest."

Fenet nodded. "Good to meet you, Chernos." Leaning on his staff, he shook hands. Lying down for a while had eased his pain.

"Are the stories true? The Church says miracles are only tales of the past."

"They are true. Elláh granted me the gift of miracles over twenty years ago. Each of these—my disciples and my friend—can testify to the truth." Fenet paused while the novim nodded. "And yes, the Church doesn't like that we do miracles. The wonders violate doctrine. Yet we must do what Elláh puts in front of us to do."

Chernos tilted his head, studying Fenet with interest. "Do you choose which miracles to perform?"

"No, sir. Elláh decides. All I can do is ask." Where did this farm leader expect with these questions? In the past, other people had similar questions. Sometimes, rigid adherents took the side of the Church and became antagonistic. Other times, the curious had a need he could help.

This man gave an approving nod to Fenet's answer. "Farm work is dangerous work, Reb. A moment's inattention, and a harvester can take off a man's arm or leg."

The farm hands looked at each other, perhaps discomfited by the reality their leader spoke.

"Three of my crew suffer with long-term injuries that lessen their pleasure in life and their ability to work. Do you think you can heal them?"

Fenet had heard so many requests like this. Sometimes Elláh said yes, sometimes no. This time, however, his heart sank into his shoes. A brief mist blew cold from the clouds above, promising more rain later. Fenet leaned on his staff, lowered his eyes to the ground, and took a deep breath.

"We can ask, sir, but I'm sorry to say Elláh took His power away from me this week. I've not done any miracles since—"

Penilos interrupted by touching Fenet's sleeve. His face glowed with expectation and eagerness.

Fenet caught the boy's meaning and changed the end of his sentence, "but it is also true that some of my disciples have sometimes been able to work them. We can ask—"

Another interruption. A buzzing sensation in the air raised the hairs on Fenet's arms. He stood straighter, looking around for the source. So did Penilos and Eregim. The novim were still clustered together behind him. While he watched, three of them stepped forward—red-headed Beneim, jovial Durnadat, and taciturn Tenpos. All three had eyes fixed on something unseen by the rest. Without hesitation, without any identification of whom to approach, they moved to the farm crew, each one singling out a different worker.

HEAL! pronounced Beneim. He touched a tall man's shoulder, and the man's crooked elbow straightened.

HEAL! echoed Tenpos, laying his hand on a shorter man, who unbent his back and stood straight.

HEAL! Durnadat shouted, waving his palm over a stocky man whose eyes grew wide as he hobbled backward. A ruddy light washed from Durnadat's hand down to the man's leg. A prosthetic lower leg toppled out of his work pants. The man shouted, nearly losing his balance while he balanced on one foot. Within ten seconds, new flesh grew to fill the empty space. A newly pink club foot appeared, then quickly produced new toes. The man now stood on two feet.

At first, everyone halted in shock. Then the farm crew jumped around, clapping each other on the back. The stocky man started dancing, unevenly with only one shoe, laughing loud enough the birds in the surrounding trees flocked to the sky in a chattering cacophony. Eregim and the remaining novim shouted praises to Elláh, lifting their hands to the sky. Chernos stumbled backwards, nearly falling when his heel caught a rock.

"Praise Elláh," Fenet shouted. Still Powrfaith, through his disciples, even if he didn't take part in this one. He would retain his powername. It would be right again someday.

Scanat had the transpath turned on the entire time. When the farmer asked for healing, Scanat had been standing with the Khadam behind Reb Fenet. He moved his eyes from nov to nov, including Fenet and Eregim. The t-path worked best when he watched the specific person he wanted to feel. Would it work this time? Would he sense a miracle?

A strange sensation of overpowering urgency came through the t-path from Beneim, Durnadat, and Tenpos. Their eyes had glazed over. The intensity transmitted by his three friends stunned Scanat, who felt Elláh's authority channeled through them. The t-path left him no doubt about the reality of this feeling; his mouth dropped open and he stepped back from the three as they moved forward.

So, this is what it feels like to be part of a miracle. His breath caught. When Elláh spoke through each of the three, a powerful sense of awe lifted Scanat's spirit like a hookbird lifting a fish. He gasped for air, watching the three farm hands become whole.

Scanat fumbled for the t-path. He couldn't reach it. These emotions were too much for him, too consuming. He unslung his pack to one shoulder and scrabbled at the side pocket to reach the unit. Desperate to stop the sensations, he scraped the switch to the "off" position with a frantic finger.

He stood, separate from the rest, panting quick breath, like escaping from a near-death accident. Sweat bloomed all over his body, drenching his armpits and torso.

Gradually, his breath calmed.

On the heels of the physical reaction came an emotional reaction. His jaw clenched. His hands tightened into fists. Resentment filled him to the brim like bitter bile.

Why wasn't *he* included?

༄ ❋ ༄

Fenet stepped forward to shake hands again with Chernos, while pandemonium still reigned among both groups.

A handshake wasn't enough; Chernos grabbed him into a bear hug so tight Fenet almost lost his staff. The farmer shouted into Fenet's ear over the noise of rejoicing. "Praise Elláh, Reb Fenet. I can hardly believe it. Thank you ... thank you!"

Fenet laughed with everyone else. "I didn't expect it, sir. But as always, Elláh has His own plans. This is for us both artha and kama, work and passion."

"It seems so, Reb." Chernos laughed almost too hard to get the words out. He released Fenet, who checked his ribs were still intact.

"I'm very pleased we could serve you and your team," Fenet said.

"So am I. These three have been crippled for over four years. We'll be celebrating this miracle for weeks to come, perhaps all winter. And we'll remember this all our lives." Then he turned serious, looking at Fenet. "But tell me, Reb, you're in such obvious pain. Why? Why didn't your novim heal you when they prayed?"

Melancholy infused Fenet in the midst of the celebration. "I have no answer, sir. I do not know the mind of Elláh, but today he has a difficult path for me to tread. All I can do is follow."

Chernos smiled. "Then keep following. Keep following, because it works." He waved a hand at the rejoicing crew.

Fenet's three new miracle workers—Beneim, Durnadat, and Tenpos—had come back to reality, as astonished and delighted at what they'd done as the rest. The farm workers surrounded them, bouncing up and down while hugging them in thanks. Eregim, Penilos and Lorefim joined in their joy. Scanat stood by himself to one side.

Elation flowed into Fenet, displacing his personal sadness. When the spontaneous celebration quieted, joy flowed through him in words he spoke to all Creation.

> *Praise to Elláh in the day, on the heights,*
> *In joy of Him, honor His time.*
> *Shouts of the world, extolling His might,*
> *May each of us strive to climb!*

The entire company had become quiet while he recited. Then laughter rang out again, from Lorefim. "But, Reb F-fenet, we're already at the t-top of the road. There's nowhere higher to climb!"

Chernos clapped Fenet on the back. "May we give you a ride into Fisher, Reb?"

The answer came inside Fenet in that warm, familiar voice.

THIS TIME, FENET, ACCEPT THE HELP.

11 – Challenge of Diplomacy

Hidden information turns the tide in many negotiations. Often, the side that exposes concealed data at the most appropriate time wins.

—*A Practical Guide to Sensitive Negotiation* by Ellen Thranadil, 426 A.T.

In the dark post-midnight stillness, a lone figure tramped through the streets of Thad City in the country of Tileus. Dark buildings loomed above him with few lights still on. The city carried a faint odor of dirt, magnified to rank humanity when he passed an alley. He raged inside, his jaw clenched in anger. Why couldn't he get the recognition he deserved?

The man he was going to meet would change that.

His bosses, Jake and Zofia Palatin, hogged all the glory. Yet they didn't deserve it. All Zofia had done amounted to a bit of clever programming, and Jake hadn't done much of the work at all. Yitzak Goren, that genius over in Verdant Prime—he invented the whole transpath and made the first prototype. He *gave* the plans to Jake. Jake simply implemented them here in Tileus. Yeah, making it big enough for the conference room required changes. Individuals on the team made those changes. Like himself.

Jake did nothing more than coordinate—and get all fussy and difficult during the process. Even Zofia had to calm him down at times.

The dark figure's steps pounded harder on the pavement. His fists clenched.

He himself had solved some of the most difficult problems during that fast-paced development. Since then, he'd done the primary work on miniaturizing the whole device. He'd taken it from a room-sized system to a palm unit. He'd changed it from broadcast to personal.

Now those stupid bosses had failed in Rathas. He couldn't believe Jake and Zofia had been so naïve as to send a woman to do sales inside the Church. Must be because they grew up isolated in Verdant Prime. They just didn't know how the rest of the world worked.

But he did. He'd sold other devices within Rathas before TechEmpath. He knew the trick to choose the right contacts, to pick the appropriate paths.

If the bosses wouldn't give him recognition, he'd take it for himself. Tonight was crucial. This Johan Wellesley fellow had approached him last week with credentials from the highest levels of government over there in Rathas. Tonight, Johan had promised to help him get the personal transpaths back into Rathas through those superior contacts.

And the credit would go to him when sales started happening. Not Jake. Not Zofia. Him.

And when he finished the development of more efficient production, the same contacts might help him start a competing business. He would build devices faster than Jake and Zofia.

Today, no one beyond the TechEmpath team knew of him. That would change.

❧ ❈ ❧

The next afternoon, Beltaret Leaderlist waited on a park bench in Praise. Cool autumn brought a light breeze blowing the faded blue leaves off the loula trees. The russet leaves on the erythers were starting to change to deep red. Beltaret enjoyed the scent of fall, the fusty smell that took him back to childhood when he'd kick the leaves on a forest path.

He smiled at the incongruity of himself, the national Minister of Security, lolling in a park. Church leaders, those who wore grey robes, rarely lounged. Of course, today he had a reason. And here it came.

The unmemorable man sliding toward him along the brick walk faded into the background—even a background of bright fall leaves. Medium height, medium age, battered briefcase, worn clothes—it would be difficult to find a combination less noteworthy. Even his gait drew no attention. All of which made him an excellent clandestine agent. Beltaret didn't mind using a spy, though he would never trust one.

"Good afternoon, Minister." Shoras Guileart joined him on the bench. "Thanks for meeting me."

Beltaret chuckled drily. "I employ you specifically so we can have these meetings. So long as you bring me items of value, then you are worth my time."

"I met with our target last night." Shoras' small smile leaked triumph around the corners. "We concluded the current transaction, an indecent payment for sample devices—and a piece of his soul for his betrayal. He hopes to gain fame."

"I doubt that will happen. Is he truly possessed with sin?"

Shoras shrugged. "Most of the people in Tileus are. They have no goals except their own selfish aims. Power, money, fame, whatever motivates their individual little race for glory. Not very trustworthy for higher goals. Having a greater purpose gives me an advantage."

"I'm sure. Knowing Elláh is always an advantage." Beltaret tilted his head, fixing the man with a hard look. "If they were trustworthy, they wouldn't be traitors. Have you compromised your cover with this man?"

"No, sir. He only knows me by the name I use there, Johan Wellesley."

"Good. So, what did you purchase?"

Shoras lifted the briefcase to his lap and touched its lock, likely also activating the touch with a command through his implant. "Two sample units, sir." The white transpath units nestled inside the briefcase like precious minerals. "Each one is personal in nature. One for you and one for anyone else you wish. I believe you know how to activate and personalize them?"

"Yes, I've seen the instructions. The deacon in Glorify sent me copies when he reported on that sales presentation." Beltaret turned the units over in his hands, impressed at the simplicity, before secreting them in the pockets of his grey robe. "Very nice, Shoras. Very nice indeed. You've done well. Payment will appear in your account."

The agent bowed his head in acknowledgement.

❧ ✳ ❧

Half an hour later, a satisfied Beltaret arrived back at Church Center One. The transpath units jostled in his robe with each step up the broad marble stairs. At the top of the stairs, he paused to admire the white façade, gold trim, and lofted arches over the doors. To think he had risen to this level in the Church. But then, he believed his advance to be predestined so long as he used his power for Elláh's advance.

He had grand plans for these transpath units. Having kept them out of common use here in Rathas, his own application would be even more powerful. And his use of them would fulfill the necessary test of whether they fit Elláh's goals. From what he'd heard, he would be able to discern the feelings of those around him. That ability should give a significant advantage in all his work, both domestic and foreign. He'd personalize one of the units in private tonight, then take a stroll around the city to sample what it could do. Who to gift with the second unit? He didn't know yet.

Beltaret set aside his thoughts and moved forward again across the wide terrace. The doors opened toward him and a short, powerfully built man strode out. Beltaret mistrusted Ripat Grufhand, ambassador to Tileus. The man worked for Pronas Dominact, Minister of Trade, and both men worked across the borders so much as to taint their loyalty to the Church. Grufhand in particular had taken on the ways of Tileus, where he spent most of his time.

"Good afternoon, Minister," Grufhand greeted him. "I've been looking for you."

Beltaret gave Grufhand his best impassive stare. "*You've* been looking for me? I would think you'd work through your own minister."

"I've just come from Minister Dominact's office, sir. He suggested I talk with you."

"Concerning what?"

"Our missionary problems in Tileus. The issues go beyond our authority in the Ministry of Trade."

"Indeed," agreed Beltaret. "My ministry has been watching the problems develop. I'm concerned we may not be able to protect our young people on mission."

"I've spoken with my counterparts in the Tileus government, sir, all the way up to Welton Moller, their Governor of Outside Affairs," said Grufhand, "and we've also called in the local police leaders in Thad City, Uptown, and Freetown. The authorities all claim the Tileus activist groups are staying within their laws."

Beltaret raised an eyebrow. The Tileus laws were indeed lax concerning activism. "They believe it acceptable for protesters to shout at our missionaries, so long as they stay across the street?"

"Yes, sir. That's the way their laws read. So, their police will do nothing."

"And what about you, Ripat? As our national ambassador to Tileus, can't you apply more pressure on them to control their wild groups?"

The bluntness struck home. Grufhand's face tightened and his words took on a more challenging tone. "We are already working with their people at the highest levels. Do you have any further suggestions, sir?"

The direct question stopped Beltaret. The ambassador didn't work for him; he couldn't tell the man what to do. Not only that, but Beltaret's own methods were often more forceful than these diplomats could accept. "Embassy methods are your responsibility, Ambassador, not mine—and *you* approached *me* with the issue. Is there something you have in mind that the Ministry of Security could do for your problem?"

"Yes, sir. Minister Dominact and I thought perhaps you could provide security agents to accompany our missionary groups. Of course, we'd have to clear it with the Tileus—"

"Out of the question. Our agents are not trained to operate there, nor are we authorized to insert armed guards into a foreign country. I will not do it."

"All we would need, sir, is the physical presence—"

"The guards we have are dedicated to the Khubar f'Elláh, not to protecting missionaries. The only way they'll enter Tileus is if we decide to declare Holy War." Beltaret brushed past Grufhand, not quite shoving him aside, and entered the building.

Missionary work in the streets of Uptown got harder each day for Morat Intelact during his week. The group protesting their mission became bolder. The protesters knew where the missionaries would be. Not surprising, because the mission leader, Roloket, had to apply each day for a permit. That made the location public information.

Over the weekend, the protesting group had grown larger, now boasting over twice as many people as the half-dozen of the mission group. The protest signs became larger and more offensive, the chants more personal and pointed, more threatening.

Morat no longer looked forward to each day on the street; instead, his hands shook when he arrived. His developing relationship with Faïlebaso Servdo remained the only bright spot in this week. Her beauty still had the power to take his breath away. The two of them paired together each day, following the call to bring Elláh to the people of Tileus.

The two had tried different techniques. At first, they'd shouted their message to the hurrying crowds, reading from *The Holiest* when they could. That did little other than make people avoid them. The next day, they'd started talking to individuals, which worked somewhat better.

Morat singled out a middle-aged woman who seemed more open than most. "Excuse me, do you have a moment to talk about a better life?"

Faï added, "It really will be just a moment."

The woman stopped and cocked her head. "Better in what way?"

"Filled with peace and comfort," Faï said, "regardless of what happens."

The woman looked at the surrounding scene, with several missionaries still shouting at the passing crowds while the protesters across the street marched, chanted derogatory slogans, and waved their signs. She gave a wry smile. "Doesn't look very peaceful to me."

Morat glanced across the street, then back. As many times as he'd had this conversation, his stomach still tied in a knot. "We can't do anything about the other groups, ma'am. We can only find the peace inside ourselves. It comes from knowing our place with Elláh."

The woman nodded. "Right. I've heard about your Elláh. The Church proctors over there in Rathas watch over everybody's shoulders to make sure you all follow the rules. Is that how you find peace, by forcing everyone to conform?"

Faï let loose a bright, happy laugh. "No one forces us to conform, ma'am. We choose to follow Elláh because He makes our lives better."

Nonetheless, he had not convinced the woman.

"Well, thanks, but no thanks." She turned and walked away.

Morat sighed and put his arm around Faï's shoulders. "I'd thought bringing Elláh to people would be easier. Isn't He supposed to work in their hearts?"

She leaned against him, tucking herself under his arm. "There's no promise as to when. All we can do is sow the seed. That's what we're doing. Just planting."

"I don't know, Faï. I see the chaos of this place, and I just don't know. Protesters against us. Restrictions on how we can talk to people. No one seems happy; they all scurry and run, chasing after money and power and fame. I'm thinking it's going to take more than missionaries to change Tileus."

She looked up into his eyes. "What more will it take?"

He scanned across the busy street and the crowds. "Maybe those people who talk about Holy War are right. What do you think about my joining the Khubar f'Elláh when we get back?"

❧ ✳ ☙

Even with the transpaths in his pockets, a foul mood gripped Beltaret. Grufhand had highlighted part of his problem: the ineffectiveness of diplomacy toward advancing Elláh's realm. Grufhand and Dominact sought compromise, the "win-win." Elláh had one "win" condition: people aligned with Him, following His path. The people of Tileus focused on their worldly goals, and their version of "win" didn't include humility before any god.

Beltaret's secretary, Caropina, followed him in. "We're getting some strange reports from the west coast, sir."

"More problems," he scoffed. "What reports?"

"That supposed miracle-worker, the one who calls himself Fenet Powrfaith—"

"Yes?"

"His group is on the road now, going south and east from Glorify through the small towns, and there are rumors of supernatural events happening around him."

Beltaret let out a sigh and lowered his head. Too many issues, all at once. The transpath, the missionaries, and now this. "I want more information, Pina. Contact the proctor forces in that area. Have them find out what's going on. Tell them to shut it down, if they have to."

12 – Wonder of Crowds

In 417 A.T., a sudden blossoming of miraculous events challenged the Rathas leadership. The One Church believed miracles had been finished in historical times when the source religions were started. New miracles in the modern terms contradicted the teaching of the leaders—and therefore undermined their control.

—An Annotated History of Verdant by Ellen Thranadil, Tileus Press 442 A.T.

After walking for three days, a ride for the last twenty kilometers into Fisher felt like luxury to Fenet—even in a utilitarian lift-truck. Chernos brought Fenet into the cab with him and the driver. With warm heat, spring suspension, and heavy-duty repellor beams, Fenet relaxed into the comfort.

Fenet put the straw hat on his lap and straightened its perennial flower while looking around. The harvest lift-trucks were large, but until he climbed inside, he'd never realized how big. The cab looked small from the outside, dwarfed by the rest of the truck. The inside surprised him with two rows of seats, each wide enough for four people. In their exuberance, the harvest crew still preferred hanging on to the outside of the truck, so Eregim and the three most recent miracle-workers were given the honor of the back seat. With the large Eregim and the rotund Durnadat, even the long seat hardly had room for Beneim and Tenpos. The other three novim joined the crew on the footboards.

"So, tell me," Chernos said when they'd gotten underway, "why are you and your crew on the road? Haven't you always been on the other side of Glorify?" Chernos sat in the middle of the front seat, between Fenet and the driver.

"We're on a mission, sir, one of the Five Pillars," Fenet said. "Elláh chastised me last week for unbelief. Then he gave us the challenge to make pilgrimage to Praise. Along the way, we also fulfill the Pillar of concern for the needy."

Chernos' eyebrows went up. "Six hundred kilometers away? With your bad legs? That must have been *some* unbelief."

Fenet shrugged. "Elláh has His own ways and purposes."

"I'm impressed. And you're just going to do it?"

"Of course," Fenet said, glancing back with a smile to the four in the back seat.

"Maybe you could make it easier," Chernos said. "They sell a repellor beam belt that can help—"

Fenet broke into laughter. "Yes, I know. That's what He chastised me for using."

The others in the cab stayed silent.

Chernos looked puzzled. "But what about this ride I'm giving you? Isn't this cheating?"

"I specifically asked Elláh just now. He told me to accept your offer."

"He *told* you? You heard him speak?"

Opportunities to witness were precious. As Fenet had done thousands of times, he recognized the opening. "Let me answer your question with a question. Do you believe in Elláh?"

"Of course, yes. I know very few people in Rathas who don't."

Fenet nodded. "There is 'belief,' and there is '*believe*.' What do you do with your belief?" Fenet felt Eregim and the three novim listening from the back seat.

"I pray daily. I go to church. I study *The Holiest*. As a farmer, I see Elláh's hand in the growth of my crops. I have no power to make it rain or to keep storms from destroying what we do. So, I work hard to honor what He does."

"These are all good things—much better than I did. In my early years, I was the kingpin of a rowdy group who did not believe. I chose my friends among other rakes and libertines. Carousing, drink, drugs, sexual promiscuity. I was addicted to it all." Fenet grunted. "Eregim knew me in that time and can vouch for it."

From the back seat came a bark of laughter. "Oh, yes," Eregim said, "I was a few years behind Fenet. When I was in secondary school, I thought his exciting life everything I wanted, too."

Fenet continued, "But Elláh touched me. I was twenty-four, on a Friday night in a wild pub. The loud music pounded into our bones; none of us could think. I'd already snorted five lines of crat, and I worked on my second bottle of whiskey. Two women clung on my arms, and a crowd of sycophants pandered to me.

"The room abruptly lit up with a blinding white light. So bright I couldn't see the girls beside me."

"A bright light?" Chernos blurted. "In the bar?"

"Some sort of spiritual light. No one else saw it. It wasn't painful; I didn't even need to squint. The clamor of the bar faded to silence for me, though no one else noticed. A sweet scent replaced the smell of liquor and broken humanity. The carousers still danced, the band still screeched, drinks were spilled, but my head went into a different place."

"Was this real?" Chernos asked.

"As real as the seat we sit on. I heard His voice say, 'I need you, Fenet.'"

"The same voice as now? How do you know it was Elláh?"

"I knew instantly, and I've known every time since. The voice comes with an unquestionable sense of power, peace and comfort." Fenet paused, remembering yet again. "I had an impulse I didn't understand. I put my arms around the shoulders of the two women. A brighter flash—how it could have been brighter, I don't know— surrounded the three of us ... and we were sober. That was my first miracle. My addictions disappeared in the instant; I never needed drink or drugs or sex afterwards." He paused. "Though, I have to say, those two women didn't thank me. They were actually quite angry at being sober."

Chernos and the others chuckled.

"Since then," Fenet said, "I've been a channel for Elláh's miracles. Thousands of them."

For a while, no one spoke. The throbbing sound of the repellor engines filled the cab.

The driver broke the silence. "What's it feel like to perform a miracle, Reb Fenet?"

"Maybe I should let one of these three in the back seat answer." He turned his head to them. "Durnadat?"

"Huh? Oh." Durnadat answered, surprised to be called on. "Back there at the pass ... uh ... the power filled me," his words accelerated "it took over my entire mind and body. Like something huge and marvelous controlled what I did. I had no idea what I was about to do. My hand felt warm, as if over a fire. When the man's leg grew back," he stopped for a moment before rushing forward. "Awe filled me like I'd been a small pitcher under a torrent of water alive with—I don't know—alive with life, I guess."

For the rest of the trip into Fisher, they spoke of the miracles they'd seen and done. The time raced by with occasional spates of misty rain, and soon they came into the town.

Chernos said, "You've given me a lot to think about, Reb. If I hadn't seen today's miracles for myself, I'd be disbelieving all your wild stories. But I saw, and I can't deny what I saw."

"Keep seeking, Chernos," Fenet told him. "Elláh will make it clear."

Fenet had never been this far from home. The town, smaller than Glorify, still lorded it over any of the farm communities he knew. He saw the central spire of a church topped by a gold trifacis; it would have been more impressive on a sunny day. The early evening of autumn approached; low clouds made the world quiet, a bit gloomy.

Chernos intended to park his lift-truck at the grain storage facility, ready to empty his harvest first thing in the morning. On the way, he dropped the Khadam at the ecclesiastical housing complex next to the church. Those who'd ridden outside were damp but cheerful. Before parting, both groups stood on the road: Chernos and his harvest crew facing Fenet and the Khadam.

"Reb Fenet, I can never thank you enough for what you've done."

"It wasn't me, Chernos. It is always Elláh."

"But you've shown me what's possible. Even more than the miracles, you inspire me to deepen my faith in Elláh."

Irrepressible Durnadat danced with delight. "Deeper faith is what does it, sir." He swept his arms out to the entire Khadam. "That's why we follow Reb Fenet. May Elláh be praised in everything."

స్ ✳ ⭒

Hard rain pounded the roof in the middle of the night. Awakened by the sound, Fenet laid in the sparse bunk pondering the path they were taking. What did Elláh intend? Why did five of the six novim— all but Scanat—now do recent miracles, all of them significant?

None of them had performed more than one or two minor miracles in their entire prior time with Fenet; Scanat, Lorefim and Penilos had done none before these events. What should Fenet be learning? Was he open to learn? No answers came before he fell back asleep.

The next morning dawned shiny, clear, and cold, a crisp autumn day. After salat, Fenet and the crew gathered in the church refectory for breakfast. The large facility could hold a hundred people, with about thirty already eating. They selected a table then went through the line to get eggs, sausage, biscuits and coffee, wonderful treats after two nights in barns.

"We all slept in this morning, boys," Fenet said, "but we should get on the road again after breakfast. Let's remember we're still on Elláh's mission."

"No c-celebration, Reb?" asked Lorefim with a smile.

"Oh, go stuff yourself," laughed Durnadat, shoving Lorefim's shoulder. "We didn't stop to celebrate each time you moved us an extra kilometer, did we?"

"Praise might be better than celebration," said Beneim.

Fenet nodded. "Good way to put it."

A grey-robed deacon entered the room. He looked across the tables, then hurried toward the group. "Reb Fenet Powrfaith?"

"Yes, sir. That's me."

"I'm the facility deacon. Didn't have a chance to meet you last night, though my friend Eregim here had called in advance to reserve your space." He put a hand on Eregim's shoulder, who covered it with his own hand and a smile. Then the deacon continued, "We have a problem."

Fenet looked across the table at Eregim, who shrugged.

"Is it something I can help with?" Fenet asked the deacon.

"I hope so. It involves you."

Fenet sat up straight in surprise.

"Would you come with me, please?" The deacon led the way from the refectory through the interior courtyard to the admin building and front door. He stopped and pointed through the windows toward the morning, where clouds wafted apart to show bits of blue sky.

Hundreds of people jammed the damp street beyond the wrought-iron fence of the ecclesiastical buildings. How could a town like Fisher have so many? They stayed in quiet order. Groups stood or squatted everywhere: families, individuals, work crews.

"What's this about?" Fenet asked, confused.

The deacon turned to him and shrugged. "They're waiting for miracles, Reb Fenet."

His heart sank. Small crowds frequently followed him these days, in the local areas where he taught and healed. In all his years of being Elláh's servant, he'd never seen a packed street waiting for him.

Fenet muttered to himself, "This must be in response to what happened yesterday."

"What was that?" the deacon asked.

Fenet shook his head, dismay rising. "My novim healed some men from a harvest crew on the way into town. The crew went out last night to celebrate; they must have told people about what happened."

"Well, Reb, there's not much our chapter can do about this. It's up to you and your novim."

Was this the price of a little fame? Perhaps Fenet's dream might be more difficult than he'd imagined.

⁂

A half-hour later, Fenet led the Khadam out the front door into the garden between the building and gate, a clot of grey robes—and Fenet's casual tunic—issuing forth to an unknown fate, soldiers of Elláh on sortie. When they appeared, people who'd been sitting or squatting rose to their feet, like a wave flowing across the street. Shock and fear rode on the faces of the novim. Eregim stayed at the back of the group. It became apparent to Fenet that Elláh also forged the others in this group.

"W-what can we possibly do?" asked Lorefim. "There's two hundred fifty of them, and only six of us."

Tenpos crossed his arms and grunted.

"That's a lot of people," said Beneim. "What if we disappoint them?"

Scanat gasped. "Yeah, that's a lot of people."

Fenet gave a quick shake of his head. "Boys, we have no idea what Elláh plans for this situation. Let's find out."

He led the group to the ornate garden gate and took a deep breath before opening it. They faced a frightening new experience.

The crowd kept order, with everyone staying in their place. People looked tentative and awed. Fenet saw some faces with hope.

One man stepped forward, his hand on the shoulder of a limping pre-teen boy. "Are you Reb Fenet?"

Fenet stepped through the gate, the novim right behind. "I am, sir."

"Are you …" he paused, uncertain, "Are you healing people, Reb?"

Fenet didn't know whether to laugh or cry. "I'm not. But sometimes, Elláh heals people through my novim." He waved his hands at the six, now spread out on either side of him along the fence as if for execution.

"My son, Reb …" the man swept his eyes across the novim. "His knee …"

Through the corner of Fenet's eye, he saw a shudder sweep through Penilos.

The youngest nov stepped forward and knelt down. He cradled both hands around the boy's knee and spoke with Elláh's voice.

CHILD, BE WHOLE.

The air around Penilos' hands sprouted a rosy glow that pulsated once, then flowed inward to penetrate the knee. The boy's eyes went wide. He jumped back from the nov and turned to face his father. For a painful, delayed moment, the boy said nothing while Fenet and the Khadam held a collective breath.

Then the boy whooped and jumped into the air, landing in a crouch. "It works, Papa! It was hot for a second, and now it works!" He jumped up again from the squat, hooting with laughter. He ran around his father, then threw himself onto the still-kneeling Penilos to hug him with all his strength. "Thank you, thank you, oh, thank you."

Before the father could say anything, a bent old woman stepped up beside him. "My aches and pains, Reb …"

Beneim, on the other side of Scanat, stepped to her and laid gentle hands on her shoulders. *MAY YOU HAVE RELIEF*, he spoke. As with Penilos, a red wash went from Beneim's hands into the woman's torso.

With no pause, others stepped forward, one by one and in small groups. Amazingly, they remained in order. No one pushed or shoved forward, each waiting their turn. When each one came up, one of the novim stepped to them, almost as if it were choreographed. Ellah's voice sounded on all sides. Hands flushed with ruddy radiance, warmth flooding into whatever damage had been sustained. Durnadat gave his merry laugh and broke into dance each time he healed someone, then turned to the next. Tenpos stood like a protecting rock, stolid and sure in each movement. No stutter occluded Lorefim's voice; he strode with confidence from one seeker to the next.

Most of the miracles were physical healing, though a few other instances stood out. One child brought a damaged doll. Lorefim laughed when the doll's head reattached itself. A young woman came to Durnadat with a broken heart and walked away with peace. A nurse came with the medical doser from her doctor's office, in tears because the technicians had declared it unfixable and the struggling doctor didn't have enough money to replace it. Tenpos healed the doser.

Fenet stood in awe at Elláh's power displayed so freely. His two decades had seen isolated incidents, a few a week. This whole scene stepped far beyond anything he'd done. Fenet traded a deep look of wonderment with Eregim, then saw his friend also taken over with the divine power.

Elláh suddenly expanded Eregim's native power to preach in confident humility. "Friends," his voice rang, "Blessed is each who has the modesty to come forward.

"Blessed are those with infirmity, for Elláh will heal.

"Blessed are those who are weak, for Elláh will give them strength.

"Blessed are those who surrender to Him, for they shall receive His vigor.

"Rejoice. Be glad, for you are here today to be blessed. You are the people of Elláh, and He is your god."

Eregim had always been an imposing figure, tall and broad with a rich voice for oratory. However, in all the years Fenet had known Eregim, he'd never heard his friend speak with such power, such forcefulness. His words rang across the street, demanding the attention of those still waiting their turn. The message drew Fenet himself. He had no doubt the words Eregim spoke flowed through him from Elláh.

The entire scene gladdened Fenet, but he also felt left out. The novim healed penitent after penitent, Eregim orated stronger than he'd ever preached before, the crowd of patient people absorbed the Spirit while waiting their turn. As for Fenet ... he stood, uncertain. What part did he have in this? Standing by the gate leaning on his staff, Fenet shook his head in amazement and wonder. His breath rushed fast, as if he gasped for thin air. Other than that, Fenet could do nothing. The event had passed him by.

Beneim brought an older man to Fenet. "Reb, this man asked for his teeth to be straight. I couldn't work a miracle for him."

A few miracles had already failed. Fenet saw them as teaching opportunities, which he could still do. "Thanks, Beneim. Go ahead back to your work." He turned to the man. "I'm Reb Fenet Powrfaith, sir. What's your name?"

"Menotos Barkeep, Reb. Why won't your nov heal me?" The man's voice held disappointment and also anger. "I need a better smile, sir. I'm courting a young woman, and these teeth have held me back all my life."

No doubt, his crooked smile would put people off. "Menotos, I can't speak for Elláh. He has His own reasons for everything, but we know He uses all things for our good. Perhaps He has a good reason for your teeth to be the way they are. Your asking to change them would then be against Elláh's will."

The man nodded, but set his jaw. "So, you can't do anything for me, even though you can fix a child's doll?"

"It's not our choice, sir, but Elláh's."

Menotos whirled and left, obviously not satisfied. But Fenet had laid a seed that Elláh would fulfill in his own time.

Fenet watched the novim work, then realized only five took part. Scanat still stood on his right. Fenet started to speak to him, but something in the young man's eyes prevented him. Scanat scanned from nov to nov, his breath even faster than Fenet's. His mouth hung open in wonder. Scanat had never performed one miracle in four years with Fenet, but something happened with him now. He turned to watching faces in the crowd. Squatting to put his backpack on the ground, he transferred a palm-sized object from a side pocket of the pack to the pocket of his robe.

Scanat abruptly moved forward into the crowd. He grabbed the shoulder of a young man, one who looked too weak to walk, and pulled him stumbling forward to Beneim.

"This one, Beneim. Do this one next."

13 – Missing Equipment

Sometimes, the best thing you can do is bring in a consulting expert.

—*A Practical Guide to Sensitive Negotiation* by Ellen Thranadil, 426 A.T.

Having lived in Thad City for a year now, Jake still sometimes shook his head at the hectic activity. "Look at this, Zofia." He pointed at the groups marching through downtown with political signs on this early afternoon. "It's so different than the ordered pedestrians we grew up with in Verdant Prime. These people shout at each other across the street. And the mad rush of people here is crazy."

They walked with their friend Soren Moller, dodging the clots of people. The two of them towered above the short, burly police detective. Soren said, "That's the sound of freedom, Jake. You never had much of that in Prime."

Jake glanced at Soren, catching the man's solid satisfaction through his t-path.

Zofia added, "It's all politics, love. Trying to affect the next little vote coming up." Her words were mild, but her emotions tangled with caution about the uncontrolled activity around them. Her eyes constantly shifted from one movement to another.

"Of course. I know that, but it's still so strange to me I can't help but smile." He put a calming hand on her arm and felt her relax.

After Soren had arrested the two of them for illegal entry into the country last year, and after they'd straightened it out, the man had worked with Jake and Zofia. Soren's father, Welton Moller, the Governor of Outside Affairs, had pulled him off police work to assist their rapid development of the t-path. Soren had used his knowledge of underhanded procurement practices to buy necessary equipment and supplies while bypassing the usual red tape. They'd worked so well together they'd become good friends. After their success, Soren had returned to his award-winning police work.

"I guess you're right," Jake chuckled. "Though there ought to be something between the totalitarianism of Prime and this ..." he waved a hand, "chaos."

Zofia shrugged and leaned into him. "What we've got here in Tileus is pretty good." Her ease pathed into his own senses. "The business is going well, too."

"Yeah," Jake said. "Even with the setback in Rathas, we're changing the way people interact with each other."

Soren's feelings came across more serious, competent, confident. "I've noticed it in my police work. Meetings flow better with a t-path in the conference room. Interrogations are easier, too, because we can impath when the perps are lying to us." He laughed, a quick, dark sound. "It's better than a polygraph." He thought a moment, eyes distant. "There's also been a reduction in crime. I was looking at statistics for Thad City yesterday, and crime is down twelve percent compared to last year." He turned back to Jake. "Do you think it's a result of the t-path?"

Jake considered it. Could they be having that much impact already? "We installed systems in just about every conference room in the city by six months ago. The Tileus government subsidized the installations for private industry."

"And we started selling personal units," Zofia's spirits pathed higher, "about a month ago. They're going like hotcakes. Everyone who's experienced it in a conference wants it for themselves."

"The impact would be greatest here in Thad City," Jake said to Soren, "because that's where we started. Installations in Freetown and Uptown lagged behind; we haven't gotten to all their conference rooms yet."

Zofia stopped walking and looked at the two of them, her eyes sparkling and her emotions buoyant. "This is marvelous. We'd hoped we were having an impact. Now, we can point to results that matter. Think of it, Jake. We can use this in a marketing campaign. *'Crime is down twelve percent.'* What a great statement to make."

"Great idea," said Jake, He stopped with her and leaned down to give her a gentle kiss. He loved how the t-path fed back her joy to him so they both rose together. He took both her hands, impathing the physical warmth and connection.

"Okay, you two," chided Soren. "I feel your love tingling all over, but let's get back to business."

Jake squeezed Zofia's hands then let go. They started walking again. "Right. So, what are we going to do about Rathas? Prime is accepting t-paths, and the islands of Winter are getting started, too."

Soren tilted his head with a skeptical look. "You both realize you were rather naïve about Rathas, don't you?"

"Not Zofia," said Jake. "This one was all my fault. I screwed up. She's working development; I'm responsible for marketing."

"I've wondered why you two split it up that way," Soren said. "You led the first development, Jake. You were good at it. A bit hyper at times, but good. Why did you move into business and leave the development to Zofia?"

Jake thought hard, trying to remember their reasoning. "Well, someone needed to do it. We wanted to maintain control. And it sounded like an exciting change to me."

"Shoot," said Zofia "it also gave us both a reason to grow. I'd never led a development team before, either. We both hope we're doing the best we can."

"Regardless." Soren shook his head. "You needed to do more research on Rathas. Bad move on your selection of agent."

"Yeah, I know that *now*." Jake sighed. "I wish I'd consulted with you or Governor Thranadil, but Elena Hahn's credentials seemed like a good choice at the time."

"Are you sure, love," chimed Zofia with an edgy smile, "you weren't just turned on by her looks?"

Soren raised an eyebrow at the gibe.

Jake hung his head. She'd brought this up to him several times in the last few days. Even worse, he had to admit the attraction had indeed influenced his decision. Irritation rose about her bringing this up again now in front of Soren. "I made the best decision I could, Zofia." He took a deep breath to calm his irritation, knowing Zofia could sense it through her t-path.

"Can't change the past," Zofia said. "I don't want to butt into your territory, but I have an idea what you can do about Rathas."

Her quiet words eased his irritation. "What's that?"

"Well, Filip Kaminski's been doing a fine job over in Winter. Why not move him to Rathas and let Elena take his position? She might not have read the situation in Rathas right, but she still has some great experience from her prior work."

The idea resonated with Jake. "Give Elena another chance, in a place where things are already going well? What do you think, Soren? You've got more knowledge of business than we do."

Soren nodded thoughtfully, and his emotions echoed his agreement. "Sounds like a good plan to me, too."

"Then we'll do it," Jake said. "I'll talk with Filip when we get back to the plant. If he agrees, I'll put it to Elena."

The three walked on, the autumn afternoon calming them. The jingling of bells from a street vendor's hot dog cart replaced the political shouting behind them. Jake smiled to see Soren eyeball the street vendor, apparently checking for her license on display; always the policeman, always watching for crime.

Then Soren turned his attention back to the pair. "I'm sure the marketing issue wasn't why you asked me to join you."

Zofia's pathed mood swooped downward. "Uh ... no. I think we've got a problem that needs your police expertise."

Jake chose to listen; Zofia had screwed up in this area, and he knew it.

"Police expertise?" Soren asked. "In what way?"

"We've had some equipment go missing. Lab prototypes, component parts. No record of where they went."

Soren pathed interest, concern, professionalism. "Have you reported the losses?"

"No, everything so far is too small to be of much value. Except for the intellectual value. And the two personal t-path units. And I'm not sure it's theft."

"Have you had any break-ins?"

Zofia cocked her head. "Not that I'm aware of. We still have the security measures in place that you installed last year."

Jake couldn't help himself. "In place, but not being used."

She flashed back at him. "Bangit, you think you could do better?"

He took a deep breath. "I *did* do better, Zofia. Remember, I worked in a classified defense lab. The security measures are there for a reason." Was his irritation at her? Or perhaps still residual from knowing his own failure in Rathas? She could certainly feel his irritation through her t-path, whichever source drove it.

"Shoot, *love*," she said, the word taking on a contrary meaning, "maybe we're *both* screwing up in our new jobs, huh?"

Soren leaned closer. "Hey, friends. Remember I've got a t-path, too. Your love tingled my spine. Conflict ain't fun at all."

"Sorry, Soren," mumbled Jake. Zofia just hmphed.

"Back to your issue, Zofia," said Soren. "You're sure the losses are real? Not enough to break threshold, but things are missing?"

She nodded, her jaw tight.

"Sounds like an inside job," Soren said.

Jake bit off words accusing Zofia again.

She jerked her head back and pathed shock. "You think so?"

"Certainly," Soren answered. "I can help. This is what I do. Let's start without making it a big deal. Why don't you invite me to a meeting? Just 'old friends, visiting.' You get the team to do what you do. I'll observe and see what I can find out."

"That'll work," she said, some relief showing through the t-path. "We've got a meeting this afternoon. Could you make it?"

"I've got time."

Jake said, "I'll let you two handle the meeting. I'll talk with Filip and Elena." It would give him a chance to back off from Zofia's security failure.

҉

An hour later, Zofia led Soren through the TechEmpath building toward the engineering conference room. Slick floors and neutral paint colors gave the interior the usual commercial feel. "Soren, this room has a full two-way t-path. You'll impath everyone's emotions, but they'll also feel yours."

He nodded. "I'm used to it by now. It'll help me identify possible culprits. This is good. You have your technical meeting, and I'll probe the emotions as a starting point for my investigation."

Fourteen engineers and technicians had already gathered in the chairs around the big table. An interior room, the walls held glossy pictures of TechEmpath products and equipment—the conference room t-path system, the personal units, the repellotron for particle wave testing, production facilities. Zofia enjoyed a level of pride every time she saw the results of her year's work.

She also loved the respect she got from this team. As soon as she and Soren entered, she felt it through the room's many-way t-path system. She also knew the people felt her own pride in the group. A couple of younger technicians made room for them at the table.

"Thanks, Nina and Pete," said Zofia. Before they could sit, however, three of the team jumped to their feet beaming with welcome. The room exploded with the pathed enjoyment of the three.

"Soren!" shouted Mos Wenstildon, the oldest one of the group. "Good to see you, man!" Mos clapped a hand on Soren's shoulder.

Soren rose out of his usual reserve to give a quick smile. "Good to see you, too. How've you been? Still nose to the grindstone?"

Randy Princeton followed, shaking hands with energy. "Where've you been? Still catching criminals?" At thirty-something and brilliant, Randy sometimes came across belligerent about what he knew. His striking blue eyes contrasted with black hair.

Soren grunted an affirmation. "Just brought in a ring of corporate thieves, stealing product from their company."

Zofia startled at the reference, something so close to why she had him here. Then she realized Soren had probably said it on purpose. She scanned the others but didn't perceive any guilty reaction.

"That's fantastic," said Randy. "Anyone who steals from their employer *ought* to be caught."

Quieter than the other two, Emigan Contrar simply grinned and stood by. "You're looking good." Emigan, dedicated to excellence, worked on the tiny antennas.

"Did your kid's team win that tournament last year?" Soren asked. "In all the excitement—stopping a war and everything—I never did hear."

Emigan just nodded. "Yeah, they did. They played well."

Zofia's heart lifted with the pathed camaraderie. These three had been part of the original rapid development team last year with Soren and her.

Soren smiled also, as much as he ever did, anyway. "Yeah, you guys. Good to see you, too. That was a hard time last year, but we did it together."

"You were the one," Mos said. "Anything we needed, somehow you made it happen."

Zofia realized the rest of the team sat with patient, expectant smiles on their faces, pathing mild anticipation. She explained. "Hey, everyone. Most of you don't know Soren Moller. Last year when Jake and I first came to Tileus, Soren arrested us for illegal border crossing and smuggling."

The smiles in the room changed to shock, which came across to her as a t-path wave.

Soren added quickly, "We got it straightened out. Asylum, not smuggling."

Zofia grinned and patted Soren on the shoulder. "Bangit, this man is amazing. He got pulled off police work to do our supply management. He knows every nefarious way in this country to get things done. He can find ... anything."

Soren shrugged off the compliment.

Zofia turned back to Soren. "As you can see, we've expanded our development team in the last year. I'm not going to introduce everyone, but I did want to point out Caroline."

"Hi," said a pretty young woman with a wave. Her smile looked nervous.

"Caroline's the newest member of the team. She joined us two months ago, fresh out of secondary with a degree in modern physics. She's helping Mos and Randy in the development. She's a great example of the kind of talent we're attracting."

Soren nodded a curt greeting. His eyes kept scanning each of the team members, likely probing their feelings with the t-path.

Zofia marveled at how he kept his pathed emotions calm while doing so. She needed to take the attention off him so he could work surreptitiously. "Soren, it's great to have you visit, but I called everyone together for some technical status. Why don't you stay? We'll talk more afterwards."

"Sounds good to me." Both he and Zofia took their seats.

"So, team." Zofia sat forward with elbows on the table. "Work's been moving along, but I'm getting concerned about completion. Demand is increasing for t-paths, and we can't produce personal units fast enough. We need more efficient production. What's holding us up?"

Emigan answered right away. "I had some trouble with the particle wave antennas, but I think I have it solved. I've redesigned them to eliminate the microscopic arcing that shows up in test."

Emigan always pathed sincerity, dedication and confidence. A good, solid team member, Zofia relied on his expertise.

Randy added, "Yeah, to get power in a small unit, we had to redesign the internal repellotron and particle wave target. We've had difficulty focusing the repellor beams. Caroline's been a help to Mos and me." He'd always been a bit nervous in meetings, which overrode any deeper emotions Zofia might have sensed.

"It's been exciting for me," Caroline said. "I love seeing how the stuff I learned in school actually works."

Mos chuckled at her young enthusiasm. "She's been so turned on, I let her take some of the work home. Bringing back new ideas the next day."

Taking work home? Zofia traded a raised eyebrow with Soren, then said, "You're bringing everything back, aren't you? We don't want our trade secrets floating around."

Caroline blushed. "Oh, yes, ma'am. I wouldn't leave stuff lying around."

Mos laid a hand out on the table. "I'm watching over Randy and Caroline, Zofia. Everything's under control."

Zofia made a note she'd have to talk with Mos later about security. She didn't want to bring it up in front of the team with Soren here; she might spook the thief.

"So, how much longer is it going to be?" asked Zofia.

Mos answered for his physics team, "We're seeing some working results on the lab bench. Maybe another two weeks to try out a new production method?" Nervousness came across while he made the promise.

"Good work, everyone," Zofia said. "Remember our vision is that everyone—literally *everyone*—would be sharing emotions. We hope we can reduce the animosity between people. Make all of us, all of humanity, a gentler race."

Soren added, "We have data. I just told Zofia we've seen a significant drop in crime in the major cities. This can work."

Mos shook his head. "That's a great goal, but it still begs the question of how we're going to convince people to buy it."

"You're right," said Zofia. "It's a tough sell, but Jake's on top of it. I hope the results from other people, the changes in society, will encourage new people to join."

❧ ✳ ☙

"So, what do you think?" asked Zofia in her office after the meeting. She had a large office with desk, a seating group, and a credenza. The surfaces held few memorabilia, reflective of her lower class upbringing.

"Just first impressions," Soren said. "I've been getting pretty good at using the t-path to probe suspects. This is a bit different, because your people are all dedicated. Mostly, I work with the scum of the city."

"Hope it doesn't rub off on you," she said with a smile.

He grunted. "Hasn't yet. Been doing this a lot of years."

"What did you get in the meeting?"

"Well, your newest member shouldn't be taking stuff home. She acted straightforward about it, but nervous. How long have you been missing things?"

"About two months."

"The same time she's been here."

"Damn. Yeah. What about the others?"

"I caught some indications, but not enough to be sure yet. It's kind of surprising, but my experience is perps often identify themselves without knowing it. They either avoid talking about the investigation, or they're too enthusiastic about it. I caught some of both in the meeting. However, it's not clear yet. Nothing like the guilt I see in our usual suspects. This person is different; whoever's doing it believes what they're doing is right."

14 – Odd Man Out

Before: Decisions made on lack of information.
After: Decisions based in deep understanding of each other.

—Before and After by Ellen Thranadil, Tileus Press
446 A.T.

Beltaret Leaderlist sat alone for lunch, waiting for company. The restaurant he'd chosen featured white tablecloths, silver settings, and fine china, an indulgence his ministerial salary could afford. The transpaths occupied his thoughts. He'd personalized one to himself and tried it out, but he'd not given it a full test. Should he give the second to Captain Forsfear? Would the captain make good use of it? The restaurant's rich paintings and padded silk wallcovering caught his unseeing eyes while he thought. Forsfear could be a loose cannon at times. Useful in the right circumstances, but the man had his own strange ideas.

Like the proposal Beltaret held for the captain's Heresy Angels to test and train missionaries. Forsfear and his elite sub-corps of proctors ran around the country chasing heretics. So far, Beltaret had given the man a free hand and reasonable funding, but the effectiveness and usefulness of such a corps remained to be seen. As for vetting missionaries, though, it seemed like the wrong direction.

A waiter ushered Captain Forsfear to the table. The man slid into a chair without asking permission, adjusting the needle gun at his uniform belt for comfort. "Minister, a protest group attacked our missionaries in Freetown yesterday."

No greeting, no deference, just right to his issue. "Captain, do you understand respect and decorum at all?"

Forsfear furrowed his eyebrows. "Do they matter to my job, sir? I do what you want me to do."

Beltaret waved the issue away with a hand. "Never mind. What's this about an attack?"

"Mud, sir. The protest group followed the laws of Tileus by staying on the opposite side of the street, but then they threw mud across at our missionaries."

"That hardly qualifies as an attack."

"It does under Tileus law, sir. We could use this as an international incident to ask for better enforcement—"

Beltaret shook his head. "No, Captain. Not big enough for international attention."

"Then, Minister, we could use it as a reason to implement my Heresy Angels screening the missionaries before they go. As in my proposal, we would make sure—"

"Yes, I know. The 'centrality of their message.' Isn't that the phrase you used?"

"Exactly, sir."

Beltaret tapped the tablecloth. "I have something more important for you to do, Captain."

"More important?"

"Yes. We have an upstart minister on the Coast Road with his novim. They're on a walking pilgrimage from Glorify all the way here to Praise."

"A long way to walk." Forsfear picked a piece of lint off his sleeve.

"Worse, the rumors say this Reb Fenet Powrfaith is performing miraculous actions. The man must be in league with dark forces."

Forsfear sat straighter, the light of interest in his eyes.

"I want you to work with the proctors in the area to find out what's going on. I've already passed the word for the proctors to stop this band, but for some reason, they've been reluctant to do so."

"Interesting, sir." The captain displayed an intense interest in the task. "So, you think we might be dealing with a band of heretics?"

Beltaret lifted a finger. "Caution, Captain. Make no assumptions. But check them out."

"Yes, sir. Do you also want me to leave some of my Heresy Angels here in Praise to vet the missionaries?"

"No. I've considered your proposal. While it has some merit, it's opposed to our practice of having every young man and woman do missionary service. Your proposal is denied. Instead, chase down this Fenet Powrfaith for me."

Noontime and dhuhr prayer had already passed by the time Fenet led the Khadam out of Fisher. Over two hundred miracles had happened in those three hours; the novim healed everyone who came forward with a problem, no matter whether large or small. An emaciated old man stood straight for the first time in fourteen years. A charming six-year-old girl no longer had a scrape on her knee. The ecstatic crowd wanted to honor the Khadam with an all-day fête. Fenet convinced them otherwise. Even so, more than thirty people followed them out on the country road, chattering among themselves, spectators hoping to see more miracles.

A glowering pair of Church proctors in grey robes and red collars cast the only dark cloud. The two stood in visual range all morning, saying nothing but watching everything. At some point in this pilgrimage, Fenet expected problems with the proctors.

But not today.

"Can you believe what we did?" shouted Durnadat, skipping and twirling, his rotund form bouncing like a buoy on the waves.

"We didn't do it, you silly man," said Penilos. "Elláh did."

"Durnadat's problem is all the pastries from his parents' bakery," Beneim joked. "I understand sugar makes you hyperactive."

Durnadat walked backwards for a moment to face the carrot-topped Beneim. "Not hyperactive at all, Red. Just normally active. Unlike old Tenpos there."

"Don't call me 'Red,'" said Beneim.

"Hey," interjected Tenpos. "Are you calling me 'old'? I'm only twenty."

Lorefim laughed. "Not b-bad, Durnadat. You m-managed to insult t-two friends at once."

"Did you see that quadriplegic jump up and run?" asked Penilos with wonder. "That one astonished me, even in the middle of all the other excitement." He looked in amazement at his own hands.

Beneim said, "Yeah. Busy as I was, I saw it, just before that withered recluse came to me. His friends said he hadn't spoken a word for thirty years. I watched the light of reason come into his eyes. When we left, he was talking up a storm, making up for all those years of silence."

Eregim walked behind the novim with Fenet, listening to the exuberance. Then he also spoke. "I felt it, too, Fenet. I didn't perform any miracles, yet Elláh filled me to preach in a greater way than I've ever done. He is working great things in this pilgrimage. I'm glad I joined. I'm learning new things about how much He can do."

The road drew nearer to the coast. This close, the salt of the ocean smelled sharper in the cool, clear day. Scanat walked in front of the two ministers, but behind the babbling excitement of his fellow novim. Fenet wondered what had happened with him. Why did Elláh not give Scanat the same power as the rest? And what power had Elláh given him? Throughout the marvels in Fisher, Scanat had repeatedly rushed into the crowd to select a particular person, then brought that person to a specific nov for healing. How had he done that?

"Scanat, would you walk with me for a bit?" Fenet asked.

He startled and turned to Fenet with guilt in his eyes. They quickly hooded, though, and he dropped back to join Fenet and Eregim. "Yes, Reb?"

"Scanat, you've been with me a long time."

Scanat nodded, taking an uncertain breath. "Yes, Reb. Four years. Longer than any of the others."

"I remember you had some great opportunities elsewhere before joining me, didn't you?"

Eregim listened quietly.

"I did, Reb," answered Scanat. "They selected me for tertiary school."

"In something very technical, I recollect."

"They wanted me to study particle physics."

"Yet you chose to join me instead." Fenet paused. "Why?"

Scanat shrugged with a small smile. "I saw your miracles. They transgressed everything school had taught about science. I wanted to know more about how you did them."

"And have you learned more?"

The young man took a moment before answering, then erupted. "No, I haven't. And it irritates me. I learn quickly. I understand things easily. That's why I did well in school; that's why they selected me for more. But this ... stuff ... you do," he waved a hand in the air, "this surrender and listening to Elláh and doing only what He tells you. I don't understand *any* of it. And I don't know why. I've been trying for *four years*, and I'm no further along than when I joined."

He ended his diatribe as abruptly as it had started, watching the ground while he walked. When he spoke again, in a small voice, he had lost his usual forcefulness. "I've been thinking about quitting, Reb. Maybe they'd take me back in tertiary."

Fenet bit his lip, thinking. Scanat didn't usually make such an outburst. How to guide the man? Giving himself a moment, Fenet took his straw hat off and fiddled with the flower. Not really straightening it, just focusing his thoughts. "I've wondered if you were reaching this point, Scanat. I've seen your frustration." He swallowed. "And now you think you've been left out by Elláh."

"Yeah." Scanat's gaze stayed on the ground.

"But I'm certain Elláh has a plan for you. You did something different than the rest back there. I watched you selecting people for treatment. Were you hearing something from Elláh?"

Scanat looked up at Fenet, his eyes hard and his lips set. "No. Never." After a moment, he added, "I'm not ready to talk about it yet." He set his jaw and quickened his pace, passed the rest of the novim, and took the lead on the road.

"That one has a problem," said Eregim quietly.

"Indeed."

Scanat's head felt like exploding while he trudged forward. He turned off the transpath he'd used throughout the healings, no longer wanting to feel the jubilant emotions of the novim around him. He'd felt the deep caring and friendly concern from Fenet. The reb's compassion made Scanat's situation worse. *Why can't I get what the other novim get? That's why I joined Fenet in the first place.* He caught himself grinding his teeth yet again, something he'd started doing recently. He forced his jaw to relax. *What am I going to do?*

More and more, he wished he'd accepted the appointment to tertiary school. By now, he'd be deep into particle physics. Maybe he'd be able to understand what that Jake fellow had done to create the t-paths. Or better, maybe he could work with him and learn more. This t-path thing offered a new technology promise for humanity. He could be part of it. Except ... now four years had passed, behind where he would have been. Would they even take him back in tertiary at his age?

The euphoria in the novim behind him eased while they walked into the afternoon. Someone stepped up to walk beside him; Scanat glanced up to see stolid Tenpos striding along with him. Neither said anything as they walked through a col lined with fading berry bushes then started up another gentle slope. Scanat didn't want to talk. How could he avoid a conversation?

When they topped the next rise, Tenpos finally spoke. "It's gotta suck."

Scanat said nothing, just kept walking and watching the ground. He swallowed a lump in his throat.

"You're so much smarter than me, Scanat. My father's a fisherman. The best I did in school went toward bodybuilding and wrestling. I can't imagine the way you think."

Scanat snorted a dismissive sound. "It's not all that special."

"Yes, it is. It doesn't feel special to you because you have it."

The two walked on in silence. Tenpos, though four years younger than he, had connected with Scanat in ways none of the others had. Maybe the man's quiet, solid nature attracted him. Unlike the exuberance of the teenagers, Tenpos gave Scanat space to be himself without the immediate demands of youth.

"Thanks, Tenpos. You're a help."

Tenpos detoured around a pothole in the roadway. When he came close again, he looked directly at Scanat. "So, what are you gonna do?"

The direct question echoed the same one rattling in Scanat's mind like a rat in a shaken cage. "I don't know."

Long pause. "Let me know when you figure it out. I'll help."

The offer softened Scanat's worries. "Thanks again."

Tenpos kept quiet company with Scanat while the four hours of afternoon faded toward dusk. They talked little, but the man's presence helped him to think. The cooling air of evening brought Scanat out of his self-absorbed thoughts. He looked around. The crowd of followers from Fisher had disappeared, leaving just the two rebs and the Khadam. Fenet had slowed down again, leaning on his staff. Sometimes, Scanat's heart went out to Reb Fenet about his infirmity. Other times, he couldn't understand why Fenet didn't just use the technology available. Or pray a miracle for himself.

With no convenient farms along this stretch of the Coast Road, the company pitched tents for the night, which turned cold. Scanat slept in his jacket.

The next day, cool and clear again, the road turned southeast to follow the coast. At times, their path rode the tops of cliffs with an expansive view of the ocean. The air temperature rose to balmy, the sun sparkling white on the waves and the salt scent of the ocean carrying to them on the breeze.

Through the day, Scanat pondered what to do with his life. Should he carry through his plan to provide t-paths to the Khadam? He turned the unit back on while they walked, getting used to the perception of feelings from the company. Would the t-paths help the Khadam, when Elláh already had everything under control? Maybe Elláh didn't? Perhaps He wanted them to use this technology? In Fisher, Scanat and his t-path had been helpful, guiding those with problems to the miracle-workers. Yet that paled in comparison to actually performing the miracles.

Or should he set aside the t-paths and continue to study with Fenet? He knew his resentment sometimes blocked him from Elláh. If he could set it aside, maybe he'd join the rest of the Khadam in their marvelous workings. He'd like to feel first-hand the amazing power he'd felt in his friends. But he'd been trying for four years, and nothing had happened yet.

His last option would be going back to school if they'd take him. Sometimes, it seemed attractive, more useful than what he'd been doing. Yet the possibility of school faded as each year passed; he might already be too late.

🙠 ✳ 🙢

The second morning out of Fisher, Scanat awoke to the sounds of Beneim preparing breakfast for the company. The Khadam had settled into a travel routine in which one nov bustled around a fire before dawn so all could eat early enough to perform the morning salat prayers. On this day, the whine of several aircars disturbed their salat. Reb Fenet led them to complete the prayers despite the noise.

When Scanat rose from the prostrate position, four aircars had stopped on the road in front of them at a respectful distance. No sooner than he gained his feet, the car doors opened. More than a dozen people poured out onto the road and approached them. Reb Fenet and Eregim stepped forward.

A middle-aged man in the group asked, "Excuse us, but are you Reb Fenet Powrfaith?"

"I am."

The man acted excited but restrained, glancing around at the entire company. "We heard what happened in Fisher. Did you really perform miracles for everyone in town?"

Fenet answered, "Not me. But ..." he swept his hand around the company, "my novim were rather busy."

Scanat considered the group in front of them. A pregnant girl caught his attention; she peeked out from behind the spokesman. The girl pathed feelings of desperation and fear mingled with hope. Scanat felt her react to a pain in her womb. His breath caught when he realized her situation.

Without pause, he stepped past Reb Fenet to take her hand, drawing her out from behind the man, likely her father. "Come with me, girl. We can help you. What's your name?"

"Donadirdu," she whispered. "They call me Dir. My baby boy..." Her free hand cradled her belly.

He gently pulled her toward the Khadam. "Yes, Dir, I know. Come meet my friends." Then he turned to Fenet. "This one, Reb Fenet. She has an urgent need for her baby."

Fenet looked puzzled. "Scanat? How do you—"

Scanat scanned the novim with his eyes, pathing their astonishment. In Beneim, however, the t-path revealed Elláh's power flowing into him while the nov stepped forward. Scanat led Dir by the hand to Beneim, who knelt and placed his hands on her swollen belly.

GROW HEALTHY, Beneim said with the voice of Elláh. The air around his hands sprouted a warm rosy radiance and pulsed twice before flowing into the girl's belly.

She gasped, her fingers clamping on Scanat's hand like vines cling to a tree. "Oh, my Lord," she cried, "He's kicking again!"

Beneim stood up with a dazed smile, shaking his hands as if relinquishing an electric shock.

Scanat's blood rushed into his face. A jolt of adrenaline accelerated all his sensations. He patted the girl's hand and looked again at the crowd. While doing so, he reached in his pocket to adjust the t-path. He clicked it on, then stopped in surprise. He clicked it off, then back on. *Was the t-path off? How could that be? Strange.* Yet people were still in front of him, so he shrugged and returned to action.

One man caught his eye, wrapped up in a heavy coat and scarf, far more than needed for this cool morning, with sweat all over his forehead. The t-path relayed to Scanat the man's sense of fear, as well as the shivering, shaking, and weak sensations of a high fever. Scanat let go of the girl and then helped the man to Lorefim for yet another miracle.

One by one, Scanat identified each of the six people who'd been brought out early by their families, the ones who needed healing of some sort. The t-path made it easy to find them. He led each to one of his friends for a miracle. While he did so, his heart filled with purpose, just as in Fisher.

While helping people, his dilemma of what to do with his life disappeared. He took kama joy in the simple artha of doing the good in front of him.

15 – Different Kind of Miracle

Most of the people of Verdant had no faith in a higher power, Rathas being the exception. When the technology of the transpath met the spirituality of Elláh, something interesting surely would happen.

—*The Making of a New Humanity* by Ellen Thranadil, Tileus Press 448 A.T.

Fenet leaned on his staff watching another set of miracles happen without him. The pain in his hips made his posture more bent than usual. He couldn't explain why Elláh continued to withhold the power, while granting it so freely to the novim. Had his choice to use the repellor belt been such a heinous sin?

Eregim intruded on his thoughts. "Fenet, are you watching what Scanat is doing?"

Fenet focused on Scanat. After leaving Beneim and the pregnant girl, Scanat walked as if with directed purpose to the small crowd of visitors and picked out an elderly woman. Exchanging a few words, Scanat led the woman to the novim. He looked over his compatriots and moved without hesitation to Durnadat, turning over the woman to a ready miracle.

"I don't understand, and I'm still learning about these miracles. How did he pick her?" asked Eregim.

Fenet furrowed his eyebrows. "And how did he know to choose Durnadat?"

Scanat didn't stay with Durnadat and the woman. He turned back to the locals and walked to an enormous bearded man with bulging shoulders, perhaps a blacksmith. Scanat took the man by the arm and brought him toward the other five novim. With his first step, the man's limp became apparent. Again, with obvious certainty, Scanat chose Lorefim. The nov reached out a healing hand when the man arrived.

"And again," Fenet said. "Scanat looks to be possessed by some knowledge the rest don't have."

Six times, Scanat chose and led a person to a nov ready to perform healing. On the seventh pass, Scanat looked over the crowd with intent eyes, then gave a firm nod and a satisfied smile. He turned back to the two leaders. "That's all, Reb Fenet. Those were the ones they brought here for healing."

"Thank you, Scanat ..." Fenet's voice trailed off. What could he say?

The locals left no time to talk. They pushed forward to shake hands and praise Elláh. Minor pandemonium filled the road in their exuberance. Man after man pumped Fenet's hand as if they expected him to issue a flow of miraculous water. Women curtseyed with tears in their eyes. Fenet smiled at each one and thanked them for coming, yet he also watched Scanat. The young man looked uncertain when he accepted the praise from the locals. Yet he also exhibited a firmness and satisfaction Fenet had not seen in him before.

Something had happened to Scanat. Fenet needed to know what.

Fifteen minutes later, still bubbling with effusive compliments, the people offered the Khadam a ride into Netweaver, the next town. After asking Elláh and hearing no answer, Fenet declined their offer. The locals piled back into their aircars, chattering like overjoyed jaybirds. The cars moved back up the road, leaving Fenet with the scent of dew and the music of morning birdsong.

Most of the novim burst into quiet, excited conversation. Scanat stood alone, smiling to himself.

Fenet tugged at Eregim's sleeve to go with him, then limped to Scanat.

The young man startled and glanced at the others a few meters away.

"What you just did," Fenet said, "astounded Eregim and me. You haven't done any healing, but you have your own form of miracles in this ability to find those who need us. Two days ago, outside of Fisher, you said you weren't ready to talk about it. It's time, Scanat. What sort of miracle is this?"

Scanat looked down at the ground and rubbed his palms down his thighs, the grey robe stretching with the force of his pressure. The nervous silence extended. He opened his mouth to speak, then stopped again. He even blushed.

Fenet kept quiet. Scanat's discomfort would force the answer out.

When Scanat finally spoke, he sounded a bit like Lorefim. "R-reb ... I ..." He stopped again and took a deep breath. When he let it out, the words burst from him. "It's not a miracle, Reb Fenet. It's the technology I told you about before we started."

Technology? Fenet hadn't considered that possibility. He and Eregim traded a glance.

The dam had burst in Scanat. "It's a *good* thing, Reb. I can't do the miracles, but I can do this. And it feels like ... purpose, like something Elláh *meant* for me to do." He paused, looking hard at Fenet. "Like the things you teach about. It happened that evening in Glorify. I left the Khadam for a while ..." He trailed off.

Fenet waved an encouraging hand for him to continue.

"I saw a poster for the new technology, Reb. The same one I tried to tell you about at your mother's house. They held a presentation, and I wanted to see what it could do. They call it the transpath." He looked up into Fenet's eyes, wonder filling his own. "It works, Reb. I can impath other's emotions. Right now, I feel your surprise and your concern." He looked at Eregim. "Reb Eregim is more controlled and has some doubt."

Scanat pulled a small white box out of his pocket. "This is it, Reb Fenet. It's so simple and so easy. I looked at the people in the crowd just now, and I felt which ones were hurting. I also felt the concern of the others, and I could tell the difference. And ..." his face filled with awe, "I experienced the miracles happening in the novim. The rush of Elláh passing into and through them. I've been desperate to know what it felt like."

He held the unit out toward Fenet. "It's just technology, Reb, not miracles. But it's very good technology."

Fenet took the box from his hands. Hard plastic, a simple volume wheel, a reset button. It looked innocuous—yet what Scanat said sounded incredible.

Eregim asked, "How did you get this unit, Scanat? Did you pay for it?"

"Oh, no, sir. They gave them out as free samples. I just asked for it."

Fenet handed the transpath to Eregim for his inspection, then asked, "Is it still working now?"

"Yes, Reb," said the nov. "I can feel your curiosity, and still your concern."

"Why don't I feel anything?" asked Eregim while he turned the unit around in his hands.

"Because it's personalized to me," answered Scanat. "Even while you're holding it, it only works for me."

Eregim handed the transpath back to Scanat with a shake of his head. "It hardly seems possible."

The more Fenet listened to Scanat, the more uncomfortable he felt. "Scanat, it's technology, just like the repellor belt I wore. You've seen what happened to me. Why do you believe Elláh would want you to use this?"

"Because this is what He guided me to do," Scanat answered.

He looked nervous, but Fenet also sensed a determination in him to convince.

"Reb, you've taught us not to believe in coincidence, that everything has a purpose in Elláh's creation. Yet there was a series of coincidences. The poster in Glorify was in the right place to catch my eye. The presentation happened just once—the one night we were in town. I'm the only one of us to whom Elláh hasn't given healing powers. I had no money, but the company people offered units for free. None of these are miracles by themselves, but when you put them all together ..." His voice rang with earnest conviction. "I believe Elláh *arranged* for me to be there."

Fenet shook his head. "I'm having a hard time accepting this. All these years, I've taught you—and learned myself—that surrender to Elláh grants us this power. You've never performed miracles, and I've watched you push yourself hard. But you've always driven yourself under your own control, following your own thoughts. Not in surrender."

"But this *feels* like surrender to me. I didn't ask for anything like this. I didn't make it happen. All I did was follow what He put in front of me, and I got these units as the result."

"These units?" Fenet asked. "You have more than one?"

Scanat nodded emphatically. "Yes, Reb. They gave me enough for *all* of us." He paused and looked at Eregim. "Uh ... not you, Reb Eregim. That night, I didn't know you'd be joining us."

Fenet looked at the ground and held up his hand to stop Scanat's rapid flow of convincing language. "Hold on, Scanat. Let me think."

He'd been standing too long already, since the aircars arrived. Fenet took a step toward a nearby cluster of rocks to sit. Despite using his staff, his right hip collapsed. He fell to the hard ground, a crashing impact on the already-painful hip.

His arm twisted and his shoulder slammed on one of the rocks. The collision knocked out his wind. For a too-long moment, Fenet's chest could not expand. He thought he'd be unable to take in the next breath. Spots danced in his eyes. Nonetheless, his body eventually knew what to do, and Fenet sucked in a huge lungful. At first, he thought his shoulder uninjured, then he realized the blow had numbed it. He dreaded what it would feel like in another minute.

Eregim jumped to help Fenet to the nearest boulder, but couldn't lift him onto it by himself. The novim crowded around him in a babble of voices. Several more hands held him steady, lifting him to sit on the rock. Fenet put his head between his knees and panted, trying to expel the pain through every breath. The hip eased, and he became aware of the shoulder while the numbness of the impact gave way to deep trauma.

"Oh, Elláh," He breathed. "I can't do this."

Fenet kneaded his right shoulder with his left hand, pressing on the muscles and joints to discover what hurt most. The bruising seemed confined to the muscles, thank Elláh, though it flared into sharp pain when he pressed the wrong places. He stretched his arm around, testing its limits.

"Some pain reliever, Eregim, please?" Fenet asked. "I've hurt my shoulder now, too."

Eregim turned toward the packs to get something.

Now that Fenet felt stable, he looked up at Scanat.

The young man still stood where they'd been, his face drained of blood, holding the transpath in his hand. He moved abruptly, stepping to Fenet and falling to his knees. He dropped the t-path to take one of Fenet's hands in both of his.

"Reb Fenet ..." he ran out of words, then tried again. "Reb, I had no idea how much pain you were in."

The other novim also gathered around. Tenpos said, "How could you not know, Scanat? We've talked about it every day. We laid on hands and prayed over him just three days ago."

Scanat shook his head. "No, Tenpos. I knew, in that way. But I didn't really *know* until now." He spoke to Fenet. "Reb, I can feel your pain. Your hips, and now your shoulder. It's awful, I can hardly bear it. I've had the t-path, but I've been avoiding impathing you. I don't know why. How can you stand it?"

Fenet let go of his shoulder and patted Scanat's arm. "It's okay, Scanat. Really, it's okay. This is what Elláh has given me to bear."

"Is it really?" Scanat gripped my hand harder. "Or are you driving yourself to this pain? Elláh told you to stop using the belt. He told you to do this pilgrimage. Remember, I was there. I heard what Elláh said through Penilos. Did He really tell you to suffer every day of the walk? I don't think so." Scanat lifted a finger in the air, his voice rising. "Or are you doing to yourself what you've just accused me of doing, living with your own idea of what Elláh wants?"

His words stunned Fenet, who thought back to that day in his mother's parlor. Elláh had said not to use the repellor belt. He had labeled it purification. Then He had commanded this pilgrimage. Hanging his head again, picturing the room and remembering the exact words, Fenet slumped further. Scanat was right. Elláh had not commanded him to suffer for the whole journey. Fenet did this to himself—pride—his own assumption Elláh wanted him to stay in this pain.

"Reb Fenet," the young man whispered, "we tried praying for you. Perhaps Elláh needs you to be humble enough to pray for yourself."

A wash of humility suffused Fenet, allowing every taut muscle in his body to relax; his shoulders dropped. He nodded and squeezed Scanat's hand. "And so, the teacher learns again from a student." Fenet gripped Scanat's hand to prevent him from rising.

He looked up at the rest. Eregim had returned with pills in his hand. "Not those yet, Eregim. Please, lay hands on me instead. All of you." When they had done so, Fenet prayed, "Elláh, I've been arrogant once again. I assumed I knew what you wanted, and I have not asked. If it be Your will, heal me. Let me fulfill Your pilgrimage with the grace You grant." Perhaps some might think this prayer too simple, but Fenet's years of experience told him a simple surrender would be all Elláh wanted of him. He closed with, "Selah."

Fenet felt warmth flow into him from the many hands on his head and shoulders. Burning flooded into his right shoulder, washing the pain away. The heat moved down his torso to settle into both hips, easing the intense pain he'd felt this morning. He breathed freely for the first time in several days.

The relief astounded him. "Thank you, Elláh." He looked up at his friends. "And thank you all. My shoulder feels wonderful. My hips—well, they're better. All in Elláh's time. I will trust in Him and keep praying."

"Praise Elláh," said Scanat softly.

The others echoed him with more force, raising their hands in the air and shouting the words. "Praise Elláh!"

Scanat still knelt in front of Fenet, the t-path on the ground where he'd dropped it. He looked once again like the disciple he'd been when he first joined Fenet, full of eagerness, hope, and determination.

Fenet shook his head in wonder.

"Fine, Scanat," he said. "I don't know what Elláh's plan is, but we'll try your way for a while and see what He tells us. Pull out your transpaths and teach everyone how to use them." He thought a moment longer, then added, "But give my unit to Reb Eregim. I'm still concerned what Elláh might do if I start using technology again."

16 – Fire and Danger

Gather the facts. Always gather the facts. And do it before the meeting, whether you will use them or not.

—*A Practical Guide to Sensitive Negotiation* by Ellen Thranadil, 426 A.T.

Zofia arrived at work while dawn painted its faintest colors in the sky. Following heavy rain yesterday, crisp air spoke of the coming autumn.

Soren hadn't yet given her any indication who might be stealing from them, but he told her yesterday he had some suspicions. He'd asked her for any records she had on the lab equipment and prototype devices, wanting to familiarize himself with the equipment that should have been in the lab.

Zofia took the early morning opportunity to work with the holo at her desk, a respite she rarely had time for these days. Managing the development team both thrilled and exhausted her. A group of people could achieve successes she could not do by herself, and Zofia prized guiding them, but sometimes she missed the individual software work she used to do.

Pulling up the lab equipment records, Zofia stashed copies in her imp memory to give to Soren later. She then opened her messages. Randy and Mos had an interesting exchange about technical details. Mos had been giving direction to help Randy make progress. The discussion became esoteric, dealing with particle physics and electronics, and Zofia lost herself checking specific technical facts. She paid no attention when others arrived outside her office.

Shouts and the sound of pounding feet intruded on her focus. Puzzled, she looked up just as the fire alarm went off.

"Fire in the lab!" someone yelled.

It took a second for the words to sink in. *The lab? That's the core of our business!* Zofia jumped up from her desk while more shouts sounded. She ran into the hallway. The fire alarm shattered the air, screaming to quicken the heart. Three doors to her left, Mos and two others jostled around the lab door. Smoke poured out, rising and spreading on the ceiling. Randy rushed past her holding a fire extinguisher. Zofia dashed to follow him. Mos held the lab door open, waving two technicians into the hall.

"Out! OUT!" he yelled. "Clear the room!"

Emigan raced out last; as soon as he cleared, Mos slammed the door shut and slapped a large red button on the wall. A heavy whoomp sounded behind the door. The door jumped against its latch when gas pressure blasted against it from the other side.

"Halon suppression," Mos hollered to the group. "Damn, I hope it works."

Zofia put her hand on Mos's shoulder while they both looked through the wire-impregnated window on the door. "Did it work? Is the fire out?"

White mist and black smoke churned inside the room like demons trapped in a bottle.

Mos answered, "I can't see yet. It's all smoke."

"I don't see any flames," she said.

Randy held up the extinguisher. "Are we going to need this?"

"Not yet, Randy," Zofia said. "Maybe not at all. Halon should do the trick."

The distant sound of fire truck sirens grew louder.

The clouds in the room began sweeping toward a duct in the wall. She felt a pressure differential in her ears and the door squeaked hard against its jamb.

"That's the suppression system retrieving the halon," said Mos. "I've never seen it work before. Pretty damn effective."

When the room cleared, Zofia saw no flames and only a few wisps of smoke from a couple of lab benches. "Looks clear. Let's go in." She reached for the door.

Mos touched her arm. "Be careful, Zofia. Halon can irritate, but it's okay to go in."

She pulled open the door with some hesitation, sniffing the air. The room emitted a sharp, acrid odor, clearing while the suppression system continued to pull remnants of the gas into the ductwork. Mos led the group into the lab, holding a cloth to his face. He headed for the burned workbenches. The room was hot. Zofia looked everywhere else for damage and saw none. The residual soup of chemicals in the air made her eyes water.

"Mos, is the fire out?" she asked.

"Looks like it, but these two benches are ruined."

Blackened and warped by the flames, the benches held unrecognizable equipment. Boxy shapes had melted. Tangles of hook-up wire shone copper instead of insulation.

Emigan looked upward. "We got it just in time. The ceiling almost caught fire."

The ceiling tiles over the benches held black Rorschach streaks like evil tentacles trying to claim the entire building.

Randy sneezed behind Zofia. "That's a pretty vile smell." He still held the extinguisher, though it wasn't needed anymore. Several other engineers and technicians had followed him, everyone holding something to their face.

"What was on these benches?" Zofia asked. She held her hand cupped in front of her nose.

Mos shook his head, frustration showing, pointing to one of the two benches. "This was our prototype bench where we worked on the new production equipment. The other bench held small parts being tested."

A sudden coldness hit at her core. "What about our prototypes? Where are they?"

Mos pointed at the melted jumble. "Gone." He picked up a mangled piece, then dropped it, shaking his hand. "Damn. Still hot." He compressed his lips and shook his head. "It'll take several weeks to rebuild them. They were close to ready."

Another setback. Zofia slumped.

Stomping and bustling sounded behind them. Zofia turned. Two firemen in full gear, faces behind large polycarbonate masks, rushed into the lab. Quickly assessing the situation, they moved forward.

"Everyone out!" the taller one shouted through his mask. "Clear the building."

Mos turned to him. "The fire's out, chief."

"Doesn't matter," the fireman shouted. "Get out. Now. We'll let you know when it's safe to return."

Zofia flashed in anger. "This is *my* building, sir. I'm staying."

"No, ma'am, you are not." The fireman moved between Zofia and the benches, then started urging everyone toward the door. "I own this building now, until it's safe. Everyone. Out." He continued to push forward with his arms held wide. The man had well-practiced forcefulness. "Is there anyone missing?"

She wanted to fight back, but he'd asked the right question. She glanced around at the people, counting heads. "No, we've got everyone here."

"Then clear out for now. Safety first."

His compatriot held a sensor in the air around the benches. "Hazardous fumes here. Halon system worked."

Mos chimed in while he reached the door, "Yeah. It did good. Put the fire out, then sucked itself away."

"Still hazardous," said the second fireman as he stepped to the blackened benches. He gestured to the charring on the floor, pointing something out to the taller man.

The irritation in Zofia's eyes spread to her breathing, and she recognized the truth of what they said. She turned to help get everyone out of the building

Zofia reached the door just as the tall fireman spoke again, obviously reporting by imp to someone outside.

"Fire's out, Chief. No hazard. Occupants accounted for, evacuating now. Meters say the air's still an irritant. Send in an investigator. We've got accelerant charring on the floor."

Zofia took a surprised step back and traded looks with Mos. A shocked gasp came from the rest of the group, now in the hallway. She turned back to the fireman. "Accelerant?" she asked.

"Yep." The fireman pointed to the floor. "See those rounded patterns on the floor tiles? That's from a flammable liquid." He paused, then turned back to her. "Looks like someone did this on purpose."

❧ ✳ ☙

Beltaret had some unscheduled time after lunch. He decided to walk out into the city of Praise to try out the transpath in a more stressful situation than he'd done so far.

Two nights ago, he'd walked down to the river park to personalize one of the units. The instructions told him to make sure no one else stayed within five meters. In the dark of evening, he'd been isolated enough.

The result astonished him. That evening, he strode around for another hour with the device turned on, experiencing the emotions of others—first in the quiet park, then past a few riverside restaurants. Unnerved at first, he grew used to the power the unit gave him. He discovered to his relief he could control it; he only impathed the emotions of the person he looked at, though others in his peripheral vision overlaid some feelings as well. Joy, fear, excitement, desperation—a panoply of human fears and desires played out in the minds around him.

Today's unscheduled time would give him the chance to practice. He strolled into the shopping district packed with people going about their personal business. The crowds in Rathas moved in orderly ways, reflecting the peace of Elláh. Taking a deep breath, though with some trepidation, he reached into the pocket of his robe and turned on the device.

His eyes locked on a harried-looking woman rushing down the sidewalk. He immediately sensed her emotions. Strong. Desperate. Rushed. Overwhelming fear. Her feelings presented a huge contrast to the order of the crowds. It felt to Beltaret like a fear of failure. She looked up at him as if sensing something of him, and he gasped. *Did she perceive me looking?* But she looked ahead again—it had just been a passing glance—and shook her head, her misery filling his mind.

At the same time, the crowd of people around her impinged on his senses. He caught happiness, more fear, determination, doubt, and much more. His senses overwhelmed with the feelings of so many people in such close proximity.

He turned the unit off with a frantic brush of his finger, his other hand clenched against his chest. He would have to be careful how he used the transpath. Learn to separate his feelings from those of others.

The experience confirmed for him the need to keep this technology out of Rathas for now, to protect the faithful from its influence. Though he stood tall among the most fervent of believers, he wanted to give in to this temptation to keep looking into others. Temptation, the strong and evil foe to spiritual growth. It offered dangerous shortcuts, ways to gain Elláh's blessings without the growth to use them properly. Sin always masked itself as a blessing, something that felt good while it attracted people away from the path to Elláh's heart.

On the other hand, this device would enhance his abilities as Minister of Security. He'd be able to influence the people around him with knowledge of how they reacted. He'd be able to advance Elláh's goals more effectively. While he walked back toward Church Center One, he turned the unit back on for a few minutes at a time, practicing.

∂✳∽

Following the fire, the TechEmpath employees hustled out of the building. The perpetrator smiled secretly to himself when he saw the two fire trucks and a host of people gathered. He'd done his best work so far, setting the fire. However, he kept having difficulty keeping his pathed emotions in control; sooner or later, someone would realize his thefts through his own displayed feelings. It helped to have bigger things for Jake and Zofia to worry about, so he'd have time to move his plans forward.

The two of them acted clueless as managers. *He* could do better. Jake and his fiasco over in Glorify and Praise. An incompetent woman agent in the Rathas culture? What a disaster. And Zofia's ineptitude at security. Mercy Mavens! He'd managed to squirrel two transpaths out of the lab without anyone noticing. The security logs were a joke.

And now, thanks to his fire, he had the *very first* prototypes of the new production systems in his bag. And no one would know they were gone. They'd just assume the devices burned up. The firemen couldn't have been more helpful, chasing everyone out.

What he'd done would set back their improved production by at least two weeks, which would give enough lead time for him to set something up on his own.

He hadn't known a fireman would detect the arson so quickly, though, and that irritated him. It put him at risk of discovery. They'd bring in investigators. Like Soren.

On the other hand, Zofia and Jake would know someone was undermining them. Good. A bit of fear, a bit of uncertainty, the knowledge they weren't completely in control. That might cause them to make more mistakes.

Next, he'd create his own company. Get the structure in place. Find good associates, people willing to do whatever it takes to be successful. Jake and Zofia hadn't done anything toward securing patents. If he changed the design somewhat, he could claim independent development and beat TechEmpath to the punch in Rathas. And on other worlds! That'd be much more rewarding than just Tileus.

He'd have to contact Johan Wellesley tonight to arrange the help he'd need. He'd demand a larger payment, for something so much more efficient. Big enough to fund his effort.

Even while expressing concern to his fellow workers about the fire, he grinned inside.

17 — Pedestrian Impediments

By the time of the colony worlds, the One Church had become rigid in its interpretation of scripture. Its primary book, *The Holiest*, had been modified many times over the years to reflect changes in the colony cultures and languages, thereby often diverging from its original message. Church leadership had difficulty maintaining its consistency across multiple worlds.

—History of the One Church by Ellen Thranadil,
Tileus Press 445 A.T.

Following his prayer, Fenet could walk again. The Khadam packed everything for travel, and they stood as a group again on the gravel road coming out of the rolling hills toward Netweaver. The cold morning began to warm.

Fenet's hips still hurt, but—praise Elláh—less than they had for several months. He couldn't hop around like a kid goat, but at least he could move with only modest help from the walking stick. Maybe the worse of Elláh's purifying would be past. What would come next? If he were Elláh's tool, then his God would have something for him to do. He looked forward to that.

Feeling jaunty, Fenet replaced the flower on his floppy hat with a late-blooming yellow *astradell* from the rocks beside the road. Doing so reminded him not all of Elláh's power had left him; the hat flower still stayed fresh. The old flower could have stayed, but changing its color gave him a lift.

As had happened several times recently, Elláh inspired him to verse. Fenet spoke the words flowing through him, singing them to the rocks and scraggly bushes of the hillside above them.

Through trial, travail and vast tribulation,
    Elláh gives us power.
In peace and plenty and trouble cessation
    We continue to flower.
Elláh give us test;
Elláh give us rest;
    We follow Elláh to His heavenly bower.

He looked down to see the Khadam smiling as one. Durnadat bowed from the waist with a laugh, then stood to spin once in place, finishing with applause for Fenet's doggerel. The other novim and Eregim joined in.

"Thank you, my friends," Fenet said, "but you know words like these only come through me from Elláh."

Eregim shook his head, still smiling. "But, my friend, they do indeed come through you. Your beautiful words honor you as much as Elláh."

Fenet nodded thanks. "In any case, it's time to get this ..." he smiled, "traveling menagerie on the road once again."

And so, they started. Fenet's spirits, lifted by the healing, floated aloft like the tiny moths that surged upward from the bushes around them.

While they walked, Scanat instructed the others on how to activate their t-paths. The process sounded simple enough, though Fenet still had an uneasy feeling about using the technology. *In any case, we can always turn them off again. Isn't that right, Elláh?*

Silence answered him. The Lord often left Fenet on his own—sometimes because the issue didn't matter to Him, but sometimes as a test. Fenet wondered which He intended this time.

"You need to be alone to personalize the unit," Scanat told them. "There should be no one within about five meters." He looked around at the empty road and rocky country. "You could drop behind the rest of us by that far, one by one."

Fenet had sufficient curiosity to watch. Eager to try it out, Penilos strode back a few paces to be first.

Fenet stopped to watch. The rest stopped with him.

At some distance, Penilos stood still. He held up the t-path, then looked down while he pushed the reset button. Activation took only a few seconds. Penilos stood still, eyes on the road, before looking up again. He cocked his head to one side as if to listen to faint noises. After a few steps toward them, he stopped again. Penilos shook his head enough his straw-colored hair flopped, then his eyes grew wide.

"It works, Scanat!" he shouted with boyish delight.

He ran back to join the rest. When he got close, he slowed and kept shifting his gaze from one to another, a bemused smile on his face. After a few moments, he shuddered. Reaching down, he adjusted the knob on his unit.

"It's really strong," he said. "Even more so when I'm close to you. Scary. This will take some getting used to."

Tenpos stepped to him and put a hand on his shoulder. "Most worthwhile things do." He looked around while the rest of the novim nodded at his words. "My turn next. Go ahead and keep walking. I'll catch up."

Moving on, Eregim walked beside Fenet. "I'm glad you're feeling better."

"I am, too. I had begun to doubt I could do this entire trek."

"I've been wanting to talk again with you about it."

Fenet glanced at him. "In what way?"

Eregim paused, scratching his neck. "I have a serious question you've not answered."

"What question, my friend?"

"The most basic one. Why are we doing this?"

Fenet stopped walking. The answer seemed obvious. "Because Elláh told me to."

Eregim shook his head. "No, that's not what I mean. I know he told you to. I heard it, remember? What I want to know is why?"

"Because He told me to. What more reason can we have?" Frowning, Fenet resumed moving forward.

"There must be something He wants you to do in Praise. Do you have any idea what it is?"

The deeper question went to the core of Fenet's own doubts. He'd set them aside during the time his hips had so much pain. Now, feeling better, this question niggled at Fenet, too. Worse, he had no answer. Since the beginning of the pilgrimage, he'd assumed Elláh would give a purpose at some point like a flash in the darkness—but none had yet appeared. If his faith were stronger, perhaps Elláh would have already let him know. Eregim asking made Fenet feel helpless.

"No. I have no idea." A tightness gripped his chest, facing this core question.

"Then why continue, when you've been in such pain?"

Fenet wished he would stop probing. The repeated question felt like poking a sore with a sharp stick. "Because Elláh told me to. What more can I say?"

"There's no need to snap at me, Fenet. I'm only asking."

"But you keep harping at it. I. Don't. Know." Fenet became strident. "Can't you understand? I just don't know. But I have to do it."

Eregim backed off, palms raised in surrender, and walked a bit farther away.

By the time they neared Netweaver two hours later, all the t-paths were active including Eregim's. Fenet kept seeing amazed looks among the Khadam as they watched each other, obviously impathing the emotions. The feelings suppressed their conversation.

Eregim walked with Scanat, leaving Fenet alone.

Somewhat larger than the last town of Fisher, Netweaver served as a center for the fishing industry on the southwest coast. Fenet wanted to see everything. The Coast Road ran alongside the famed packing plants lining the west end of the harbor, where boats would unload their daily take before returning to their berths. Today, despite it being the middle of the week, many boats rested in their moorings. They hadn't gone to sea. The plants sat idle.

Instead, people waited for Fenet Powrfaith and his Khadam.

When they cleared the last bend and started down the slope into town, shouts resounded from the crowds awaiting them. Children ran forward to meet them.

"Reb Fenet! Reb Fenet!" they shouted with exuberance. "Come do your magic!"

He hardly knew what to say. "Not magic, children. Elláh's work." The hundreds in front of them, twice as many as the last town, dismayed him.

The children danced around them, wheeling and grouping like a flock of sky-bound swillows. Holding hands in circles, they sang wild refrains of "Magic, magic, Elláh, Elláh." A few also threw in "Fenet, Fenet."

The adults followed them. Fenet's miracles over twenty years had sometimes brought small crowds, but never anything like this. Intimidated, he looked at the novim to see them even more so. Several of them reached to turn down their t-paths because the feelings were too strong.

"W-what do we do, Reb?" pleaded Lorefim.

"What *can* we do, boys?" Fenet answered, bolstering his own confidence as much as theirs. "We serve them. That's why we're here."

When people came close, Fenet raised a hand to forestall them from approaching him, gesturing toward the novim. Eregim stood separate with a wondering look on his face, likely experiencing the emotions.

The novim soon separated, each one surrounded by eager supplicants. In front of Fenet, Beneim scanned the people, then settled on one teenage boy. He stepped forward and laid hands on the boy's shoulders, having a short conversation. The boy nodded with his eyes lowered. Beneim responded with a nod, then raised one hand in the air. The power of Elláh flowed through him, a red haze around his uplifted hand followed by a rosy glow around the boy's shoulder. Startled, the boy looked up with eyes wide—then he grinned and started dancing under Beneim's hand.

Fenet had no idea what Beneim had healed, but the boy treated is as something important.

All around him, similar scenes played out. The six novim stayed busy, sometimes performing miracles, sometimes praying with someone. Fenet's mouth fell open as he watched. He remembered the thrill of those first weeks of miracles many years ago, the excitement and wonder of it, and saw it all again in these disciples. Yet a deep sadness settled in his heart at being no longer part of these miracles. Was this what it felt like, to pass on a legacy?

Scanat also didn't perform any miracles. Instead, he served by praying with people and leading supplicants to the others.

After a time, Eregim rejoined Fenet to watch. He frequently gasped, perceiving the pathed emotions of both recipients and donors. He spoke little, until at one point he remarked, "Fenet, I had no idea what your life of miracles felt like ..." His voice trailed off.

Fenet nodded, lost in the wonder of it and sad at his loss.

☙ ❋ ❧

It took an hour to reach the town center, slowed by swarms of people. The Khadam had healed or comforted everyone who'd stepped forward—and many who had been too shy to ask—but the novelty of what they did fascinated the onlookers. The town had effectively declared a spontaneous holiday.

After the noon dhuhr prayer, vendors came to Fenet with free food. The vendors took the opportunity to sell to the crowds, and feeding the Khadam became part of their marketing. Several offered fried fish and chips, some of the best Fenet had tasted. Others had sandwiches or hot pasties.

After consuming a pasty, Durnadet laughed and broke into his usual dance. "Best food I've had on this trip. We should come back here."

Tenpos shook his head, smiling for once. "Don't get too used to it, Durnadat. We've still got a long way to go."

"Where are you going?" interjected a man from the crowd. "We can help, if you'll come back when we need you." The short man had rumpled clothes and hair, and he smelled of raw fish.

"I got better transportation than y'all, Inger," shouted another. "I can fit their entire party in my hoverbus." This man wore a billed cylindrical hat with a metal badge on the front.

Inger shoved the second man. "Get away, Pincely. I thought of it first."

Pincely turned to Fenet. Tall and gangly, he spoke forcefully with a bit of twang. "How about it, Reb? Would y'all rather ride in a bus or a couple of beat-up old autotrucks?"

Fenet held up his hands and smiled, hoping to ease the minor conflict. "It's not up to me, gentlemen. We're on pilgrimage. We can only ride when and how Elláh tells us."

Inger glowered at his answer.

"Well, g'wan and ask!" Pincely pointed a finger toward heaven. "Go ahead. I'm sure the Lord will give favor to my bus." He shoved Inger's shoulder in a playful way. Apparently, he often got his way with people around him, and Inger may have been a frequent target.

Fenet laughed and nodded. "Okay. Let's see." Praying came so naturally to him he had no concern about taking the man's advice.

"Lord, what is Your will here? Should we ride at this time? And how far?"

The noises of the crowd filled the air, but nothing else sounded.

Fenet shrugged to Pincely. "Elláh gives me no guidance. This is a walking pilgrimage, so I believe we'll continue to walk." He put a comforting hand on the man's shoulder for a moment.

Pincely sighed. Inger nodded and turned away, petty triumph on his face about the negative answer to Pincely.

The crowds still packed close, but Scanat pushed his way toward Fenet.

"Reb Fenet, Reb Fenet," he called.

"I'm here, Scanat."

"Reb, I just had the most puzzling occurrence," Scanat said breathlessly when he got to the teacher. "I heard a voice in the crowd, but could find no one who spoke to me."

Fenet leaned on his staff and beckoned Scanat to continue. "What did they say?"

"Strange." Scanat shook his head once. "The voice only said, *RIDE FOR THE AFTERNOON*. The voice had more penetration than I've ever heard."

Fenet shared a glance with Eregim, then broke into a merry laugh. "Scanat, my friend ..." he stopped while he waited expectantly for Scanat to realize what had happened.

Pincely, still standing by, suddenly lit up. "There's the answer to your question, Reb! Elláh spoke through your boy here."

Awe filled Scanat's face.

Still chuckling, Fenet wrapped his arms around the young man. "Congratulations, Scanat. You've just experienced your first touch of Elláh's hand. I asked the question here, and He gave you the answer."

☙ ❋ ❧

Half an hour later, Fenet and crew had worked their way through the town center. The crowds had lessened, but the remaining people stayed persistent—asking questions, seeking understanding, offering unnecessary gifts. Pincely now stood by his hoverbus, his tall frame radiating pride. He'd brushed some small crumbs from his clean clothes and busman's hat, waiting for them.

However, getting away presented two problems.

First, they'd come across a more hostile group. Waiting on this side of the town square, these people faced the Khadam with stolid expressions and pumped fists. One held a home-made sign highlighting the repeated symbols "MS":

"Miraculous Scams—Mark of Saitan"

The second problem might have been worse. A line of a dozen proctors stood to one side of the naysayers. In a collective mass like this, their faces chiseled from rock, the grey robes and red collars appeared far more threatening than any past experience with one or two. They were positioned so as to use any conflict as an excuse for arrest. Or, as they sometimes did, exercise their heavy-handed violence to suppress events.

Fenet's heart jumped and started racing.

When they got closer, a spokesman for the protesters stepped out to orate. He wore black clothes and had greasy hair trailing onto his collar.

"Be *very* careful," he intoned in a penetrating, strident voice, "not to *fall* into the trap of Saitan." He emphasized strange words in his message. "Arrogance *comes* before the Fall. Even Jaysus told us, 'I *never* knew them,' when asked about *those* doing supernatural works. Remember also the Islamic *ijaz* of old Earth, when men claimed *scientific* miracles. *Beware* that you not fall into the same thinking, that *you* can do what only Elláh can do."

He continued at length, his eyes darting across Fenet's group and around the square, leaving no gaps for counter-argument—not that Fenet had any impetus to dispute with him. What the Khadam did spoke for itself. Theological discussion became a refuge for those who wanted to *understand* Elláh instead of follow Him.

The crowds closed in, those following the Khadam and those gathered with this preacher. Fenet's supporters shouted, "Oh, go shut up!" Angry faces showed on both sides.

Conflict sparked in the air like rutting beasts. Fenet's breath quickened. The hostile orator and his group generated tension like electricity in the air. The crowd following the Khadam responded with angry support for their mission. Between those two groups, the proctors prepared to bash heads to restore order.

Fenet and the Khadam were caught in the middle. Fenet wanted no conflict of any sort. In prior incidents, he had miraculously displaced proctors several times to remove them. Without Elláh's power, he could not do so again.

Tenpos spoke beside him. "Reb, that orator paths dangerous. His feelings are scattered, hostile."

"Gather to me, Khadam," Fenet shouted. "Come together. Board the bus. Quickly, peacefully."

Fenet's young men pushed through the crowd toward him and the bus, looking around them with wide eyes. Violence might happen at any moment.

Fenet avoided speaking either to the orator or the threatening proctors. He had one single purpose now, to get out of Netweaver.

"Eregim, please help us get clear," he said. "Can you separate the novim from the followers?"

"I'll do that." Eregim moved into the crowd around the Khadam, using his large size to separate paths for the novim.

The proctors moved forward as the Khadam reached the bus, inserting themselves to control the crowd. Their grey robes flowed between the black-garbed speaker and the agitated crowd. The proctors raised heavy black stuncheons, forcing the groups apart. One stuncheon rose and fell with a crunch.

Fenet wasn't clear whether the proctors were there to protect the Khadam or to threaten them. He didn't want to find out.

"Quick," he said again. "On the bus."

Scanat also helped. "On the bus," he repeated over and over, stopping the conversations around the novim.

Fenet boarded the bus, his heart still pounding.

Pincely had taken the driver's seat, his eyes holding alarm. "I don't want no trouble here, Reb."

"We don't either. Let's get everyone on and drive away, please."

"Will the proctors stop us?"

"I don't think so, as long as we don't see physical violence break out."

The novim rushed into the bus, their robes sweeping past Fenet while he stood inside near the entrance. When the last came on board, Pincely closed the door and eased the bus into a slow crawl forward.

People still crowded around, impeding their progress. At least they'd already done all the healing asked for. No one clamored forward, desperate for yet one more miracle. These curious followers only wanted to be with them. While the bus crawled forward, the crowd eased apart. Gradually, Pincely found a way.

Fenet looked out at the proctors and the hostile orator with his protesters. Both groups still stood in their places, the proctors keeping the main crowd away from the protesters.

Fenet's heart still raced, but a single deep breath began to calm him.

"Thank you, Pincely. I don't know what we would have done without you."

"No problem, Reb Fenet. I jes' hope I don't face some charges when I return."

"Trust in Elláh, sir. You have done a good thing."

Fenet turned to face the Khadam and saw some tentative smiles, relief evident on every face. Then he gasped. Eregim was not on board.

18 – Incident in Uptown

Like many religious groups before them, the One Church moved from loving, spiritual teachings to rules and laws. Their teachings became laced with the firm underpinning that only *they* had truth, that all other ways were deficient. The first Holy War started centuries ago on the planet of Elistan shortly after the Church celebrated its two hundredth birthday.

—*History of the One Church* by Ellen Thranadil,
Tileus Press 445 A.T.

By the fifth day of their mission, Morat Intelact and the other missionaries had spoken to at least three hundred individuals, not to mention the thousands of passersby. Not one had come to Elláh. The culture here in Tileus made them immune to Elláh's message. People laughed at them when they spread prayer mats for salat. Even Faï's exuberance had dimmed.

Not only that, this afternoon threatened to rain again. Cold, wet wind whipped around the streets, pushing dark clouds above the buildings.

The mission leader, Roloket, continued to encourage them at every opportunity. However, he admitted, "I've never seen it this bad before. Tileus has always had conflicts among groups with different political opinions, but not like the protesters we're seeing this week."

"Yeah, Rolo, *that's* pretty scary," said Gadet, pointing across the street.

Morat hadn't needed the leveled finger to notice the protesters, impossible to miss. The half-dozen missionaries faced close to a hundred antagonists on the other side of the narrow autocar lane. The angry crowd marched in a constant circle waving signs.

"Church: Shut Up!" "No Missionaries!" And the worst of the lot: "Jaysus Lies!"

Who were they? Morat had asked Rolo, who looked them up on the InfoNet with his imp. The core group, calling themselves The Freethinkers, expounded the use of strong methods to suppress religion, which they characterized as "misleading babble." The demonstrators across the street had grown more numerous each day, apparently with other organizations now supporting them.

The protesters kept up a steady stream of shouts, spraying spittle on the occasional passing autocar. Sometimes, their yells coalesced into chants.

"Back to Rath-as, Back to Rath-as, Back to Rath-as."

In unison with the chant, those holding signs pumped their placards up and down. The voices of their hundred people filled the street.

Morat had a hard time staying calm. He responded to the chant with one of his own, shouting as loud as he could, "Jaysus Saves the Lost." He shouted it over and over, giving it a rhythm, and the rest of the missionaries joined him.

"Jaysus Saves the Lost—Jaysus Saves the Lost."

Faï leaned in to tell him, "Great idea, Morat."

He glowed at her praise and watched her while they kept it up. Her long, red curls bounced as she just about danced in time with the chant. She focused her green eyes at protester after protester. She seemed to *will* her faith into them. *Elláh, I love this girl.*

Other passersby avoided the chaos. Some people turned around to go back the way they'd come. Morat had come to believe this country completely crazy. They prided themselves on "freedom" and "democracy," but that meant they had chaos in the streets— and insane laws to keep the conflicting political groups from constant warfare.

After a moment, the protesters mocked the missionaries' chant, joining in the same tempo:

"Jaysus Saves the Lost—Jaysus Save the Lost" now competed with

"Jaysus Sells a Book—Jaysus Sells a Book."

Faï screamed at the blasphemy. She rushed across the car lane and put her *Holiest* in the face of one of the protesters, shouting, "This book *saves*."

"No, Faï! Don't go there!" Morat shouted in surprise. His gut jerked in fear at her boldness.

The protester reacted with complete surprise. Dozens of others stopped chanting around Faï, disbelief showing in their eyes.

Morat jumped across the lane to protect her. The other four missionaries followed him, shouting verses.

Rolo grabbed and missed each missionary as they left the curb. "No, no, no. You're not allowed to cross the street. Come back, stay here." No one paid attention, so he crossed the lane to grab Gadet by the shoulder. He pulled Gadet back to their side of the street, then came back for another.

Meanwhile, after stopping in surprise around Faï, the protesters resumed marched in their circle, ignoring the missionaries. "Jaysus Sells a Book." Faï, Morat, and the other missionaries put the books in the faces of the marching protesters, trying to stop the offensive chant. Morat slapped his *Holiest* with his other palm, a sharp pop, hoping to break through their irritating mixture of hostility and aloofness. With no reaction, he finally nudged one of them to get the man's attention. Abruptly, the man dropped his sign and punched Morat squarely on his left cheek, knocking him to the ground.

"Back off, fool!" the protester shouted. He kicked Morat in the ribs. "Know the laws! You touched me. Now, everything is self-defense!"

The confrontation became a melee. Rolo tried to get his flock back across the street, but the protesters had turned themselves loose. Punching and gouging and grabbing, they pummeled the missionaries from every direction.

Rolling on the ground, Morat protected his head with his arms. Each time he tried to stand, someone knocked him off balance again. Grunts and screams sounded above him. He'd lost his *Holiest*, and he crawled around to find it. Someone kicked him again just as he picked it up. Frantically, he jumped to his feet and limped back across the street. His face ached and his ribs were bruised. One hip burned where a kick had landed hard.

Rolo pulled the last of the missionaries back into his group. They all panted from the exertion.

In the middle of the pandemonium, Morat heard a stifled scream. He looked for Faï and didn't see her. "Faï!" he shouted.

"Where's Faï?" He barged through the people on this side of the street, searching for her.

In the hotel conference room hours later, battered and bruised, changed to dry clothes, Morat paced the floor, muttering to himself. None of their searching had found Faï. The protesters must have spirited her away; nothing else made sense. His mind spun widdershins, trying to find some memory, some clue how to find her.

Morat brooded on their treatment by the Uptown police, who had focused on enforcing Tilean law. They treated the protesters gently and let them go. While the rain poured down, the same police blamed the missionaries for instigating the incident, saying the law required them to stay on their side of the street. *As if crossing the street could justify kidnapping!* Concerning Faï's disappearance, the officers took the data without great concern, saying they'd look into it. They took names and detailed statements from each missionary, a permanent record of their "transgression." The police held them for two hours, standing drenched in the cold street.

Meanwhile, Rolo had used his implant to get advice from the Mission Ministry back in Rathas. In a hotel conference room, he gave them the news. "We're heading back to Rathas. An autobus will pick us up in an hour. Pack your things and return here. Your mission is being cut short."

"Will it still count for Church membership?" asked Gadet.

Morat stopped pacing to snap at him, "You've got to be kidding me. I can't believe you'd ask that. Faï's gone, and you're only worried about checking a box?"

Rolo palmed the air in a calming gesture. "We all need to stay at peace. Elláh will work this out."

Morat took in a deep breath, let it out, and nodded. "Thanks, Rolo. But I'm frantic with worry. I'm not leaving until we find her, and I want your help."

"There's nothing more we can do here," the leader said. "You can't stay. You'll only make the problem worse."

"I can search. I'll do it by myself if I have to."

Rolo gave a hard shake of his head. "No, You won't. The Mission Ministry demands we return now. You have no choice."

As much as he wanted to fight the decision, Morat realized the wisdom. His shoulders sagged. "Okay."

Still fretting, Morat went to his room to get his bag. He asked Faï's roommate to pick up her things, too.

They returned to Rathas. Without Faï.

19 – Incident in the Mountains

Throughout history, major wars have often started upon trifles. A deranged individual shoots a minor political figure; one country believes something different from another; activists believe now is the time to end a practice already dying. The events on Verdant were no different.

—*The Making of a New Humanity* by Ellen Thranadil, Tileus Press 448 A.T.

Back home in his dormitory, Morat thrashed in his bed that night like branches in a wind. First he roasted, then he froze. All his covers found their way to the floor, then he'd chill and have to pick them up. The familiarity of his room provided no comfort.

In the mirror, his face looked red and bleary by the time the group met the next morning for yet another grilling, this time by the school officials from the Mission Ministry. The officials had taken over the dormitory study room for the day, keeping the missionaries sequestered for interviews. This time, they pulled the group into the study room together.

"What were you people thinking?" shouted the Mission Coordinator. "Or were you thinking at all? You can't win converts to peace by punching them out."

Morat kept his eyes on the floor, except when he looked up in shame at others in the group. He wanted to shout back, to explain. None of the missionaries had done any fighting or thrown any punches. A part of him, however, knew his own small push on the protester had precipitated the physical confrontation.

He asked the question closest to his heart. "Where's Faïlebaso Servdo? Does anyone know?"

The Mission Coordinator softened his tone. "We have no information. The Uptown police haven't found her."

The next hours were excruciating. As part of the sequestration, the school had denied InfoNet access to the missionaries' imps. They had little to do but sit in their rooms while the Ministry called them out one-by-one. The whole group fell into feelings of disconsolate defeat.

Morat still heard nothing about Faï. He paced from one end of the room to the other, his steps slapping the floor harder at each pass. He began to pound a fist into the wall at each end of his track, his teeth gritted.

Mid-morning, a tall, older man knocked on his door. With an air of confidence and authority, he obviously had a position greater than any school administrator. An unusual orange collar surmounted his grey robes, indicating a national official. The man had an intent gaze, as if he could see everything inside Morat.

Abruptly, Morat recognized the man, and he sucked in a breath. He stood straight and nodded his head in deference. "I know you, sir. I saw you on the news, speaking to the Bishopric Enclave about violence in Tileus. Aren't you the Rathas national Minister of Security?"

The man nodded. "Yes, I am. Beltaret Leaderlist. And you're Morat Intelact."

"Yes, sir. But how would you know—"

The man waved a hand. "Never mind about how. I sense you're very upset, frantic with worry."

Morat leaned back. How could this man know so much about him? Did he see inside Morat's own emotions? How could he do that?

The minister continued, "The others identified you as being close to Faïlebaso Servdo. Is that right?"

"Yes, we're close." Morat blushed.

"We need your help." Beltaret's voice charged with determination. "This whole thing is a horrible incident of international scope, because Servdo's father is one of our leading Bishops. A good friend of mine, he's devastated and broken. We need to find her.

"We also need to know what happened. Our people are no longer safe in Tileus. Our national leadership is considering what to do about it, everything from closing the borders to Holy War."

Morat startled at the thought the minister could seriously consider starting a Holy War. But perhaps he was right; perhaps the time had come. In the meantime, they needed to find Faï. "How can I help, sir?"

"We've been working with Tileus authorities to find her, but they aren't very cooperative. Officially, those authorities tell us our missionaries work in Tileus at their own risk, and the authorities are not responsible for keeping track of them. Unofficially, those same authorities tolerate violent groups like those Freethinkers.

"Yesterday afternoon, after your incident, the InfoNet got a location on her implant going up the hiking trail from Tileus to Magnum Gap on the border. Unfortunately, there's a large area around the mountain pass with no connection to the InfoNet. She hasn't left that dead zone … or her imp hasn't."

"So, she's been up there all night?" Morat clenched his fists and pounded them into his thighs.

"We're organizing a search party. You'd be an asset, if you're willing to come. If and when we find her—"

"*When*, sir, not if."

"Yes, *when* we find her, it would be good for her to see a friend."

❧ ✳ ☙

Two hours later, Morat hiked the mountains above Praise with the search party. He and Minister Leaderlist climbed a steep trail wending its way up toward the Gap and the border with Tileus. A dozen searchers formed a line above and below the trail on the steep mountainside, paralleling each other while they climbed. Each one had been issued a walking staff and a hiking knife. Even without InfoNet coverage, Faï's imp would respond if someone got within twenty meters. Frequent shouts disturbed the quiet of the forest.

"Faïlebaso!"

"Speak up."

"Where are you?"

Everyone looked. Everyone listened, both with ears and with imps.

Despite the bright sun above the trees, the same mountainside that looked so beautiful from down in the city now loomed as a dark threat around Morat. He thought about Faï's condition after a night here in the mountains.

He spoke to the minister. "I'm concerned, sir. What if she's hurt? Do we have medical help in the team?"

The minister glanced at him. "You should be concerned. Doing good is becoming dangerous. It's always that way when we follow Elláh." The minister faced forward again. "Yes, we have a paramedic on the team—and a surgery team standing by."

Morat shuddered.

Near the top, a gap in the forest revealed a precipitous field of huge boulders, one to three meters in size. The trail disappeared among the rocks. A hundred meters away and thirty meters higher, the trail resumed where the trees started again. Morat had little idea how to cross the gap.

Climbing the boulders took all of Morat's attention. He jumped from one rock to another like an unsteady goat. His heart pounded with the exertion; fear took a large part. On his third jump, his foot slipped on a patch of lichen. He fell to the left and slammed his upper body into the wall of rock beside him. The impact took his breath away and his eyes glazed. Sweat suddenly suffused his body. For a moment, he froze in place, picturing himself slipping the other direction, careening down rock after rock like a twisted marionette, losing limbs along the way.

The minister cautioned, rather late, "Watch yourself, Morat."

Morat caught his breath. Weakened from the fall, he crawled up the next few rocks—which led to him not keeping up with the search line. He stood up again and risked a few quick jumps to get ahead.

He stopped, sniffing the air. "Do you smell something foul, sir?"

"No, nothing," said Beltaret behind him.

Morat took another two steps forward. His imp pinged him with a notice about a new person.

He shouted, "I'm getting a signal!"

Beltaret had everyone hold the line while the two of them advanced another few meters. Morat moved around one of the larger boulders and saw a shallow recess behind it. Inside the hollow ...

"Oh, Elláh," he whispered. Then his voice rang out. "I've found her."

The whole group started converging on the spot, working their way through the rocks.

Morat rushed into the recess. "Faï, we're here." Then he stopped in horror. When he saw her more clearly, bile rose in his throat.

His girlfriend sat in an awkward position with her head hanging. Ropes tied to stakes pounded between the rocks held her arms high and wide. Her feet were tied together, stretched out in front of her. Her hair straggled down past her closed eyes.

Exposed for a cold night and most of a day with clothes ripped open, her skin looked red and raw. Bruises blackened her face, arms, and legs. Dried blood covered her hands and face. Worst of all, her bare belly had been cut with the symbol of Elláh, a circle within a triangle. Blood had flowed around the shapes and hardened there. It blackened the ground at her hips. The wounds still gaped open and foul. Flies buzzed around her and landed on the blood. An awful smell filled the air, a mix of coppery blood and urine.

Morat's arrival and the noise of others elicited no movement or response. As frozen as she, he could not move for the horror of the scene. Her chest still rose and fell.

A large hand suddenly rested on Morat's shoulder.

"Sweet Jaysus," Minister Leaderlist said. "Go to her, boy."

The words released Morat from torpor. He jumped to Faï's side, knelt, and cradled her face with his palm. "Faï, we're here. What have they done to you?"

He pulled his knife from its sheath to release Faï, supporting her weight while he cut each rope. Her wrists were bloody and scarred from her efforts to pull free before she passed out. He waved away the persistent flies.

His mouth filled with the sour spittle of anger. This Tileus protest group had beaten Faï, carried her up through the pass into Rathas, staked her out in a hidden place, then cut the symbol of Elláh into her belly. All because they resented her sharing about peace. They hadn't cared whether Faï lived or died; their message worked either way. He raged inside while he worked to ease her position. *The people who did this are sick.* He ground his teeth. He wanted to retaliate. Violence would work. He wanted to slam them against these rocks, to cut them the way they'd cut Faï.

One of the searchers reached them with a canteen and moistened her lips. Faï moved her head to suck in the water. The man then wiped her forehead and eyes with a wet cloth. Another searcher carried a medkit and started scanning her for damage. She was alive. The practiced team would get her back safely.

Faï opened her eyes, encrusted with tears and sweat, and looked at him.

Morat wondered whether she could see anything. "We're in Rathas, Faï. You'll be okay."

Faï nodded and closed her eyes again.

The team moved in with a stretcher.

Morat got out of the way to let them work. He raged inside, transforming into new determination.

He looked at Faï and the cluster of people helping her, then turned to look down from the mountain toward Rathas and home. The peaceful city of Praise rested in the valley below, unaware of this disaster above. Morat thought about how ineffective their mission had been.

He wanted to do something greater, something that would change the way Tileus treated people. He had felt unready for mission, lacking any confidence. Now ready, he wanted a new purpose.

Morat took a deep breath and made a decision. He would join the Khubar f'Elláh, the "Experts of God," the national holy army.

When he'd spoken to Faï about it, he'd been uncertain. No longer. If this incident didn't spark Holy War, something else would. Then he'd have a chance to change those crazy people in Tileus. They must learn to respect Elláh and His people. Righteous anger would be a powerful tool for good, and he would be part of it.

20 – Potholes in the Road

The conflicts between the technological way of the transpath and the way of spirituality showed themselves early.

—*The Making of a New Humanity* by Ellen Thranadil, Tileus Press 448 A.T.

Fenet couldn't see Eregim. He hobbled as fast as he could to the back windows of the hoverbus while Pincely maneuvered the vehicle through the crowds and into the open. The line of red-collared proctors had shoved their way between the contrary preacher and the mass of Khadam supporters. The proctors had their stuncheons out, threatening the throngs on both sides.

"He's gone," Fenet exclaimed, searching the entire crowd.

"Did we lose somebody?" Pincely hollered back.

Fenet returned to the seat in the front row. "Yes. My friend. I don't know what happened." His heart pounded. "Let me call him."

He directed his imp to contact Eregim and waited for a response, his breath shallow. What could have happened to the man? No response came while he waited through ten impatient rings. He cut off the call.

Scanat had the seat across the aisle from Fenet. "No response, Reb?"

"None." Fenet thought about the proctors' ability to jam and disable imps. What had happened? Had he been captured by proctors? Kidnapped by protesters? What might the proctors do with him?

"What do you want to do?" The concern in Scanat's voice suggested he impathed Fenet's emotions, something that still made Fenet uncomfortable.

"I don't know what we *can* do, Scanat. I'm torn between going back and keeping on."

The driver stared at his sideview mirror. "We got us another problem here, Reb. Half a dozen autocars, following us. They're waving and cheering."

Great. Now they've got an entourage. Fenet always hoped he would be known by history, like the Zikri, perhaps become famous. Yet the crowds made him uncomfortable.

Fenet turned back to Scanat. "I want to go back and find Eregim. But I'm afraid that mess would turn into mobs with the proctors bashing heads. I want nothing to do with that. Or, we could keep going and hope Eregim can join us again." He pointed a thumb back at the cars. "It shouldn't be hard to find us. But I hate to leave him."

"It's a tough choice." Scanat softened in his attitudes with the impact of the t-path, a good thing.

Fenet paused to consider, then shook his head and said, "Let's keep driving for now, please. Pincely, how far are you willing to go?"

The driver guffawed. "I'm havin' the time of my life, Reb. Never have seen anything like what you and your people can do. When I first offered, I just thought of taking y'all to Richearth, the next city on the Coast Road. But who knows? Let's see what happens."

"Well, remember Elláh's in charge here. He only gave us guidance to ride for the afternoon."

"Then Richearth it is," Pincely said. "You'll have plenty of time before dark to heal a bunch of people there, too."

"We'll see what Elláh has in store for us." Fenet activated his imp once more to call Eregim, his heart falling further with each unanswered ring.

Just as Fenet almost gave up, Eregim answered. "Fenet, I'm here." He grunted hard, as if struck. "Let go, let go. I'm trying to talk here. Ouch!" Muffled, he talked to someone else. "Yes, I'm coming. Just let me—" His voice cut off.

Fenet caught his breath and stared out the front window of the bus.

His imp came alive again with an incoming call from Eregim. The hurried words sounded fearful. "Keep going, Fenet. Don't come back. The proctors have me, but keep going. I'll be—"

Again, his words cut short.

≈❋≈

Over the next hour, while driving toward Richearth, Fenet agonized over Eregim. What could he do? Nothing came to mind.

They left the coast behind. Despite its name, the Coast Road turned east into a broad valley of farmland. Behind them, hills and coastal arroyos grew a scrub covering of bushes. Ahead, the land transitioned to manicured fields and bands of fading blue-leaved loula trees. Farmhouses with the distinct Rathas style of rounded eaves dotted the fields.

He had to let go of his worry over Eregim and return to leadership of the group. Elláh wanted surrender to Him, but He also gave each person intelligence and capabilities to use. Fenet needed to use again the meager leadership gifts He'd given. Perhaps use would strengthen them.

While Pincely drove, Fenet engaged the novim. "Listen up, everyone. Eregim pointed out we've been drifting on this pilgrimage since our meeting in Glorify. That's been my fault. I've been too lost in pain. I'm thankful to Scanat," Fenet nodded acknowledgement to him, "for adjusting my attitude this morning. I'm feeling better now, and I'll continue to pray for myself, which I should have been doing all along." After a pause, he added, "We have some decisions to take to Elláh."

Lorefim spoke first. "W-what do we n-need to decide, Reb?"

Fenet counted on his fingers. "First, what do we do about Eregim? Second, how should we continue to travel? Third, what do we do about healing along the way?" He paused, frowning. "And the biggest question: Why are we on this pilgrimage at all?"

Penilos answered the last immediately. "We're on the pilgrimage because Elláh told us to."

Fenet chuckled. "That's the same answer I gave Eregim this morning. He pointed out it's not enough, and he's right. Elláh never wants us to lean on a shovel and pray for a hole. We need to be active, *doing* what Elláh wants us to do. Is there something we're supposed to accomplish on the way? Or is there some task awaiting us in Praise? We don't know yet because we haven't asked."

The humming of the hoverbus filled the silence while the novim pondered the questions.

Tenpos spoke in his quiet, deep voice. "Those are hard questions, Reb. I think the answers to all of them must come from Elláh, not from us."

"Thank you. We could make all four decisions, and be wrong in every case. So, how do we find out what Elláh wants from us?"

"We pray," several of them answered in unison, which raised smiles.

"Not only that," Fenet said, "but it's important for us to pray together. Let's divide in pairs. Scanat and Penilos. Lorefim and Beneim. Durnadat and Tenpos. Each pair pray together for answers. I'll call us together again in half an hour."

Everyone nodded. The novim divvied up the questions, then moved into three separate groups to pray. The bus filled with paired voices and an occasional, "Selah."

Fenet settled back in the front seat. He missed Eregim. They'd been friends a long time, but in these few days of pilgrimage Eregim had become his sounding board. Now, he had no one. He closed his eyes and prayed for his friend's safety and quick release.

After a few minutes, Pincely spoke in a low voice so as not to disturb the others. "Reb Fenet, I got some thoughts about your first two questions."

Fenet opened his eyes and smiled to encourage the man.

"I don't think there's much y'all can do about Eregim at this point. The proctors in Netweaver can be scary. They've been known to beat prisoners just 'cause they didn't like them. Hardly spiritual behavior, but power does that to some. I had a cousin..."

Fenet's chest tightened. "Had?"

"Oh, well, guess I still have him. In any case, he got in some moral trouble with a girl—young guys and all that—and the proctors broke his arm to teach him a lesson."

Fenet winced. "Do they do such things regularly?"

"Well, not all the time." Pincely glanced over at him. "If he's not done nothing illegal or immoral, I'm sure they'll let him go."

"From your mouth to Elláh's ears, my friend."

"And about traveling, I'm willing to drive y'all as far as you'll let me. I wanna see what happens."

⁂

Before entering Richearth, Fenet called the novim back together to discuss what prayer had brought them. He turned the front-row seat around to face them.

"Let's talk first about Eregim," he said. "Did any of you hear guidance from Elláh about him? I've gotten nothing new."

Scanat raised his hand while he spoke. "Penilos and I had a strong sense we have to leave Eregim in Elláh's hands for now."

Penilos nodded agreement.

"W-we got a similar f-feeling," said Lorefim. "There's n-nothing we can do about his situation now."

Fenet took a deep breath. "That's the same answer I had before we broke up to pray, so we'll have to trust Elláh on this one. But we can also pray for Eregim, for him to be safe and return to us."

The Khadam agreed.

"Now," he continued, "what about our mode of travel?"

Silence fell. No one had received an answer.

Tenpos almost smiled, as close as he ever came, before adding in his deep voice. "Sounds like we need to keep asking on that one. Perhaps it'll be a daily decision."

Fenet agreed, then moved on. "Our third question. What about healing on the way? What about these transpaths?"

Scanat answered with force, "I still have a strong sense of purpose to use the t-path to find people for healing."

Fenet expected his answer. Without his own miracles, Scanat had a vested interest in making the t-paths part of our ministry.

"They do help," said Beneim, "but Lorefim and I didn't get any guidance on it. Healing, yes. We should continue to heal. The t-path? We heard nothing."

Durnadat enthused, "I like having the t-path. I feel closer to all of you with it."

"But did you get any guidance about it from Elláh?" Fenet asked.

Durnadat shook his head.

When no one else spoke, Fenet said, "We'll continue to look for answers about it. But obviously, healing is a large part of what Elláh expects of us." He paused. "So that brings us to the big question. What about our purpose? What are we to do on this pilgrimage?"

Beneim spoke again. "It was clear to Lorefim and me we should be healing, spreading the knowledge of Elláh's power among the faithful."

"M-maybe that's our primary p-purpose," said Lorefim. "M-maybe there's nothing more w-waiting for us, other than what we do on the way?"

Pincely chimed in from the driver's seat. "Well, y'all better get ready. We still got a dozen cars following us, and now we got a bunch of people in front, too."

21 – Technology Issues

Adherents to the One Church can cite frequent cases where Elláh appeared to take back something given—yet claim such cases nearly always lead to something better.

—*History of the One Church* by Ellen Thranadil,
Tileus Press 445 A.T.

Fenet turned to the front and gasped. Where the farm fields gave way to the outskirts of Richearth, masses of people crowded the streets and yards. The biggest city they'd gone through since Glorify, the size of the crowds daunted him. No sooner did the bus appear than people moved forward to greet them. To one side, a military-style hover truck held a cadre of proctors watching over the gathering.

"Holy Elláh," Fenet muttered. "Is it going to be this way at every city on the road?" Then louder, to the Khadam, "Pincely's right, boys. Get yourselves ready to heal."

They drove to the first opening in the road with sufficient room to work, the crowds parting to let them through then closing in behind. Fenet advised the Khadam to form a widely-spaced line beside the hoverbus, with Scanat working within the crowds to find those who needed healing. After the experience in Netweaver and on the road, their faces shone with confidence.

Fenet wished Eregim were still with them. He could use the support. He sent a quick prayer for his friend's safety.

Pincely opened the door. No sooner did the novim step off the bus than people swamped them.

Fenet took a position in front of the Khadam, walking back and forth and organizing the crowd. "Back up, folks. Elláh has sufficient grace for everyone, and we'll work with each person in turn. Queue up, please."

He gently held the arm of a woman pressing forward and put her in line. "Durnadat will get to you, ma'am. It'll be fine."

When some order came into existence, Fenet marveled again at how Elláh worked. The wash of His power showed as a red glow entering each nov's head and leaving again through his hands to the supplicant. People cried out with astonishment and praise.

Scanat continued his role of bringing specific individuals to one or another nov, somehow connecting their precise ailment with the power given to that nov.

With their prior experience, the Khadam handled this larger crowd with ease. Each nov stayed busy, and Fenet stood by the bus to watch. A part of him echoed again sorrow at not being the one doing the miracles. The power had passed on to his disciples. Would it ever return?

The proctors stayed close but separate. Their hover truck had moved with the bus, parking forty meters away, and the proctors continued to stand in the bed of the truck watching the proceedings from above.

Fenet closed his eyes to pray for Elláh's protection, for the proctors to stay separate and not interfere so long as the crowd continued to be calm. Though Elláh had taken away Fenet's healing powers, he felt the usual moment of internal peace in answer to his prayer. However, a flash of puzzling anxiety followed the moment of peace. He cocked his head to watch the novim, wondering what might happen.

The problems showed up first with Beneim. He had his hands on the shoulders of a young man with a bent back. Beneim lowered his eyes in prayer, but nothing happened. He lifted his head with a confused expression, then prayed again. Scanat stood by, having brought the man to Beneim. The two novim exchanged some words, Scanat waiting patiently. Fenet couldn't hear what they said, but disquiet showed on their faces. Beneim lowered a hand to the t-path on his belt and tapped it with his finger.

Tenpos, a bit closer to Fenet, had also seen the exchange. He said, over the noise of the crowd, "Bring the man to me, Scanat." When Scanat and the young man came to him, Tenpos received the usual red glow and the recipient's face lit up with awe.

The three of them—Beneim, Scanat, and Tenpos—came to Fenet.

"I couldn't do it, Reb Fenet." Beneim rubbed his hands together. "Nothing happened when I prayed. I still impathed the man's emotions, but I couldn't heal him. And my hands itched on his shoulders."

Fenet narrowed his eyes. "Wrong thinking, Beneim. Elláh does the healing, not you. It's always up to Him."

"And yet it worked for me," said Tenpos.

A murmur rose in the crowd around the other novim. Durnadat stood in place, shaking his hands and waving supplicants to stand away from him. "Hold off, folks. I don't know what's happening."

Beyond him, Penilos and Lorefim had also stopped healing. Penilos rubbed his hands on his robes. Lorefim had his hands clasped at his waist. The townspeople around them watched with concern.

Fenet stepped over to Durnadat. "What's going on?"

"The power stopped, Reb. My hands burned. It's fading now, though. I can try again." He turned to the next supplicant in line, apparently scanning her with the t-path. He nodded and spoke to her, then put his hands on her shoulders, starting to pray.

Immediately, he ripped his hands away as if from a hot pot. "Ow!" His eyes were wide, and he spun in a circle while shaking his hands again.

The novim had gathered around Durnadat and Fenet, all of them watching. Several of them winced with the pain they perceived through their t-paths.

"This isn't working, Reb," Tenpos offered. "Something's wrong."

"What's happening?" demanded the woman. "Is he going to heal me or not?"

"We've all been waiting for this," chided a tall man behind her. "We stayed in town just to meet with you."

"Is this a scam, or what?" asked a third.

Fenet stood tall to address the crowd. Before he could speak, a heavy hand fell on his shoulder.

"You're the leader of this motley group, right?" The harsh voice of a senior proctor sounded behind him. "You're Fenet Powrfaith?"

Fenet turned to face him. "Yes, sir, I am. We're trying to work out what's happened—"

"It's pretty obvious what's happened." The proctor shook his head, denying Fenet's words. "You people have promised things you can't deliver. The entire city has taken off Elláh's appointed artha as a holiday in response to your false promises."

"Not false, sir. Please talk with those we've already healed."

"But you're not *healing* any more, right?"

"We don't know. Only Elláh knows."

"Easy enough to blame Elláh for the things you've set up." The proctor moved his hand from Fenet's shoulder to grip his upper arm. "We've been warned about you and your group from authorities above us. Disrupting work, creating conflict, sowing false doctrine. I'll give you two choices, *Reb*. You can get on your bus and leave now, or I'll take your entire entourage to my jail."

Behind the senior proctor, his troop of a dozen had offloaded from their hover truck to form a threatening line. Each proctor held his stuncheon at the ready, the tips sparkling with unspent energy, their cruelty and strength obvious in their stances. To one side stood another puzzling and threatening figure. Short and slim, the man had a red proctor collar but dressed in a dark grey military-style uniform. In only a glance, Fenet felt a wave of threat from the man.

Fenet looked around. The novim had settled in behind him, seeming younger than they were. The crowds had moved away, leaving a gap between themselves and the incident with the proctors. Some people were hurrying away by side streets.

He bowed his head. "Yes, sir. We'll leave." Fenet turned to the Khadam. "Follow me, boys, let's get back on board.

Pincely already had the door open. At the bus, Fenet felt like a chastised prisoner returning to the lock-up. He waited by the door for all six novim to enter, then stepped in last.

"Drive away, Pincely, as safely as you can." Fenet took the usual front seat while the driver eased the hoverbus forward. Townspeople scurried out of the way, leaving the road open to go through Richearth and onto the Coast Road beyond. The novim chattered with questions, but Fenet held up his hand for quiet, watching the grain towers and processing plants fall behind.

Evening approached. They'd have to find a place to camp, or perhaps spend the night in the bus. He thought ahead to those mundane tasks while the Khadam waited.

The more he thought, the more Fenet realized he held the responsibility to deal with this. He took a deep breath, sat up straight, then turned to face the Khadam, now quiet and downcast.

"Okay, boys. What happened back there?"

"It j-just s-stopped, Reb." Nearly in tears, Lorefim shook. "I impathed the need in the boy in front of me. W-when I tried to help him, my hands started b-burning."

Penilos nodded. "The same happened to me. That older man's pain filled him so much I had to turn down my t-path. But when I reached out to touch him, the itch in my hands was like fire."

Fenet looked at each of their faces. Concern, anguish, distress echoed in the bus. "Who was first? I saw Beneim's reaction. Did anyone else have a failure before him?"

Everyone looked at each other. No one spoke.

Tenpos broke the silence with his deep voice. "I healed the young man's back after Beneim failed."

"Did you feel his healing through your t-path?" Fenet asked.

Tenpos shook his head. "No, I had my t-path turned off at the time. The emotions distracted me."

Several of the Khadam sat up. A couple had startled looks.

Lorefim glanced around at the others and frowned. "Is it p-possible the t-path interferes with our healing?"

Scanat rushed to answer. "No, the t-path has been good for us. It's brought a way for us to know who needs healing and what they need."

Durnadat shook his head, scowling. "We healed people before we started using the t-path."

Beneim's face got red. "That's right. Now, we're trying to use the t-paths and the healing power has left us. It's like being spanked."

"It's like what happened to Reb Fenet," Tenpos added, "when he relied on the repellor belt instead of on Elláh."

Durnadat pointed a shaking finger. "It's your fault, Scanat. You brought these things into our midst, and they've taken us away from Elláh."

All the others reached down to turn off their t-paths. Scanat looked as though he'd been slapped.

22 – Testimony

Throughout human history, even before the destruction of Earth, religious military orders attracted the devout to defend their faith. The faithful joined holy armies for many reasons: to prove themselves, test their faith, escape life problems, meet peer pressure, or even for love.

—*History of the One Church* by Ellen Thranadil,
Tileus Press 445 A.T.

Morat climbed the steps of Church Center One in early morning, each tread making the grand building façade more imposing. He'd visited the center of the Rathas nation on a school tour years ago, but never expected to be called here for a presentation. Butterflies invaded his stomach. He swallowed several times, trying to calm the impulse to throw up.

Following Faï's rescue yesterday, Minister Leaderlist asked Morat to speak to the Service Ministry. The Service Ministry, the central council of government! The minister wanted Morat to give his eye witness account of the missionary experience in Tileus. Morat spent last night in a panic, organizing his thoughts and making implant notes to guide the presentation. He hoped what he'd put together would satisfy the minister, but feared it might not. Morat told himself the truth would suffice, yet he had no experience with men this powerful.

He'd much rather be sitting at Faï's side in the hospital.

And why does the minister need a presentation from a secondary school student? Dismay crouched in the back of his head.

Through the stone-arched doors, the foyer lofted three stories high, marble in different colors shaping scenes of the early One

Church. Images of merging Islam, Christianity and Hinduism. The Zikri writing *The Holiest* from those prior holy books. Travels of The Zikri around Earth to preach the faith.

Unlike ordinary society in Rathas, in this building nearly everyone wore grey robes. Morat had entered a strange world. A yellow-collared receptionist registered his implant for entry, then a male functionary with a pale blue collar, perhaps a secretary, approached him. "Are you Morat Intelact?" The rodent-faced secretary, short and fortyish, had a haughty look in his eyes showing the petty power he wielded as a Church bureaucrat.

Morat doubted this secretary dealt often with a mere student. "Yes, sir. That's me."

"Follow me, please. You've cut the time short." The man turned away, veered to the left, and scurried down a narrow hallway.

Morat rushed after, wincing at the idea of being late. Had he screwed up already? Before starting? He checked the time in his imp. "I thought I was supposed to be here now."

The secretary chided over his shoulder. "Then you are ill-prepared. You should have arrived early. We need you in the room and ready before the Ministers arrive."

"The Ministers? All of them?" Morat's mouth went dry.

"Yes, indeed. Your presentation is to the entire Service Ministry in the Seat of Elláh conference room." The man hurried him to a lift tube, then up to the top floor.

Halfway down the upper hall, a pair of huge arched doors displayed a deep, intricate carving of the triangle-in-circle trifacis of the Church. The secretary pushed his way through. Morat entered, then froze, intimidated by the grandeur. A long dark-wood table stretched across the room, inlaid with patterned marble. The entire opposite wall, one large window, overlooked the city of Praise, where the spires of the many churches dotted the urban scene. Carved wood arches repeated around the walls, each one framing a scriptural frieze of Church history: the Creation, the Mahabharata epic, the passion of Jaysus, Muhamet's ascent to Heaven, and the Zikri's synthesis of the One Church.

Morat wondered how he could possibly have something to offer in this magnificent place—and to the powerful men who would be here.

The secretary turned, his irritation clear. "Hurry up, son. They'll be here soon." The man showed Morat to a lectern at one end of the table. "You'll make your presentation from here. Of course, you have some visual materials for the holo display, right?"

"Uh … no." Morat stammered, tongue-tied already in the face of a mere secretary. "I have an outline in my imp, but nothing to show."

The man huffed. "Yes, ill-prepared indeed. Son, you're presenting to the leaders of the country. Can't you at least show an agenda? That would be better than nothing."

"I can reformat it, yes."

"Then do so, quickly, and connect it to the holo projector on the local InfoNet. The code address is on the podium."

Morat nodded. With something concrete to do, he broke out of his stupor. It took only a moment to reformat, and the small success felt like passing a pop quiz.

The secretary examined the agenda when it appeared. "Acceptable at least. Can you cover all this in fifteen minutes? That's all the time you'll have."

"I can."

"The ministers will also have questions, perhaps quite a few. You should remain standing from now until you leave. I'll tell them you're here." The man hurried out, muttering, "for what it's worth."

Others began filing into the room, everyone in robes except Morat. Most had the white collars of leadership. These people knew each other, chatting while they took seats around the room periphery. No one sat at the table, apparently reserved for the most important people. Several glanced at Morat, though no one spoke to him. He shifted from one foot to the other, trying to tame the butterflies.

Moments later, the double doors opened again. Minister Leaderlist entered, and those around the room all stood, honoring his presence. The minister came directly to Morat with an encouraging smile. "Good morning, Morat. I'm glad you came. Are you ready for this?"

Morat cleared his throat and nodded. "Yes, sir. I can tell the story of what happened in Uptown and how Faïlebaso was kidnapped. Do you also want me to tell how we found her? You should tell that part instead."

Leaderlist shook his head. "No, you should tell the whole bloody story. It will be more powerful coming from you."

Talking about it with the minister calmed Morat. He could do this.

While they talked, another eight ministers entered with casual conversation and took their seats at the table. Minister Leaderlist patted Morat's shoulder. When all the ministers had seated themselves, the others around the room also sat.

All except Morat, standing alone at the lectern, the only man in the room without a robe.

Minister Leaderlist started the meeting. "Gentlemen, we're here today to decide what to do about Tileus. We cannot countenance the increasing menace our people experience there. In the last two days, a violent group kidnapped and tortured the daughter of Bishop Oratus, one of our leading citizens. Tileus is unwilling to punish the criminals, and more, is disinclined to correct the continued danger." He raised a hand toward Morat. "I've brought young Morat Intelact here as an eyewitness. He can tell you how horrible it is, and why we have to do something about it."

Over the next quarter hour, Morat described the events of the previous days in Uptown. He told of their ineffective missionary actions during the week, of the hostility of the people in Tileus, of his bewilderment at the chaotic culture there. He mentioned, with some embarrassment, his relationship with Faïlebaso Servdo and how they'd worked together to enliven the mission.

One minister seemed hostile with questions. Short and stocky with thick black hair, he sat behind a placard labelled "Pronas Dominact—Minister Trade." He spoke fast and with emphasis, his hands distracting in meaningless gestures. "Remind me again, young man. Why were you there?"

Morat blinked. Could the minister not know of mission? Or did he have some point he wanted to make? "We were on mission, sir. It is our duty."

"Yes, yes, but what was your purpose?"

Now Morat understood. "Our purpose was to present Elláh to the lost, to give them a chance to find Him."

The minister nodded, as if his point had been made.

Morat continued, telling the story of two days ago, when Faï had rushed across the street and the entire mission group had followed.

Minister Dominact cut in with a demand. "And did none of you think of how you were violating the laws of Tileus? And how that would take away from presenting Elláh to the lost?"

Morat felt faint, not wanting to answer the accusation. "Uh … Minister, we were pretty wrapped up in the moment. I know I wasn't thinking of what was legal or not."

Morat continued telling of the incident and how, when they re-gathered on their side of the street, they discovered Faï missing. "I wanted to go looking for her, but Roloket, our group leader, said we needed to clear out."

To complete the story, Morat told of the search party and the horrible condition in which they found Faï. "She'd been mutilated …" His voice caught. "She was covered in blood. If we hadn't found her, she'd be dead. They'd carved the trifacis into her bare belly, and they'd left her tied to the rocks—to die or not—they didn't care." Bitterness and outrage rang in his voice.

When he finished, silence fell. Anger hardened on the ministers' faces. One had eyes closed and fists clenched on the table. Another glared at Morat as if it had all been his fault.

"Thank you, Morat," said Leaderlist while he took charge of the meeting again. "Any questions, gentlemen?"

The glaring minister lifted a hand off the table. Grey-headed with intense eyes, he leaned forward to speak without awaiting recognition. "Morat, did anyone at any time train you on the laws of Tileus?"

"Yes, sir, they did. I remember Roloket telling us our responsibility to stay on our side of the street. But we didn't."

"Why not?"

Morat winced. "It was a frustrating time, sir. We wanted to do what right, to please Elláh with our witness. But the people there were so horrible. Loutish. Harsh to us. Every day on the street, the protest group got larger and more aggressive. They shouted obscene and demeaning things at us. I'm sure they were trying to entice us into doing something wrong." Morat clenched his jaw for a moment, controlling his resentment. "I guess Faï just … snapped, when she ran across the street. By that time, we were all ready to crack."

The entire group of ministers nodded.

Another one spoke up. "Would you go back?"

Morat shuddered at the idea. He looked directly at the man. "Not unless I had better guidance from Elláh, Minister. I want nothing to do with their culture anymore." He paused for a moment. "Except to correct it. I'm going this afternoon to join the

Khubar f'Elláh. If I can go back to Tileus to avenge what they did to Faï, I'm more than willing."

Minister Leaderlist thanked Morat for his witness, then excused him. When he stepped into the hallway, adrenaline forced a whole-body shudder. He wondered what he had just done, what effect it would have on the country.

23 – Bound for Glory

When any religious institution becomes self-protective, they have lost touch with their god. If a Supreme Being exists and provides for those who believe, why would the individuals think they needed to protect themselves?

—History of the One Church by Ellen Thranadil,
Tileus Press 445 A.T.

Beltaret Leaderlist waited for Morat to leave, then turned to the assembled ministers and their staff. "Gentlemen, you've heard the reality of what we face. The people of Tileus are so disrespectful they incite these incidents, then use them as a reason to torture our innocent students. Then, the country leaders countenance all this by doing nothing to correct it. Prior to this event, we've confined ourselves to a series of diplomatic protests. Now we're faced with the results of our inaction. What do we do about it?"

Beltaret already knew the momentous action they needed: Holy War. They needed to influence the country of Tileus, bring them closer in line with Elláh's ways. War offered itself as the only way to influence an entire country, to convert them from their free-wheeling chaos to something with more order.

He'd been working toward this decision for several months, as incident after incident flooded the news. Beltaret used every opportunity each day to sway the ministers' thinking. In this last week, his hidden transpath showed its worth, allowing him to divine the best arguments to use with each minister.

Now the opportunity presented itself, the unspeakable event to force the decision. The laws of the Church required a unanimous choice by the Service Ministry. One holdout remained: Pronas

Dominact, Minister of Trade. *Ellåh, Lord, help me get this unanimous vote.*

The Minister of Education, Brevet Curio, jumped at the opportunity to voice his anger. "I'm incensed at this whole affair." His deep voice reflected the powerful oratory that had brought him to the Ministry. "We bring up our children, our young men and women, to treat people well. We send them out to help others, and they're treated in Tileus with contempt, disrespect, and now torture. We must institute the strongest possible response to Tileus, to demand their respect."

Curio's rage rang clear through the t-path. Beltaret counted on the man's support.

Without waiting for Curio to finish, Pronas Dominact responded. "Let's not be so hasty, friends. We still have diplomatic avenues available to us, and we need to maintain a good business relationship with Tileus."

Dominact's caution and fear came through the t-path. Beltaret would have to explore that fear, use it to change the man's position. Dominact's reactions to the discussion might reveal what triggered his fear.

Time to get the bold proposal on the table. Beltaret nodded to Bishop Menos Evangel to go next. The Minister of Religious Affairs, the highest post in the Church, would be the seemliest person to propose Holy War. Beltaret had spoken to Evangel last night and pre-arranged for the bishop to introduce the motion. Arranging someone else to propose had worked well many times for Beltaret. This way, he could support the action from apparent neutrality, even though he had been the actual originator.

Bishop Evangel stood up to speak, his immense charisma apparent. "Gentlemen, we stand at a crucial point for the One Church and our country. Two hundred thirty years ago, the Church separated from the repressive rule of Verdant Prime, part of the initiative to create a new country of freedom on this, Beta Continent. Our civil war created the country of Tileus with high hopes for us all. While that initiative succeeded in separating us from Prime, it did not work for the Church. The wild freedom of Tileus became filled with immorality and license. As a result, members of the Church quietly moved over the Gortooth range to separate ourselves. Fifty years later, we had to take our own drastic action: we declared Holy War on Tileus to form this glorious preserve of Rathas, where the Church guides our actions and our society. Our newly-formed Khubar f'Elláh won the day and earned our separation from the Tileus chaos.

"Once again, we find ourselves severely impacted by their corruption. The Church cannot live with the insolence and disrespect given to our people. Our missionaries bring back concepts from Tileus that conflict with our teaching. And now, Tileus countenances this most egregious attack on one of our innocents. We need to change Tileus' perception of us. It is time once again for us to fight for Elláh. We must fight in the mountains, we must fight in the fields, we must carry the fight into their cities. It is time we do again what we did one hundred eighty-four years ago. I move to declare Holy War on Tileus, and to mobilize our Khubar f'Elláh for blessed combat."

When the bishop's firm words ended, the room burst into applause. Nearly all took part—the ministers at the table and most of the staff surrounding it. The rewarding wash of righteous anger pathing into Beltaret's head took over his own thoughts while it lasted. Then he looked at Pronas Dominact and his staff, sitting with stoic faces fixed in resistance. Surprisingly, Dominact's major feeling pathed as fear rather than anger or resistance.

When the bishop seated himself, Gravidim Orgfors, Minister of Interior, seconded the motion, adding, "How can we continue to send missionaries when they're in physical danger? And yet, our faith compels us to reach out. What Tileus has done is unacceptable at a national and at a Church level. It's time to act."

Dominact shook his head. "Ministers, I plead with you to exercise caution. Our country relies on many technologies coming from Tileus. This motion would send thousands of our young men into danger and untold numbers to their death. Surely, it's better, safer, to work through diplomacy."

When Dominact spoke of young men, Beltaret impathed a jump in the man's fear. In a flash of realization, Beltaret knew what held Dominact back. The issue of trade hid the man's real fear.

"Pronas," Beltaret said, choosing to use the familiar given name, "you have two young sons, don't you?"

Dominact startled, sitting up straight. His fear spiked in Beltaret's t-path.

Beltaret continued, "Would you counsel them to take the coward's position of refusing to serve? Would you remove from them their chance to act for Elláh, to seek the glory found in Holy War? Have they yet volunteered for their service in the Khubar f'Elláh?" Beltaret knew the two boys had not, that Dominact had held them back. "This action is something Rathas and the Church need to do, and your sons must be part of it—for their honor and yours." He turned to the entire Ministry. "I call the question, Ministers. Shall Rathas and the Church mobilize for Holy War against Tileus?"

Eight hands went in the air. Pronas Dominact sat, red-faced, looking around the table at the vote. Beltaret impathed his shame coupled with resentment. However, Dominact let loose a heavy breath, lowered his eyes, and raised his hand.

Success. Beltaret had done it.

The Service Ministry then authorized the Rathas ambassador, Ripat Grufhand, to convey a strongly-worded message to the Tileus council of Governors. Following its noontime delivery, the Church news blared the declaration within Rathas that very afternoon.

24 – Exposing Obstacles

Sometimes, Elláh slams a door in our face—yet He always has a good reason.

—*Sayings of Reb Fenet* by Ellen Thranadil, Tileus Press 448 A.T.

Fenet and the Khadam stopped once more in the afternoon, in a small town east of Richearth surrounded by fields. Beneim identified the recently harvested neowheat. A few modest shops supported the area. With implants widespread, the news of their ups and downs preceded them. Crowds had disappeared, though this town offered a small group. Fenet had Pincely stop, then stepped out of the bus.

Three scowling proctors stood behind the group. "None of your black magic here, Fenet Powrfaith. We've heard about you."

"No black magic, sir. Only the miracles Elláh may grant."

One of the waiting townspeople stepped forward. He tried twice to speak before he could get past a speech impediment. "R-reb F-f-fenet, I ..."

Fenet waited for the man's words, a painful process. Lorefim stood beside Fenet.

"R-r-reb, c-can you h-help me? I c-can't t-t—"

"Talk." Waiting hurt too much. "Yes, I can hear your problem. Perhaps Elláh will let one of my novim help you." He waved a hand. "Lorefim, please try."

Lorefim gave a sad smile. "I h-have a similar p-problem, friend. But s-sometimes, Elláh uses me." He laid a hand on the man's arm and prayed.

Nothing happened. Lorefim gave a great sigh.

"Let me try," said Tenpos, who gripped the man's arm and Lorefim's, linking the three in a triad. Tenpos lowered his head. "Please heal this man, Elláh."

Thankfully, the accustomed carmine wave of spiritual force descended on Tenpos and flowed into the man.

At the same time, Lorefim jumped back with a yelp. "That hurt!"

Surprised, the man also jumped back, watching the two novim. "Hurt? What hurt?" Then he stopped speaking in shock before trying again with wonder. "I'm talking. Talking normally." He whirled to face his friends. "I'm talking normally!" he shouted. "I've never done that in my life. Thank you, oh thank you." He flung his arms around Tenpos.

Tenpos gently retrieved himself. "Give the thanks to Elláh, sir."

"That's enough," said a proctor. "You've done your dark deed, tainted this poor man's soul. Now get out."

No one else stepped forward, so Fenet and the novim reboarded the bus. Lorefim's face darkened. He took the t-path out of his pocket, walked to the back of the bus, and dropped it in Scanat's lap. One by one, the others followed suit.

This problem had become a leadership issue. What could Fenet do about it? Though he'd been teaching novim for all these years, he wasn't really a leader. Just a man who followed Elláh. Torn between soothing Scanat and upholding the other novim, he chose to address it with gentleness. "Go ahead and put them away, Scanat. Perhaps Elláh will use them later."

Beltaret strode back to his office with a firm step and a grim smile. He'd gotten what he wanted, what he believed Rathas and the Church needed. Now, however, a new problem confronted him.

His secretary stood in the outer office, her eyebrow quirked. "I heard you coming down the hall, Minister. Did you succeed?"

He gave her a triumphant smile. "Thanks, Pina, we did. Holy War it is, and we'll have the God-given chance to take the Word to those heathens in Tileus."

"Excellent, sir." She put her hands together in quiet applause.

"But now, please get Shoras Guileart for me. I've got a new task for him." He continued past Caropina into his office. Settling himself at his desk, he pondered his new issue.

Beltaret's success in the Ministry meeting just now derived from the t-path technology. Only by knowing Dominact's feelings could he have found the way to trigger the minister into a positive vote. Yet Beltaret had a conflict. He now had the t-path banned in Rathas and he'd kicked out those Tileus entrepreneurs. Yet he had a trial unit, thanks to Guileart, and it proved itself to be essential in Beltaret's backdoor politicking.

His conscience bothered him. Hypocrisy of any form violated Elláh's principles. He'd have to release the ban, if for no other reason than to legalize his own use of the device. Hence the new problem. He did not relish the idea of someone impathing his own emotions. That would remove the advantage he currently held.

His imp pinged. "Yes, Pina?"

"I have Shoras Guileart for you, sir. Shall I transfer him?"

"Please do." A click in his inner ear indicated the shift.

Guileart said, "You wanted me, Minister?"

"Yes, I did. I've got something else for your Johan Wellesley alias to do. I want you to propose a new development to our caged traitor, if the man can do it."

ȣɳ ɳ ȣ

Zofia met Soren Moller in the TechEmpath lobby. A small space for a small company, the reception desk sat empty with a holo display welcoming visitors to sign in. An interior door kept them in the lobby until retrieved by an employee. Attractive logo on the wall, potted plants, and wide windows made the space attractive.

It had been three days since the fire.

"I believe I've identified your traitor, Zofia." Moller's face was grim. "I don't have all the goods on him yet, but I'm pretty certain. As I told you, perps often identify themselves for us. In this case, your man's been giving us frequent information. But it's always red herrings."

"How do you know you've got the right person?"

Moller grunted. "It's what we do. After he raised my suspicions, we started forensic research. Found his DNA on the accelerant container. Got a record of him buying it. His financial records show huge deposits in the last couple of weeks."

"I still find it hard to believe any of our people would be doing this, Soren. Theft? Arson? Who could be so disgruntled? We're paying everyone well."

"Yeah, and he's one of those who've been with you all along. I remember him when we all worked together last year."

She shook her head. A part of her wanted to know, another part just wanted it all over. "I'm not ready to get involved in a bunch of legal proceedings, Soren. We've got too much work to do."

He shrugged. "Not uncommon. Whether we arrest him depends on who else he may have hurt. Our job is to protect the public."

Zofia gazed at the blue plants in one corner, her mind racing. Did she really want to know? They couldn't let this go on. "Okay, who is it?"

❧ ✳ ❧

That evening, Morat sat in the hospital chair beside Faï's bed, holding her hand. She had spent four hours in surgery yesterday, repairing the damage. Bruises marred her face and hands, but she would recover. White spray-on bandages covered her wrists, face, and neck. Groggy but aware, she smiled at him. His heart soared.

"Have you heard the news, Faï? The ministers declared Holy War on Tileus and have pulled back our ambassador."

She nodded. "The nurses talk." Her voice, beautiful to him, stilled slurred with drugs.

"It seems you and I had a part in making it happen. The attack on you became the final straw, and Minister Leaderlist asked me to give an eyewitness account to the Ministry."

"To the Ministry? What was it like?" She squeezed his hand.

"Scary. Those are men of power, used to presentations by important people." He shrugged. "But they listened to me. To me, a simple secondary student."

"Not so simple." She smiled, but fatigue had closed her eyes.

He blushed. "Apparently, they voted to declare Holy War right after I left the meeting. To think I might have had a hand in the Church's history! What a thought."

"What if ..." She dozed off for a few seconds, then awoke again to ask, "Did they have ... any questions?"

"Only a few." He looked down. "They did question me about whether we'd been trained in the Tileus laws. One of them—I think Minister Dominact—treated me with some contempt for having broken the law there."

Her eyes opened. She gave a weak chuckle. "Oh, my fault." Her eyebrows furrowed. "I think ... did I go first?"

"It was all of us, Faï. Those protestors were just horrible."

"Yes." Her face screwed up in pain and she gave a sigh. After another moment of silence, she awoke again to ask, "So, what now?"

He held his head up, straightening his shoulders. "I've already done it. I went today to sign up for the Khubar f'Elláh, even before I heard the news about Holy War. I report tomorrow. Now, they tell me they're going to accelerate basic training. And with my education, they put me in a track to become a fireteam leader."

Faï smiled and squeezed his hand again.

25 - Traitor

On ancient Earth, a wise orator once said, "In times of war, the law falls silent." Intelligence-collecting activities during peacetime may be unsavory, clandestine, even dangerous, yet nations approve and fund them. The same activities during war are often punishable by death.

—*A Practical Guide to Sensitive Negotiation* by Ellen Thranadil, 426 A.T.

This morning, Randy Princeton returned to work. The lab already had equipment and tables back in place, ready for operation. The blackened ceiling tiles showed the only remaining evidence of the fire, and workmen would arrive today to replace them. A slight sharpness in the air lingered. Today, Randy would start rebuilding the new production devices, inferior copies of the ones he'd stolen and given to Wellesley. Zofia wanted the new units by next week, but Randy slow-rolled the build. He snorted to himself. She'd never notice.

He suddenly got an imp summons from Wellesley, a signal to meet the man right away. Randy looked around nervously. The agent had never contacted him at work before. Leaving work wouldn't be good, because suspicions had flown around the building since the fire. Yet Wellesley always came through with money, and Randy needed more to set up his own lab.

Damn the suspicions. This was more important. Randy stood and stretched. "Gotta go out for a bit," he said to Mos.

"Today?" Mos raised his eyebrows. "We're still trying to catch up. We need to push hard." Mos' apprehension displayed through Randy's t-path.

"Yeah, but it's important." Saying no more, Randy slid out of the lab. He tried to avoid interacting with anyone. With his emotions visible, he feared they'd discover his role in the thefts and the fire.

In the foyer, he stopped short. Zofia and that police detective stood together, talking. What was his name? Miller? Milstead? No, Moller. When they saw Randy, they stopped talking. Moller's eyes looked cold and he pathed distrust and anger.

Zofia glanced at Moller before asking Randy, "Where are you going?" Her seething anger overwhelmed Randy's t-path.

Randy gritted his teeth, his mind racing. Did she have solid reason to be angry at him? Still the fire? Or did she have something new?

He focused his emotions on a sense of desperation to hide his guilt. "I just got an emergency call, Zofia. I've gotta go out for a bit. I'll be back in an hour."

She cocked her head at him, lips set thin. "See that you do. I need those prototypes rebuilt."

He ducked his head and made for the door. Moller's eyes bored into him the entire time.

Randy ground his jaw while he walked through the city toward where he would meet Wellesley, a public park not too far away. The situation kept getting worse. Zofia talking with that detective. Danger. He'd have to be more careful, and this trip might be too revealing.

He'd already extracted all the data he needed from the TechEmpath files and squirreled it away in a secure InfoNet location. He'd like to take some more samples with him. They'd save development time after he got his business started. But it wasn't essential. He could get access to the prototypes he'd already given Wellesley.

Wellesley waited on the usual bench. "Hey, Randy. You doing okay today?" His feelings pathed as eagerness; he must have something good. That would be a nice contrast to the conflict back there in the lobby.

Randy plopped down beside him and huffed out a breath. "Not good. Lots of distrust. Everyone's being treated with doubt, even those of us who've been around the whole time."

"Well, I've got some good news for you. The Minister needs something else, and he's willing to fund you bigtime. He's offered to set up a new lab for you in Praise, over in Rathas."

Randy smiled and sat up straight. "What's he want?"

Wellesley glanced around the park before answering. "Your knowledge and capability, my friend. Can you build a jammer?"

⁂

Randy floated over the sidewalk on his way back. The agent had offered exactly the kind of situation Randy needed. A funded facility over in Praise. Access to capable technicians. Streamlining the business setup under the laws of Rathas. A sole source decree to supply t-paths within Rathas. And the agent wanted something simple. Jam a t-path? Ha, the difficulty came in *making* one work. He would have a jammer in a few days.

Hell, he could even put up with the religious nuts to get the business going. He'd create the jammer, then focus on building and improving t-paths. He'd have a lock on Rathas. Then he'd expand to compete with TechEmpath internationally and to the other planets. What a great opportunity to show up Jake and Zofia, to get back his own pride by winning out over them.

Just before reaching the TechEmpath building, he got a text from Zofia. She wanted to see him in her office as soon as he returned. This didn't sound good. She'd been talking with the detective when Randy left the building. He stopped to compose himself, get his emotions under control, then entered.

Both Jake and Zofia stood in her large office waiting for him. This wasn't going to be a quiet meeting at her conference table, nor an employer-employee discussion across her desk. Both had arms crossed, scowls on their faces, anger overriding any other pathed emotions.

Zofia started in with a hissing rage. "What the hell, Randy? What were you thinking? When Soren told me this morning you were the one, I didn't believe him. Then you waltzed past us to go meet someone? Didn't you know we'd feel your guilt?"

Jake echoed. "I can't believe you'd betray us this way. You've been here since the beginning. Soren says your contact is a known spy."

Randy considered the offer he'd just gotten from Wellesley, and his simmering anger exploded. "The man's not a spy, Jake. He's a businessman here in Thad City. With contacts in other countries. At high levels. And he's made me a great offer, something you two never have seen fit to do."

Jake shook his head, jaw firm, emotions implacable. "The man's a spy for Rathas."

Randy whirled on him. "I don't care what Soren thinks. Wellesley's got money behind him. Lots of money." He turned back to Zofia, enraged. "Last year, you two were nothing but refugees with some technical plans for a device that didn't work. Hell, Zofia, you'd just been tortured and couldn't even function without Jake's assistance. Without our help, you'd never have gotten anything at all. Damn it, the t-path only works because of me. Jake didn't do it, and neither did you."

"No, Randy," she barked. "It was a team effort if I've ever seen one. Everybody did their part. Until you started stealing."

"Yeah, right. Team effort. 'Everybody did their part.' But some of us did more important parts than others. I did the testing to extend Yitzak Goren's work, under the crush of time. Me, not Jake. He was too busy 'coordinating' and tending to your fragile condition."

Randy jabbed a finger at Jake. "You're not the only particle physicist here. Hell, I designed the cavity repellotron, the heart of our signal driver. You two always talk about 'Mos's signal driver,' never me, but I was the one who made it. Me! Then, I did the miniaturization for the personal t-path. I've done all that and more, and you only talk about Mos and 'team.' Never give me credit. Damn it, I want the credit."

"Credit?" Zofia shouted. "You're getting a generous salary for your work. What better credit is there?"

He snorted. "Wages. Just wages. No piece of the action, no piece of the business." Randy waved his free hand around at the building, then shook his finger toward Zofia. "You and Jake are keeping it all for yourselves." He shook a finger at the two of them. "It's time for a reckoning. And now I'm going to get mine elsewhere."

Zofia had fire in her eyes. "What, by stealing from us? By setting a fire? By meeting with spies?"

Jake's anger filled his voice. "And what's this about Rathas? Dammit, their minister kicked us out of the country."

"Shows how badly you mishandled it, Jake. That same minister is talking to *me* now, and wants to fund me. So there. Screw you and the refugee train you rode in on."

Zofia threw her hands up. "I've had enough of this trash, Jake. I want him out of here, and out of our hair. Call Soren to pick him up."

Jake nodded.

She turned back to Randy, "You're fired. Get out. You can wait for Soren outside."

"You can't fire me. I quit."

"And I want you to return the prototypes you stole," she gritted.

Randy shook his head. "Sorry. No can do. They're already gone."

Jake balled a fist by his side.

Heart pounding, Randy discovered his own fists ready, too. "You wanna go physical, Jake, bring it on."

Zofia shook her head and put her hands between the two men. "Knock it off, guys. Randy, you just leave. Get out. Soren Moller will find you, and you'll suffer for what you've done."

Fists clenched, teeth gritted, Randy pivoted to the door and left. He would have slammed the door on the way out, but its pneumatic closer softened the action.

In the street, Randy imped Wellesley while he stomped back toward the park. "Are you still around? Can we meet again?"

"I'm not too far away. What's going on?"

"Bad stuff. I've been fired. The police know I've met with you. They have you identified as a Rathas spy."

Wellesley said nothing.

"You still there?"

The agent said, "Yeah, I'm here. So, what are you going to do?"

"They're coming to arrest me, for theft and arson. Maybe you, too, and they'd add on espionage."

"Nah, they've got nothing on me or they would have arrested me before now. Intelligence gathering in peacetime is okay; everyone does it."

"Whatever. We need to move right away. How quickly can we set up a lab in Praise?"

"How soon can you be ready to travel?"

Randy started to cool off, walking fast, his mind racing ahead. He already had everything he'd squirreled away. He had some small assemblies hidden in his apartment. He'd have to get those out right away in case that detective got a search warrant. "Why don't we meet at my apartment in a half hour. Can you get us across the border to Praise?"

≈ ✳ ≈

Thirty minutes passed faster than any he'd known. A public autocar took him first to a packing store for boxes, then home. For once, the streets were mostly clear, with no protest groups. He hurried himself to gather the personal things he wanted, clothes and mementos, as well as the tech assemblies. Everything fit into four medium boxes, which he then staged down the lift tube into the lobby of his building, two at a time.

While packing, Randy fought inside himself. The year of mistreatment by TechEmpath angered him to the point of breaking a precious figurine from his mother. When it cracked in his hand, his rage exploded and he threw it to shatter against the wall. However, the next moment, the opportunity in front of him made him soar. He'd create his own business, hire his own employees, and compete against Jake and Zofia. He'd create this jammer for the Rathas minister, and that would be only the beginning.

On his second trip to the lobby, Randy put the last two boxes by the first. A minute or two later, Wellesley arrived at the curb in a sleek, dark blue autocar.

The agent hastened up the stoop to the front door. "Ready to go, Randy?"

"Just these four boxes." The two men picked up the boxes and loaded them into the trunk.

While getting into the car, a nondescript black sedan pulled up behind them. Randy glanced at it and saw Soren Moller and his huge partner Manny Hong inside.

Randy jumped into the car and slammed the door. "Quick, Wellesley. Go now." He turned in his seat to watch Moller and Hong get out of their car. Moller shouted something at them.

"Damn," breathed Wellesley. "Him again." He punched the start button on the autocar and it lifted from the pavement.

"You know him?" asked Randy.

"Yeah. Moller's been a nuisance to me. I'm a respectable businessman here, but he keeps harassing me because I come from Rathas."

The car lifted higher than the buildings around them. Randy's stomach swooped with the acceleration. "Whoa. This is quite a car."

Wellesley shrugged and turned his chair to Randy while the car continued on its way. "It's an international autocar. It'll take us all the way over the mountains to Praise."

Randy's imp rang. "Uh-oh. I've got an incoming call from Moller. What should I do?"

"Answer it. See what he wants."

Randy accepted the call, and also routed it to Wellesley.

Moller said, "Where're you going with Guileart, Randy? You realize you're in deep trouble here, don't you?"

"That's why I'm leaving," Randy said.

"We came here with a search warrant. Running away just makes you look guiltier."

"It doesn't matter, Soren. I'm out of here, moving my operations to Rathas. I'll be out of your hair." *And out of your jurisdiction, too.* "But who the hell is Guileart? And what kind of name is that?"

"Wellesley, whatever," said the detective, "you don't know? Shoras Guileart's his real name, over in Rathas. The religious freaks use last names to celebrate their character traits. That worm you're with? His best traits are being artful and getting his way through guile."

"Is that true, Wellesley?" Stunned by the detective's accusation, Randy shot the question to the agent. From the look on Wellesley's face—or was it Guileart?—the agent didn't appreciate it, either.

"Yeah, it's true, Randy. I go by a different name here in Tileus so I can do business without everyone knowing I come from Rathas. But my business is straightforward and successful, and it's completely legal here in Tileus." Wellesley pathed full confidence.

The car continued to fly west. Randy glanced outside to see the outskirts of Thad City passing below.

Moller said, "Aside from being a front for your occasional forays into intelligence work, right?"

Wellesley held his ground. "I'm a respected businessman, Moller. If you had anything more on me, you'd have arrested me by now. So, stop us or not. It's your choice. But we're heading for the border."

Randy's fears eased when he sensed Wellesley's confidence. Yet he'd learned new caution in this man's hidden aspects. *I'll have to watch him more closely.*

"You two go ahead," said Moller. "We'll fulfill our search warrant and then decide whether to call in someone to stop you. We've got plenty of time before you reach Rathas." The connection clicked off.

"That was close," Randy said. "They might have arrested me if I'd still been there. That's what Zofia said. Theft, arson, and espionage."

Wellesley shrugged. "If he's got the right evidence, he could make the arson stick. But not the espionage, unless he's also got the goods on me. And he doesn't."

Randy turned in his seat to look ahead. Farmland and blue forests led the way to the Gortooth Mountains, still out of view.

At that moment, his imp rang an urgent news alarm followed by a bulletin.

War! The Rathas ambassador has just delivered a declaration of war to the council of Governors. Rathas claims justification for a Holy War based on treatment of its innocent people visiting Tileus.

Randy looked at Wellesley, whose face reflected Randy's own shock.

"War?" said Randy. "So, now I'm working for the enemy? When does espionage become treason?"

26 – Heresy Angels

While the technology led to a far greater, more complete communication for humanity, the road sometimes held danger. Some people resisted it, resenting the forced openness. Others used it to excess, as a constant invasion of privacy.

—*The Making of a New Humanity* by Ellen Thranadil, Tileus Press 448 A.T.

What do you mean, you're not ready?" Beltaret Leaderlist shouted toward the holo display above his office desk, his implant picking up his voice as audio for the holoconference.

In the holo, General Comfors displayed resentment at Beltaret's attitude. "Of course, we're not ready, sir. The Ministry only declared war yesterday."

"As head of the entire Khubar f'Elláh, it's your job to have those forces ready whenever we need them."

"It would help a great deal, Minister, if you'd given us some advance warning. We've anticipated some sort of action, and we've had forces exercising at an increased rate, but—"

"But nothing, General. Build up your forces. Make your plans. Get ready. We need to act on Tileus *now*, not at some vague future time." Beltaret terminated the call. His blood pressure had probably peaked. He found it hard to believe their military forces just ... weren't ready."

The holo lit up with an incoming call. Captain Forsfear. Beltaret put a hand to his forehead. Guiding the security of this country within the grace of Elláh put him in contact with the most unsavory, incompetent people.

"Yes, Captain. What now?" he spit out when he activated the call.

"I wanted to let you know I've gained enough information to take action on this errant minister, sir."

"What sort of action? Are you going to remove that irritation from our heart?"

"I've motivated the reluctant proctors in their path, Minister. They're being watched at every stop, looking for heresy. And I've mobilized my Heresy Angels in Center. If we get the evidence, we'll stop them there."

The man so easily went overboard. Beltaret needed a balance on Forsfear. And he had just the man to do it. "Proctor Major Stolwatch has a large force in Center. Contact him, Captain, and allow him to provide a second set of eyes on what you're doing. He can help you if you need it." And Stolwatch will slow Forsfear down if necessary.

Scanat woke repeatedly in the night after the Khadam had rejected his t-paths. The voices in his head yammered. *Useless, Scanat, you're useless. Inadequate. You haven't done any miracles. No one likes you. You're older than everyone.* Over and over, he shoved the thoughts aside only to have them return. He'd sweated so much, despite the cold night, his sleeping bag smelled clammy.

He got up well before dawn, picked up his backpack, and stalked into the trees behind their campsite. The woods, hemmed in by farmlands, didn't allow him to get very far away. At the far edge of the copse, he sat down against a tree with a dim view across the dark fields. The smaller moon, Silver, put a soft glow on the crops. He had no idea what kind of plants; the murky light made it hard to see, and Scanat knew very little about farming anyway. He'd grown up in town, tending his family's electronics stores. Nonetheless, the plants—vercorn, maybe—swayed in furrowed rows in a cold breeze.

He ground his teeth at the rejection of last night. The t-paths nestled inside his pack, no longer in use. *Whatever had I been thinking? That I heard a message from Elláh to get the t-paths? No way.* He'd screwed things up for everyone. Now the proctors were angry at them, people had stopped following them, and the Khadam had lost faith in themselves. All because of his arrogance, thinking he could improve on Elláh's miracles with technology.

He'd turned off his t-path last night. He thumbed it back on and turned the volume up all the way. Then he turned it off and back on again, a nervous movement. The action reminded him of the incident five days ago on the road outside Richearth, when he'd used empathy to select the pregnant girl and found his t-path had been off. Or had it been on? He couldn't be certain. Could that have been a miracle? Or just a faulty switch?

In the pre-dawn gloaming, the quiet emptiness of this place, with the t-path at maximum, he sensed nothing at all. Maybe that's the way it should be. Perhaps Elláh never intended humankind to listen in to each other's feelings.

Did he have some flaw in his character keeping him away from Elláh? Perhaps his intellect did indeed get in the way, as Reb Fenet kept saying. But shouldn't he be able to apply his intelligence to ministry, too? Back there on the road, he hadn't been thinking at all, just feeling the empathy—and it worked, switch on or off. Again, miracle or not? Did it happen because he'd set aside his intellect? Or did he remember wrong?

He looked up at the bright stars, twinkling in the still-dark sky. The sight calmed him, and he took several breaths.

Maybe he'd misinterpreted Elláh's life goal for him. Perhaps he didn't have the character to be a minister. He shouldn't have turned down the offer for tertiary school and particle physics. Now, four years later, it was too late to go back.

Perhaps another path would open. After all, he still had many years in front of him. But he couldn't see it tonight.

❧ ✳ ☙

Fenet's hips had bothered him again in the night, though far less than before his prayers. He awoke while the Khadam still slumbered. Dawn stained the sky with brilliant peach at the horizon blended upward into clear indigo skies. Cold air in his nose hinted at the winter to come. He laid in the sleeping bag for a few minutes, thanking Elláh for the cycle of the year and for His constant guidance.

The sadness of yesterday evening washed into him. Failed miracles. Despondent novim. Resentments. This schism around Scanat. And then, the news from the InfoNet about Holy War.

Unbelievable. The Service Ministry must have gone insane. While the novim stirred, Fenet focused on his own breathing to calm his mind.

KEEP GOING, FENET. TAKE THE BUS. YOUR PURPOSE WILL BECOME CLEAR.

Peace fell over him. Meditating on his breathing often brought such answers from Elláh, in a voice always kind, loving, gentle, comforting. Doubts and fears fell away with Elláh's reassurance. All events would be as He willed. Fenet got up with a residual ache in his hips. Enough to make him reach for the staff, but he looked forward to today's events, whatever they might be.

During fajr prayer and breakfast, he noticed a nov missing. "Anyone know where Scanat is?"

Beneim tilted his head toward the woods. "He went off by himself earlier. His stuff's still here."

The novim ate without their usual banter. Fenet hoped today would revitalize them. Toward that end, he shared the words he'd heard from Elláh. The message did little to cheer them.

Fenet finished his breakfast, recalling his easygoing young days, before Elláh had gifted him with miracles. He'd been very different from these novim. Carousing, drinking, chasing women. In some ways, his life under Elláh had been as carefree as those early days. He rarely made his own decisions. On this pilgrimage, however, the stress of leadership had grown, disturbing his soul as much as his hips pained his body.

Yet the leadership task Elláh had given him still called. Fenet told everyone to board the bus. While they embarked, Scanat appeared out of the woods, picked up his gear, and moved to sit in the back of the bus.

The Coast Road wound through rich farmland that rose to rolling hills. Ahead, a plateau with trees rather than fields separated them from the productive valley around the capital. They'd come halfway on the journey. Pincely and the bus provided a blessing from Elláh not to have to walk all this distance. Ahead of them, the city of Lowly Rise would mark the junction with the Center Road toward Praise.

A changed character in the rising land became evident. Instead of a single city serving large areas, the rolling hills fostered many hamlets both on and off the road. Poverty showed in poorly-maintained homes and frayed clothing. Pungent smoke rose where people burned animal dung and their own trash.

Entering the first such town, Fenet didn't know what would happen. To find themselves bereft of miracles, to have Elláh turn his face away and reject their work, to feel His disfavor, all made his stomach curl despite Elláh's comforting words at dawn. This whole situation echoed what had happened to himself during the last year, how his abilities had dwindled when he relied on technology. Would the Khadam follow his path of error? Or would they regain here their ability to help people?

Before the novim exited the bus, Fenet gathered them together for prayer. "Dear Elláh, Guide and Father, be with us today. We've set aside the technology. Please allow us to help anyone who requests. Let us all work in humility to use Your power for others."

The novim echoed, "Selah." Scanat stayed silent and glowering at the back of the group.

A handful of people, poor farmers, waited for them in simple attire. The town smelled of stirred dirt and chopped hay. Farmyard noises made a background to the sound of their footsteps. A single proctor watched from one side. When they moved forward, he put a hand to the side of his head and spoke quietly, obviously reporting by imp to someone.

A man stepped forward. "Are you Reb Fenet? We gots some folks badly hurt. Kin you help us?" He paused, looking uncertain. "We hearda you and your people, but got some mixed stories from Richearth."

Fenet looked at the few individuals. One young boy with his arm in white bandages, a woman collapsed to sit in the dirt, a man leaning on a staff. His heart went out to them. "Whether we can help is up to Elláh. Let us try and see."

Penilos stepped up to the boy. "What happened to you?"

The boy whispered, "Got too close to the thresher. Lucky I still gots my arm."

Penilos nodded. "Machines are like that. Unforgiving." He closed his eyes and put his hands on the boy's shoulder. After a heart-rending pause, Elláh's red warmth came over Penilos and washed down into the boy.

Relief filled Fenet, and he saw relaxation wave over the novim when the miracle happened. The boy jerked upright, eyes wide. He shouted out and tore off the bandages to show an unblemished arm. Then he jumped to his feet and ran around showing his arm to everyone.

The morning continued in this way, town after town. Tiny villages with few people waiting. Through success, the Khadam regained their confidence in what Elláh would do through them.

Scanat's face grew darker and darker. And a proctor, face scowling, watched them in every town.

Lowly Rise, a larger place, held a small crowd, though less than half the size of Richearth. As in the smaller villages, Fenet had them stop and exit the bus to heal. The five active novim stepped forward.

Scanat confronted him. "What should I do, Reb?" His belligerent attitude slapped Fenet in the face.

"Whatever you can," Fenet said. "Perhaps Elláh will choose you this time."

"Right," he answered, his voice tainted with bitterness.

Scanat did help in Lowly Rise, using his t-path, though he hardly spoke to the rest. He moved into the crowd to select certain individuals for specific novim. The young man never smiled during this time, though, and Fenet caught him scowling when no one watched.

"That one's still in trouble, Reb," Pincely murmured.

Fenet nodded. "I don't know what he'll do, or what Elláh has planned for him. But you're right. He's in trouble."

In this larger town, four proctors stood by glaring at the Khadam. One of them had the same dark military-style uniform as the one in Richearth, though he was a different individual. They talked among themselves, often stopping to make reports through their imps.

Pinceley said, "That dark uniform. Them's Heresy Angels, Reb. Bad news."

Fenet watched the proctors with his stomach uneasy, remembering those who had taken Eregim away in Netweaver. Their presence increased with each town. What might they be planning?

Following Lowly Rise more villages dotted the Center Road while it climbed onto higher ground. Elevation and steep terrain forced the farms into river bottoms. Trees covered the hillsides. A riot of bold fall colors and earthy scents made the forest feel alive.

Their ministry continued in each community. While they ascended, however, the number of proctors increased—even in the small villages. The problem came to a head in one unnamed place;

when Fenet stepped off the bus, two proctors pushed in front of the supplicants.

"No, no," they shouted. "Get back on your bus. We're not having any of your supernatural stuff in our town."

Fenet pointed at the five people standing behind the proctors. "But these people are waiting for us. Perhaps we can help them."

One of the five raised a hand and a malformed arm. "I'd like to try." His voice shook.

A proctor spun to confront him. "Shut yourself, Graffis. You've lived with your arm all your life. Do you want to lose your soul by accepting what these people have to give?"

The man cowered.

The other proctor shooed Fenet back to the bus. "Go on. Get out of here. None of your evil stuff here."

He returned to the bus, where Tenpos summed it up. "We can't fight ignorance, Reb Fenet. Only Elláh can do that."

In the next town, they were again able to help people.

❧ ✳ ☙

The next morning dawned clear and cold, Fenet's breath steaming while they prepared for the day. They'd slept on the ground under the trees, the hoverbus parked beside the campsite. Fenet tried to pull Scanat aside for a short talk after prayers, hoping he could encourage him, but Scanat avoided him. Fenet let him go, thinking they'd have time later. He was proved wrong.

The others bantered with each other during breakfast, their spirits much improved with the successes of yesterday.

On the upper Rise Plateau, successful farms covered the gentle rolling land again, now intermixed with industry buildings. Who knew what each one manufactured? Probably only the people who worked there. Fenet chuckled at his own ignorance.

He'd heard of Center, the second largest city in the country after Praise. The roadbed beneath the hoverbus changed from graded dirt to asphalt. Storm gutters and curbs marked the approach of civilization.

Time to exercise some leadership again. "Pincely, have you been to Center before?"

The driver nodded. "Y'all are in for something different here, Reb. I've driven this bus to most places in Rathas, but Center's got the most industry of 'em all. Lots of factories. I'm glad we've got clear air today, 'cause sometimes the air's not so good here."

"Do you know the best place for us stop and help people?"

Pincely screwed up his lips as if in thought. "There's several places. A coupla large squares. A central park."

Fenet looked ahead at the gathering city while the novim talked. Tall buildings in the central district towered above the homes and businesses in front of them, which themselves crowded out the green and russet spaces of country. A burned taint in the air evidenced the detritus of industry. Pincely guided the hoverbus through increasing traffic of autocars into an area dominated by five- and six-story buildings. Ahead of them, Fenet saw an opening several blocks away. Ordinary people on ordinary business crowded the street and the open space. In a city this size, they dressed in many styles and colors, looking like a festival to Fenet's country eyes.

"That's Holy Square coming up," Pincely said.

The traffic in front slowed. Cars entering the square stopped, one by one, before proceeding.

"What's going on?" Fenet asked.

Pincely shrugged. "Looks like proctors, doing some sorta search. They're usin' the proctor override, Reb. They command each automated car to stop, and they release it again on their say-so."

Three cars remained in front of them. One proctor stood tall and pointed at the hoverbus. Another hurried to a corner of the building on the right.

A short warning tone sounded from the dashboard and a red light appeared.

Pincely pointed at the light. "They've taken control of the bus."

The two cars in front moved on through the square. The hoverbus moved forward on its own into the square, turned right and stopped.

Twenty armed proctors stood at attention along the sidewalk, a sober splash of dispiriting grey-and-red in the colorful surroundings. In front of them, three others were in command. They wore the threatening uniforms of Heresy Angels: trousers and gold-buttoned jackets. With name badges, shiny visors, needle guns and stuncheons hanging from the belts, they looked military. Their red collars identified them as proctors, but far more intimidating than any Fenet had ever seen.

Pincely's eyes went wide. "Holy Elláh. Them Heresy Angels again. We don't wanna mess with them. I've heard they'd just as soon shoot as look at you."

The one in front, gold pips on his shoulder, stood short, slim, and powerful, the same man they'd seen in Richearth. He carried himself with contemptuous pride, his jaw set, his dark eyes cold. He tapped an impatient hand on his needle gun.

The other two held a large figure in grey robes slumped between them while they held him up. *Lord Elláh, what's happened to that fellow?* His head hung low on his chest. One of the Angels jerked up his head by the hair so Fenet could see him. The man's eyes were swollen shut by livid bruises, dark against the ashen pallor of his forehead. Blood stained his robes.

Fenet gasped. His friend Eregim, last seen four days ago and two hundred kilometers away in Netweaver, hung battered and beaten.

27 - Arrest

The concept of heresy is the last refuge of a central Church. Anything other than orthodoxy can be defined as heresy and therefore condemned.

—History of the One Church by Ellen Thranadil,
Tileus Press 445 A.T.

The day after his testimony to the Service Ministry, Morat Intelact reported to the Khubar f'Elláh. News announcements about the war declaration filled everyone's imps, so the induction center had more volunteers than they knew how to process. He had some pride in the fact his testimony may have swayed the decision.

Morat had arrived early, fifth in a line now stretching four city blocks. At dawn, he watched some of those in line lay down mats for prayer. Morat shrugged. Sometimes he prayed, sometimes he didn't.

In the induction center, a sergeant who'd taken his name looked him up and down. "What can you do, Morat Intelact?"

"I can fight, sir. Those Tileus people kidnapped my girlfriend. I can't let them get away with it."

"Your girlfriend? It was your girlfriend?" The sergeant turned to another who handled the next queue. "Hey, Teras. This guy knows the girl."

Teras shouted back, "Sign him up. He oughta be ready to fight."

"Not just that, Sergeant," Morat said. "I need to change my powername, also. They kidnapped her and tortured her. I want vengeance, not intelligence."

"Hoo-rah," said the sergeant. "You're in the right place, boy. What's the new name?"

"Sign me up as Morat Vengeact."

By late afternoon, Morat marched with a platoon of new recruits, feeling like his mind had been replaced with someone else. He had new uniforms, new gear, and a new cocktail of chemical additives already building him up. The Khubar f'Elláh base outside Praise teemed with soldiers, most of them new recruits like him. Sergeants yelled, recruits yelled back, they did everything in lock-step unison, and he hardly remembered his life of one day before.

Still on the bus, looking out at his shattered friend, Fenet tried to contact him with his imp. Something blocked his entire connection to the InfoNet. The proctors had that kind of control. When the hoverbus settled to the ground and opened its door, the Heresy Angel captain crashed his stuncheon several times on the door frame, "Out of the bus. Now!"

The violent noise made Fenet jump up from his seat in the front row. He leaned forward to read the man's name badge.

"Why, Captain Forsfear? What've we done?" He kept an eye on the man's weapon. Fenet understood the stuncheon packed quite an electric jolt in addition to its brute force.

The captain screamed at Fenet, "Are you questioning my authority? Get out. All of you. Line up facing the bus." He reached in to grab Fenet's sleeve, pulling him down the steps. Fenet barely had time to grab his staff and maintain balance.

"Go, go, go," the captain urged, slamming his stuncheon against the bus.

The Khadam followed. Durnadat glared at the Angels and their high-handed treatment; most of them showed shock and fear. Fenet stood facing this officer. The novim flowed past him to line up by the bus.

Behind the captain, still supported by the other two Angels, Eregim moaned. Fenet started toward him. "What've you done to my friend?"

Forsfear smashed Fenet's shoulder with his club. "Back in place. Turn around, all of you. Can't you obey simple commands?" He looked inside the bus at Pincely in the driver's seat. "And you. What are you doing still in there? I said *out.*" Forsfear took one step into the bus and jammed the weapon into Pincely's side.

Pincely jumped up and screamed. He must have gotten the electric jolt. "Damn! That hurt."

"You'll get a lot more if you don't get off the bus. Move!"

While Pincely scurried out to join the group, Forsfear whacked him. Pincely stood beside Fenet facing the bus while rubbing his side.

"Tanglecuffs," the captain yelled.

Eight robed proctors moved forward, one for each member of the group. They yanked everyone's arms behind their backs and fastened tanglecuffs on their wrists.

"Hey," shouted Durnadat. "Not so rough."

Scanat growled when the proctor grabbed his hands.

Fenet's staff clattered to the ground.

"I need my walking stick, Captain. I can't stand long without it." Fenet's heart pounded, but he kept his voice under controlled calm.

The officer ignored his request. "All of you, I'm in charge here. As Reb Fenet has so *adroitly* figured out, I am Captain Frinat Forsfear, and you will do exactly what I say. Turn around and face me."

They did so.

Forsfear looked at Pincely. "You. You're not wearing robes. Who are you?"

"Just a driver, Cap'n. I own the bus."

"Are you one of these so-called *miracle* workers?" The captain gestured at the rest of them.

Pincely glanced at Fenet. "I can't work no miracles, sir, but I been driving these people since Netweaver." With a gleam in his eyes, he added, "Yeah, they do miracles."

Forsfear glared at him, then turned to one of the robed proctors. "Take him away alone. We'll interrogate him first."

Pincely gasped, "Interrogate? I ain't done nothin'!" His voice shook.

The proctor gripped Pincely's arm to lead him away. Pincely resisted, tensing, and the proctor heaved him forward into a stumble.

Forsfear turned to Fenet. "So, you are the famous *Reb* Fenet Powrfaith." He turned the honorific into a sneer.

"Yes, I am. What have we done to deserve this treatment?"

"We've been following your exploits for years, Powrfaith, and particularly your little jaunt here from Glorify. Some *chats* with your friend Eregim Steadknow have been quite revealing as to your supernatural connections. We have evidence we can no longer ignore. You and your entire entourage are under arrest for heresy."

"Heresy?" Fenet exclaimed. "How can it be heresy to heal people of their infirmities? To ease their burdens?"

The captain leaned forward, spitting his words into Fenet's face. "The question is not whether you're causing supernatural events. That's pretty obvious. The heresy resides in what power you're drawing on to make them happen."

"The only power we use is that of Elláh."

The captain gave him a look of contempt. "That will be for us to determine, not you."

Pincely's hoverbus lifted itself off the curb. The bus repellor beam caught Fenet's staff and flung it outward. The staff slammed across the back of his legs. He cried out at the pain and nearly fell. Then the staff whirled across the sidewalk into a brick wall, just missing two proctors. It rebounded back to Forsfear's feet. The bus drove off with everyone's packs and belongings.

The captain picked up the staff and looked at Fenet. "So, you need this staff to stand? Let's find out what kind of power you have." He slammed the staff down on his knee. With a sickening crunch, the wood bent. Grabbing it by one end, Forsfear slammed the other end onto the pavement. The staff broke.

Fenet's stomach sank at the loss.

"If you're so good, heal that," Forsfear shouted at Fenet. He flung the part he still held onto the ground with the other half.

No staff. Fenet's shoulder ached from the stuncheon blow. The pain in his hips flared. With hands cuffed behind him, he couldn't even rub the sore spots. His heart raced like it would explode. Fear. Every message in *The Holiest* said "Do not fear," but at this moment Fenet could not shove the fear aside.

A black hover truck with barred windows pulled up behind them.

"Get in," commanded the captain, slapping Fenet again with his club. He turned to his two black-garbed mates. "Put Steadknow in there, too. And don't let them talk."

One by one, they boarded the truck at its rear-facing door. Fenet entered last, struggling with the steps. A Heresy Angel dragged him upward into the truck. Longitudinal bench seats received them. Two Angels were already on board, slapping their stuncheons into their hands. The two holding Eregim brought him in behind Fenet and dumped him on a bench.

Forsfear appeared at the door. "You'd better take this with you, Powrfaith. You'll need it to stand." He threw the two halves of Fenet's staff onto the floor.

With two Angels at the front and two at the rear, the metal door clanged shut on them.

Inside the black metal box, Fenet sat next to Eregim. His heart ached.

"Eregim, I'm sorry." He put an arm around his friend's shoulders to hold him steady while the hover truck lifted and moved.

"No talking!"

The Angel jabbed Fenet with his stuncheon. A thunderbolt of electricity jolted Fenet's body, straightening him in a rictus of quick pain. When it passed, he slumped beside Eregim, breathing hard.

Fenet couldn't talk to his friend, but he could support him. He prayed inside for Elláh's guidance and help, but heard nothing. The novim watched, also silent, then hung their heads. Their implants were disabled from any contact either with each other or with the InfoNet.

Fenet took to silent prayer. *Lord, I thought we were past the worst of the forging? What now? What do you wish of us?*

The trip took a mere twenty minutes. They arrived at a blockhouse of a building in the city, devoid of decorations other than the steel bars on many windows. Shouting and demanding, the Heresy Angels drove them into the building with prods and pushes like frightened ruminods. The Khadam scurried through an official-looking lobby into a cellblock. The Angels rapped Fenet several times with stuncheons when he couldn't move quickly enough. Removing the cuffs, they placed the group two-by-two into four cells. Plasteel walls, solid doors with small apertures, fixed furniture, and high barred windows defined each three-meter cell. Fenet shared one with Eregim.

With the Angels gone, Fenet and Eregim sat on the two fixed cots. Eregim's weight made the cot sag with a creak when he moved.

"What happened to you, Eregim?" Fenet spoke with caution, fearing someone would burst in and beat them.

"It was okay at first." His voice trembled in a broken whisper, a far cry from his usual ringing oratory. "The proctors broke up that damned group protesting against us. They dispersed the crowds in Netweaver." He paused, catching his breath. "Then it was questions. The proctors wanted to know about us. Simple things. Where we came from, what we'd done." He had to stop, panting for breath.

The cell had a metal sink and toilet. Eregim's robe had a rip at the hem. Fenet tore off a piece and wet it to cleanse the blood from Eregim's face and ease his wounds. "Don't talk too much, my friend."

"No, I need to talk about it. The proctors were curious, skeptical. Firm but reasonable."

Fenet gave him a sopping piece to suck, to wet his mouth.

"They held me overnight, waiting for these Heresy Angels." He hung his head and shook it from side to side. "The Angels are terrible, Fenet. Their questions are full of hate and suspicion."

Fenet put a hand on his shoulder.

"I told them all I knew, but ..." He gestured at his face. "They did this to me." He took a deep breath and looked up at Fenet. "What's happened with the Khadam?"

"Amazing and difficult things. Using Scanat's t-paths stopped the miracles."

"What?"

Fenet nodded. "Yes. Stopped in mid-healing. We got chased out of Richearth by the proctors. The other novim threw their t-paths back in Scanat's lap one night, and the miracles started again the next day."

Fenet wasn't sure Eregim would respond; he looked so tired and worn, his head hanging.

But he spoke anyway. "Gotta be hard on Scanat."

"That, too. The young man's been distant and difficult ever since. He won't talk to me. His actions seem filled with resentment."

"Has Elláh forsaken us, Fenet?"

Fenet shook his head. "We're still doing miracles. I choose to believe this is all part of His plan."

They sat for several hours while daylight from the tiny window moved across the floor.

❧ ❋ ☙

Scanat shared a cell with Penilos, the oldest and the youngest of the novim together. He'd rather have been placed with Tenpos, but the Angels gave him no choice. With Tenpos, he'd be able to talk about his issues, his fears about himself and what Elláh wanted from him. With the boy so naïve, talking with Penilos would be useless. It galled Scanat that this *boy* did things Scanat couldn't.

"What are they going to do to us?" Penilos' voice quavered. "They're gonna kill us."

"Shut up." Scanat waved off the question. "Just shut up."

Penilos said no more. Minutes later, he started crying quietly.

Scanat sat on one of the two cots, his head in his hands. Arrested. Could things get any worse? In the quiet of the cell, his head burbled on his own problems. No miracles. No schooling. And now no t-paths, either, except for the one on his belt. They'd left everything on the bus, and who knew where it had gone? Everything had gone wrong. All his hopes had died, and all his fears rose ascendant.

He'd joined Fenet thinking he could be somebody important, do Elláh's work, be respected by others. It looked like an easier path than studying particle physics. He ground his teeth while he thought about it. Fenet had taught him *nothing*. And now, damn it, they were all arrested and in the hands of the Heresy Angels. He no longer wanted to be part of this.

An hour later, the door rattled and a stern, uniformed Angel stepped in. He looked at the two of them, then pointed at Scanat.

"You. Come with me."

Penilos cried out, "Don't leave me alone."

"Don't worry, kid," said the Angel. "You'll get your turn." He led Scanat out, relocked the door, then prodded him to move down the corridor.

Scanat had seen crime shows featuring interrogation. They placed him in a classic room: bare walls of non-descript pale green with a large mirror set into one, a single table and one chair fastened to the floor, two others loose on the other side, and two vidcams in the ceiling corners. The Angel sat him in the hard chair and handcuffed Scanat to a D-ring welded to the table.

"Wait here." The Angel left.

And so Scanat waited, as if he had any choice. Nothing happened other than the sound of air in the ventilation system.

After a time, the door opened. Captain Forsfear strode in to take the chair opposite him. Another Angel stood guard in the corner.

Scanat glared at them and tugged at the cuffs. "Do you think I'm going to break free and hurt someone?" He wasn't surprised at the deep bitterness in his own voice. Anger at his situation colored everything.

Forsfear tilted his head and watched Scanat through narrowed eyes. "Are you?"

Scanat sneered. "No, of course not. I'm fed up with the whole business. I don't belong. I don't do miracles. I just want out."

Forsfear had come in looking ready to beat Scanat into submission. At this outburst, he paused. Then he nodded to the other Angel, who released Scanat from the handcuffs.

"Is that better?" the captain asked.

Scanat shrugged. "Hardly. This is only one more in a long chain of 'not better.'"

Forsfear cocked his chin, his eyes boring into Scanat. "So. Scanat Forsenquire. A powername that speaks of learning about power. Yet you claim not to use any power. Tell me about it." The man's posture still spoke volumes of threat, though withheld for the moment.

"I had a promising career. Did well in school. Then I got enticed into joining Reb Fenet. Changed my powername. Thought I'd do amazing things." He stopped and hung his head.

"Didn't you?"

"No." Scanat's word dripped with cynicism. "In four years, he hasn't taught me a single thing. Not one. I'm in the wrong place. I want out."

The captain traded a glance with his associate. "Maybe we can help each other."

At every step, Beltaret ran into obstacles. The Khubar f'Elláh kept delaying their readiness to act. Missionary trips had terminated. He wasn't sure what actions Captain Forsfear would be taking. And his tame traitor floundered in setting up his t-path lab in Rathas. Every issue needed Beltaret's direct hand, and he could only touch one thing at a time.

His secretary buzzed his imp. "Minister, I have Minister Dominact here to see you."

Beltaret sighed. "Invite him in, Pina."

Dominact's face screamed of the man's doubt. He fumbled with the belt on his robes, in the usual physical misdirection, while he stepped across the room to take the chair in front of Beltaret's desk.

"What can I do for you, Pronas?" Beltaret asked, keeping his voice neutral.

Dominact paused and looked at the floor. He waved a hand in one of his distracting useless gestures. After a pause, he looked up. "You can explain to me why we're going to war with Tileus."

Beltaret gave a tiny shake of his head. "We went through this in the Ministry. Tileus disrespects our missionaries. Their laws make it impossible to reach out to save people. This latest incident—"

"Is an excuse, Beltaret. Yes, the girl is related to Bishop Oratus—"

"His daughter, Pronas. His daughter."

Dominact waved a hand again. "Of course. But that makes it a personal issue, and an issue for laws. Tileus has laws against kidnapping and torture. They will enforce those laws and find whoever did this. Why does it take a war?"

Beltaret paused, giving Dominact's words time to settle. "You have doubts, my friend. I know that. As Minister of Trade, you'd rather see us negotiate."

Dominact nodded.

"But Pronas, our national security is at stake—and that is my responsibility. It's more than just missionaries. It's a disrespect for the Church, and for Elláh. Our karma suffers when we let others define what we should and should not do. Only Elláh can do that."

"But—"

"Stay the course, Pronas. The Ministry has decided. It's up to all of us to support the decision."

When Dominact left, Beltaret turned back to the issue of Randy Princeton. He'd have to motivate the young man more. Give Guileart some more money, let him push Randy. Beltaret wanted a t-path jammer, and he wanted it now.

28 - Interrogation

While the techniques of interrogation have changed with technology, the basics have not changed in five thousand years of recorded history. Interviewers use deception, hostility, sympathy, rotating interrogators, mind-altering drugs, and even torture, to elicit verbal and non-verbal cues from the subject.

—A Practical Guide to Sensitive Negotiation by Ellen Thranadil, 426 A.T.

Fenet sat on one of the two cots in the cell, holding the broken staff in his lap, while Eregim laid on the other. Eregim's halting tale of torture horrified him. Fenet had cleaned Eregim up as much as he could. He didn't appear to have any broken bones amidst all the bruises, cuts and scrapes. He fell asleep, to Fenet's relief. Sleep was the best thing for him. Eregim sounded like he'd given up, though Fenet knew his friend would return.

His story of brutal beatings made Fenet's stomach clench. Who were these Heresy Angels, anyway? He'd never heard of them before, though Pincely had known of them. With their red collars, they looked to be some kind of super-proctor, or perhaps a completely different group? They appeared to be sanctioned by the Church, yet they reminded Fenet of the totalitarian police of Verdant Prime.

The farther they traveled from home, the more brutal the authorities. The proctors at home sometimes gave them trouble. In Netweaver, Pincely said the proctors had a reputation for beating people. Fenet had seen a heavier hand in Richearth, when the miracles failed. Then proctors watched them in every town;

sometimes the proctors hadn't let them stop. These dark-garbed Angels, however, seemed to be over the top.

And Fenet had no opportunity to exercise leadership. Forsfear had isolated them all. Fenet and the Khadam were in his power.

That thought caught Fenet's breath. He prayed for peace, but fear kept taking hold.

Several times, the hallway echoed with raised voices and slammed steel doors, sounding like individual novim being taken elsewhere. Sometimes, the voices elevated to shouting matches ended by thuds that made Fenet wince.

Yet no one came for Fenet. He sat while Eregim slept, his thoughts careening in circles of pray and fear, pray and fear.

The light from the high window dimmed and moved up onto a wall before the cell door crashed open.

Captain Forsfear stopped in the doorway with a scowl on his face. He looked at the sleeping Eregim with contempt before gesturing to Fenet. "You. Powrfaith. It's your turn, come with me."

"Yes, sir." Fenet stood, uncertain whether his hips would support him. He left his shattered staff on the floor.

Forsfear took two steps in and struck Fenet on the upper arm with his stuncheon. "Not fast enough, *Reb*. Move it." Again, he spit out the title as if it tasted foul.

"I don't move well, sir."

"Then I'll give you motivation." He hit Fenet in the lower back. Fenet's spine flashed with fire.

Fenet limped as fast as he could out the door, holding his arm. His hips flared in pain. He hissed breath through his teeth. Walking fast made his hips feel like wading through long-spiked brambles.

Down the hall and around several turns, Forsfear put him into an interrogation room. Puddles of water dotted the floor. Disinfectant assaulted his nose. Who'd been in here last? What happened? Forsfear shoved him down onto a hard metal chair bolted to the floor, then fastened his wrists to a fixed ring on the table edge.

"Now, Powrfaith," he spit the words into Fenet's face, "Tell me where you get your power."

"Faith, sir. All our power comes from Elláh."

Forsfear slammed his palm across Fenet's cheek hard enough to spin his head sideways. Sharp pain shot through his neck. Before he could cry out, the captain slapped his other cheek just as hard.

Fenet's ears rang with the impacts. A muscle spasm in the back of his neck forced him to hang his head.

Fenet lifted his head against the pain of the spasm and looked up into Forsfear's eyes. "That was a true answer, sir," he said. "Why did you hit me?"

"I don't need a reason, *Reb*. Remember that, and don't play with me. Your disciples talk about healing diseases, re-growing lost limbs, teleporting people here and there, even changing the weather. The Church says such things don't come from Elláh."

Fenet opened a palm. "What are you going to believe, the Church teachings or the reality of what we've done?"

This time, the man swung his fist. The cartilage in Fenet's nose exploded. Then the captain left, while blood dripped down Fenet's lip.

⤞ ✳ ⤝

Left in his interrogation room for hours, Scanat wondered what would happen next. The Angels had taken him to the bathroom once. He paced around the room, flexing his hands like a boxer who'd already been knocked down twice. Fresh air circulated in the room, not quite covering the copper taint of old blood. He most hated the times when they left him alone with his thoughts. He'd been such an utter failure in everything, and now he couldn't close this deal, either.

Forsfear kept coming back with more questions. At his next visit, the captain brought Scanat's backpack.

"Is this yours?"

"It's got my name on it, doesn't it?"

He had to be careful with snippy answers. Captain Forsfear treated him as an associate, perhaps as a friend, but he certainly wasn't a friend. *It's a ruse. Interrogation technique.* The captain's voice often carried unfathomable depths of danger on the edges of his courtesy.

Forsfear raised an eyebrow. "I'm trying not to make assumptions here."

Scanat nodded and hung his head. He'd been doing a lot of that today. "Yes, it's mine. What do you want to know?"

Without answering, the captain reached in the pack, pulled out a t-path, and set it on the table between them.

"It's a transpath, Captain. A device to sense other people's feelings."

What should have been a startling revelation didn't even make the man blink. He either had an amazing poker face or he already knew about the t-path.

"Show me how it works."

"I can't. First, it has to be personalized to you, and you have to be alone to do that."

Forsfear stared at him, obviously waiting for something more.

"But I also have one personalized to me under my robe. I can turn it on and tell you what you're feeling."

The captain nodded. "We've already inventoried everything on your person. We knew about your electronic box. I've been waiting for you to bring it up. It didn't look like a weapon, so we let you keep it." He paused, eyes narrowing. "Okay. Do it. But you'll be ground meat if there's a trick."

Scanat reached under his robe and turned on his t-path. He hadn't had it on since the last village healing session; his friends' emotions had been too painful to feel. He adjusted the volume, then looked at Forsfear. Scanat's heart nearly stopped in fear. The depth of the man's depravity festered like a volcanic pit. *I can't tell him all I sense. He'll explode. But I've got to give him something. Prove myself.*

"Captain, what I feel from you ... uh, I sense your distrust of me, anger ..." He found it difficult to keep looking at the man. "contempt for us in your hands ... a sense of emotional manipulation ... but also you have a small hope. I don't know what these emotions are about. The device doesn't give me thoughts or words, only the feelings."

"Keep watching." Forsfear cocked his head while he glared at Scanat. "What am I feeling now?"

Scanat snorted. "Amusement ... and speculation."

"Turn it off again, please."

Scanat did so.

"Why do you have five of these things in your pack? What were you planning to do with them?"

The question touched on the core of Scanat's problem. He let out a sigh and lowered his head, talking into the table. "I thought they'd help me do miracles. I thought they'd help everyone. Instead, using the t-path shut down Elláh's miracles. I haven't been granted a single miracle in all these years." He paused, remembering the incident in Netweaver, then shook his head, denying. "I had one time when I thought I heard Elláh's voice—but I heard only my foolishness and wishful thinking. That's why I'm ready to make a deal, ready to leave Reb Fenet. I'm useless to them, and I have no future there."

He also told Forsfear how he'd gotten the t-paths from a marketing presentation in Glorify, that the devices had been manufactured in Tileus. He gave him the names of Jake and Zofia.

"What can you do for me, Captain? I'm not one of them anymore. Can you help me regain a good life?"

"That depends on what you're willing to do for us." The captain left him alone yet again.

Fenet's wrists ached where the handcuffs still held him to the table. He'd gotten his nose to stop bleeding, but now he had trouble breathing through it. The captain came in and out of the interrogation room, shouting hard questions at Fenet and striking him when he didn't like the answers. He never liked the answers.

He seemed to believe Fenet some sort of magical wizard using dark forces. Time after time, Forsfear tried to trick him into revealing some dark secret he didn't have. Each time, Fenet told the simple truth. In response, Forsfear kept hitting him.

Then he'd leave Fenet alone in the room, sweating, head hanging, unable to soothe his pains because of his bound hands. Fenet prayed, asking Elláh to give His strength, to give His peace in whatever Forsfear did. He tried hard not to question Elláh's path, though this particular part of the path seemed too rocky to withstand.

The next time the captain returned, another man came with him, a tall, corpulent proctor in the usual grey robes. His red collar carried the special insignia of a Proctor Major. The man said nothing, only stood to one side of the door while Forsfear repeated the demands.

"Tell us, Powrfaith." He leaned so close his spittle hit Fenet's face. "Your supernatural events aren't sanctioned by the Church. Where do they come from? Who do you worship?"

Fenet shook his head, knowing and fearing what came next. "I worship only Elláh, Captain. He provides all the power."

Instead of hitting Fenet, the captain shocked him with the stuncheon, electricity that stopped his breathing for long seconds and sent his whole body into spasmic convulsions. Fenet fell off the chair, straining his shoulders because of his fastened hands. Afterward, he had to pull myself back up into the chair by his wrists.

Forsfear stood over him with a red face. The Proctor Major frowned, his face dark. Forsfear bludgeoned his club across Fenet's back with an angry cry, then the two turned and left him alone again.

Shortly after, Fenet heard shouting in the room next door, behind the one-way mirror. He thought such rooms were sound-proofed, but at least two people were out of control. One voice sounded like Forsfear. The other was deeper, more measured. At no point could he understand the words, but the argument frightened him more. What might it portend?

Fenet had been praying all day. During the argument, he focused on praying for peace. "Elláh, dear Lord, I'm frightened. The things of this world are not Yours, but I hurt and they cloud my judgment. It's hard to follow You when the flesh is abused. Please, fill me with Your peace. Let me do right no matter what these Heresy Angels may do. Give me courage to endure. Allow me to reflect Elláh to this errant man."

When the captain next returned, Fenet gasped at the darkness of his face. Something about the argument had angered the man to the point of frenzy. His motions were jerky as he slammed his fists onto the table in front of Fenet.

Hands still fastened to the table, Fenet could only flinch. It wasn't enough.

Forsfear repeated pounding with his fists to punctuate his words. "*Damn* you, Fenet Powrfaith. Your supernatural doings are *beyond* anything the Church condones, and yet you still *claim* it's all the work of Elláh. Your words are *blasphemy*. What do you expect me to do but charge you with heresy?"

"I don't know what you'll do, Captain. I hope you'll let us all go so we can continue our ministry."

"It's a black ministry you do, for sure. And I want to find out how you're doing it, if it takes days." He stepped to a blank wall and slammed his fist into it.

Fenet imagined he heard bones crunch. *What kind of man can do something like that?*

Without any cry of pain, the captain stormed out of the room again.

༺ ❊ ༻

Scanat wandered in the confined space of the room, shaking his head to himself. *Gotta get out of here. Make this work. Might be my last chance to make something good of my life.* He'd been thinking for hours about particle physics, refreshing the knowledge he'd gotten in secondary and renewing his interest in the field.

Forsfear returned. He pointed to the chair.

Scanat sat. When he did so, a document came into his imp from the captain.

"Read that," said the man.

Scanat focused on his inner eye to scan the document. *Whereby … In the event that … The accused shall … In return …* The more he read, the more his eyebrows rose. This paper documented a formal agreement between Scanat and the country of Rathas. It required him to gather information about Reb Fenet and his followers, to report the information to Forsfear and follow any directions given. In return, the State offered to reinstate him into tertiary school.

"I … don't understand. This reward is everything I want. But I'm not sure I can do what you ask."

Forsfear shrugged with an angry edge tempered by certainty. "If you want the reward, then do the deed. You know what I want."

Scanat shuddered. "You want me to discover evidence Reb Fenet is consorting with evil."

The captain nodded, lips thin.

"But I've been with him for four years, and I've never seen any such evidence. He always claims his powers come from Elláh. So do the others."

"If the evidence isn't there, our agreement will still stand. BUT YOU BETTER FIND IT." The man abruptly slammed both fists onto the table. Scanat's glass of water jumped, fell over, and spilled.

Scanat leaned back, eyes wide. Forsfear had treated him gently all day. This sudden violence and shouted words highlighted the danger Scanat had sensed throughout. The captain might wear the collar of a proctor, but Scanat had come to believe Saitan worked through Forsfear.

The captain shook a finger at him. "We will know."

❧ ✳ ☙

The Angels returned Fenet to the cell hours later. He collapsed onto the cot as his entire body released its adrenaline charge.

Eregim was taking a couple of shaky paces back and forth in the tiny space. The sky through the narrow window showed a few stars. "Sleep helped me, Fenet. I'm not well, but I'm better. I'm ready to continue with whatever Elláh has for us. I'm sure His path is—" Then he looked at Fenet's face. "Holy Elláh, you look terrible." He wet the torn rag Fenet had used earlier and knelt next to his friend.

Fenet put a hand to his aching face and used the rag to blot his nose. "I don't know what's going to happen to us. Elláh's forging seems too hard to take. This Captain Forsfear is dangerous. Raging angry one moment, probing with intelligent questions the next. He's strong in his faith and believes the Church can do no wrong."

Eregim let loose a heavy breath. "A dangerous combination. How does he view what we've done?"

Fenet waved a helpless hand. "He thinks we do miracles by witchcraft, because the Church says miracles by Elláh don't happen anymore." Saying the words choked him.

Eregim's eyes went wide and he said nothing. The two of them simply existed in the hush and looked at each other. Accused of witchcraft. Yet the voice of Elláh has guided and enabled everything Fenet had ever done.

Fenet tried to say more. "I don't know how—"

With a metallic rattle, the door swung open. Forsfear stood in the hallway, his features contorted in a grimace. For a long moment, he could not speak. His right fist tapped over and over against his hip.

Fenet waited in fear for whatever he might do next.

Finally, Forsfear got words out. "Apparently, *Reb* Fenet, we don't have enough evidence yet." His voice sounded strangled. "You … and your entourage … are free to go. Your driver is waiting outside."

Forsfear turned to Eregim. "And you … Reb. Here's your transpath back. Go find something useful to do, something better than consorting with these heretics."

29 – International Parley

Good negotiations build compromise that can be accepted by all players, assuming the players are willing.

—A Practical Guide to Sensitive Negotiation by Ellen Thranadil, 426 A.T.

Riding the bus out of Center in darkness, Fenet had questions. Why did Forsfear let them go? Did that argument behind the mirror force him? Or did he have some deeper, nefarious plan? Fenet had trouble thinking with the throbbing soreness throughout his body. The dusty scent of the bus eased his worries like petting a familiar cat.

All the entourage bore bruises and cuts from the rough treatment. Beneim had a broken wrist he cradled in his other hand with tears in his eyes. All, that is, except Pincely and Scanat. Why did those two have no harm?

Clear of the city, he asked Pincely to stop the bus.

Fenet stood to get everyone's attention. "Dear Elláh," he prayed, voice carrying through the bus. "We thank you for deliverance, for moving the hearts of these Heresy Angels to let us go. May we continue to live in Your peace and do Your work. Please, Lord, keep us in your protection."

Everyone echoed, "Selah."

Young Penilos stood up with his eyes wide, listening to something the rest could not hear. The familiar red glow washed over him from above. Then he moved to each person, Beneim first, and miraculously healed their wounds. He even picked up the halves of Fenet's staff and melded them together.

Removal of Fenet's new pains—the broken nose, aching joints and bruised bones—relieved him so much he felt all the muscles of his body relax. He'd thought himself beyond astonishment after all these years. Somehow, though, it felt different when he became the subject of a miracle. Seeing it from outside, or even being Elláh's conduit, could not compare with the liberation of feeling the results.

He spoke for everyone. "Thank you, Elláh, and thank you to Penilos for his humility to You."

Penilos' action, though, reminded Fenet the power he had lost now passed through these novim. He ached at the loss. A part of him cringed, yet he still had the responsibility to be the godly leader they needed.

"Pincely," he said, "can you find us a suitable place to camp for the night?"

"I'll find one, Reb." The driver started the bus moving again.

"What happened to you, Pincely? Why did they pull you away from the rest of us?"

"Reb Fenet, them Angels hardly spoke to me at all. When they dragged me away for 'interrogation,' I thought I was in for it, so scared I nearly peed my pants. When I told them I wasn't doin' no miracles, though, they treated me like no account. I was back out of there in less than an hour, sittin' in my bus and wondering what to do. I worried 'bout you all, but couldn't figure out how I could help. Hours later, that proctor came by and told me to go to the Enforcement Center to pick y'all up."

Fenet shook his head. Behind him in the bus, the novim were telling each other horrible stories of being questioned and beaten without mercy. Eregim and Fenet had suffered much. Yet they treated the driver with kid gloves? Why the difference?

"Well, I'm glad for you—and pleased to know you're still available for us. Elláh spoke to me again, made it clear we should be riding with you, though He's not made clear the reason."

Eregim said, "Elláh's not required to give us reasons, Fenet."

"I know that. But sometimes I'd like to know."

"Wouldn't we all?" Eregim cocked his head. "And what about Scanat?"

"Good question." Fenet waved Scanat to come forward.

The young man's eyes were hooded and he spoke with a cautious manner. "Yes, Reb Fenet?" The ordeal with the Heresy

Angels hadn't changed the sullenness Scanat had taken on since the other novim had rejected his t-paths.

"What happened to you in there, Scanat? Why were you not beaten like everyone else?"

He paused a long time, looking at the floor, before he raised his eyes again. "I don't know, Reb. They had me in an interrogation room for hours. Sometimes, they locked my hands to the table. I'm sure they watched me through the mirror. That Captain Forsfear kept coming in and out, firing questions at me. He threatened me and frightened me, but he didn't beat me like the others talk about. I told him I hadn't worked any miracles. I guess he finally believed me." His eyes lowered, shame suffusing his face.

"There's no shame in not performing miracles, Scanat. Miracles are unusual, not ordinary. Elláh grants them at His will."

Scanat's jaw tensed as he nodded, but he said nothing more.

"Okay, thanks for telling me. Let's talk more tomorrow."

Scanat returned to his lonely seat at the back of the bus.

Eregim scratched his chin. "So, where do we go next? What do we do?"

"We continue to follow Elláh on pilgrimage to Praise. He keeps presenting us with opportunities to serve people with His miracles."

"And what will we do when we get to Praise?"

This question had plagued Fenet since the first time Eregim asked it nearly two weeks ago. He raised a palm. "We'll do whatever He tells us to do. In the meantime, we do the best we can with the gifts He's given us."

Pincely interrupted, "Reb Fenet, we've got a black car following us."

⁊⧉⧉

Two days later in his office at Church Center One, Beltaret Leaderlist looked up from his desk when Caropina entered.

"Sir, I had an urgent call from Minister Dominact. He's on his way here."

Beltaret had become quite adept at using the t-path. His secretary's unease with the sudden meeting came across. "Why does that worry you, Pina?"

"It's unlike him, sir. He usually demands meetings in his space, on his schedule. That's part of his power game."

The minister chuckled. "You're right at that. But if he's coming here, we'll receive him. Thanks for warning me. I always have to treat Dominact with care. We're both officially equal in the Service Ministry. I usually carry more power than he does, but there are areas where he has influence I don't. It's all the politics I enjoy."

"And you're good at it, sir, if you don't mind my saying so. I'm always glad to be part of what you do."

He nodded thanks. "In the meantime, would you please arrange for Holy General Comfors to report to me on force readiness? I want an update on how soon he can launch our forces into Tileus."

"Yes, sir."

"And also ... have we heard anything more from Forsfear about that problematic miracle-worker?"

"The captain reported this morning, sir. He had the whole group arrested in Center. Then, your Proctor Major Stolwatch overrode him. The major told him he didn't have enough evidence to charge them. Forsfear says he now has one of their group gathering information to confirm the heresy. He also said the group had some of those transpath devices you outlawed two weeks ago. The names Jake and Zofia came up." She paused in thought. "Weren't those the Tileus people you had in here?

Beltaret sat straighter and stroked his chin. "Interesting. Yes, they were. Thanks. That'll be all for now."

While waiting for Dominact, Beltaret spread his hands wide on the firmness of his desk. The cool wood often gave him a sense of solidity and purpose while he thought. He pondered the transpath and what to do with it. He'd now had the unit for over a week and had grown accustomed to its capabilities. It offered immense benefits, an advantage over his peers. Yet he still had reservations about the way he'd gotten it through the spy Guileart. Through his own decree, he made the device illegal in Rathas—and he was still using it.

This past weekend, Guileart told him about a more efficient production method for t-paths. With reluctance, Beltaret had funded Randy Princeton. Beltaret didn't care about efficient production, but he did want that t-path jammer.

However, the man had created more trouble. The police in Tileus wanted to charge Princeton with arson. Beltaret snorted. He'd treat that request with the same urgency Tileus police had applied to the kidnapping.

Loud footfalls sounded in the outer office like a crowd of rabble. The office door burst open at the same time Pina buzzed his imp. Dominact hadn't waited to be announced. Ripat Grufhand, their ambassador to Tileus, came in with him. Both men were much shorter than Beltaret; Dominact stocky with frenetic gestures, Grufhand built like a solid blockhouse. Beltaret stood to greet them.

"We need to talk right away," said Dominact. "We've got a new urgent communication from Tileus." He waved his hands as if swatting bees.

Beltaret snorted. "Of course. They'd rather talk than *do* anything." He ignored Dominact's distracting gestures; the man always used them to hide his true purposes.

"They're serious. Willing to do whatever it takes to forestall a war."

"Too late. We already voted on it."

"But we haven't done anything yet other than prepare. And besides that," Dominact said, irritated, "you pressured me into joining that vote. If we can resolve these international issues without sending our young men off to die, we'd all be better off."

"We may have different understandings of 'better.'" Beltaret emphasized his words with a glare. "As Minister of Trade, your job is to preserve and improve our trade relations. Mine is to protect Rathas and our people from the kind of unwarranted attacks we've had. Often, sending men off to die is *better* than giving in to constant abuse. So, what is this new communication?"

Dominact looked to the ambassador.

Grufhand answered, "Sir, their Secretary Susanna Nintuk has offered to host a negotiation meeting day after tomorrow. She wants to explore ways to forestall an actual war."

"What good would such a meeting do?" Beltaret asked. "We've already coordinated with their national police forces, and they refused to treat the girl's kidnapping and torture as a serious crime. And her kidnapping is just one more in a long series of violent incidents to our missionaries in Tileus, like the young man who came back with broken bones last month—and the entire missionary group that had to flee from protestors before that."

"Negotiations are always worth trying, Minister," said Grufhand.

"Not necessarily. There comes a time for action. Who is this Secretary Nintuk? Do you know her?"

"Yes, sir," said the ambassador. "She's my counterpart there. Her title is Secretary for Rathas Affairs, and she works for Welton Moller, their Governor of Outside Affairs. Both of them would take part in the meeting. They are the Tileus equivalent of Minister Dominact and me."

Dominact added, "We're sitting in a position of power right now, Beltaret. Even more so if the other side is desperate to come to terms."

"But are they desperate?" Beltaret's voice dripped with sarcasm.

Grufhand leaned forward, his face eager. "Yes, sir, I think they are."

Dominact joined in. "I believe we should give it a try, Beltaret. What do we have to lose?"

Beltaret hmphed. The two radiated confidence, the kind of audacious arrogance often felt by diplomats before some disaster. On the other hand, the last report he had from General Comfors said the Khubar f'Elláh would not be ready to invade for another week.

After a moment of thought, Beltaret nodded. "All right. Let's accept their offer, though I don't have much hope of success." He again fixed his glare on the two diplomats. "And remember the entire Service Ministry has already declared Holy War. Retracting it will also require a unanimous Ministry vote. I'll take part in this meeting along with you two."

In Tileus, the day before the meeting with Rathas dignitaries, Jake stepped into the conference room on the seventh floor. Freedom Aerie—the Tileus central government building— had a portico carved with figures from Tileus history. He'd brought Zofia with him to get her out of the self-condemning mire into which she'd fallen since the incident with Randy. It had been months since they'd been here, the site where the t-path had stopped war between Tileus and Verdant Prime last year. He smiled to be back. This room had been their first big success.

Jake paused to admire the room again. Fresh air scented with jasmine made for a warm welcome. Beautiful marble floors matched inlaid marble panels in wood-framed wainscoting. A glistening conference table for twenty filled the room, a pair of sprawling stained-glass chandeliers hanging above. Around the walls stood chairs for another forty. The scene out the windows displayed an expansive view across the diverse buildings of Thad City.

"Why do we need to use the conference room version of the t-path?" Zofia asked. "I thought by now the personal versions would take its place."

Jake sat down and opened the padded case filled with test equipment. "Governor Moller asked us to make sure it's working. The Rathas contingent won't have t-paths, remember? Their Service Ministry outlawed them. The only way these negotiations can benefit from two-way empathy will be by using the full-room version we developed last year."

Zofia winced. "Bangit, you're right. I've been so focused on the new development, I forgot that factor."

Jake looked up at her with caution tempered by what he hoped was kindness. "You're forgetting a lot these days. That security business with Randy; not good. You've got to bring it together. You're better than this."

Her eyes got wide and her lips thin. She pathed quick resentment. For a moment, he thought she might slap him.

Jake looked back down at his case. "I'm sorry, Zofia. Not appropriate. I didn't do anything about Randy, either. I'm just peeved we've lost one of our best engineers with all his knowledge. I don't know what he's going to do, but it can't be good for our business." He looked back at her. "So, help me test out this system again, please? I didn't want to trust the testing to anyone but you and me."

Her pathed anger subsided, and she nodded. "We need the nano-processors. They were necessary for the particle waves to synchronize while filling the conference room."

"I've got a set here," Jake held up a small vial of grey dust. "And we have another set for tomorrow's meeting."

"Are we going to stop another war, Jake?" She raised an eyebrow, eyes twinkling in amusement.

"I hope." He uncapped the vial and flung the dust into the air, where it floated and dissipated into invisibility. The air filled with millions of tiny but capable computers, able to communicate with each other and the t-path room system. "Let's turn off our personal t-paths and turn on the room system. Then we can enlist the help of a few others as a test."

She found the t-path system control in a cabinet and handed it to him. "Do you get to be here during the meeting tomorrow?"

"Yeah. Governor Moller asked me to run it like I did last year."

Pathed amusement rose in her. With taunting eyes, she said, "And are you going to dive across the table to tackle an ambassador again, like you did last year?"

He laughed out loud. "Yeah, I did that. Director Denmark had been my old boss, but he couldn't handle the effects of the t-path. The man pulled a gun in the middle of negotiations!" Still chuckling, he shook his head. "I hope nothing like that happens tomorrow."

30 – Perfidy from Within

Negotiation can be defeated most thoroughly from the inside. One of the famous Christian writers on old Earth said it best, "Each betrayal begins with trust."

—*A Practical Guide to Sensitive Negotiation* by Ellen Thranadil, 426 A.T.

Scanat kept to himself in the back of the bus after the Heresy Angels released them. Two days passed before he could figure out what to do. He'd signed the contract, he knew what he needed to do, but he didn't believe he'd be able to fulfill it. Reb Fenet's powers clearly came from Elláh, and so did the powers granted to the novim. How could he gather evidence of heresy when none existed? Or as an alternative, would it be possible to convince Captain Forsfear there wasn't any?

They stopped in every farm town down the Rise Plateau and into the Praise Valley. The shiny black aircar stayed in sight. At every visit, one of Forsfear's Heresy Angels got out and stood by like a carrion-eater waiting for someone to die.

The Angel's presence reminded Scanat to fulfill his deal with Saitan. He needed to stretch himself to gain the promise of getting back into tertiary school; he imagined himself as a long-necked bird leaning forward more and more until striking at a fish. Being a nov didn't work for Scanat. Elláh hadn't given him anything. His mind worked better in the science and engineering fields. Thinking didn't help in this business of miracles.

The other novim chattered on without him, while Reb Fenet and Reb Eregim had a quiet conversation in the front row.

Durnadat bounced in his seat, his exuberance overflowing. "Did you see me fix that aircar? I can't believe I did it."

"Yeah," said Penilos. "A different kind of miracle for sure."

Tenpos shook his head. He didn't often join in this kind of banter. "Be careful, Durnadat. Reb Fenet's busy, but he'd take you to task for saying *you* did the miracle."

Durnadat ducked his head. "I guess you're right. It's always Elláh, not me."

Beneim screwed up his mouth in puzzlement. "But how did you do it, Durnadat? You don't know anything about engines. You worked in a bakery."

"M-maybe the car was like a b-breadbox," laughed Lorefim.

Durnadat threw his hands in the air. "I don't know! I just did what Elláh told me to do. I have no idea what got fixed."

After voicing his caution, Tenpos had gone quiet again. When the conversation moved on, he turned in his seat to look back at Scanat, a kind look that conveyed compassion.

Scanat wished at this moment he had his t-path on. He had avoided using it around the novim. He never wanted to feel those miracles again. They reminded him too much of what he missed. He held Tenpos' gaze for a moment, then shook his head and lowered his eyes.

Tenpos had been Scanat's closest friend within the Khadam. The two had deep, searching conversations at times. When Scanat tended to isolate, Tenpos had reached out to draw him into the camaraderie. It didn't feel right to cut out that friendship, but Scanat already felt accused by what he'd agreed to do for Forsfear.

The conversation he'd just heard brought Scanat an idea. Durnadat had talked about *him* performing the miracles instead of Elláh. Not very sinful, but on the edge of the kind of heresy Forsfear wanted. Perhaps Scanat could use tidbits like to satisfy Forsfear, though they'd never qualify in a fair ecclesiastical court. Even Reb Fenet might occasionally say something like that.

Scanat nodded to himself. This could work.

Energized with renewed purpose, Scanat activated his imp to record the conversations he heard. He would go through them a couple of times a day to pick out things that might fulfill his contract without actually harming his friends.

⁊❋⁊

Fenet kept surrendering his fear. The sky ahead blustered with dark clouds, threatening a cold fall storm. His nightmares reverberated with their treatment in Center. Over and over, he gave it up to Elláh only to have it return. His responsibility for the entire group weighed on him. And now ... "Eregim, what are we going to do about this Heresy Angel in the black car?"

"I'm not sure there's anything we *can* do. So far, he's not being difficult."

"His presence has been sufficient to create a problem in some of the towns. When he showed up in that small community yesterday, the town elders asked us to leave without doing any healing. This morning in Farmfriend, two others in those hideous dark uniforms joined him. It's getting worse. What might they have planned when we get closer to Praise?"

Because the two sat just behind him, Pincely often became part of their conversation. "They mostly just stand around and watch so far, Reb. But they're dangerous."

Fenet took a deep breath. "I'm scared. Being arrested is not something I want to do again."

Eregim shuddered. "Same here. I thought I'd never get away."

"But, Reb," said Pinceley, "don't you teach to rely on Elláh? That's what I hear from you all the time. And Elláh did set you free again."

"You're right," Fenet said with a soft little laugh. "I know that, and I keep falling back onto it. It doesn't stop me being afraid."

"Well, we'll be coming into Artha soon." Pincely said. "It's a bigger place, almost a suburb of Praise. Let's see what happens."

The three fell into silence, listening to the conversation of the novim, while the Center Road took them into yet another city. Word of their mission had swept ahead of them. Once again, Fenet caught his breath at the size of the crowds awaiting them. Time to rise to the challenge of being the leader of this crew.

He raised his voice. "Be ready, everyone. We've got another big task in front of us. Pray for Elláh's guidance."

⤳ ✳ ⤳

Scanat nodded to himself. He had recorded some words from Reb Fenet sounding like the Reb advised the novim to do the miracles on their own power. Maybe words like this would satisfy Forsfear. He packaged this and a few similar recordings and sent them by imp to the captain. Not without trepidation. He had become a traitor to the Khadam, and he now, he also misled the Angels. Not exactly the good behavior of one of Elláh's true followers. Would he be caught in his two-faced handling of this?

He kept his mind on the goal. Back to school. Back into science.

In the meantime, he had to keep up appearances. When the bus stopped and settled to the pavement, he turned on his t-path to do his usual task of guiding supplicants to the novim.

When he stood to follow the rest, Scanat put on his jacket. Then another strategy hit him. What if the novim sometimes failed? Would that also provide grist for Forsfear's grinder?

Scanat stepped off the bus last. Artha looked larger than any place they'd seen since Center. The city square had shops and restaurants lining three sides. On the fourth side, an ornate building reached for the darkening clouds with carved lintels and a bell tower.

The other novim lined up outside the bus facing the packed crowd, as they'd done in each city along the way. The black autocar parked to one side, and the single Angel inside joined another five Angels already watching the crowd. Scanat glanced at the Angels. He hoped they would report his actions to Forsfear, adding to the positive weight of what he did.

The people in this city behaved well. Instead of rushing forward, they formed queues at each nov. They'd apparently gotten advanced word from other towns.

He moved into the queues to select people, the t-path showing him the desperation and the hope inside each person. The scent of disease wafted around him, bandaged blood and festering wounds closed in by the jackets and coats they wore against the threatening weather. Family members and friends supported the ill and maimed, keeping their spirits up.

Behind Scanat, the novim started doing their miraculous work. Scarlet waves of Elláh's power washed downward into and through them, accompanied by shouts of joy, amazement, and relief. Hopeful conversation grew loud throughout the crowd.

A gust of wind drew Scanat's attention to the clouds above. Swirling blackness swept over the square. The temperature dropped, and he tugged his jacket closed. Others also glanced up at the power in the sky.

Lightning suddenly struck a chimney down the street, followed at once by the deafening crack of Elláh's power. Scanat jumped in nervous fear. Thunder rolled, echoing from buildings farther away. Bricks flew into the air, arcing outward toward the street below. Screams sounded at that edge of the crowd when pieces of masonry hit the ground—and people. Rain burst from the sky like a flow of condemnation on Scanat's actions.

Most of the crowd remained. Rain, lightning and thunder didn't have enough threat to keep people away from miraculous healing.

Tenpos hurried to the edge of the crowd to help anyone hurt by the bricks.

Scanat raised his hood for protection. Shaking off his nervousness, he thought about his problem. Failures. How could he cause failures? The solution came to him in a flash as sudden as the lightning. Scanning the people in front of him, he selected a family member, someone who did not have the desperation and pain of a supplicant.

"Come with me," he said to the woman. "I'll take you to one of the healers." He took her arm to lead her forward.

She spluttered and pointed at a man beside her. "But it's not me. Jonim is the one who needs healing."

Scanat shook his head. "No, ma'am. Elláh wants you to come forward." He winced at his own lie, continuing to lead her.

He chose one of the novim: Lorefim, the simplest and easiest to fool. "Lorefim, I've brought you this woman for healing." His mouth tasted sour.

Lorefim simply nodded. "Th-thank you, Scanat." He put his hands on her shoulders and closed his eyes.

"But ..." the woman said. "But ... it's not me."

Lorefim raised his face to the sky, as Scanat had seen him do many times.

Nothing happened.

Lorefim looked back down at Scanat. "Are you s-sure?"

Scanat shrugged. "I guess this time, it's not working." He led the woman back to rejoin her family in line, while he put the recording into secure storage in his imp.

The cold rain poured down and lightning flashed. Scanat returned to the novim with supplicants and, occasionally, healthy family members. He had to be careful not to overdo it, because Reb Fenet would notice the failures if he brought too many.

The third healthy person Scanat chose pathed some nervous agitation, though his concern centered on the woman and child who'd been beside him. The man had a pock-marked face and tangled teeth.

While Scanat led him forward, the man kept asking, "Why me? I'm fine. It's my child."

Scanat chose Beneim this time. While Scanat started recording in his imp, the nov lowered his eyes and rested a hand on the man's shoulder. Scanat ground his teeth at his own deceit. As before, nothing happened. At first.

Then, to Scanat's amazement, the familiar rosy glow washed down through Beneim. *But Elláh, there's nothing wrong with this man!* The glow moved to the man's face. The disfiguring pox faded away, leaving his skin clear.

Scanat let go of the man's arm and stepped away in shock. He nearly cried out aloud, which would expose his duplicity. *What is this, Elláh? Are you toying with me?* He turned off the imp recording and took the man back to his family. The wife exclaimed in joy to see the man's smooth skin.

Now, Scanat didn't know what to do. Elláh had foiled his plan with a trivial healing. His stomach churned and he muttered to himself while he worked through the crowd.

He chose the next five people from true supplicants. After a time, he decided to try again, picking a healthy woman standing beside a bent old man. The false incident went smoothly this time. No miracle, instead "evidence" for Forsfear of the novim not always able to heal. When he took her back to her place, though, anger rose in Scanat—anger at Elláh, at Forsfear, at Reb Fenet, at the whole situation. He hated what he did.

For the next hour, while the violent thunderstorm continued, Scanat fought with himself to continue this path he'd been forced into. He never knew what Elláh would do. Miracles happened sometimes; other times, Elláh let Scanat's trickery stand.

When the rain finally eased, he had drenched robes and a string of failed "miracles" ready to send to Forsfear. He also had a deep, abiding anger at the capricious god who played with him.

31 — Jammed Hopes

The ancient Sun Tzu said, "Know the enemy and know yourself."
When negotiations break down, it is time to return to basics. Re-
assess your knowledge of yourself before blaming the enemy.

—*A Practical Guide to Sensitive Negotiation* by Ellen
Thranadil, 426 A.T.

Jake would control the conference room transpath tomorrow,
supporting Governor Moller. Jake needed to know what he faced
in the meeting. After he and Zofia confirmed proper operation of
the system, they returned to her office and spent the afternoon
reviewing the international news. The political situation, with the
Rathas declaration of Holy War, blared from every media source.
They sat side-by-side looking into the holo displays.

"I can't make heads or tails of it." Zofia slapped a palm on the
table. "Tileus has too many conflicting sources. Bangit, sometimes I
wish we were back in Verdant Prime with only one news source."

"Yeah, but there all the news was false." Jake gave a wry smile,
then turned back to the holos. "Conflicting, yes, but I see some
common threads in all these reports." The more Jake explored, the
more his anxiety rose. "Rathas is gathering its Khubar f'Elláh army
right against the border."

Zofia looked at him, concern in her eyes. "Damn, I wish I could
be in the meeting with you. I understand, though. Governor Moller
needs to control attendance. Is this situation worse than last year?"

"I think so. Last year, Verdant Prime was ready to invade Tileus,
and they had my antimatter bomb. I don't see anything about
Rathas having an advanced weapon like that, but—"

"But they've got over a hundred thousand troops. Did you see the satellite pictures?"

Jake nodded. "Yeah. That's what makes it worse. The situation's scary. Some of the media are shouting dire warnings. Automated drone weapons, armored vehicles and more."

Zofia swept her hair over her shoulder and pointed at her own holo. "Tileus has our defense forces gathering. They look puny compared to the masses on the other side." She paused and squinted into the display. "What are the distances here? How quickly could they move?"

"Their army is at the base of the Gortooths, no more than ten kilometers from the border. Uptown, our second largest city, is in the foothills on this side—about thirty kilometers from their forces."

She gripped his arm. "That's really close." Her voice spoke volumes about her concern.

"Here in Thad City, we should be safe. We're eight hundred kilometers away. How fast can their war machine move? Then again," Jake winced, "some sources say Rathas has weapons in orbit. There might be danger right over our heads."

"Isn't that illegal?"

"Yes, by international treaties. But who can enforce them?"

❧ ✳ ☙

The next day, Jake sat in one of the conference room chairs against the window wall, watching the principals gather. He clamped his jaw, nervous about what might happen. The day impended as a re-creation of last year's climactic event. Diplomatic negotiations. One side shouting for war, the other side asking for peace. He hoped it would go smoother this time.

Today had a difference. Jake had confidence in the t-path system. It had been so new last year they'd only finished testing one day before the meeting. None of them had been sure the whole thing would work. Since then, t-path success in industry and government had demonstrated its worth. Now, they trusted the system to help the diplomats understand each other. And yet, something could always go wrong.

Governors Welton Moller and Ellen Thranadil entered. Jake had a rush of warmth and trust about both. Moller, Governor of Outside Affairs and father to Jake's detective friend Soren, had funded the original tech development last year in order to stop the impending war. Afterward, Thranadil, Governor of Commerce and Industry, had advised Jake and Zofia how to get their TechEmpath business up and running. She still helped them. Jake stood to greet them.

"Are you ready, Jake?" asked Moller with his usual broad smile, warm handshake and deep voice. The powerful man always presented himself as a good old boy, friendly and open, though Jake had experienced the iron underneath.

"Yes, sir. We checked the system yesterday."

Thranadil nodded, a warm smile on her face. "You and Zofia are one of our success stories, Jake. I'm glad you're on this."

"Thank you, ma'am."

Moller gestured to a middle-aged woman with them. "I'd like you to meet Susanna Nintuk, Jake. She's our Secretary for Rathas Relations. This meeting will be hers to control."

"Nice to meet you, ma'am," Jake said, holding out a hand.

Tall and slim with sparkling red-brown hair and chiseled features, Nintuk gave him a firm nod while shaking his hand. "I've heard a lot about you and your devices, Jake. We're pinning our hopes on them working today."

"Our test showed them working," he said. Behind his confident words, he had the normal doubt of any engineer facing a crucial proof.

Nintuk cocked her head at him, making him wonder if she saw through his display of confidence. Diplomats were a long reach above where he worked, with intuitive capabilities beyond him. And she might be wearing a personal t-path, reading his emotions. Which reminded him …

"Secretary, we need to tell the Tileus people to turn off their personal t-paths if they have them. They'll interfere with the room system."

"That's fine," she agreed, then raised her voice. "Attention, everyone, please." Nintuk paused to let the conversations die away. "I need to let everyone know—if you have a personal t-path operating, please turn it off during this meeting."

A rumble of muttered exclamations ran through the room. "Why?" echoed several voices.

The secretary answered, "Because the Rathas diplomats will not have t-paths, we'll be using the whole-room system here. Your personal t-paths will interfere with it, so you'll need to leave them off. Please be assured: you will still have the transpath effect."

Welton Moller's voice followed hers. "Secretary Nintuk is right, folks. You'll be without your transpath effect for the first part of the meeting, until I signal Jake to turn on the room system." He turned back to Jake. "And you'll do the same procedure we used last year, right?"

"Yes, sir."

"But without attacking someone across the table?" Moller's eyes twinkled when he asked, and most of the room laughed. Everyone had heard the story.

Jake blushed. "Yes, sir. No attacks this year."

Jake faded into the background when the Rathas people arrived. Three principals, with a contingent of five more to support them. Secretary Nintuk introduced the principals to the room as Ripat Grufhand, Pronas Dominact and Beltaret Leaderlist. Several people furrowed their eyebrows at the strange Rathas names. Jake didn't hear their roles, but he caught his breath when he recognized Dominact and Leaderlist. These two had orchestrated Jake's disastrous marketing meeting in Rathas. Leaderlist carried himself into the room like a key authority, while Grufhand acted as the primary speaker and Nintuk's counterpart. None of them looked at Jake.

Nintuk and Grufhand sat to face each other over the center of the table, with the other two principals of each side flanking them. The support people, Jake included, all took seats around the room periphery. After some preliminary politeness, the meeting got down to business.

"You asked us here," said Grufhand in a firm voice. "We'll let you talk first. What is it you propose?"

Susanna Nintuk leaned forward. "We propose to stop a war that might devastate both our countries. I'm sure we can find solutions better than sending our young people to die."

Grufhand tilted his head. "I hope you have ideas more concrete than just a desire to stop. Our young people are already being maimed and harmed in your country. It's been a violent and disconcerting trend for over a year, orchestrated by your Freethinkers fringe group. Last week, your people kidnapped and brutally assaulted our bishop's daughter. They left her to die in the mountains! Our Service Ministry declared war because we saw no other solution to make you stop."

Nintuk looked down at the table for a moment before raising her eyes again. "We have different understandings of what's been happening—and particularly about the recent kidnapping incident in the mountains—"

Welton Moller gave Jake the sign to activate the room transpath. Jake turned it on and gradually increased the volume.

Nintuk continued, "Our understanding is your young missionaries have often broken our laws, either through ignorance or by design. You and I spoke of this last week, before you returned to Rathas. Ambassador, we don't condone kidnapping or attempted murder. But even in this extreme case, your missionaries instigated the incident. We showed you proof last week."

Grufhand gave an emphatic shake of his head. "Yet when we tried to have someone investigate the kidnapping, to find the girl, to save her life, your police forces brushed us off. All the information your police had gathered centered on the unwitting, minor crime committed by our people. Your police did *nothing*," he pounded a fist on the table," to investigate the greater crime, and *nothing*," he pounded again, "to help us save her life."

Jake looked down at the room t-path control in his hand. He had the volume at midrange but felt nothing, even from Grufhand's obvious strong emotions. His stomach clenched. Why wouldn't the system work as it did yesterday? The control had no technical readouts to give him details, nothing but a green activation light. He turned it off and back on again, watching the light operate normally. Nothing. Jake's mind raced through possible solutions.

He looked up. Governor Moller had his eyes on Jake, eyebrows raised and head cocked, a silent question. Moller repeated his covert signal for Jake to turn on the system.

"Ambassador," Secretary Nintuk said, "we understand you did indeed rescue the girl, and she will heal. We're very glad of that. In the future, we are willing to take stronger actions to help your missionaries ..." Her voice had an edge of uncertainty while she glanced at Jake. "Including giving more training to them when they arrive."

Jake tried a third time. He switched the system off then back on. Panicking, he turned the volume control to maximum. That level often overloaded people with too much empathy. A different reaction happened this time. Several people shook themselves as if startled. Jake impathed a tangled sense of emotions from the entire room. He couldn't separate whose from whom. The feelings battered his senses. No useful information. The muddle of emotions confused his thoughts. In alarm, he turned the system back off.

Governor Moller still watched him. Jake raised his hands helplessly. *Someone's interfering with the system. The Rathas people?*

The extreme emotional sensations, spread through the room, had brought the exchange to a halt. Minister Leaderlist narrowed his eyes at Secretary Nintuk and Welton Moller, then turned to follow their gazes to Jake.

Leaderlist snorted, a dark sound of amusement. "Jacoby Palatin, I believe? We meet again. What arcane machinations are you attempting in this room?"

Pinned to the wall by the man's scrutiny, Jake froze. Being noticed so publicly in this high-powered meeting sapped his confidence. Worse, this particular man had thwarted their marketing in Rathas. Leaderlist's direct attention left Jake's tongue empty of words. "Uh … Minister … I …"

Governor Moller saved him. "Mr. Palatin is here at my request, Minister. We had thought the use of a transpath system might smooth our discussions."

Leaderlist compressed his jaw. He turned back to Moller. "Yes, we thought you might try something like this. We've heard the tale of your surprise technology foisted on the Verdant Prime diplomats last year. The technology unhinged one of your opponents, didn't it? Allowed you to get what you wanted."

Moller matched Leaderlist's intent gaze with one of his own. "The technology allowed all of us to understand each other. It was essential to our negotiations."

The governor's ability to shift from hail-well-met bonhomie to hardened steel left Jake breathless. Without a t-path, Jake floundered to understand the motivations. He'd gotten used to having the empathic connection with others. If the room system wasn't working, he would try his personal unit.

Moller continued, "In the year since, we've seen the transpath proven in—"

"No, Governor," Leaderlist interrupted. "We're not having any of it. If you've asked us here to trick us, to work tech magic on us, rather than to make the concessions Tileus needs to make, we'll return to Rathas and prepare for war." He stood up and the others joined him. "Perhaps force will bring you to the table with a less devious mindset."

Jake turned on his personal t-path. When he looked at Leaderlist, however, his mind filled with a jumble of conflicting emotion. He couldn't think. Rage, sorrow, pain, compassion, love—all intertwined in a twisted combination that made no sense at all. When the disturbing sensations increased, dizziness overwhelmed him. He gripped the arm of his chair to keep from falling.

Last year, during the problematic development of this room's transpath, they'd had immense difficulty getting the system to synchronize different peoples' emotions. During that testing, they'd gotten this same mishmash from all the people in the room. Something interfered with the whole t-path technology.

Desperate for relief, Jake turned off his t-path again.

Despite protestations from Moller and Nintuk, all of them now on their feet, the Rathas diplomats hastened to the door. Grufhand and Dominact carried expressions of dismay, while Leaderlist led the way ranting about traitorous actions and betrayal of trust. The contingent swept out the door and disappeared.

The Tileus people remaining in the room burst into heated conversation.

Governor Thranadil shook her head. "There goes our chance for trade. Our economic base will be ruined."

Secretary Nintuk turned to Moller, her face filled with ire. "That was an extreme reaction, Welton, and it looked orchestrated. As if Leaderlist had planned it."

"You're right, Susanna." The governor turned to Jake, his normally warm eyes filled with steel. "What happened, Jake?"

Jake remained sitting, his mind racing. What could have caused a lack of synchronization on the personal unit? Suddenly, he knew.

He jumped to his feet to answer Moller. "Something jammed the system, sir. Something they brought with them." He had a sudden, wide-eyed realization and his mouth dropped open. He clamped it shut again and closed his eyes. "Randy Princeton. This was his doing."

32 – Stellar Opportunity

Following its initial success in Tileus, expanding knowledge of the transpath to other countries and other worlds became essential. The new empathic technology could have only limited effect until all of humanity used it.

—The Making of a New Humanity by Ellen Thranadil, Tileus Press 448 A.T.

Coordinator Deniz Serban sat in his raised, padded chair behind the bridge crew of the speedship *Orca Three* during the approach to the planet of Verdant. They had traveled for two months to get here from Brightness, their home planet, on this first leg of their colonization recruiting trip. Serban had high hopes for the future of humanity and for the results of this trip. After visiting Verdant, they'd also go to Newland before returning home to finish fitting out the much larger colony ship *Orca Blue*. The ship had been named for the stirring opportunity to start a new human world named Bluewater.

Subdued conversation filled the quiet bridge. The air smelled of aromatic oils from home, a reminder of what they would soon leave forever. The colorful uniforms of the watch standers made Serban smile; color brightened and made cheery a space that would otherwise be dull and grey. The color also contrasted nicely with the brown skin of the colonists. While a few Brightness people had fair coloring, most displayed dark eyes and black hair like Serban himself.

Automated systems handled the orbital insertion around Verdant. Coordination with planetary authorities, centered in Verdant Prime, cleared their path.

Serban turned to the speedship captain, Cohar Derian, who sat beside him. "Cohar, what be you thinking of our chances here on Verdant? With this new declaration of war, be we finding welcome or rejection here?"

The captain rubbed his chin. "Not knowing, friend. The situation be similar to that twenty-one years ago on Branch, before they launched biological war that did extinguish their entire planet. Verdant be nearing its end, like so many other planets have done."

"Will their problems make people want to leave, to join us on a new world?"

"Maybe. Or maybe they will bring onto the *Orca Blue* their same problems."

The *Orca Blue*. Serban had overall responsibility for the huge effort of shepherding humanity to the new world of Bluewater. His leadership team had decided to extend the invitation to all three remaining human worlds: Brightness, Verdant, and Newland. He hoped with all his heart they would launch Bluewater in such a way it would not deteriorate into warfare in a few hundred years. Human technology offered so many paths to global destruction, Branch being the most recent example. He shuddered to think of what war could do.

The captain spoke again. "We will know soon, Coordinator. Entering orbit in an hour, then our staff will start working with the country of Tileus for our first presentation."

"Do you still agree Tileus be the proper starting point of the four countries?"

"Yes, I do," said Derian. "We did be monitoring the political situation for months. Verdant Prime be too controlling and difficult. The religion in Rathas be off-putting to the other countries. Winter lacks technology. Tileus be open. They also be fragmented and unruly, but I think our people can work with them."

Serban nodded. He had his hopes, but he also shared the captain's doubts about working with Verdant. This world seemed so far down the path to destruction that coordination would be difficult.

❧ ✳ ❦

"A jammer, Zofia. They brought a t-path jammer." Jake fumed while he paced her office. "It must have been Randy."

"Yes, he escaped to Rathas. That makes sense. But how did he get the resources to design and build one so fast?" She rolled her eyes in sudden understanding. "Oh. Leaderlist. How duplicitous. The man rejected our t-paths for the whole country, but he must have one of those Randy stole from us. Then he brought Randy in to build a jammer."

"And what else might Randy build? If Leaderlist accepts the use of a jammer, might he not also be using those prototypes Randy stole from us?" Jake pounded a fist into his palm. "Damn. We should have had him arrested right away. I took him out of the building instead and let him go."

"Yeah, but I told him to get out. Beating ourselves up about the past won't change it, Jake. What can we do about the jammer? Can we defeat it?"

"I don't know." Jake shook his head. "It's so difficult to synchronize the particle waves to make the t-path work at all. Jamming it is easy. I can think of a dozen ways to disrupt the t-path signals. We'd have to get hold of one of his units to find out how it works. Is it okay with you if I talk with Mos and give him some ideas?"

"You bet. Then you get back to marketing. We'll have to stay ahead of Randy now."

Jake closed his eyes. Just what they needed, a competitor at this critical stage.

"And talking of marketing," she said, "have you heard the news about the Brightness colony ship?"

Jake stopped pacing and looked up. "No. What's going on?"

"A ship arrived in orbit this morning, while you were in the meeting. They're recruiting people from all three worlds for a new colony. A public presentation tomorrow evening, here in Thad City, will tell everyone about it. I think it might be an excellent opportunity to spread the t-path to the other planets."

"Interesting. I like the idea. Let's go."

❧ ❋ ☙

The following evening, Jake and Zofia went to the Eluxor Hotel for the presentation. Jake had never been there. The opulent resort hosted political rallies, indoor concerts, and high society.

Entering the hotel proved a problem. A protest group had already gathered across the street, marching back and forth and waving signs denouncing humans desecrating another virgin world. Thankfully, Tileus laws kept them on the other side of the street.

Zofia nudged Jake's elbow. "We can cross the street here to avoid them. How do they gather so fast?"

"Any issue, Zofia. There's somebody in Tileus ready to protest any issue."

The presentation filled the gaudy Earthrise ballroom, boasted as the largest room in Tileus. The hotel prided itself on its immersive experience. The walls displayed a continuous Earth sunrise over snow-clad mountains. Crystal chandeliers refracted dancing rainbows around the room. The air carried the scent of pindel forests and ocean breezes, while quiet music filled the background.

A thousand people packed the place. Jake nudged Zofia while they found seats near the front. "Look at the backdrop. They've got pictures of the new world. And there were samples in the back of the room of plants I've never seen."

"Settle down, Bucko," she chided. "It's exciting, but we're here on business."

"I don't know. The more I see, the more thrilled I get. A new colony is a big deal."

An older man with charismatic authority took the podium. Obviously from Brightness, because everything about him differed from Verdant norms. He spoke Standard with a distinct syntax. The bold aqua and purple in his clothing clashed.

"Good even, all," the man said. "I be Deniz Serban, and I be coordinator for the Bluewater colony. My confrères," he gestured to the six others on the stage, "be here to tell you of our plans. We hope many of you with us will join."

Jake leaned forward to view the large holo behind the man showing the image of a blue-green world surrounded by distant stars. Overlays showed graphics and information. The world had characteristics suitable for humanity—a larger world with heavier gravity, much slower rotation than Verdant, and year about the same length.

"Bluewater be our new world," said the coordinator.

Over the next hour, Jake listened intently while Serban and his team told them about the colonization. The planet promised an excellent new home. Air and water were within human range. The important plants humanity used could grow there. Bluewater did present some challenges. Native plants grew aggressively and some produced airborne toxins.

"However," Serban hastened to say, "the search team did find some controls effective; they did clear a ten-kilometer area where they could go without protection. They be confident the same techniques will make large areas livable. Over decades, the toxic plants can be brought under control."

Serban showed videos of the planet. Four major continents divided vast areas of ocean. The largest continent had more land area than the entirety of the planet Verdant. Bluewater's sun, further down the main sequence, shone with a reddish tint, creating unusual colors. The scenes were spectacular, an untouched world with natural beauty.

Zofia leaned over to Jake. "It's beautiful, but we can't leave our business. If we introduce them to the t-path, though, they could take it back to Brightness—and on to Bluewater."

"That would certainly move our dream forward."

After the presentation, Zofia pushed her way to the front with Jake following. They waited in line to talk with the speaker. When their turn arrived, she edged Jake forward.

"Coordinator Serban," he said, "my name is Jake Palatin. We have some new technology that may be essential for your Bluewater initiative, technology that will help your colonists understand and get along with each other during your voyage and colonization. We'd like to meet with you tomorrow. Is that possible?"

The next morning, the two returned to the Eluxor to meet with Serban in his spacious top-floor hotel room. Serban rose from a comfortable seat to greet them. Close up, the man's features looked like people on Verdant with only slight differences—bushier eyebrows, longer ears, a wider mouth. He wore even more colorful clothes than last night, bold yellows and oranges interlaid with purple bands. The room carried a strange sweet scent.

"Thank you again," said Jake. "I know you're busy, so I'd like to show you what we have without delay. We think you'll find it nothing short of incredible." He held up one of their units. "This is a transpath, a device that allows people to sense each other's emotions."

The coordinator blinked, raising his head. "Feeling other's emotions?"

"Yes, sir," answered Zofia. "Our devices are spreading here in Tileus, and they do what we claim."

Jake waved at the t-path with his other hand. "We developed this technology a year ago. The t-path has proven itself time and again in business and government, smoothing interpersonal communications by allowing people to understand each other at a deeper level."

"A year ago?" Serban raised a finger. "Be this related to the near-war incident between Verdant Prime and Tileus? We do follow the news from your planet."

Jake had never considered these people from Brightness to be aware of politics on Verdant. He glanced at Zofia, who looked as startled as he. "Uh … yes, sir. We developed the t-path specifically to affect the pre-war negotiations last year. It successfully stopped the war." Recovering himself, he added, "That's how good this device is."

Zofia asked, "May we show you, sir?"

"I be willing," said Serban.

"This is a special unit, sir. Our current production devices require you to be alone to personalize the unit to you. This one personalizes by being close. If you'll hold it about ten centimeters from your head and press this button, it'll work just for you."

Serban cocked his head but acceded. When the t-path activated, surprise flooded his features.

Through his own t-path, Jake sensed the coordinator's curiosity and interest—then the man's startled reaction to sensing Jake's own eagerness. Serban regarded Jake intently, taking in his emotions, then turned to Zofia, reacting again to the different emotions the coordinator saw in her.

The man straightened in surprise. "You be right. Incredible. I feel your excitement, your competence, your honesty. The possibilities be immense. How we will be getting this technology for Bluewater?"

"We're manufacturing them now, sir," Jake said. "I'm imping you a link to full information. We'd enjoy giving you a tour of our facility if you have time. In addition, we can give you a set of samples, as many as you wish, to take with you back to Brightness."

"Samples be an excellent idea." Serban kept looking back and forth between Jake and Zofia, impathing the emotions. "We don't have time for a facilities tour, though. Our plan be to make presentations in your four capital cities, staying a few days in each. Unfortunate it be, however, that Rathas has declared war. Did you not use the transpath to solve this conflict?"

Zofia put a supporting hand on Jake's shoulder.

Jake lowered his eyes and took a deep breath before looking up again. "We tried, sir, just yesterday. The Rathas people created something to defeat the t-path effect. We still hope the t-path may bring the negotiators together again."

The coordinator rubbed his chin. "So. There be a way to block the effect. Have you a solution?"

Zofia said, "Not yet, sir. We only discovered the problem yesterday. But we're working on it."

"So, more development be needed. And manufacturing on Bluewater." The coordinator cocked his head and pointed at the two. "Be you two willing to go with us?"

Jake stiffened. *Go on a colonization voyage?* He and Zofia looked at each other. His surprise and shock echoed in Zofia's wide eyes and in her pathed emotions.

Serban chuckled. "Your answers be evident in your emotions, my friends. We'd like to have this technology. Do come with us."

33 – Shaky Experience

How big does a miracle have to be for people to recognize it as a miracle?

—*History of the One Church* by Ellen Thranadil,
Tileus Press 445 A.T.

Morat Vengeact had been in army training for ten days. He hardly believed the change in himself. Chemical augmentation had accelerated the growth of muscle bulk, toned further by constant extreme exercise. Forced learning through his imp and a brain stimulator had given him knowledge he'd never expected to need.

"Hey, Corp," called out Private Manmove. "When do we form up for graduation?"

Oh, yes, and Morat had also been promoted to corporal of a fireteam of four men. He checked his imp. "In another two zero minutes, Manmove. Get your gear." He triggered his imp to the entire fireteam. "Graduation is in full gear, men. Get it together."

"HUNH," they responded in unison. He'd made that up, and it worked.

He shook his head, occasional bewilderment coming over him.

Morat no longer recognized himself. Basic training had been brutal—and very effective. He'd never considered himself an athletic man, so his new conditioning and build filled him with pride. He could run five hundred meters in full gear, drop to a prone position, and fire his weapon without pausing. Not only that, but he could hit his target.

He drove himself to excel in the combat training. He wanted nothing more than revenge, to exact vengeance on the Tileus people for their complicity in what had happened to Faï. She had become the rallying cry for the entire army, the proximate reason for the upcoming war. He'd become famous in his battalion for his close relationship with her. Morat knew Faï to be only one example of the abuse Tileus people had heaped upon missionaries for years. Yet she was *his* example.

Morat yearned to start the attack. Rumor said they'd do it within days.

❧ ✳ ☙

The final stage of Fenet's pilgrimage, from Artha to Praise, moved as slowly as the glaciers in the northern Gortooth fjords. Fenet and the Khadam had only advanced a hundred kilometers in three days.

People crowded everywhere they stopped, hope filling their souls. Fenet's heart went out to the masses clamoring for healing—of broken limbs, broken hearts, and broken machines—wanting to fulfill the Third Pillar of caring for the needy. Excited but orderly, the multitudes gathered ahead of them, awaiting the simple hoverbus carrying the promise of better life. The country of Rathas had always had faith, but Fenet's Khadam transformed faith into reality by their health-giving restoration.

The novim? They rode high on the exuberance of their service. Fenet himself found that taking leadership fulfilled him, too. Each time he guided the Khadam to do something worthwhile, he found satisfaction in doing Elláh's will. This pilgrimage did more to uplift Fenet than all of his twenty years of being a channel for local miracles around Glorify.

The surrounding farms had given way to suburbs—housing developments, churches, clots of tall buildings, industry. Ground traffic impeded their hoverbus on every major road, and the air teemed with vehicles flying in all directions. Scent in the air changed from manure and animals to industrial reek. Despite the masses of people, the normal order and politeness fostered by the Church prevailed.

Fenet pointed ahead toward an open square surrounded by twenty- and thirty-story buildings. "Here's another town center coming up, Pincely. People are already queued."

The large Eregim tapped on the rail in front of his seat, a nervous gesture that had become more common as his impatience increased. "Is this trip ever going to end, Fenet? We set out to do a pilgrimage to Praise, and we're getting close. Can't we just press on?" He spoke in subdued tones.

Fenet chuckled and brushed his long grey hair off his shoulder. "As you've said many times, Elláh has His own ways. Be patient, my friend. We'll find out what He wants of us when we get to Praise. It's only another fifty kilometers."

"Sorry about that, Fenet. I think sleeping in the bus last night made me grumpy." Eregim stretched his shoulders. "Not to mention a morning washup in a town park restroom."

"I'm sure we can find a Church hostel in the outskirts of Praise for tonight."

More leadership. While Pincely drove toward the city square, Fenet pulled *The Holiest* out of his back pocket, looking for support and comfort in the role. He turned to a well-worn page and re-read the passage: *Leaders should pardon their followers, ask Elláh to forgive them, and consult with them.* Humility in the face of challenge. A good reminder.

Pincely brought the bus to a stop. Fenet put his floppy flowered hat back on his head, hefted his healed staff and pulled himself up to stand. His hips had worsened again. *Be the leader, Fenet.* He raised his voice. "It's a beautiful morning for miracles, boys, and we've got opportunities in front of us. Let's do it again."

❧ ❈ ❧

By an hour later, with the novim healing townspeople, Fenet needed to sit. Standing too long made his hips ache.

He rested on a park bench to pray and watched Scanat. The nov still did his self-assigned job to bring special supplicants to the other novim for healing. While the day wore on, however, Fenet noticed an anomaly. From the beginning of this journey, a few miracles hadn't happened. Elláh always controlled it, and sometimes He had different plans than immediate healing. What Fenet observed today, though, went beyond a few. Perhaps a quarter of the supplicants Scanat brought received no miracle.

Did Scanat's use of the t-path suppress miracles? Did Scanat perhaps misread the supplicants? Were the novim less able to channel a miracle for a supplicant brought to them by someone else?

Fenet turned to Eregim. "Something strange is happening around Scanat again."

Eregim started awake. "What? Oh, sorry, Fenet. I was dozing. This may be the last warm afternoon we'll have this fall, and I've been enjoying it."

"I've been watching Scanat, and I'm puzzled. Quite a few of the people he brings forward receive no miracle."

Eregim sat up and shook himself awake, his eyes seeking Scanat in the packed square.

Fenet's vision of the crowd suddenly blurred and the bench started to vibrate. Forgetting Scanat, he cocked his head. "Do you feel that, Eregim?" Fenet put a hand on the wood slats of the bench. The throbbing continued, followed now by a deep rumbling sound.

"Yes," said Eregim. "That's strange. What—"

Abruptly, the entire bench slid sideways. Eregim fell off his end; only Fenet's hand gripping the bench kept him in place. More than the bench; the entire world moved around them. The crowds staggered as one. Half the people lost their balance and fell to the ground. Shouts and wails filled the air.

"Earthquake!"

Most of those who had fallen stayed down. Others started running, staggering through the crowd like erratic goats. Toward what? Fenet had no idea.

The towering buildings swayed like grasses in a non-existent wind. Fenet hung on to his bench with a desperate grip. He saw waves of motion move across the buildings from right to left. Windows broke. Huge sheets of glass fell from the buildings. People below screamed. Fenet stiffened, watching death gather speed in the air. Long moments of severe shaking tested his grip on the bench. He extended a hand in a vain attempt to stop the tumbling glass.

The sheets hit the square, shattering on impact. Thousands of shards spewed outward. None of the glass flew as far as where Fenet sat. Near the buildings, though, the sharp edges wrought carnage through the crowd. Many people died in the instant. Others lost arms and legs. Fenet gasped when blood sprayed in all directions. Piercing screams tore at his heart.

Time dilated. Seconds of reality became minutes of destruction. Fenet hung on to his bench for dear life. Eregim struggled twice to get up from where he'd fallen.

As suddenly as it started, the quake stopped. The groaning of the earth and splintering of glass gave way to sharper screams and cries from the people. Fenet recovered on his bench; the thought of trying to stand again left him breathless. All around the square, the sound of fear rose in a collective screech of agony.

GATHER THE KHADAM. NOW.

Fenet jolted when the voice resounded in his head. Jumping to his feet, he swept his arms toward the novim and shouted as loud as he could, "To me, Khadam. Join me!'

Apparently, the novim had also heard from Elláh—all but Scanat, who was lost somewhere in the pandemonium. The rest were already on their feet and making their way toward Fenet with shaky steps.

"We're coming, Reb Fenet," called Tenpos, his deep voice carrying through the clamor.

They were halfway to him when the ground rumbled again. A deep, threatening sound felt more in his gut than his ears. Gasping, Fenet flopped onto the bench. The novim broke into a run. The ground slewed violently under them. They fell like toppled tenpins.

"Keep coming, boys. Gather to me!" Fenet knew Elláh had some good plan. He needed to follow it.

The noise of the quake assaulted Fenet's ears. The novim crawled toward him. None could stand. One by one, they gathered. The bench swept from side to side.

More than glass started falling. The infrastructure of the buildings began to fail. Plascrete, bricks, and blocks fell from upper stories. They filled the air with deadly hail toward the helpless crowds. Moaning and cries changed to desperate screams. The ground itself groaned in echoed agony.

NOW JOIN HANDS AND PRAY.

Fenet, Eregim, and five novim—less Scanat— sat on the ground. They clasped hands in a circle. The quaking ground threw them left and right. Holding each other with a tight grip became the only way to keep from falling over.

"Lord Elláh, save your people!" shouted Fenet over the clamor. "Not for us, but for them."

The falling masonry neared the ground. Deadly missiles loomed seconds from crushing hundreds of people.

"Amen," chorused the others.

"Help them all," added Tenpos.

The quivering air around the Khadam turned thick and blood-red. It filled the space between them, under them, and over them.

Darker than any manifestation Fenet had seen, yet it excluded Fenet. Then tendrils of the visible color exploded to spear outward in all directions. The congealed, spiritually-charged air gripped masonry in midair. The falling missiles stopped, holding their threatening positions as if by magic.

"Save," shouted Penilos.

"Protect," cried Beneim.

The plascrete and blocks started to rise. So did the glass. Heaved upward by the red manifestation, the materials accelerated into the air back to their original positions in the buildings. Glass sheets reassembled from shards. The towers swayed themselves back into position. Masonry and glass knitted back into place. The ground held still.

Fenet's mouth fell open. He gripped the hands of Tenpos and Beneim on either side of him with all his strength, somehow also feeling the grip of all the others as an unbreakable ring. This miracle loomed bigger than anything he'd known.

"Good Lord," he breathed. "What have You done?" Forging, purifying again, Elláh now showed them the possibility of collective miracles.

He lowered his eyes to the crowds on the ground. People were rising to their feet. Brushing themselves off. Smiling. No dead lay mangled on the ground. No blood showed anywhere. A few individuals still cried, but the wails of the injured and mutilated were gone. No one seemed to be badly hurt. How could this be?

Fenet whipped his head back and forth, looking at everything, and jumped to his feet, pulling the others up with him. Amazed, he discovered no pain in his hips at all—yet another miracle in the midst of the rest. The Khadam stood and raised their linked hands to the sky.

"Praise Elláh," shouted Fenet.

The others echoed, "Praise Elláh!"

Eregim displayed a look of pure wonder. "I took part. I felt that miracle work."

Fenet shouted to the sky and the crowds, "Look what Elláh has done. He stopped the earthquake. He repaired the buildings. He healed the injured. He used us as His vessels for the biggest miracle Verdant has ever seen."

A man in the crowd, standing nearby and brushing himself off, stood up straight. "Don't get too full of yourself, old man. It was just a little quake."

Fenet shared a shocked look with Eregim.

"Little quake?" asked Fenet. "What about the blocks falling from the buildings?"

"What blocks?" The man waved a hand upward at the towers. "Everything's still up there, ain't it?"

Eregim asked, "How about the glass and the casualties? Didn't you see the healing of those masses of people?"

Another man, standing beside the first, spoke. "What healing? What casualties?" He looked around the square. "Do you see anyone hurt? I don't."

The first man laughed in derision. "Hurt people. Right."

"Of course not," said Eregim, agitated. "We healed them all. And the buildings, too. Didn't you see all that? The quake was huge."

"I don't know what you people are smoking," said another. "One little shake, and you think you've healed people and buildings? Charlatans, that's what you are." With a dismissive wave of his hand, the man walked away.

A Heresy Angel watched the interchange, head tilted, eyes boring into Fenet's. The man said nothing.

"Th-they don't believe us," said Lorefim.

Penilos said, "Didn't they see what we saw?"

Fenet turned in a circle, taking in the whole square. People going about their business. A few queues reforming for the touch of the novim. A blue sky, with clouds sliding by like cotton fluff. Tall buildings standing as firm as ever. "Elláh, what just happened?"

Life continued like normal—except the pain in his hips had gone.

34 – Empathic Colonization

Businesses reach growth plateaus. The characteristics that feed growth in each prior phase become the restrictions to cause the next plateau. One of the hardest plateaus to get past is when the owners must let go of direct control to foster the next growth.

—*The Making of a New Humanity* by Ellen Thranadil, Tileus Press 448 A.T.

Jake laughed when he stepped into Zofia's office. He held what looked like a small version of the t-path. "One day's all it took, Zofia, just one day. Gotta love technology development. Sometimes it's so frustrating as to consume your mind. Other times, it's a breeze."

"What are you talking about?" Sitting at her holo desk, Zofia wrinkled her eyebrows.

"The jammer. I talked with Mos yesterday about it. We tore our hair out and couldn't figure out how to stop it. Just too many ways for Randy to disrupt the particle waves, and we don't know which method he used."

"Yeah, I checked with Mos after your conversation. He still struggled for ideas."

"He had an epiphany last evening. A different solution. This, my dear," Jake waved the device around, "is a jammer *detector*. It won't stop the jamming, but at least it lets us know when it's happening and where it's coming from."

"A detector?"

"Yep. All Mos had to do was create the particle waves, then see if he could also receive them. If a jammer's operating, it'll disrupt the connection. Then he added a function to test the connectivity in all directions, to see where it's worst."

Zofia rolled her eyes. "Of course. How simple."

"I've already gotten us another appointment with Deniz Serban for this afternoon, to tell him about this solution. Wanna come along?"

"You bet. But what are we going to tell him about his offer for us to go with them?"

Jake winced. "I'm not ready to pull up stakes and go to another planet. Particularly a new one, where people still have to carve a safe place for themselves."

"I'm not either. Do we know of anyone we could send?"

"No, we don't. Our employees are the only ones with knowledge so far." A wave of anger washed up in Jake. "And since Randy turned on us, we need everyone we've got."

"Well then, Bucko, we'll have to find more people. It's time to expand. Maybe Serban can help us recruit suitable candidates for training from the other planets."

≈ ❋ ≪

A long maghrib prayer and comfortable night's sleep in the Artha hostel did little to ease Fenet's confusion. When he woke the next morning, his head still spun with perplexity. How could such a huge miracle happen, and the people who received the boon not even know it happened? Did the miracle also erase their memories?

Fenet looked around the bunkroom. Rumpled bedclothes. Familiar packs on the floor. No one else here. He'd been so exhausted last night he'd not seen the room. No one had any energy to talk about the day. A few had showered; most had just crashed.

Durnadat walked in rubbing his head with a towel. "Reb Fenet, everyone else is already up and headed to breakfast." The nov grinned. "But trust me, you'll want to take a shower first. After our camping, it feels like pure luxury." The plump young man did one of his delighted spins.

Despite Fenet's bewilderment, he couldn't help but smile. "I'm glad we have this place for the night."

"You did good, Reb. Thanks." Durnadat pulled on his underclothes, wrapped himself in his robe, and tightened the cincture that had been presented to him at his novitiate. "I'll see you at breakfast." Laying the towel over a rack, the nov left.

Leadership's not so bad after all. When I get it right, the appreciation's a reward in itself. Fenet picked up his towel and headed for the shower.

Later, Fenet joined the Khadam at breakfast at a table large enough for all nine. He set his tray in the place they'd reserved for him with Eregim and Pincely at one end of the table. "Good morning, boys. How's everyone doing this morning?"

"S-still puzzled about y-yesterday, Reb." Lorefim said.

Beneim nodded, his eyes outlined by dark circles. "Yeah. I was so tired last night, I fell asleep right away. But this morning, I can't stop thinking about it." He ran his hand through his red curls. "It just doesn't make sense."

Fenet called out to Scanat at the other end of the table. "I'm very sorry you couldn't join us to be part of that amazing event, Scanat."

Scanat sighed. "One more missed opportunity, Reb. I was too far away in the crowd to get back in time."

"It might have been the chance for you to take part in a big miracle. Your turn will come." Fenet gave him an encouraging smile. "I'm sure."

Eregim set his fork down. "But what about yesterday, Fenet? The people around us didn't see what we saw. How could that be?"

"I'm as puzzled as anyone," said Fenet. "I've been wondering this morning whether *we* all saw the same thing. How about it, boys? I saw the buildings falling down, people killed and maimed by falling glass, blood all over the place, and then a red ... mist? I don't know what to call it. The manifestation stopped falling blocks in mid-air, reassembled the buildings, and healed the people. It even brought those killed back to life." He searched the faces in front of him. "Now tell me. What did you see?"

Penilos' eyes darted from nov to nov. "That's what I saw, too, Reb. And when it ended, no one was hurt and the people thought it had been only a mild shake."

"Wasn't it amazing? Awesome," breathed Durnadat.

Tenpos nodded. "Truly incredible."

"But all of you were part of the circle," said Fenet. "What about you, Scanat? What did you see?"

Scanat lifted his shoulders, his eyes amazed yet sad. "I saw the same thing, Reb. And right afterward, most of the people were talking to each other about how lucky they'd been they'd had such a small quake. Except ..." Scanat tilted his head, bewilderment on his face. "A couple of people not too far from me talked about the miracle. They saw the buildings fall apart, they saw the pieces reassemble, and they couldn't understand what had happened. Other people laughed at them."

Eregim huffed. "Well, that's good to know. At least some of the people saw what we saw. Could you tell what difference existed between those who remembered and those who didn't?"

"No, Reb, I couldn't. I did notice the ones still talking about the miracles seemed eager to get back in line for healing from the Khadam."

"Maybe it's a matter of faith. Those with stronger faith still remembered?" Eregim shrugged, then turned to Fenet. "Where do we go next?"

"On to Praise, my friends. Elláh willing, we'll get there today."

☙ ❋ ❧

When the door opened, Jake followed Zofia into Coordinator Serban's hotel room at the Eluxor. Once again, the outlandish color combinations on Brightness people struck Jake. Today, Serban sported a green-and-yellow striped shirt under a bright red jacket.

They'd decided Zofia—as VP of Development—should tell the colony leader about the jammer detector. Jake would follow up with more about interplanetary distribution.

While they shook hands, Serban brought up a piece of news. "Did you hear of the earthquake yesterday afternoon near Praise?"

Jake looked at Zofia. "No, sir. Quakes are rare on Verdant. A little more prevalent around the Gortooth Mountains, but still rare. Was it bad?"

"We did be wondering whether Verdant be tectonically active. What be most interesting, though, be the conflicting reports on it."

"Conflicting?" Zofia asked.

"Some witnesses did be claiming it a mild quake, not worth reporting. Others did be saying it a disaster, with buildings falling down and hundreds of people killed."

"Not so unusual, I think." Zofia said. "These witnesses were in different places, right?"

"No, that be the unusual part. They did be reporting from the same location. Someone claimed it be a miracle from Elláh. The ground shook so violently buildings did be falling, but then it stopped and the buildings was repaired in moments."

Zofia traded a glance with Jake. "Well, it would indeed be a miracle if it happened. But others said nothing like that occurred?"

Serban shrugged. "Those be the reports, yes."

"It'll be interesting to find out what really happened. In the meantime, we have some good news for you," Zofia said. "We've found a solution to the t-path jammer from the other morning."

Serban lifted his head, looking surprised. "Just since our meeting yesterday? I do know something about technical development. How did you be having success so fast?"

"It was a combination of Jake's knowledge of particle physics and a most creative engineer on our team. Stopping the jammer is impossible without knowing what method it uses. However, our engineer created a way to detect and locate the jamming, so you know when it's happening and who's responsible."

Serban pursed his lips and nodded approval. "Good solution. Knowing of the interference be nearly as powerful as stopping it."

"That's what we thought as well."

Jake stepped into the conversation. "We're very keen for Brightness, Newland, and now Bluewater to know about and use the transpath, Coordinator. Are you and your team favorable enough to take samples with you?"

"I did talk about it with my team. I with them shared my astonishment. We be all quite favorable. But we also have a couple of questions."

"We can answer them," said Jake.

"First, we like to know what different versions you be having."

Jake nodded. "A reasonable question, sir. The one we demonstrated to you yesterday is our newest, a t-path that personalizes by proximity. It locks onto one user, and provides empathy for that person. As you saw, it's small enough to carry on a belt or in a pocket. When we demonstrated it to you, both Zofia and I had such units."

Serban nodded. "And other versions?"

"The new version will replace our current personalized version. The current version has the same functionality in the same size, but requires a more rigorous personalization procedure.

"The first type was a fixed installation suitable for a conference room. It provided multi-way empathy for all people in the room. As with all the versions, individuals focus on another person by looking at them. When they do so, they can feel that person's feelings—like you did yesterday. Familiarization happens quickly as our brains learn to interpret the new sense. The room-sized version requires some larger equipment and a cloud of nano-processors in the air."

The coordinator rubbed his chin in thought. "Fine. I understand our options. The most recent personal unit sound like the best choice for us. It be something we can both to Brightness and Newland take samples. In the next months, before our colony departure, we can decide what to do about Bluewater. So, how many samples can you be providing?" asked Serban.

Jake chuckled. "How many would you like? We'll give you half again that many."

The coordinator laughed. "You two must be eager."

"We are." Zofia joined the laugh. "We have a dream of all humanity understanding each other. Maybe we could stop destroying our worlds. Business considerations fall second to our dream."

"Would two hundred samples be too many?" asked Serban.

Jake smiled. "Let's make it three hundred—a round hundred for each planet."

The coordinator turned serious. "Which brings me to the most difficult part. Each planet will be needing manufacturing and distribution. Travel times of several months between planets be preventing a central distribution from here on Verdant. You will need knowledgeable people on each other planet."

"We've thought about that problem, too," said Jake. "Brightness and Newland can select people to our qualifications and send them here for training. We'd love to set up related businesses on each planet."

"But what about Bluewater? I still be thinking we need someone to go with us. If not you two, then who be that person?"

35 – Treachery Revealed

A stern vision is told to me; the traitor betrays, and the destroyer destroys.

The Holiest, book of Isaiah

Quiet had fallen among the Khadam after their awe-filled conversation about the earthquake of yesterday. Fenet looked around at the members of his group; each one knew the depth of being Elláh's vessel for amazing works. He touched his healed walking staff, leaning against the chair beside him. His hips had no pain this morning, not a twinge, another part of the big miracle. He would no longer need the staff, but he'd keep walking with it as a memory of Elláh's grace. A smile ghosted across his lips.

Fenet lifted his hand for attention. "Boys, we have no idea what Elláh will do with us today. He told us to make pilgrimage to Praise, and our journey should complete today. Join with me to ask His guidance."

The group joined hands around the table.

"Dear Elláh, we follow only You. We've always known of Your power and Your eternal grace. Yesterday, you showed that incredible power. You've led us over hill and valley, through joy and fear. You've used us to heal people and to stop an earthquake. Now we near the end of this journey. I'm sure You have a plan that goes beyond today, a reason for this pilgrimage that will fill us with awe. We wait upon You to reveal it."

He paused a moment mid-prayer, remembering the beginning of this trip. Penilos, the youngest of his novim, had first spoken Elláh's command. The thought of walking seven hundred kilometers had daunted Fenet, an impossible task for a crippled man. Then Elláh had provided Pincely and the hoverbus.

"Elláh has given us much to be thankful for." Fenet raised his hands, taking Eregim and Pincely's hands upward with his. "Selah."

The Khadam echoed, "Selah."

Fenet stood, amazed at how easily his body worked. He brushed a few crumbs off his tunic and picked up his staff and floppy hat. The yellow *astradell* from the hills above Netweaver shone as fresh as ever. "Then let's get to it, boys."

ᘓ ※ ᘔ

Scanat stood with the others. He'd joined them in prayer, and it touched his soul. A part of him still wanted very much to be a member of the Khadam, yet he knew his betrayal had already separated him. He turned on his t-path, checking the emotions of his friends, looking for approval and fearing condemnation. None of them yet suspected what he'd been doing.

He took a deep breath and followed them out.

A message from Captain Forsfear came into his imp. Scanat stopped walking in fright. The captain had not mistreated him during the arrest in Center, but he knew how violent and dangerous Forsfear could be. Scanat's trepidation continued to grow. He regretted signing the agreement, but what else could he have done? Every duplicitous action he took since then, every kilometer closer to Praise, brought him nearer to being exposed for the traitor he'd become.

Useful information so far. Guide your heretics to Church Center One.

Scanat remembered a part of the agreement required him to take the group to a designated place. The captain now prepared another arrest based on the evidence Scanat had provided. Scanat paused and closed his eyes for a moment, girding himself to do what he'd agreed, reminding himself of the prize: a return to tertiary school despite his age. He acknowledged the imp message.

How could he convince Reb Fenet to take the Khadam to Church Center One? An idea came. He hurried to join the others leaving the refectory, so as to speak to Fenet right away.

Following his friends, Scanat's heart felt like a glacier frozen between impassable mountains. They walked in happiness. He did not. Their second arrest loomed, and none of them knew.

⁂

Fenet strode confidently on the way out to the bus. His body felt healthy for the first time in several years. Buoyant and joyful, he looked forward to whatever came.

The novim shared his ebullience. Behind him, Penilos said, "How about a contest today, Durnadat? I'll bet I get to heal more people than you do."

Durnadat gave a merry laugh and swayed his bulk back and forth. "You're on, little boy. Count 'em up."

Fenet spun with a grin, emulating one of Durnadat's pirouettes. "Contests, boys? You're feeling that confident? Life might be good today, hmm? We'll see." He winked and turned forward again when Pincely opened the hoverbus door. Fenet stood outside the door, encouraging each nov while they climbed aboard. He patted shoulders, spoke to them, laughed with them. Leadership duties. Today would be the day Elláh would make His purpose clear.

Scanat stepped up last. "Reb Fenet, can I sit beside you up front for a moment? I've got some information for you."

"Certainly, Scanat." A surge of warmth swelled Fenet's breast. Scanat had isolated himself so much such a request pleased Fenet. "Join me." Maybe the young man would come out of his funk.

The two boarded the bus and took their seats. Pincely checked everyone on board, then drove away.

Eregim, sitting across the aisle, looked at Scanat with raised eyebrows.

Fenet smiled back at Eregim, then gave his attention to Scanat. "Thanks for joining me. What kind of information do you have?"

"I talked with people in the crowd yesterday," Scanat said. "They told me about Praise and what to expect." Usually confident, the young man avoided Fenet's eyes, picking at threads on his robe. Obviously still uncomfortable.

"Sounds like good preparedness." Fenet wondered what the young man had to say. His manner spoke of some secret. However, his reticence might be that he felt defeated. The events of the last few days had been hard on Scanat.

"They said the best place for us to offer miracles in Praise would be the large park in front of Church Center One. The highway goes right downtown. There's an area just in front of the building where people gather to pray."

Fenet turned to the driver. "Pincely, what do you think? Have you been there before?"

"Sure have, Reb. He's right, it's be a good place. Lots of room. And as filled with faith as any place can be."

Eregim reached from across the aisle to touch Scanat's shoulder. The nov jumped. "Is there something more, Scanat? Something you need to share?" Eregim had also picked up on the nov's nervousness.

Scanat shook his head quickly. "No. Just that the people I spoke to …" his voice faltered, "thought the location would be best. I think they're right. That's where we should go."

"Then that's what we'll do," said Fenet, cocking his head at Scanat's strange behavior. "Maybe you'll get your chance for a miracle there."

"Maybe, Reb. I hope so." Scanat lifted his eyes. The young man's normal confidence warred in them with some sorrow. Then he abruptly stood and made his way to his usual seat in the back.

Eregim watched him go, then leaned across the aisle to Fenet. "Strange behavior," he murmured. "Can we trust him?"

Fenet shrugged. "It's as good a place as any, and should have the benefit of being visible. Going to the very center of Praise sounds appropriate. If we can also encourage Scanat, that's a good thing."

While he said the words, his mind went back to how Scanat had come out of the jail in Center with no injuries. Why would that memory come to him now?

≈ ✳ ≈

The roadway to Praise became wide and busy and now had limited access, bypassing other town centers where people might have gathered. This final leg would pass quickly, putting them into the center of the capital city without delay. Anxiety crept into Fenet's heart as he considered what Elláh might ask next. If Elláh used them to quell an earthquake, what else might He do with them? The Church still disbelieved Elláh's miracles; perhaps they would change that attitude. War with Tileus loomed within days. An InfoNet rumor said a colony ship had appeared, recruiting to populate a new world; would a miracle help the colonization? The t-path technology Scanat had brought might transform them all, if Elláh wanted it to.

He had no idea what Elláh's plan would be. It might be for any of these—or for something else, perhaps something very local and not world-shaking. Waiting on the Lord required faith, but often also brought the temptation of unease. Fenet had done more than his share of waiting.

Pincely pointed behind them. "That there black car with the Heresy Angel is still followin' us, Reb."

Fenet glanced out the rear window and confirmed it. "Thanks, Pincely. They will do what they will do. Elláh's in charge."

After passing a series of off-ramps, the broad highway ended in the midst of city streets with twenty-story buildings. Pincely pointed ahead. "That open area about ten blocks ahead, Reb. That's the main square. You can just see the white marble walls of Church Center One."

Fenet leaned forward. "I've never seen it before, except in pictures."

"I was here once," said Eregim, a touch of awe in his voice. "It's a spectacular temple."

The conversations in the bus quieted while they made their way through a series of traffic controls. As each block passed, the opening in front became wider. Fenet watched the autumn sun shine full on the façade of the majestic building. Six stories of white marble glinted with gold trim. Statues of prophets lined alcoves like soldiers of the Church. Four minarets at the corners reached high, overtopped by a central dome and towering spire that held aloft a gold statue of the archangel Israfel blowing his horn.

"Wow," whispered Lorefim behind Fenet. "That's impressive." For once his voice held no stutter.

Pincely pulled the hoverbus to a parking area near the front and settled it to the ground. People had already gathered, though Fenet didn't know whether they came to meet his Khadam or to pray at this central shrine. Some nudged others and pointed at the bus as if they recognized it.

Fenet stood in the quiet bus. "Boys, this may be the end of our journey. Only Elláh knows for sure, and He hasn't told us yet. We'll do what we've done, and we'll wait on Him to—"

Movement caught his eye. The black car that had followed them had just pulled in behind to block them in place.

The door suddenly slammed open. Black-garbed Heresy Angels pounded stuncheons on the sides of the bus. Fenet's heart raced at the unnerving clatter. Three Angels charged onto the bus. They shoved Fenet aside and stormed down the aisle. Angels struck their clubs on the shoulders of several novim. The third and last stopped at Fenet's seat. The huge man's head brushed the roof of the bus. His shoulders filled the aisle. The scowl on his face spoke volumes of contempt and control.

Farther back, Beneim and Lorefim cried out in pain when the second Angel slammed his stuncheon from one to the other.

"Out!" the Angels shouted. "Everybody out. End of the line."

"What's going on?" demanded Fenet.

"You're all under arrest for sedition and heresy. Get out now." The Angel nearest him whacked Fenet across the shoulder blades.

Fenet bent forward, his bones bruised, and his floppy hat fell to the floor. He started to pick it up.

The Angel flipped his club in an uppercut to Fenet's chin. "Leave it. You won't need it where you're going."

Fenet's jaw exploded in agony. Was it broken? He stood again, heart pounding, and held his jaw. No, not broken, just badly bruised. He said nothing, just grabbed his staff and made his way off the bus. Behind him, the Angel shoved Eregim, who fell down the steps into Fenet. The impact of his friend's large body tumbled them both to the ground with tangled limbs and jarred elbows.

Pincely rushed off the bus and helped them both up. "We'll straighten this out again, Reb."

Before Fenet could find out how badly he and Eregim were hurt, Heresy Angels pulled the three apart.

"No gathering. No talking."

An Angel yanked Fenet's hands behind his back. His staff clattered to the ground. Tanglecuffs secured his hands. His chin throbbed in time with his back. Each heartbeat pounded pain into his bruises. Now his knee and shoulder, scraped by the fall, joined the cacophony of damage.

Heresy Angels dragged each nov away when they stumbled off the bus. Even the muscular Tenpos had no chance to resist.

"Hey," shouted Durnadat when they grabbed him. An Angel drove a stuncheon into his ample stomach. Durnadat doubled over.

Two more Angels pulled him forward to fasten his hands behind his back. Durnadat gasped for air.

In less than a minute, the entire Khadam stood cuffed and helpless. Yet the Angels continued. They positioned steel collars around each man's neck and fastened them with electronic padlocks. A muzzle and gag dangled from each collar. A moment later, an Angel shoved the gag into Fenet's mouth. He tasted the foul tang of leather composite. The muzzle held it in place, straps over his mouth and nose, fastened behind his head.

"Wouldn't want you heretics chanting any magical incantations now, would we?" sneered the Angel while he buckled it, yanking the muzzle tight against Fenet's face.

The Angels pulled steel chains from a box. They linked the collars together, person to person, with the chains. Another chain went to the front of Fenet's collar, with its open end clanking on the ground.

It all happened so fast Fenet had no chance to think. The muzzle obstructed his peripheral vision like blinders on a pack animal, so he had to turn his entire body to see anything. The crowd had backed away as soon as the Heresy Angels appeared. The people now stood, watching, expressions torn between outrage and horror. Two voices spoke out against the treatment, immediately falling silent again when the Angels threatened them.

Fenet's face flushed as he realized what a horrible sight he and the others must be to this crowd that had anticipated them. He, Eregim, and the novim formed a ragged line, linked two meters apart by the chains. Each one collared and muzzled, they looked like a pack of feral dogs being led to a kennel.

"Well, and here we are again." The sneering voice rang loud. Captain Forsfear strode past the other Heresy Angels to stand in front of him. "Released and recaptured, *Reb* Fenet, like fishing in a preserve. This time with more ... *evidence*." He leaned in to emphasize the word.

Fenet remembered the overheard conversation in the Center jail, the raised voices through the interrogation mirror, and Forsfear releasing them for lack of evidence. What more evidence could they have gathered?

Forsfear shoved his stuncheon into Fenet's chest, causing him to stumble backward. "We'll take you and your crew of heretics inside in a moment, Powrfaith. Before that, we're going to make sure the public knows your true worth."

The captain turned to shout at the crowd. "Citizens, good Church members, we level the charge of heresy against these charlatans. Heresy is serious, not just because of what it does to the heretic but because of what it does to the faithful. They've been deluding people from Glorify to here, claiming miracles that could only have come from Saitan. Fenet Powrfaith and his people will be stripped of their ministry and purged to cleanse both them and the Church."

Forsfear turned back to Fenet with a wicked smile. "Oh, I almost forgot. We also need to thank the one responsible for your capture."

The captain stalked past Fenet toward the bus. Pincely still stood by the front of the bus, unbound and looking bewildered. Yet Forsfear ignored him and waved a *come-on* gesture toward the door. Scanat came down the steps, his body posture screaming reluctance and shame.

"Thank you, my boy," said Forsfear in a voice loud enough for the entire Khadam to hear, as he shook hands with Scanat. "Your information and recordings have been invaluable. You have earned your payment."

36 – Uptown Down

The biggest problem humankind faces is the power of our weapons. We can't seem to stop fighting, whether over territory or ideology or resources. For centuries, our weapon technology dominates our existence. When war breaks out, we destroy our worlds.

—*The Making of a New Humanity* by Ellen Thranadil, Tileus Press 448 A.T.

We've got to do something to stop Randy." Zofia paced the floor of the police conference room, her voice as agitated as her gestures. She'd made a special trip to meet with Soren Moller. He'd cleared her past the desk sergeant and into the utilitarian conference room.

"Sorry, no jurisdiction over there," Soren said. "We've put in a diplomatic request for extradition, but it's up to them. And Rathas has declared war on us. They're not likely to honor the request."

"You don't understand, Soren. It's related to the war. Randy created a t-path jammer, and it blocked the Tileus governors from being able to negotiate out of this war."

"Yeah, I heard about that from my father. He was pissed."

"We don't know what Randy will do next. He's damaging our entire plan for the transpath."

Soren shrugged, one of his gestures that irritated Zofia.

"Can't you send a police force over there to capture him or something?"

Soren flipped his head as if surprised. She didn't think she'd ever surprised the detective before. "You've got to be crazy, Zofia. Send a force of our policemen into another country? With a war looming? Come on, get your head on straight."

She stopped pacing and hung her head. "Yeah, I guess you're right. We had hoped so much the t-path would stop this, like it did last year."

⤸ ✳ ⤷

Morat Vengeact sat with his entire forty-man platoon inside the belly of a jump-vee personnel carrier. Hundreds of identical jump-vees lined up on the pavement of the Khubar f'Elláh base outside Praise. Each vehicle flew as an armored box using repellor beam propulsion, bulging with beam weapons and filled with death in infantry platoon form.

Morat crowded face-to-face sideways with all the others on four benches running the length of the vehicle. Shoulder to shoulder, knees interlaced with the man opposite. No room to stretch, not enough to move. Encased in a steel cocoon. He'd already become used to the smell of ozone from the powerful repellor propulsion system. Hot inside the jam-packed vehicle despite the cool fall weather, sweat poured from Morat's face and he tried to keep his thoughts positive.

Their attack on Uptown would commence in moments. As a corporal, Morat had leadership of a fireteam of four holy soldiers. The shoulder of the youngest, Private Grinhand, pressed against Morat's.

"What's it gonna be like, Corp?" Grinhand asked, his voice shaky.

What the hell to answer, when Morat had never done this before? "We'll find out when we get there, Grinhand."

He clutched his weapon between his knees. What a weapon he held! It could fire heavy duty flechettes that ripped through a body like the five rows of teeth on a slasherfish. It could operate as a beam weapon, projecting short bursts of directed energy powerful enough to burn through a half-centimeter of steel—and the entire thickness of a human. It could also throw fragmentation grenades a distance of seventy meters. The kit on his harness included five grenades and five hundred flechette rounds.

The jump-vee lifted from the ground, a swooping motion that swayed the entire platoon as one. Someone across the way cried out in surprise, getting an elbow in the rib in response.

"Settle down, you grunts," growled Staff Sergeant Pushman. "Focus on what you're gonna do when the hatch opens. Get out fast and spread by squads. That's the only thing that matters. Put everything else out of your minds."

Morat trusted Pushman, their platoon sergeant. The man had never been in a full-scale war—none of the Khubar f'Elláh had—yet he was a veteran of a dozen punitive skirmishes with Verdant Prime, Tileus, and Winter. He'd seen combat. Morat's platoon leader, a lieutenant who rode in the jump-vee bubble with outside view, had no such experience. The lieutenant, however, did have extensive training in tactics and military capabilities.

The flight over the Gortooth range took a mere twenty minutes. Morat's skin crawled with anxiety. He didn't know whether to look forward to combat or to fear it. Probably both. His responsibility as a fireteam leader added to his anxiety. Would his fireteam make it through unscathed?

He couldn't see out of the jump-vee, but Morat imagined the infantry carriers in tight formation growling along at treetop level over mountains and down into valleys. It would be a sheet of steel death undulating over the terrain. He'd love to be able to see that sight, a demonstration of Elláh's tangible power. Instead, he was an integral part of it.

"Thirty seconds, men. Get ready." The voice of the lieutenant came through imp.

Explosions sounded in the air around their jump-vee, loud enough for Morat to hear over the roar of the vehicle. With a final swoop, the infantry carrier grounded. The entire front of the vehicle, a single armored door hinged at the bottom, dropped to the ground as a ramp.

"Go, go, go," shouted Sergeant Pushman.

The platoon raced to move. Starting at the front of the jump-vee, men stood and rushed forward. Morat and his fireteam, Squad Three Blue, had to wait until Squads One and Two went out. The wave of movement sped back toward him. A few seconds passed before Morat and his team jumped up like the rest. Several enemy rounds zipped in the wide front hatch while they waited, ricocheting around the metal box with a loud clatter. Staying inside would be a death trap.

"Blue team, move it! Now!" he shouted to his team.

They responded in unison, "HUNH!"

Private Gutstrong added, "Let's get 'em, Corp."

The fireteam answered with another, "HUNH!"

Banter made for a good sign. His team worked together.

The platoon fanned out while it bolted from the vehicle. Morat and his Blue team peeled off to the right, joining Red and Green to make up their fighting squad Three. Glancing to his right and left, he confirmed the two other jump-vees of Company Bravo had grounded in line abreast and also disgorged their platoons.

Something whizzed by Morat's ear. "Hit the dirt, Blue!" he yelled, echoing the words through his imp.

His team flattened on the ground, weapons forward, looking for the enemy. Blazing metal zinged overhead, coming from somewhere in the trees ahead of them, across an open field. Morat couldn't see the location of the enemies firing at them. Repellor beam weapons had no muzzle flash.

Private Manmove fired twice.

"Whadda ya see, Manmove?" Morat demanded.

"Movement, Corp. In those trees."

"Keep a watch, team. You see something, take it out."

Squad Three leader, Sergeant Headwary, organized directions through imp. "Three Red, advance *now*. Three Green, be ready. Three Blue, cover fire."

Morat passed the command on to his team. Staying prone, they fired flechettes into the area below the trees while team Three Red rushed forward. Bark and leaves scattered with each hit, but they didn't see any enemies in there.

Huh. The open field where they'd landed looked like a normal sports field. Ordinary and prosaic, now a battlefield. Trees surrounded the field. Beyond that, roofs of shops and homes looked like a neighborhood. Taller buildings of a city center showed over the tops of the trees. From the pre-brief, their entire Company Bravo targeted a communications center five hundred meters away.

"Three Red, cover fire. Three Green, advance." With short intervals, squad leader Headwary commanded a rapid pace of advance by fireteams.

When their turn came, Morat raced his team forward. They covered fifty meters in a breathless eight seconds. Throwing themselves prone again, they resumed firing on the trees while Red jumped up to advance. Grinhand sounded like he was hyperventilating, but Morat's team remained intact despite incoming fire.

A jump-vee growled overhead. Rathas or Tileus? The vehicle blasted the trees with its beam weapons, setting the upper foliage ablaze. Then it veered off behind them. Ours.

A sudden explosion detonated thirty meters in front. Morat ducked his head. Pebbles clattered against his helmet. As soon as it ended, he resumed firing. They weren't close enough yet to launch a grenade to the trees. Another advance might do it if they pushed it. They had to get through this resistance and make it to the comms center before the Tileus forces brought reinforcements.

"Blue team," he barked through his imp, "We'll go farther next time. Close enough for grenades."

"HUNH," grunted his team, to which Grinhand added, "Love it, Corp."

When their turn came, Morat jumped to his feet at the instant Headwary gave the command. He raced like a longcat, holding the advance for a count of twelve instead of eight.

"Three Blue, whadda ya doin'?" came from Headwary.

Morat snapped an answer. "Grenade range, Sarge."

His team stayed with him. Just before diving for the ground, something thumped Morat's left shoulder.

He ignored it and grabbed a grenade from his belt. He shoved it onto his weapon's muzzle. "Three Blue, spread grenades." Center man of the five, he aimed straight ahead. "Ready ... Fire!"

Morat hadn't bothered to check their readiness. He trusted his team. They did well. Five grenades launched within a half-second, arcing across the field toward the trees. The explosions boomed. Flaming branches blew off the trees. Body parts flew outward from the cover.

"Squad Three, charge!" shouted Headwary.

The squad of twenty vaulted to their feet and raced the remaining distance to the trees. Some sporadic firing faced them, hitting no one.

Morat sprinted past the first trees. A line of a dozen Tileus soldiers had been shattered by the grenades. Only five still remained active. Morat and his fireteam took them out with flechettes.

"Re-form the line," came a command from platoon Staff Sergeant Pushman. "Advance at quickstep."

Morat checked his fireteam. They were still with him, in formation, ready to go. "Great work, Blue. Let's keep on." He set the pace to match the rest of the squad.

True to his powername, Grinhand gave Morat a broad smile that faltered when the private looked at Morat.

"Hey, Morat," said Manmove. "Didja know you're bleeding?"

Morat looked down at his left arm, where he'd felt something earlier. A projectile had pierced through his deltoid. He'd hardly noticed.

❧ ❀ ☙

Two hours later, Company Bravo had secured the comms center. Specialists entered the building while the grunts—Morat's team included— took defensive positions outside.

The specialist team shut down the normal Tileus programming and filled the airwaves with demands for surrender. Prepared messages flew outward to the city of Uptown and the entire country of Tileus, extolling the success of the Khubar f'Elláh and declaring a new set of morality for Uptown.

Medics dressed Morat's shoulder wound and wanted him to retire to the field hospital. He refused, wanting to stay with his unit. Eventually, they approved. An ointment held the pain to a faint twinge, and he had near full movement of his left arm. Lifting the arm higher than his shoulder wouldn't happen in the next few days, but he could still do what he needed to do.

Morat and his fireteam held a defensive position between the comms center and the tall buildings of Uptown city center. The strategy assumption from above claimed any counter-attack would come from the city center, because that's where the transit lines met. Morat wasn't so sure. He'd seen flying vehicles crisscrossing in multiple directions. He had to believe Tileus better prepared than he'd seen so far. They'd found a plascrete drainage ditch, three meters wide with sloped sides, that made a perfect defense.

Staff Sergeant Pushman strode up behind their position. "Corporal Vengeact. Where are you?"

"Here, Sergeant." Morat raised his hand, keeping his eyes on the perimeter.

"I came by to say well done this morning. Headwary told me about your fireteam's extra push. You men cleared the way for the whole company. That resistance might have stopped our advance, and you broke it free. Might be a holy medal in it for you."

Morat flashed a smile. "It was the entire fireteam, Sarge. We did it together." The other team members were all grinning.

"Yeah, but you led them," said the sergeant. "Nice job. I understand you also took a round, but kept going."

"Sarge, what do you hear about the other targets?" The question came from Grinhand, still a gung-ho blond boy of seventeen.

Sergeant Pushman nodded. "We did well. Alpha Company secured the government buildings and Charlie captured the power utility plant. Delta's still fighting their way into the transit hub. We've just about got this city sewn up."

"Incoming," shouted someone from the adjacent fireteam.

Everyone, the sergeant included, hit the ground. A Tileus aircar dove toward them out of the afternoon sun. Energy beams blasted from its bow, streaking across the field toward their emplacement.

"Holy damn!" Morat yelled. "Beams! Give it everything you've got." The flechettes would be useless against a vehicle. The hand-held beam weapons wouldn't be much better, but they had to try.

Manmove yelled wordlessly at the aircar while swiveling his beam all around it.

The incoming beams, much more powerful than their hand weapons, swerved as the vehicle twisted in the air. The aircar came directly toward Morat, who kept firing at it. Ten meters in front of him, the beam veered to his right. It raked across Private Grinhand, disintegrating his body from head to hip. Sweeping further right, the beam slewed across fireteam Three Green, hitting every member, then ranged back to take out Staff Sergeant Pushman. The entire incident happened too fast to believe. Morat's jaw dropped and he stopped firing, appalled at the sudden carnage.

The air vehicle pulled up and away, wheeling for another approach. Morat raised his weapon again and aimed at the fast-moving target. He couldn't tell whether he hit anything at all.

Suddenly, a powerful beam shot down from above. It hit the enemy vehicle dead on, and the car exploded. Pieces of shrapnel tore outward, winging their way to the ground in wide curves. The concussion hit Morat and drove him into the plascrete. The air stank of hot metal.

Morat had heard rumors of orbital weapons stations. Now he knew they existed.

37 – Midnight Event

The wonder of the One Church rested in the record of miracles performed by Muhamet, Jaysus, and Hindu believers. After more than two millennia, that wonder had faded. More miracles would be needed to rekindle it.

—History of the One Church by Ellen Thranadil,
Tileus Press 445 A.T.

Fenet's teeth clamped on the composite leather gag. The combination of muzzle and gag made him lift his head to breathe. His mouth filled with acrid saliva he swallowed with difficulty.

The crowd in front of Church Center One drew back from the spectacle of seven ministers chained together like slaves of old.

Forsfear strode back from congratulating Scanat, picked up the end of Fenet's neck chain, and dropped it onto a hitch on a small hoverbot. "We'll be taking you inside now, Powrfaith. Whether you come out again depends on your humility."

The captain picked up Fenet's walking staff and laughed. "Oh, look. You fixed it. More black magic arts. You might be needing it, right? Of course, it's not very useful with your hands cuffed. So, you'll just have to limp along without it."

The hoverbot slid forward to pull him by the chain. Fenet stumbled, and Forsfear gave him a whistling smack across his rump with his own staff. Behind him, Eregim and the novim cried out while the bot dragged them along. With hands bound behind him, Fenet struggled to keep his footing. He prayed no one would fall.

Scanat had not been bound and gagged. Instead, Forsfear thanked him. Fenet turned to look back at the young man. Scanat still stood by the bus looking shattered. What had Scanat done?

The Heresy Angels formed lines on each side of the shamed, bedraggled crew. Captain Forsfear led the way beside the hoverbot, not bothering to look behind.

Suddenly, someone behind Fenet screamed through his nose, a terrible wrenching sound. The chain went taut. Pulled forward by the hoverbot and yanked back by whoever had fallen, Fenet nearly fell also. He pushed forward and upward to help whoever had gone down, and gave thanks for the new strength in his hips. He twisted his body to see.

Penilos, last in line, dragged full-length on the paved path. The boy scrambled with his legs and feet, trying to find purchase to stand. In front of him, Beneim strained to keep his own feet.

With expressions of disgust after several moments of dragging, two Angels stepped in to haul Penilos back to his feet. The boy whimpered through his gag, tears streaking his cheeks. He followed Beneim with a limp.

Instead of aiming for the main entrance to Church Center One, Forsfear took a path around the right corner of the building. The hoverbot continued at a steady walking pace, down a set of stairs to a basement entrance. Four Angels moved forward to lead the group through the door.

Inside, pale green walls and a bare, composite floor presented an institutional look. The spartan surroundings looked nothing like the grandeur of Church Center One. Halfway down the hallway, one of the lead Angels unlocked a door on the left. He leaned hard to open it; the door must have been heavier than most. The hoverbot led them in.

Fenet's heart stopped in his throat. Torture equipment filled every space of the large area. They crossed the room to a door on a side wall, but the few short steps destroyed the little ease left in his soul. Devices loomed massive and threatening. A rack with motorized draw wheels, a spiked iron maiden, a Spanish donkey to split the body from below. Others, just as menacing, were more obscure. Some had modern computer controls and obvious electrodes.

The devices filled Fenet with horror, even more so because he had no idea Rathas possessed such things. A morbid curiosity rose within him about those he did not recognize; he shoved aside that repellent reaction. The room smelled antiseptic, but a darker, foul odor lingered. Making it worse, none of the equipment looked like museum pieces from centuries before. All of it shiny, new and well-maintained, a modern Verdant Inquisition.

Forsfear opened the side door, just as heavy as the first, and led the way into another hallway. Plascrete walls held barred doors. Bare floors gathered dirt in the corners. With his mind in shock from the devices in the first room, Fenet tripped on the threshold of this obvious dungeon. Two Heresy Angels kept him from falling, their fingers digging into his arms.

Fenet wanted to ask about the torture equipment. He wanted to know why, who it had been used on. The gag left him helpless to do so.

At the end of the hallway, Forsfear opened the last barred door. Beyond it, a large round cell with scarred walls showed itself as the end of the line. A strong smell of sewage slapped Fenet in the nose.

"Welcome to your future, heretics," Forsfear sneered. "You'll stay here until we're ready for you."

Angels unfastened each chain from the person in front, refastening them to rings set low in the wall around the room. The captors made no attempt to remove the muzzles, gags, or tanglecuffs.

"I'm sorry there's no furniture," mocked one Angel when he attached Fenet to the wall. "You'll just have to sit on the floor. Hope its comfort is to your satisfaction."

The Angels left, all but Forsfear.

"I don't know how long we'll be," he scoffed. "We'll try to take care of you when we find the time." He looked at Fenet's staff, still in his hand. "Oh, by the way, I brought this for you." He laughed and threw the staff clattering to the floor at Fenet's feet. With that, Forsfear left and slammed the door. A loud clack announced the lock engaging.

Still standing, Fenet looked around at Eregim and his novim. Six pairs of terrified eyes looked back at him. He suspected his own eyes showed the same.

Leadership. He turned to examine the space. Bare and utilitarian, the cell stretched five meters in diameter. By extending their chains to full length, each prisoner could just reach down a slight slope to the cesspit in the center. He had difficulty breathing with the muzzle over his nose, yet the stench of the open pit filled Fenet's head. No windows broke the grimy threat of the plascrete walls. A metal cage adorned the single light fixture in the center of the ceiling. Grit on the floor scuffed under his shoes.

Now he saw Penilos, Fenet's heart went out to the boy. Penilos' robes were ripped from the knees down and had scuffs around the hips, all from being dragged. His scraped bare knees oozed blood.

They all watched Fenet for guidance. The untenable responsibility of leadership weighed on his shoulders. Yet Fenet had been learning, through incident after incident, Elláh's purifications did indeed lead to better. He took a deep breath and chose to believe in Him once again.

The chains were too short for Fenet to reach Eregim opposite him, or Penilos and Beneim fastened adjacent to Eregim. With hands bound, gag in place, and a hated muzzle, he could do little to succor his group. Yet Fenet still guided the Khadam. He moved toward the center, extending his chain, and gestured with his eyes and head for the others to join him. They nodded and also moved toward the stinking center. In a moment, all seven stood in a circle as close together as they could.

Fenet closed his eyes and raised his face toward heaven. He couldn't talk, but he intoned a common hymn through his nose. Others of the circle joined him. At the end, he lowered his face and nodded acquiescence.

He gave a great sigh through his nose. Then he shrugged and moved back to the wall. He settled himself to the floor. The others followed suit. Fenet leaned against the wall, closed his eyes, and prayed silently.

⁂

Hours passed, Fenet's imp marking the slow minutes. The facility blocked InfoNet access, so he had no idea what happened in the world outside. Had the war started? Did someone oversee Forsfear's excesses?

Fenet's shoulders cramped. He tried lifting them, squeezing them back, pushing them forward. Nothing eased the spasm. Over time, the demands of nature began to bedevil them all.

Penilos whimpered while he squirmed. The boy finally stood up, moved to the end of his chain, and squatted over the edge of the cesspit. With some difficulty, Penilos used his hands to lift the back of his robe. Fenet closed his eyes rather than watch. Sooner or later, he would also suffer the humiliation of having to relieve himself without the ability to remove his pants.

After a time, the door clacked open and a single Angel came in. The man said nothing, though the disgust in his curled lip spoke of the unbearable reek in the room. He moved from prisoner to prisoner, releasing both their cuffs and their muzzles. When he got to Penilos, the Angel pointed at the boy's damp, torn robes and shook his head with a sneer.

Immense relief washed over Fenet when the Angel released his hands and muzzle and pulled out the gag. The muzzle and gag dropped to his chest, still fastened to the steel collar.

"May Elláh bless you," Fenet rasped, his throat sore. "Thank you for this relief. What happens next?"

The Angel snorted and moved past Fenet to Tenpos, saying nothing. When he had released all of them, he left and locked the door again.

"Reb," demanded Lorefim, his coarse voice filled with anger, "H-how can you d-do that?" The young man had never before spoken this disrespectfully to Fenet. "They've ch-chained us, shamed us, b-beaten us, d-dragged poor Penilos on the ground, and you *thank* them?"

Fenet shook his head with a sad smile. "What would you have me do, Lorefim? Rail at them in anger? I would fill with the negative spirit of Saitan, and only give them satisfaction. Plead for mercy? They've shown no indication of mercy, and doing so would only affirm their power. Curse them in the name of Elláh? Evil from Elláh comes from each person's own choices, not from someone else cursing them. By blessing him, I've given that Heresy Angel insight into Elláh's grace and mercy."

Across the room, Eregim coughed when he tried to speak. He cleared his throat. "Let me repeat Lorefim's question to you, my friend: how can you do *that*? In this situation, in the midst of this filth, how can you still maintain your peace enough to teach these novim?"

Fenet shrugged and gave a quiet laugh. "It's what I do to follow Elláh. I've been learning, during all this pilgrimage, more about being a teacher and leader."

"The bigger question," said Tenpos, his voice raw, "is what are we going to do?"

Fenet started to speak, then had to swallow and clear his abused throat. He raised a finger, pointing above. "As always, we will wait on Elláh. We can talk about possibilities, and we can plan for contingencies, but His plan will be greater." Fenet stretched out to retrieve his staff from the floor. He pulled the staff back against his shoulder—a source of spiritual comfort—and settled against the wall. "So, what possibilities are there?"

Two days later, Fenet and his people still had no good answers. The Angels left them chained to the wall, living in the stench of their own effluvia and the grit of the floor. They did what they could to observe salat. Twice a day, a silent Angel brought them enough bread to ease their hunger for an hour and a few swallows of water to slake their thirst. Once during those two days, the Angel brought two bowls of rancid, congealed slop for the seven of them to share. Only Fenet's aching hunger allowed him to force down the gobs of unidentifiable meat.

The Khadam knew nothing of outside. Their world constricted to five meters of round cell, collars and shameful dangling muzzles, and their empty bellies. A single harsh light illuminated the cell night and day. Their imps showed the slow passage of time. Their second midnight in this cell approached.

"We've mostly avoided talking about the hooliphant in the room." Beneim had found a pebble that he scratched on the floor. "There's someone missing here. What did Scanat do?"

"He turned us in to get arrested again." Penilos' bitter voice sounded as raw as his scraped knees. They'd scabbed over and no longer bled.

Looking in the boy's eyes, however, Fenet saw his soul still oozing pain.

Lorefim clanked two pieces of his chain together, an angry sound. "W-why go over it again? What m-more can we say? We know w-what he did. What makes you th-think we can find something new?"

Fenet's hips were still clear of pain, but the stress of these two days—physical, mental, and spiritual—beat him down. Yet he still had leader responsibilities. "Pray, boys. Pray for peace in your souls. Pray for Scanat. Anger serves no purpose unless it is Elláh's righteous anger."

Durnadat slumped against his segment of wall. "We've been praying for two days, Reb."

"Elláh has been guiding humanity for seven thousand years," Fenet answered. "Two days seem long to us, but they are a wink of a blind bat's eye to Him." He looked around at the despondency in all of his crew, and his heart ached. "Another three hours have passed. It's time for all of us to pray together again. Please slide forward so we can join hands."

Several novim grumbled this time. With each passing hour, their faith weakened. Yet they obeyed, each one moving far enough they joined hands in a circle. A sickly thought struck Fenet: they gathered around the stench of the cesspit as if it were an altar. He set the image aside. *Elláh, keep my mind clear and my attitude on You.*

"Lord Elláh, we come to you again—"

The air thickened around Fenet. He found it difficult to take his next breath. He waved a hand in front of his face. It felt abnormal resistance.

Now, it is time. Elláh's voice sounded palpable in the room for all to hear. *Time for your next obedience.*

Fenet's heart lifted. He gripped the hands of Durnadat and Tenpos. They squeezed back. Another collective miracle in the making?

The air around the five novim became visible as scarlet swirls. It condensed into a thick column as it had during the earthquake, excluding Fenet. Delight and wonder filled the eyes of the novim. The column spun in the room, floor to ceiling.

Eregim called out, "Praise Elláh!"

While the column spun faster, it darkened to a deep burgundy. Then curved arms shot out to rap each collar. The end of each arm sparked a discharge of ruby color. The collars released and fell to the floor. The hated muzzles and chains dropped with them. The curved arms disappeared with a flash followed by a wash of ozone odor.

The column continued to accelerate, swirling around the novim and Eregim. A wind sprang up in the cell. Dust whirled around the group. Fenet's hair lifted, blown by the gusts. A roaring noise filled the room. A sense of danger closed Fenet's throat. He hunkered closer to the others, gripping their hands. Something clattered behind him, then he saw his walking staff whizzing through the air near the walls. The staff twisted around the room three times, faster and faster, whooshing as it spun. It grazed Durnadat's head. He clung to Fenet's hand while he ducked.

Now deep maroon, the column sent out a thick arm that grasped the staff. The arm whipped the staff through the space, driving it with incredible force into the wall opposite the door.

A blinding vermilion flash overloaded Fenet's vision. The blast hit him in the chest, flinging him onto his back. His hands were torn away from Durnadat and Tenpos. The air moved in mad patterns around him, laden with the acrid scent of broken and crushed limestone. Sounds of falling plascrete filled the room in all directions.

When Fenet's vision returned, clear night shone through an arched doorway in what had been a solid wall. The door edges sported glowing decorative carvings in the plascrete, including an intricate trifacis—Elláh's symbol—as the keystone. The smaller moon Silver shone over the buildings. The thickened red column disappeared. A gentle breeze from outside replaced the fetid air in the room with the fresh night scent of pindel trees. Piles of plascrete shards mounded the edges of the room; none had landed on the Khadam. Gradually, the glow in the decorative carvings faded away.

Fenet's staff clattered to the floor in front of the door.

NOW, FENET, GO FORTH AND STOP THIS WAR.

38 – Prodigal Discoveries

Sudden spiritual awakening is a tradition documented in the long history of The Church and its precursors, from the illiterate woodcutter Hui-neng to the apostle Paul.

—*History of the One Church* by Ellen Thranadil,
Tileus Press 445 A.T.

Earlier that same night, Scanat tossed and turned in bed. His shame-filled conscience wouldn't let him sleep. In his trying to regain a fulfilling life, his friends had been treated brutally—then Forsfear had landed the blame in public on Scanat's shoulders. His mind ran over and over the events of the last week, since the first arrest. *What else could I have done? Forsfear put me in an impossible situation.* No other solutions came to him.

He shoved the pillow into shape. Again. Rolling over to his stomach, he pulled it under his shoulder and closed his eyes. The bedding in this ministry hostel smelled old and rancid. Thoughts raced. Soon, his eyes opened again.

"Damn it all." He gritted his teeth to cut off the quiet exclamation, not wanting to disturb the other strangers in adjacent beds.

Could I have held off against Captain Forsfear? Not taken his offer? The man's threats had been as clear as the one-way glass in the interrogation room. Take the offer, or the consequences would redound back on Scanat. The physical damage to all the others testified to the reality of the captain's threats.

The man had singled Scanat out by treating him with kindness. When Scanat had gotten back on the bus, hale and hearty and undamaged, his different treatment set him apart. This past week, the others kept giving him suspicious looks. Or had he imagined them, in his own guilt?

Or, should I have stayed with the Khadam? What a useless proposition! Four years of his life wasted, trying to learn to do miracles. The most he'd ever done amounted to that strange voice back in Netweaver and the puzzling incident with the t-path switch, and he wasn't even sure whether either was a miracle at all. How do those compare with the Khadam stopping an earthquake and putting the buildings back together!

But not me. Never participated in a single miracle. Damn.

Enough. Tossing and turning in this stinky bed didn't solve anything.

Scanat got up and quietly dressed. He picked up his pack. The transpaths rattled against each other, and he sighed. Getting those had seemed like a worthwhile effort at the time. Now? *They separated me from everyone else.*

The kind proctor at the door looked at his pack with raised eyebrows. "Are you leaving us at midnight?"

Scanat closed his eyes. Wearing his robes felt like a sham, and staying in this hostel felt like cheating, because he wasn't a nov anymore. Not really. "Yes. I'm going to find someplace else to stay."

"Is there something wrong with the accommodations?"

"No, sir. The problem is me. Thanks for providing a place the last couple of days."

The thin light of Silver provided enough illumination to walk the streets toward the place of his shame, the location of his public humiliation. Scanat returned to the wide park in front of Church Center One. He'd been there several times each day since the arrest of the Khadam, trying to assuage his conscience.

At night, the park stretched empty, the benches and landscaping glowing pristine under the stars. Automatic lights hovered through the park, gliding under the trees, giving a peaceful shine to the grounds. His presence alone polluted the beautiful surroundings like a patch of offal.

Sitting on a bench near the building, the basement entrance accused Scanat, the one into which Reb Fenet and the Khadam had disappeared two days ago. They'd looked like animals, chained together.

And it had been his doing.

∽ ✳ ∽

In the suburbs of the same city of Praise, Randy Princeton also had second thoughts about what he'd done. Tonight, they kept him awake, running through his head like an earworm song. He had a comfortable bed, a snug apartment with nice appointments, yet the entire situation didn't fit right with him. He laid in bed, eyes wide, listening to the midnight church bells.

Shoras Guileart, whom he'd known as Johan Wellesley, had come through with everything he promised. Minister Leaderlist provided the money to get a new business started, even increasing the funding after Randy gave him the t-path jammer he wanted.

The start-up worked astoundingly well. In just over a week, he had a suitable building with office spaces and lab. Shoras helped him find three employees so far, people competent enough to design and build devices under Randy's direction and expertise. Three sufficed for now, as Randy built up new versions that wouldn't be copies of the TechEmpath units from Jake and Zofia.

But that named his problem: Jake and Zofia. After getting away, Randy's anger at the two dissipated, replaced by a growing sense of guilt. He'd never realized what they'd done in starting a business. The difficulty appalled him. With so many things to consider, he'd had to divert from doing the technical work he loved. The obstacles challenged him in new and uncomfortable ways. Randy had expertise in the field of particle physics, as good as Jake, but he ran up against his inadequacy in business management every day.

Had Jake suffered the same problem? Randy recalled Secretary Ellen Thranadil giving hours of her time to Jake and Zofia in this last year, helping them start TechEmpath. Maybe Randy needed a mentor, too.

The midnight church bells outside sent his thoughts in a different direction. Who rings church bells at midnight, anyway? Awkward in their religion, he had trouble interacting with his employees. They did what he asked, but he had the sense they considered him second-class because he wasn't part of the Church. That consideration colored everything here in Rathas. He'd known it existed, yet it wasn't until he arrived here that the pervasive nature of it came home. They stopped work at noon to lay down prayer mats—toward some imaginary place called Mecca or whatever—and prostrated themselves to pray. Randy couldn't imagine himself joining them. The separation from these religious freaks felt no better to him than his isolation at TechEmpath.

His new life didn't hold all the attraction he thought it would. Did he have any way to go back? Had he burned his bridges too far?

❧ ✳ ☙

Sitting on the park bench, Scanat closed his eyes and lowered his face. Thickness gathered in his throat. He fought a rising nausea. He couldn't pray. Somehow, he had to get past this shame. He thought back through the last four years and all the teaching he'd gotten from Reb Fenet. Over and over, the Reb had told Scanat to stop thinking so much and feel for a spiritual connection. This night, in the emptiness, he tried again to reach for that bond.

What should it feel like? He'd asked the question many times. Fenet told him to be open to feel anything Elláh may send his way. It had never worked for him.

Scanat scrubbed a hand over his face, then tried again. He relaxed his body as Fenet had taught. Starting with his toes, he let go of any tension. Then he concentrated in slow sequence on his ankles, calves, then thighs, easing the tautness in each limb. He worked his way up his body. When he got to his chest, he took a long, deep breath, then let it out completely. As relaxed as he knew how to be, he put every thought out of his head. When new thoughts intruded, he set them aside, too.

Night birds made occasional song around him. Something scurried through the bushes. The scent of pindel and acacia wafted across him.

He kept his eyes closed, body relaxed, and mind empty. *How silly is this? Alone at midnight in the park?* He let the thought go. Reb Fenet kept telling him to get his intellect out of the way.

Tenpos came to his mind. He pictured his friend's deep voice, green eyes, the only one of the Khadam who truly became his friend. A soft smile came to him. He tried to put the memory aside, as he had other thoughts.

What made me think of Tenpos? Scanat probed the thought. Strong feelings had come with it, similar to what he felt using the t-path. His friend suffered in terrible depression and discomfort, to the point of giving up on life. But he couldn't see Tenpos; impathing only worked when you looked at the person.

Whose feelings are these? Mine or Tenpos? What's going on?

Scanat lifted his head but kept his eyes closed. He continued to probe the feelings. His own shame and guilt were there, his desperate desire to get out of his dilemma. Separate from those were the feelings of pain, disgust, total defeat. Those weren't his, and they felt just like Tenpos. The reception seemed real and current, just like other impathed emotions. Scanat cocked his head; somehow the motion strengthened the feelings, like tilting an ear to a sound.

Abruptly, the emotions he attributed to Tenpos changed. The sensations became more peaceful, more surrendered, as Tenpos often did while praying with the group.

Is my friend praying now? How can I know this? Is my t-path working through the walls? Scanat became more certain he was indeed impathing from Tenpos. Somehow. Too familiar to be anything else, these emotions echoed what he'd received from his friend many times in the last two weeks.

Tenpos scintillated under the overwhelming strength of whatever was happening to him. The feelings took over inside Tenpos, becoming the totality of his being.

The strength of the sensations overwhelmed Scanat, also, but he recognized this, too. *Tenpos is in the middle of a miracle, a big one.* Scanat had impathed similar feelings when Elláh worked through his friends. Scanat sat straighter and his eyes popped open. He looked around the park, frantic to see something. Yet nothing had changed; everything looked as peaceful as before.

Yet he rode along with Tenpos in the all-consuming sense of awe while the consuming emotions accelerated. *How can Tenpos contain this?* For that matter, Scanat himself didn't know how to hold the awe of it. Then Scanat gained a sense of the others, all filled with amazement. Durnadat flinched at something with a wild moment of fright. Scanat's breath quickened. His head lightened. He seemed to be floating off the bench, though he still felt it under him.

A sudden red blast lit up the area near the basement door, flashing brilliant and dying again. A concussion sounded across the park, followed by the rattling sound of debris falling. Scanat jumped to his feet and froze.

A new arched doorway existed where the wall had been intact. An detailed, decorative opening, with carved edges and the Church trifacis prominent at the keystone. *An explosion created that?*

After a moment, Tenpos appeared in the arch, looking out at the Silver-lit night. Following him came Reb Fenet and the rest of the Khadam, their steps slow and tentative.

Scanat retreated behind a shrubbery. None of them noticed him. When he looked at each one, Scanat impathed their feelings—extreme weakness, fatigue, yet filled with wonder and amazement. Penilos came out last, his robes torn and knees scabbed. The boy seemed weakest of all, his emotions stretched paper-thin. Eregim supported him.

When they all reached the pathway, Tenpos turned to Fenet. "What now, Reb?"

Shame kept Scanat hidden, listening.

"You heard Elláh," said Fenet. "He's given us our next task—stop the war."

"I d-didn't even know the war had s-started," Lorefim brushed off dust from his robe.

Beneim ran his fingers through his red hair, smoothing it out. "Apparently so."

Scanat continued to scan the emotions of his friends, but it felt like spying while he stayed hidden. With his face burning, he reached in his pocket to turn off his t-path.

It was already off.

Scanat gasped. He'd been impathing the emotions from his friends while they channeled a powerful miracle. With his t-path off. Through the walls of the building.

Awe lifted his heart like the upwelling of life from a grave. Scanat sank to his knees on the turf. Elláh had finally granted him an undeniable miracle.

39 – Into the Mountains

Acceptance of the empathic technology that changed humanity seemed like climbing a difficult mountain. Some events moved forward smoothly, like the flat meadows on a level flank. Others challenged the participants to the extreme—perhaps all of humanity.

—*The Making of a New Humanity* by Ellen Thranadil, Tileus Press 448 A.T.

The night air smelled so fresh and clean, Fenet turned his face up to the stars to take a deep breath. What a relief from the fetid air of that dungeon. The stars laughed with twinkling eyes. At half moon, Silver made the shadows glow. Trees gleamed, underlit by the many floating lamps that wandered the park. His Khadam gathered around him outside Church Center One, blinking at each other in wonder.

"Shouldn't we get away from here?" Beneim growled. "After that explosion, the Heresy Angels might come after us."

Emotions still soaring, Fenet laughed aloud. "Are you speaking your fear, Beneim? After what Elláh just did, do you think it's His plan for us to be captured again?"

Tenpos spoke quietly. "What just happened amazed me, Beneim. I'm sure Elláh wants us to be free, praise Him."

Beneim glanced at Tenpos. After a moment, he nodded, a frown still on his face. "I guess you're right. But I don't want to go back there."

"We've g-got InfoNet access again," said Lorefim. "The n-news is bad. Our K-khubar f'Elláh attacked Uptown today. Or … I guess it was yesterday now. J-just on the other side of the Gortooth range. T-ten thousand holy soldiers supported by air forces and space-based b-beam weapons. They c-captured all the key centers in the city."

Durnadat added, "Yeah, I've been looking at it, too. Minister Leaderlist made the excuse that Tileus abuses our missionaries. A young woman was kidnapped and tortured, left to die in the mountains. Our security people rescued her, but they say Tileus blamed our own missionaries for the girl's kidnapping." He looked at Fenet, eyebrows furrowed. "How can that be?"

Fenet shrugged. "Politicians make wild claims when they want something." He noticed Eregim still supported Penilos. "How's the boy, Eregim?"

"He's pretty weak, Fenet. But he's young. He'd be back on his feet already if we'd been able to treat him." Eregim moved toward a nearby bench.

Instead of sitting, Penilos straightened and cocked his head as if listening. He nodded at something only he heard. Then he stood tall, pushing off Eregim's helping hand. Wobbling a bit on his feet, he put his palms together in front, them swept them gently outward, the same motion he'd used two weeks ago in the hostel at Glorify. He laughed aloud when he got the same response: scarlet air washed around him, then moved outward from his hands to flow past the Khadam. In its wake, robes puffed as if from a light zephyr.

A billow of air stroked Fenet's face. A tingle effervesced across his body. The foul odor of the pit disappeared in a fresh, clean scent. The filth encrusted on his pants and tunic vanished. His body gained new strength.

Penilos grinned. "Elláh told me to do that, Reb." The boy's robes were once again whole. "He even healed my knees." He lifted his robes and clean slacks to show whole skin.

"There's no doubt Elláh is more present with us now than ever before," said Fenet. "All the more reason for us to do His will. Let's hike over the mountains to Uptown. That's where the war is. That's where we need to be. It's another thirty kilometers." Fenet turned to the east and started them on their way.

"Wait." The deep voice of Tenpos stopped him. "There's someone watching us." Tenpos stepped off the path into a small copse. The park lights gave little illumination into the dark area.

A man knelt in the darkness. Fenet furrowed his eyes. *Kneeling? Is he praying?*

Tenpos stopped two meters short, his body posture screaming surprise. Then he rushed forward and dropped to his knees with the unknown man. Tenpos put both hands on the man's shoulders.

Puzzled, Fenet walked toward the trees. He sucked in a sharp breath and his body tensed. *Holy Elláh, that's Scanat.*

Scanat gripped Tenpos' arms. The young man shook, his muffled words rushing in abject apology. "I didn't mean for it to happen, Tenpos. I never thought it would be like this. Forsfear gave me no choice. I couldn't think of any way out. Oh, Elláh, I'm so sorry. So sorry ..."

Tenpos wrapped his arms around Scanat's shoulders and the stream of words trailed off. Scanat's whole body convulsed while he sobbed against Tenpos' shoulder.

"Scanat?" Raw accusation scraped in Beneim's shout. "He has the nerve to be here?"

"What?" said Penilos. "Scanat? No, that's not right. Not right at all." The young nov's voice resounded with anger.

Despite his own indignation, Fenet spun to face the rest of the Khadam. He interposed his walking staff to block their way. "Hear him out, boys. All we know is what Forsfear told us. Do we trust that man?"

"No, but we know Scanat did something." Durnadat stood his ground just beyond Fenet's staff. "And we've all suffered for it. Didn't he convince you to bring us here where Forsfear arrested us?"

Eregim answered for Fenet. "He did, yes." Eregim hadn't joined the heated anger of the four novim, but his expression showed seething discontent.

"Still," insisted Fenet, "we don't know the whole story." Though he'd stopped the novim, Fenet's insides roiled along with theirs. *What did Scanat do?* Elláh's way is one of forgiveness, but this would be a lot to forgive. Two days in that dungeon had been a nightmare.

"A miracle, Reb!" Scanat cried out from behind Fenet. "Elláh finally gave me a miracle."

Fenet swiveled again.

The young man's eyes were wide and his voice filled with wonder. "Just now, Reb. I impathed all your emotions while Elláh freed you. Through the walls, without seeing you." Scanat gasped. "And my t-path was off."

Fenet's heart froze, then soared. For four years, he'd tried and failed to guide Scanat into Elláh's ways. The man always stayed in control, never surrendering his entire self to Elláh. Yet here Scanat bubbled with the joy that comes from such a surrender. Forgetting the rest of the Khadam behind him, Fenet ru to Tenpos and Scanat. Settling his staff against a tree, Fenet put a hand on each man's shoulder.

"It's about time, Scanat. You finally let go, didn't you?"

Scanat looked up at Fenet and nodded. He glanced back and forth between Tenpos and Fenet, then gathered himself. "I owe you all an apology, Reb."

Tenpos snorted. "Perhaps more than an apology. We might need a full explanation."

"You bet we do," sneered Beneim. "How do we know this is real? Damn it, they broke my wrist back in Center because of him."

"Language, Beneim." Reaching out a hand, Fenet helped Scanat to his feet. He and Tenpos flanked Scanat, arms around his shoulders, and led him back to the frigid reception of the other four novim.

Durnadat stood his ground. "Beneim's right. How do we know this isn't another ruse?"

Scanat lowered his eyes, then raised them to look at Durnadat. "Just before the explosion that broke the wall, you were distressed by something in the air. Maybe dust in your eyes or smoke in your lungs. Then you had a sudden fright, as if something had struck you."

Durnadat clapped his hand to the top of his head. "Fenet's staff." His eyes widened. "It tapped me on the head as it whirled through the air." His belligerence changed to wonder.

The park around Church Center One loomed around Fenet. Healing the breach in the Khadam would be important. Should he get Scanat to address the issues now? Or should they get away from this place first? No, first would be to honor Elláh.

Fenet spoke. "Give our thanks to Elláh, everyone. But do while we move. He has forged us, brought us to the cusp where He wanted us. Now we are His tools.

"Enough discussion. We're leaving here now, before the Heresy Angels follow us out." Fenet made the words both a command and a warning. He looked each of the men in the eyes. "We have a mission to perform for Elláh. While we go, we'll listen to Scanat's side of what happened. Elláh's hand is obviously still on him, so we need to find out why."

Fenet turned again toward the east, one hand on his staff and the other on Scanat's shoulder. Tenpos rested his hand on the man's other shoulder. Together, they led the crew of fuming novim away from the prison—a crew who still wanted their pound of flesh.

A few hundred meters away, the trees, gentle lights, and park benches changed to harsh city streets.

At the park edge, Lorefim exclaimed, "Hey, isn't t-that our hoverbus?" He pointed at the lone bus parked in a lot, illuminated by the street lights.

"It is!" Durnadat rumbled into a roly-poly run, his robes flying. Scurrying ahead of the rest, he pounded on the closed door. Nothing happened. He pounded again. "Pincely! Open up."

A light came on. One curtain flipped aside, then the door opened.

"Durnadat!" the driver yelped, then jumped out of the bus to give the nov a hug. "How did y'all escape?" Pincely saw the rest. "All y'all. What's going on?"

Fenet joined Durnadat and hugged the driver. "Elláh released us, Pincely. A transcendental event in answer to prayer."

"I been waitin' two days, Reb." Pincely let go of the hug and looked at the group. "What took y'all so long?"

"Only Elláh knows His timing. But what are you doing, still here?"

"I couldn't leave, Reb. I just couldn't. The first time y'all were arrested, I gave up and looked for other work. I felt so bad with myself, I couldn't stand it. This time, I waited. I don't know what for—your return, some sign from Elláh, whatever—but I just couldn't leave."

Fenet laughed. "Well, I'm glad you didn't, because here we are. Are you still available?"

"You bet, Reb."

"We have a new mission. Can you get us over the mountains to Uptown?"

Pincely drew back and clapped a hand to his heart. "There's a war over there."

"Exactly. Elláh wants us to stop the war."

Pincely rubbed his eyes, then ran his fingers through his hair. He looked at the group, seven robed clerics led by a maverick has-been miracle-worker in pants and a tunic. "That's a tall order, Reb." He shook his head. "But if that's what Elláh wants y'all to do, I guess that's what you'll do. But you'll be needin' something."

Pincely got back into the bus, rocking it on its supports, then returned a moment later with Fenet's floppy straw hat.

"Put this on, Reb. You ain't right without it."

Fenet laughed again. Pincely reached up and affixed the hat on Fenet's head. As a final flourish, he tweaked the yellow *astradell* to a jaunty angle.

Scanat boarded the bus with the rest. During the next hour, he told the painful story. He fought to talk through tears several times. The miracle he'd experienced had released a well of deep emotion inside him—feelings he didn't understand. Tenpos sat beside him, a silent comfort.

He finished with, "I've felt so useless, guys. All of you were blessed with supernatural events. I had nothing. I wanted out, but I'm too old to go back to what I had. Then Forsfear ..." He couldn't continue, but had to say one more thing. "I'm sorry. I'm so sorry."

No one spoke. The steady rumble of the hoverbus continued. Most of the novim had softened while listening.

All but Beneim, who burst out, "Scanat, you have no idea what we just went through. Dammit, you threw us into a torture dungeon for your own selfish purposes."

Fenet raised a finger. "Language, Beneim."

"We could do with a bit more compassion here," urged Durnadat.

"I don't care," Beneim fumed. "I've watched Scanat since I came to the Reb three years ago, and I've never understood why *he* was with us." He waved a dismissive hand. "He's too old to learn. He doesn't follow directions from the Reb. He never gets the benefits from Elláh, and he's always trying to think things out. He doesn't belong."

Scanat's pulse pounded in his neck. A sour taste filled his mouth. Tenpos put his arm around Scanat. After the attack by Beneim, Tenpos' support felt like a clean shower.

Durnadat and Penilos started to respond heatedly to Beneim, speaking at the same time.

Fenet cut off the argument. "Hold on, boys. Argument isn't going to get us anywhere. Beneim is entitled to his opinion. Is there anyone else who shares it?"

Silence claimed a moment, then Penilos said, "I'm for Scanat. He's been in a very hard place and he's apologized."

The others nodded, then Tenpos' deep voice filled the silence. "Scanat's been my friend, and he still is."

Durnadat added, in a serious tone he rarely used, "Besides that, Elláh has fixed every consequence of what Scanat did. And the events, as bad as they were, have led us to marvelous happenings."

Relief washed over Scanat. Weakness made him quiver. Yet he still impathed the antagonism from Beneim.

Reb Fenet spoke before Beneim, still scowling, could reply. "Thanks for your thoughts. And many thanks to Scanat for explaining what happened—and for his apology. This isn't a vote, boys. I chose each of you as novim, and it is still my choice. Beneim, you'll have to work through your resentment. I can help. But I welcome Scanat back with us for as long as he wishes to continue."

Unable to contain his tears again, Scanat lowered his face and choked out thanks to the Reb and the others. "I don't know …" He paused and recomposed himself. "I don't know what I'll do long-term, but I want to be part of whatever is happening now. With His new grace on me, I believe Elláh has a purpose for these stupid t-paths I picked up."

Tenpos continued to hold him. Several others reached over the seats or across the aisle to touch him. Beneim alone stayed in his seat leaning against the window away from Scanat. His lips were set thin.

The support from the others touched Scanat's soul as much as the miracle from Elláh.

❧ ✳ ❧

The hoverbus climbed the twisty highway from Rathas to Tileus. The road served heavy vehicles that couldn't take to the air, so it was rough-paved and jostled Fenet while he dozed. Fenet had never seen mountains. He wanted to enjoy the scenery, but darkness and light rain prevented any view. The temperature had dipped to below freezing. When dawn sneaked a grey hint into the clouds, Fenet caught glimpses of steep hillsides around them.

"Those peaks are over two thousand meters." Pincely had noticed Fenet awakening. "We're close to Magnum Tunnel that cuts through the border ridge."

"Are you familiar with this way, too?" Fenet rubbed his eyes.

"Only been this way once afore, Reb. Them Tileus people don't care much for Rathas, so I ain't had much opportunity. I carried a bunch of missionaries over there."

Deep forests covered the slopes above and below the road. The forest smelled very different than the farm fields Fenet knew. In the rain, these had a rich fragrance of loam and evergreens.

They rounded the last bend to the flashing brilliance of red and blue lights flashing through the mist. Army trucks blocked the tunnel entrance, with armed guards beside them. Fenet's heart sank. *How are we going to get to Uptown?*

Pincely slowed the bus, approaching the roadblock at a walking pace. A guard with sergeant stripes on a glistening poncho stepped forward and gave them a "halt" gesture. When the guard stepped toward the bus, Pincely lowered his window to ask, "What's going on, boss?"

"There's a war going on," the guard answered, "dontcha know? Nobody goes through until we've secured the area."

Fenet stood to see the guard through Pincely's window. "Sergeant, we have Elláh's business in Uptown. Related to the war." For once, Fenet wished he wore regular ministerial robes so they'd know he had authority.

The guard apparently recognized him as a minister despite his unusual attire. "Sorry, Reb. No one goes through. That's our orders. You'll have to wait on your business."

"How long, sir?"

"Don't know. Two or three days. That's what we've been told."

"Is there any other way?" The man seemed helpful. It wouldn't hurt to ask.

The sergeant shook his head. "Nope. We've blocked every road through the Gortooths until things are clear over there. As I said, you'll just have to wait."

"Hmm." No way around it. Fenet tapped Pincely on the shoulder. "Okay, Pincely. This doesn't work. Take us back." They'd find another way. Elláh would provide.

"You bet, Reb."

Fenet turned back to the guard. "Thanks for your service, Sergeant."

The man nodded, still standing his ground.

Pincely turned the hoverbus on its repellors to face back the way they'd come. He closed his window. When the roadblock disappeared behind them, he offered. "There is another way, Reb."

"What might that be?"

Pincely flashed a secretive smile over his shoulder. "There's a hiking trail over Magnum Gap. I saw the trailhead just a couple of kilometers back. We could walk."

Fenet smiled. "Take us there, friend. Sounds like a good idea, a gift from Elláh. We were already about to hike anyway when we found you." He paused. "But why do you say, 'we,' Pincely?"

The driver laughed. "You think, after all this, I can leave you on your own? I gotta know what happens."

40 – Last Ditches

While often viewed as an opportunity for glory, war is nothing but ugly. Human beings annihilating other human beings never solves anything. It is a mystery why the human race indulges in it so frequently. This is changing. The coupling of spiritual growth with the new empathic technology is beginning to help us understand how we can be better.

—*The Making of a New Humanity* by Ellen Thranadil, Tileus Press 448 A.T.

In the cold, wet dark of morning, Morat Vengeact brooded, wondering what he had gotten himself into. War no longer seemed glorious. The remaining three members of his fireteam lay curled in a muddy plascrete drainage ditch. Light rain and near-freezing temperatures overnight kept them miserable despite supposedly waterproof field blankets. So did the necessity to maintain a rotating watch. They couldn't light fires or use heaters, for fear the enemy would know their position. No one got much sleep.

In the wee hours, the rain stopped and a few stars showed themselves. Morat had taken the last watch for himself. The dreary night echoed his mood while he brooded over the sudden aircar attack yesterday. The beam had cut down Staff Sergeant Pushman, the entire adjacent fireteam, and Morat's own Private Grinhand.

Morat avoided thinking about Grinhand. Barely nineteen Verdant years old, the kid had shown a rare glee for life. He'd always had a ready joke to liven any event. Those jokes wouldn't be heard anymore. The image of the aircar beam cutting Grinhand in half seared in Morat's mind. As corporal, Morat felt the responsibility.

He roused his team when dawn stained the sky to the east. "Get ready, guys. Shake yourselves out and look sharp. The new platoon sarge says we can expect a counter-attack at dawn."

Gutstrong, Manmove, and Windo rolled out of their blankets.

"Ah, Corp, do we have to get up?" Manmove shivered, sounding as depressed as Morat.

"No." Morat snorted. "You could just stay down and die in your sleep."

That got a dry laugh from the team. They rubbed their faces, drank some water, and pulled out ration packs. Morat pointed out positions for each at the edge of the ditch, facing Uptown center. He took his own position and waited.

∾ ✱ ∽

At the same moment, dawn had already burst in Thad City. Jake had been awake for two hours, trying to make sense of the war. Zofia came into their breakfast room yawning, dressed in a sheer nightie.

"Good morning, love," he said, reaching out to wrap an arm around her waist. "I fixed breakfast for you." The feel of her skin under the nightgown tingled in his fingers.

She leaned down to give him a lingering kiss, her hair falling around his face, then sat down to join him. "Thanks, Bucko. Been up long?" Outside the window, clouds scudded away to reveal blue sky. She picked up a fork and shoveled eggs around.

"Too long. I still don't understand. Why would Rathas attack us?" Jake ran his hand around the back of his neck.

"I listened to their Minister Leaderlist give a speech yesterday. He claims mistreatment of their missionaries here in Tileus," said Zofia. "There's got to be something more, though. Everyone in Tileus gets mistreated, citizens and foreigners alike. It's such a shambles here. Better than the tight controls we knew in Verdant Prime, but like a wild pendulum swinging in the other direction."

"Maybe Rathas people don't understand how fickle democracy is. We didn't before we came here."

"And got arrested." Zofia laughed, then took a bite of sausage.

"Yeah." Jake grinned with her, then turned serious again. "So, are we going to risk this trip to Rathas today?"

"It was your idea, Bucko. Now, Coordinator Serban is expecting us. We have to go through with it."

"Well, at the time, it sounded like a good idea." Jake rubbed the mole on his chin. "When the off-planet people were asked to try arbitrating peace, it presented an opportunity. We can take some equipment with us to find out what Leaderlist is doing to the t-paths. The coordinator hopes we'll break through Randy's jammer and heighten mutual understanding. That way, he and his people get honest empathy during the meeting—and we get technical information about the jammer. Win-win."

"Until Rathas attacked and started the war."

Jake slumped. "Yeah, there was that."

A sudden actinic flash outside the window grabbed Jake's attention. A vertical violet beam, so brilliant it hurt his eyes, stabbed from the sky into Thad City a kilometer away. Their apartment power went out. Lasting but an instant, the beam left an afterimage in his retina. It also left a fast-spreading spray of debris arcing into the sky, followed by a black cloud billowing upward. Seconds later, the window pane rattled with a boom.

"What was *that*?" Jake blinked to clear his eyes.

Zofia jumped to her feet, looking out the window. "Space-based beam weapon. We talked about those last week, remember? They're real." She turned back to him. "If Rathas is using them to attack Thad City, the colony team will get out right away. We've gotta move fast to join them."

❧ ✳ ☙

Fenet stood with the novim in front of the hiking information display. "This map shows the trail goes over Magnum Gap and down into Uptown."

"There's a download available for your imp," Tenpos rumbled. He pointed out a side trail on the map. "It says this path leads to someplace called East Knob Lookout where you can see the whole city. If Elláh wants us to affect the entire war, we'd need to be someplace like that rather than down in the city where we can't see anything."

"How far is the hike?" Durnadat patted his girth. "I'm not exactly built for mountain climbing."

"The download says it's a moderate trail," answered Tenpos, "The distance is only three point eight kilometers. Even on mountain trails, you should be able to handle it in a couple of hours."

Fenet listened with one ear while the novim discussed this lookout and its suitability for whatever they had to do. He had a problem. Elláh had not yet given any specific direction. He didn't know whether they should be at such a lookout point or down in the heart of the fighting. *Where should we go, Elláh?* No guidance came in answer.

Elláh's continued unresponsiveness debilitated Fenet. He missed the constant conversation that had been part of his gift of miracles. That capacity had defined him for the last twenty years, and Elláh had still not restored it. His life dream had been to teach the ability to others, to be recognized as a spiritual leader, even gain some fame over it. Yet for years, none of the novim he'd taken on had been granted any significant capability. Most had left him again. Now, he'd lost his ability to channel miracles, and simultaneously this current group started displaying awesome powers. It didn't seem fair.

What do you want of me, Elláh? How do we stop the war? What part do I have in it?

Spiritual silence granted him no answer.

He returned his attention to the current issue. "Four kilometers is a tiny fraction of what we hiked before we ran into Pincely. We can do this. If no one receives any different direction from Elláh, then let's head to where we can see the entirety of Uptown."

Pincely came up behind the Khadam. "I've locked the bus. Are we ready to go, Reb?"

Fenet nodded. "Let's do it."

❦ ✳ ❧

Jake had his personal t-path hidden in a pocket for this meeting. Zofia carried an instrumentation package in a small case. She'd designed the software to work with their imps hands-free. Following Serban's direction, he and Zofia boarded the airvan with the colony leaders.

"We did receive a change in plans," the coordinator told everyone while he got on the airvan. "Minister Leaderlist did invite us to join him at their war command center in Uptown, instead of in Rathas."

"Be they still open to arbitration?" asked one of the colony diplomats.

"He says so, yes. But the location of this meeting tells me they did commit to the path of war." Serban shook his head. "This looks not good. We will still try."

"Will the other Ministers be there, also?"

"I was told some of them be there, and the others attend remotely from Rathas."

Jake raised a hand while the airvan lifted off. "In that case, is our equipment still useful, Coordinator?"

"Perhaps, Jake. We will not know until we try. I was told Leaderlist be their primary decision-maker for this. You was at the first negotiation. What was his attitude?"

"He seemed smug, sir, as if he had everything under control, moving in the directions he wanted."

"We can expect that attitude to be continuing. Their military success yesterday in Uptown was significant. He will see himself to be in a strong position. It will help if he perceives the situation through the emotions of others."

Jake settled back for the hour-and-a-half trip from Thad City to Uptown. Zofia took his hand. He shared a concerned look with her and sighed.

❧ ✳ ❧

Fenet strode upward along the mountain path with ease. The glorious forest expanded around them. Visible through the understory, tree boles walked uphill and downhill like soldiers of faith. At this elevation, all but the evergreen pindels had lost their autumn leaves. The rich combination of growth and decay filled his nose like a musical. Birdsong joined the rustle of leaves in a breeze. Despite the situation, being here felt like moksha, a release from the samsara cycle of life and death while in the middle of the cycle.

His newly-returned physical capability elevated his spirits despite the loss of his lifelong capability for miracles. The Khadam, even rotund Durnadat, kept up. However, every time Fenet looked back down the path, Beneim trailed behind the rest. The man trudged along with heavy feet. Fenet understood. Beneim had not let go of the resentment over what Scanat had done, and it likely still ate at his peace.

"Eregim, please continue to lead the group upward."

"Of course, Fenet. Where are you going?"

Fenet motioned with his head toward Beneim, and Eregim nodded. Fenet stopped by the side of the path. He patted each nov on the back as they went by, offering encouragement and hope. When Beneim came abreast, Fenet joined him.

Beneim looked up, then back at the path in front of his steps.

"You're going to have to give this up, you know." Fenet spoke in a kind tone. "Resentment will block whatever Elláh has for you to do."

Beneim flashed him an angry look. "I don't want to give it up, Reb. I don't understand how the rest of you can. What Scanat did was unforgivable."

Fenet raised his eyebrows. "Unforgivable? That's a tall order. Has not Elláh forgiven your sins?"

"I don't care. I'm not Elláh, I'm human. I can't be together with *him*."

Fenet walked on beside Beneim, letting the man's words float in the air like a dark cloud.

After a long silence, Beneim said, "Yes, I know my attitude is wrong, Reb. But for now, it's the only attitude I've got."

41 – Holy War

He who knows when he can fight and when he cannot, will be victorious.

Sun Tzu, *The Art of War*, 5th century BC (Old Earth)

After noon, Morat and his fireteam lay in the plascrete drainage ditch watching Uptown center. The flat bottom of the ditch reeked with wet mud and rotten vegetation. Staying prone on the rough-surfaced upslope seemed to be the only comfortable place. Everything was wrong. They'd trained as a unit of five, and now they were down to four. All their exercises had been under Staff Sergeant Pushman, and Morat had come to trust him. Now, Pushman had been killed and some new sergeant had taken charge. Morat didn't even know the man's name. The sergeant hadn't yet visited their position, just sent orders by imp.

Morat's stomach clenched, his breath shook—nothing he could reveal to his team. He had to be the leader.

Without warning, two attack aircars dove out of the bright sun straight toward them. Energy beams reached out from the front of the cars to rake the ditch.

"Down!" Morat shouted to his team.

Everyone slid lower, deep in the ditch. The beams blew off bits of the plascrete rim above their heads, shattering the top edges of the ditch. Molten material flew outward, narrowly missing Morat's helmet. The aircars streaked overhead and continued out of view behind them.

Morat's heartbeat raced. He called out, "Report. Everyone okay?"

"Okay," answered Gutstrong and Windo.

"Still here, Corp," said Manmove, "but there's people coming toward us."

Morat heard it, too, the yelling of ground troops approaching. He lifted his head above the ditch. A line of green-uniformed men charged up the grassy slope toward them.

"Holy Elláh," he whispered, then shouted to his men. "Enemy closing in. Fire at will." He also activated his imp comms so the whole platoon would know.

While his men rose to shoot over the edge, adjacent fireteams also took positions. From relaxing in the ditch to fighting for their lives had taken five seconds.

Morat focused his weapon on one of the advancing Tileus troops and pulled the trigger. The man stumbled and fell, his weapon flying into the air. Morat re-aimed and fired again. And again. And again. Flechettes, beams, and grenades streaked from their ditch positions toward the enemy line, cutting them down like a scythe through hay.

The two aircars circled for another pass. This time, they lined up to Morat's right on the length of the ditch. The entire platoon would fry. The men had no weapons effective against cars.

The Rathas forces, however, were on it. A mobile beamer behind their line took down one aircar. When the second rolled level to fire, a beam shot down from the sky. Both cars exploded. The main bulk of each car crashed to the ground short of their position, plowing long furrows in the grassy parkland. Deadly chunks bombarded Morat and his team.

Miraculously, the shrapnel hit none of the team. Nor did the incoming fire from the attackers, though bullets and flechettes hit the plascrete close to them. Morat returned his attention to the Tileus soldiers coming closer. His breath came hard and fast like he'd run a mile. He and the team continued to fire until the remaining enemy troops gave up and retreated.

Morat had never imagined combat would be like this. Brutal. Destructive. Fast. Dangerous. The romantic notion of fighting for the right wasn't evident here at all. He suddenly realized he'd just killed at least five men, human beings like himself. His heart pounding, he wished he'd never volunteered.

🙰 ※ 🙰

Pillars of smoke rose from key points in Uptown when the airvan holding Jake, Zofia and the colony leaders arrived. The afternoon sun shown on destroyed buildings, active flames, and occasional streaks of weapon trails. Jake's breath stopped as he looked out the airvan window. He'd been here several times on marketing trips, but never like this. The visible reality of war rose to the sky in each black plume.

"This is really bad." Zofia sounded nervous, her voice more breathy than usual.

"Yeah." Jake turned to Serban. "Coordinator, do you think your arbitration team has a chance to stop this?"

"We always be having a chance. Trying be what matters."

Their vehicle flew past the city toward a resort hotel on the slopes of the Gortooth range. The contrast with the war-torn city could not have been greater. The four-story hotel sported flowered balconies and etched-glass windows overlooking broad expanses of grass toward the spacious view of the lower lands. The van landed beside the main portico, where two robed clerics awaited them.

When they exited the van, Zofia pushed forward with her usual desire to jump in to action.

Jake held her back. "Not now, love. Remember, we're not part of the arbitration team. We need to be invisible here."

"Oh, right." She gave a sheepish smile and rejoined him at the rear. "Thanks for reminding me. We're just here to find the jammer."

"What do you get on your t-path from these two?"

Zofia looked at the clerics. "Sincere. Officious. Feeling powerful at the moment."

"Yeah, that's what I impath, too."

The clerics greeted Coordinator Serban and the group, then led them into the hotel to a well-appointed conference room. A marble-topped table and grey wainscoting continued the luxurious feeling Jake had observed passing through the columned lobby.

Yet this room served another purpose; it had become the Rathas war center. A 2-D projection screen on one wall showed a map of Uptown annotated with military markings. The holo over the table gave a 3-D representation of the entire country of Tileus, again with martial annotations.

Jake's eyebrows rose at the sight of multiple battle tags over Thad City and Freetown. Apparently, the beam weapon attack he'd seen this morning wasn't the only action in those other cities.

Grey robes and uniforms packed the large room. Rapid conversation rattled everywhere, focused on various military objectives.

Jake recognized Minister Leaderlist standing at the head of the table. The man filibustered to two other men with national minister collars. Jake remembered Minister Dominact from their prior meeting, and he thought the third man had also been in his first meeting.

Abruptly, all the impathed emotions from the room cut off. An annoying emotional confusion filled Jake's head. The sudden change made him stumble. He reached in his pocket and turned down the sensitivity on his t-path. Zofia looked surprised and reached for hers, too.

Leaderlist turned to the newcomers. "Ah, you must be Coordinator Serban, I believe? We are pleased to receive you, but we're quite busy here. You'll have to be quick. You asked for this meeting. Why?"

Serban stepped forward to shake hands. "Yes, I can see you be busy. Be you having a short time to discuss two important issues?"

Jake stayed at the back of the group. "We've been jammed," he whispered to Zofia.

"Yeah, I got that, too." She turned on the small detection unit she carried. "Let's see what our equipment can find out."

Leaderlist scanned the faces of the colonial party. His eyes rested on Jake and his lips turned up in a slight smile, superior and smug. Then he turned back to Serban. "What are your two issues, sir?"

The coordinator responded with calm to the minister's brusqueness. "First, and most important, be to pass on to you our invitation to join the colony effort to Bluewater. I believe you may already did be hearing that news?"

Leaderlist nodded. "We'd be interested. A chance to spread the good news of the Church is always welcome."

"We be liking that also, sir," said Serban. "Diversity of opinion on our new world will be good. Be it possible, therefore, for us to bring our team to Rathas for a series of presentations on the colony effort?"

"We could authorize it." Leaderlist looked to Dominact for affirmation.

Minister Dominact nodded. "It would be our delight to host you in a tour of our cities, though our attention is obviously on this Holy War."

"Excellent. We be on Verdant for another two weeks, so we can work together to arrange days to do so."

A man in uniform tapped Leaderlist. Leaderlist turned away and held up a "wait" finger to Serban while the military man pointed to several icons on the 2-D map.

Zofia nudged Jake. "We've got it, Bucko. The jamming is coming from Leaderlist. Randy's jammer desynchronizes the particle waves. Just like last year without the nanoprocessors."

"Can we do anything about it here?"

She winced. "Nope. Don't have any nanoprocessors. Or the equipment to coordinate them."

Jake nodded.

Leaderlist finished with the soldier and turned back to Serban. "What is your second issue, sir?"

The coordinator waved a hand at the resolute bustle in the room. "The second issue be this Holy War, sir. We be peace-loving people, and it pain us to see others in such dire conflict. We only be having two weeks here on Verdant, and it will be difficult to make our presentations in the middle of war. We therefore offer our services, if at all possible, to arbitrate the issues that have Rathas and Tileus in such a divergence."

The two ministers, Dominact and Leaderlist, looked at each other.

Serban continued, "We did talk with several of the Tileus Governors while we was there. They have concerns, but be willing to change their practices. If Rathas also be willing to hold off further war actions, perhaps we can help the two countries to be reaching a peaceful agreement."

Minister Dominact nodded. "This would be a good opportunity—"

Leaderlist put a hand on his shoulder. "Pronas, I believe we should talk further among ourselves before agreeing to anything."

Dominact stepped back, irritation flashing. "We have young men fighting and dying out there, Beltaret. If we can find a different solution, we should try."

Leaderlist said to Serban, "Excuse us, please, Coordinator. We need to talk privately." He then drew Dominact to a far corner of the room along with the third minister.

Though Jake could not hear what they said the two were in violent disagreement.

Zofia nudged him. "Tell Serban about the jamming, Jake."

"Right. Good thinking."

He interrupted Serban's side discussion with an advisor. "Coordinator, we have an answer about the transpath jamming," he said quietly.

Serban raised an eyebrow.

"We now know how the jammer works. We could override it but don't have the equipment here." Jake nodded toward the Rathas ministers. "And we know who it's coming from."

Jake had not been quiet enough.

"Transpath jamming?" said Minister Dominact, stepping back toward them. "Someone here is jamming your transpath?"

Serban extended a hand, inviting Jake to explain.

"Yes, Minister. We're not trying to impose the t-path on your command center, but one of your people is carrying an unauthorized jammer—"

Dominact straightened to his full height, eyes flashing. "One of our people?" He moved closer to Jake and jabbed a finger into his chest. "Which one, Mister Palatin? Which one? The transpath is outlawed among our people."

"Well, Minister—" Jake hesitated.

"Don't prevaricate." Dominact swept his hand over the crew behind him. "Who is it?"

"Tell him," urged Zofia.

Jake shrugged and pointed to Minister Leaderlist. "Your lead minister, sir."

❧ ❋ ☙

Jake sensed any chance at arbitration falling apart at the internal conflict that ensued. Dominact and Leaderlist shouted red-faced at each other. The war coordination continued around them. From the heated words, Jake understood the t-path issue had become the tipping point in a deeper conflict within the Rathas Ministry.

The Rathas soldiers forced the arbitration party out of the room so fast Serban had no chance to affect the internecine clash. They escorted the entire party back to the resort lobby, where the colonists joined each other for a difficult planning session.

Jake and Zofia stepped away from the group. Five-meter-high picture windows gave them a view of the ongoing destruction. Fighting vehicles wheeled over key points in the city below. Beams shot down from orbit. Explosions detonated unpredictably.

Zofia grasped his hand. "This and worse is what we stopped last year."

He sighed. "But it doesn't appear we can stop it this time. If we could get effective t-paths into the mix, I know people would understand each other."

"Maybe. At least they'd have difficulty continuing to fight."

Events moved too fast for Jake. His mind raced between the war and the t-path, trying to find a solution.

A familiar voice came from behind. "Uh ... Jake? Zofia? I owe you an apology, if you'll accept it."

Jake turned. "Randy Princeton! You snake."

Randy wrung his hands, sorrow in his eyes.

"You!" Zofia cried out. "What are you doing here? Get away, we want nothing to do with you."

"An apology, Randy?" The man's words replayed in Jake's head. "What makes you think we'd accept an apology? You stole from us. You tried to burn down our lab. What apology would make us think you're anything but a traitor?"

Randy tucked his hands under his arms. He looked down at the floor. "Nothing could suffice, Jake. I did wrong, and I shouldn't have done it."

"You're going to *talk* to him?" Zofia whirled on Jake and shoved his shoulder. "We want *nothing* from him." She stabbed a finger at Randy. "Except to send him to prison."

"Everyone deserves a second chance, love."

Zofia bristled, arms crossed.

Randy lifted a hand. "I don't *deserve* anything, Jake, but I've learned a lesson. All the selfish things I did—I tried to be as important as I thought I was. But it's gone wrong here in Rathas, and I've realized how my flawed thinking led me to wrong actions. So, regardless of what happens, I'm sorry for what I did to you. How can I make it up—if I can?"

42 – Return of Miracles

The unknown prophet Fenet Powrfaith became famous in an instant.
Risking his life, his actions proved the power of Elláh.

—History of the One Church by Ellen Thranadil,
Tileus Press 445 A.T.

From East Knob Lookout, Fenet looked down on the city of
Uptown. With the bright afternoon sun behind them, Elláh's
beauty pealed like bells from this mountain bluff. Rugged
peaks towered above. The hiking trail widened into a meadow and
an overlook surrounded by a low stack-rock wall. Tall trees blew in
the breeze, birdsong praised the day, the scent of growth infused
the air.

All this magnificence swept down the valleys to the human-
made scar of war. Clouds of black smoke towered to the sky from
buildings and homes. Fierce explosions punctured the clouds. The
condition of the city filled Fenet with anguish. Though too far away
to see the men fighting and dying, Fenet's heart wrenched at the
anguish he imagined.

Eregim and the Khadam stood wide-eyed and silent around
him, their backpacks dropped in an untidy pile.

Tenpos finally broke the silence. "Good Lord. What can we
possibly do?"

"Nothing." Beneim's bitter voice dropped like lead. "We're too
late."

Several other novim whispered prayers, darting glances at the
active war below.

"Wait, boys." Eregim's rich voice grabbed their attention. "Don't
give up. This whole trip has taught me never to give up on Elláh.
His miracles continue."

Fenet nodded. "He's right. It's never too late for Elláh. He can always find a way for those who trust in Him. Gather together. Join hands like we did in the prison cell. Who knows what He will do?"

The novim formed a circle, hand-in-hand.

When Fenet lowered his eyes to pray, Elláh's muse took him over again.

When war fills the hearts of men
*   And conflict fills the air,*
We turn to Elláh again:
*   Lord, heal what we cannot bear.*

Eyes closed now, he continued in a firm voice tinged with anguish. "Lord Elláh, we come to where You wanted us. We see below the result of man's transgressions to You. Horrible devastation, ruinous loss, lives at risk—"

The buzz of an incoming aircar grew loud. Fenet kept his eyes down and continued praying, though Lorefim's hand tugged on his.

"—destruction of people and ideals. Elláh, how can Your people take such an action? Change their hearts, O Lord, change their ways that they may surrender to You—"

From the sound, the aircar landed. Many booted feet approached, crunching on the gravel path and thudding in the grass.

A loud, raspy voice shouted, dripping with sarcasm. "*There* you are, *Reb* Fenet Powrfaith. You and your motley crew of escapees."

Fenet knew the voice: Captain Forsfear. Refusing to look up, he kept praying, "—that all may know the peace You have for us, peace in our souls leading to peace on Verdant."

Forsfear's sneering voice came closer. "Did you think you could elude us, false prophet? Did you forget we can track every movement of your implant?"

The boots came closer.

"Peace is Your goal," Fenet prayed, eyes still closed. "That all may—"

Elláh's internal voice stopped Fenet's prayer. *YOU SERVE ME WELL, FENET. STOP THESE DELUDED CHURCHMEN.*

Fenet staggered at the immense love washing into him. He felt the miraculous power of Elláh fill him as it once did. Shoulders straight, he received back what Elláh had taken away, and more.

His heart burst like fireworks. The power flowed into him stronger than he had known in years. Opening his eyes, he looked to the sky and let loose a booming laugh.

"Thank you, Elláh. Thank you, Lord," he shouted.

When he looked down, the cadre of Heresy Angels, led by Forsfear, strode toward them from a black aircar that crushed the mountain meadow. The Angels walked in line abreast, moving to trap Fenet's group. All the churchmen gripped stuncheons, several slapping them on their thighs, hostile leers on their faces.

The novim still held hands, darting glances between the looming Angels and Fenet's strange behavior.

Surprisingly, Fenet could impath their doubt and fear as he looked from nov to nov. Another miraculous power. Somehow, Elláh had given him the same transpath capacity Scanat had tried to gift the group through technology. Sliding his gaze over Scanat, Fenet impathed a lingering flush of resentment from the young man. Stunned, Fenet also perceived a much deeper anger and resentment from Beneim, likely about Scanat's continued presence. He'd deal with both of those later.

The Angels closed to within five meters, those on the ends advancing farther to surround the Khadam.

From the center of the line, Forsfear scoffed, "Foolish people. And now, in addition to the charges of heresy, we can add your escape from confinement. You will rot in our heretics' prison."

Fenet let go of the novim's hands and stood tall. He straightened his floppy-brimmed hat, then pointed an extended arm and finger at Captain Forsfear. When he opened his mouth, Elláh spoke through him: *STOP THERE! WE HAVE ELLÁH'S WORK TO DO.*

Forsfear and the Angels froze mid-stride, unable to move, surprise cemented on their faces.

Were they not so intimidating, Fenet might have found them comical. He impathed from individual Angels their terror, dismay, anxiety, their struggle to force their limbs to move.

The Khadam broke apart with jumbled cries.

"Reb Fenet!"

"What did you do?"

"How—?"

Fenet laughed, bright and cheery. "We're fine, boys. Everything is just fine. Elláh is in charge, as He always has been, and He has given me back His power to use."

300

Durnadat leaned forward to look at Fenet, then roared with laughter. "Reb Fenet, I can impath your joy, your strength!" Durnadat jumped up and twirled in the air. Landing awkwardly, he scrambled to regain his balance, crying wide-eyed, "And I don't even have a transpath."

Tenpos' deep voice resounded with awe. "Me too." He flicked his gaze from person to person. "I can impath all of your emotions without any device at all. Good Lord, Reb Fenet, you are glowing!"

"Yes, I am," Fenet said with merriment. "I've been renewed."

"You're s-standing straighter, Reb." Lorefim leaned back, awe in his eyes. "And you look t-ten years younger. But ..." Lorefim waved toward the raging war below. "D-do you k-know what we should do now, Reb? C-can we stop that?"

Fenet paused to view the ongoing destruction and sighed. "Don't know yet, Lorefim, but I trust Elláh will show us."

"Can we do something about these Angels first?" asked Beneim. "They give me the frights."

"I'm sure we can." Fenet faced the ragged line of frozen militia, the scowling Captain Forsfear in the center. Fenet took a deep breath and waved his hands forward in a push-away gesture.

"Be gone."

The familiar scarlet wash of color propelled forward from his hands. It expanded to cover the Heresy Angels and their aircar. With a burgundy flash, they all disappeared.

"Whoa," intoned Pinceley. "Never seen that before."

Eregim shook his head and chuckled. "You are indeed back, my friend. You've done it before with one or two proctors, but two dozen Angels and an aircar? Do you know where they've gone?"

"Not a clue," said Fenet, smiling, "but I do know they're safe and unfrozen wherever they are. They might decide to fly the car back here, but we'll see." He turned again to the valley and the war-torn city. "Now let's do something about this war. Rejoin hands, please. All of you this time. Pincely, Eregim, you're part of this, too."

"What, me?" said the driver. "I don't have no powers."

Fenet impathed Pincely's doubt and uncertainty. "You don't need power, friend. Elláh has it all."

The group regathered in a circle on the high overlook.

Fenet prayed. "Elláh, show us what You would have us do." This time, he kept his eyes open, impathing the emotions from each person around the circle. Deep red glowed in the air around each pair of clasped hands. Fenet felt hope from Lorefim, joy in Durnadat, a solid expectation from Tenpos. The burgundy glow spread from hand to hand around the circle, through the chest and head of each person.

Until it came to Scanat and Beneim on the other side of the circle. The wash of color built up on both sides of the two, swelling around Durnadat and Eregim whose hands they clasped, but refused to touch either Scanat or Beneim.

Fenet nodded. He'd almost expected this. He focused deeper into Scanat and impathed latent resentment over the young man's separation from the rest of the Khadam. Fenet perceived Scanat did not foster the resentment, yet it remained anyway. Eyes closed, Scanat had a furrowed brow. He gave every physical indication of determination, striving to be part of this nascent miracle. Yet his attitude blocked what they needed to do.

Next to Scanat, Beneim's red-headed anger flared in his emotions. Fenet realized Beneim still held outrage at Scanat being allowed back in. The man's jaw clenched and he stood as far as he could from Scanat while still holding hands.

Fenet sighed, letting the miraculous power fade. "Scanat," he said, "and Beneim. We need you both to be part of us."

The clasped hands broke apart while Fenet talked.

Scanat startled. His eyes opened. He glanced around the circle. Everyone watched him. "I'm trying, Reb. I'm really trying."

"Yeah, Scanat." Beneim's voice dripped with sarcasm. "Just keep ... *trying.*"

"Stop it, both of you." Fenet shook his head. "Scanat, it's time for you to let go of trying. I've told you many times: it's not up to you to make it happen, my longest and best nov." Fenet gave the young man a gentle smile. "And Beneim, your anger over Scanat is keeping us from where Elláh wants us to be."

Scanat looked away. Beneim huffed and looked at the ground.

"Scanat, what's blocking you?"

Scanat looked away, his emotions seeking to fix the past. "I keep thinking of the t-paths, Reb. How I thought it Elláh's had guided me to get them. How helpful they were to us at first, and then how they blocked us. I thought I was doing right, but it all went wrong."

"Yeah, so wrong we ended in prison." Beneim had not relaxed at all.

"Beneim, pray to Elláh to forgive you for your lack of compassion. Do it. Now."

Beneim set his jaw again but complied. He took several deep breaths, eyes closed and hands clasped.

"Scanat, I don't believe Elláh gives guidance for nothing," Fenet said. "If you perceived His guidance in what you did, then there may have been a reason for—"

Elláh's voice spoke in Fenet's head again. *USE THE TRANSPATHS NOW, FENET. I HAVE THEM HERE FOR THIS MOMENT.*

Fenet gasped. An unexpected turn of events. The Khadam waited on him while he processed the command. Then he nodded. "Scanat, Elláh has just given me new direction. Your transpaths fit into His plan after all. Elláh has told me to use them in this miracle. Get them, please."

Appearing surprised and shocked, Scanat nodded and went to the pile of backpacks.

"What?" Beneim responded in shocked outrage. "But Reb ... they stopped our miracles before. That's why we gave them back to Scanat."

"Yes, I know," said Fenet. "But Elláh always has plans beyond what we can understand. He put those t-paths here, now, for His purpose. You once saw me stop rain to prevent flooding. That's what brought you to me as a nov. Continue to trust in Him."

Beneim took a surprised step back. His pathed emotions skittered from anger to surprise to contemplation ... and then to surrendered peace.

Scanat returned with hands full of t-paths, his emotions filled with relief, satisfaction, even joy at being useful after all.

"Everyone," Fenet said, "take your unit from Scanat and turn them on to full power."

Scanat passed out the units. Each man turned his on and clipped it to his clothing.

Fenet impathed no change from those with t-paths. Already imbued with the miraculous transpath power, turning on the technological units made no difference.

"Join hands once more," Fenet directed, and they did. He looked down at the city, centering his thoughts. "Dear Elláh, use us—"

Red glow snapped into place at the joined hands, all of them. Fenet staggered. Deep vermilion surrounded their circle, thicker than morning fog in a mountain dell. The air moved into a circular whirl. The breeze lifted hair and robes, like it had in the dungeon. While the zephyr built into a tornado, the transpaths sparkled brilliant white, seven dazzling gems in the thick circle of crimson power. The smell of ozone filled the air; the gale rushed around them in a celebratory howl.

The whirlwind grew in power and height, now towering far above Fenet and the Khadam. It threatened to tear them apart. Fenet shouted "Hold on!" and clenched the hands on either side to hold them together.

"Holy Elláh," cried out Tenpos.

The ground shook, a sudden earthquake. Fenet staggered when the earth moved. The Khadam held tight to each other as they swayed. Penilos fell to his knees. Eregim and Pinceley maintained their grip on his hands and pulled their friend back to his feet. Dust rose from the disturbed ground in waves, joining the carmine swirl around them. Beneim coughed. The ground continued to move. The trees around their meadow swayed like grain.

Fenet tried to continue his prayer. "Elláh, show us what—"

The incandescent gleam of the t-paths shot out bars of blazing silver to join in a seven-pointed star. The bright t-path at each apex blinded him. Then swirls of the same brilliance intertwined with the garnet whirlwind to create a vast spiral that shot to the sky.

Vermilion air, dust, and sparks roared upward in the sky. Squinting to follow them, Fenet filled with awe at Elláh's power. The rotating column reached to the upper clouds lofted above. Somewhere far above, red fingers spread east and west, reaching down again kilometers away. One broad streak shot into the war-torn city below.

Fenet had trouble breathing. His hands vibrated with heat energy like holding a hot buzzsaw. When he thought he could stand no more, that he might die, he tried to let go and found he could not. Tenpos' and Lorefim's hands grasped his like iron grips that would not release. Bound together, he had no choice but to follow Elláh's will.

The event took over his body and mind. Fenet couldn't even try to pray. He could only trust Elláh.

43 – Full Empathy

One time, only once, empathy became widespread, not relying on the technology of the transpath but on a miraculous gift.

—The Making of a New Humanity by Ellen Thranadil, Tileus Press 448 A.T.

Morat Vengeact hunkered into the plascrete ditch, wanting to get away from the terrifying battle. He hated the idea of killing people, but he remembered the aircar taking out Sergeant Pullman, Private Grinhand, and the entire adjacent fireteam. Here, his choice had to be kill or be killed. He escaped by thinking of Faï, back in Praise, the initial excuse for the war. How beautiful she was! How she cared for him. He fought back tears, wondering if he would ever see her again.

Shrieking artillery shells from the Tileus forces fell around his fireteam. Continuous explosions roared, pummeling his chest with pressure. The air filled with electric energy. Fear plastered his eyes closed. He squeezed his face against the hard surface.

Another attack would surely follow such a barrage. The moment the bombing ceased, he gritted his teeth and rose to peer over the edge of the ditch.

"Get up, men," he shouted. "They're coming again."

A longer and thicker line of soldiers in Tileus green already advanced up the shredded parkland toward them. Morat checked his team. Gutstrong and Windo had joined him at the edge with weapons aimed. He didn't see Manmove.

Alarmed, Morat looked below and to the right. The private's body lay torn in the stinking ditch, a terrible sight. "Good Lord," Morat whispered, horrified. His shoulders slumped. One of Manmove's legs rested two meters away and a bloody hole gaped in the man's chest. Morat ground his jaw, sucked in a long breath of blood-laden air, and turned back to the attackers.

He steadied his weapon on the edge of the ditch and took aim at one of the leaders. They'd done this to his friend.

Without warning, the ground shook violently back and forth, threatening to roll Morat down to join Manmove. He braced his feet against the slope and pressed himself to the plascrete.

Yet the enemy approached. He lifted his weapon. In the quake, his gunsight lurched back and forth across the target, unable to settle. He couldn't aim. But the attackers had trouble advancing, too. They staggered. Some fell.

After a half minute, the ground settled into its normal stillness. Morat lined up the sights on the leading enemy when the man started moving forward once more.

An odd sensation gripped Morat. He squinted at the man in his sights. He felt the man tremble with fear and the determination that drove him forward. Receiving the feelings of his target? How could that be? Feelings were private, not broadcast. Morat gasped. *Another person. Human. Just like me.* Now, with his sight on target, he couldn't pull the trigger. The enormity of shooting someone stopped him. He shook his head and re-aimed at another. This man evidenced panic, which Morat felt directly. The man would turn and run if possible, except for the shame of letting down his fellows.

Over and over, Morat aimed at an enemy and found him to be *not* an enemy. Just a man, frightened, driven and lost like Morat himself. Repeatedly, he was unable to pull the trigger. Neither of his remaining team members were firing, either. He sobbed in frustration. How long would it be until they swept over his position? He would die, yet he couldn't bring himself to shoot.

Unable now even to aim, he let his weapon drop, waiting for the end.

Then the attack faltered. One by one, then in hordes, the Tileus attackers stopped charging. No one fired on either side. Morat impathed amazement, regret, compassion from the enemy line. Men on both sides shook their heads and threw their weapons on the ground. Some collapsed, crumpling as if in grief.

The attack ended. Morat had no idea why.

❧ ✳ ❦

Above Morat, the pilot of a Tileus warfighting aircar rolled into position over the front lines, finger on his trigger. He settled in to his fourth pass, and he had ammo for more. The men below in Rathas grey were sitting ducks. He laughed to himself, feeling the unassailable power of his position above them—and rage at the temerity of these forces to invade his country.

Abruptly, something new impinged on his consciousness. Emotions from the men below. Determination, doubt, fear. In his surprise, he took his finger off the trigger. He felt their humanity, their compassion for others. Just like himself.

The entrenched soldiers dropped their weapons. They feared death in the same way he did. Somehow, he'd connected with them. How could he fire on people he understood? Tears came to his eyes and he was unable to finish the attack.

The pilot wheeled his aircar upward and away from the battle. Torn with doubt, he turned toward his base. In the distance, he saw three other aircars break off their attacks.

Yet what would he tell his commander? The pilot was a professional, doing the job he'd trained to do, and he'd just quit?

No. He turned his craft back toward the lines. The empathy returned. Each of those men had lives, families. Again, the pilot couldn't bring himself to fire.

Screw this. He didn't know what sort of weapon they used on him, but he'd at least report it. He returned to base.

⁂ ❋ ⁂

Beltaret Leaderlist shouted at Dominact, "What I've done was necessary, Pronas! If I hadn't gotten that Tileus defector to develop the jammer, we'd all be under their emotional control. You've felt what the t-path can do. You know how evil it is."

"But you developed and used the same technology, Beltaret! That makes you just as evil as them. You can't take on a little sin to prevent—"

The floor slid sideways.

"Earthquake!" shouted one of the soldiers.

Dominact stumbled and fell. He cried out when his wrist bent backward. The coffee service on a side table crashed to the floor, spilling scalding liquid over Dominact's hand. He yelled in pain again, rolling away from the searing pool.

Beltaret grabbed a doorframe, swaying. The room swept back and forth, dizzying, unsettling. A strange scent of dirt came to him. The hologram display over the table wavered and blurred.

On the heels of the quake, the war center conference room infused with deep red air. Sparks of white brilliance whirled in the carnelian fog.

Something burned Beltaret's hip. He jumped and looked down. The t-path jammer in his pocket glowed through the fabric. With a shout, Beltaret snatched it out. The unit was so hot it seared his fingers. He threw it to the floor.

"Good God," he yelled.

The jammer ignited in a white flash, then melted into a puddle. The glowing material slid around on the moving floor. Beltaret's breath rasped in his throat.

The room stopped moving and Beltaret sighed.

Dominact struggled to his feet and looked ready to resume his flaming accusations.

Immediately, though, Beltaret's relief at the earthquake cessation gave way to incredible feelings from all around him. He wasn't carrying a transpath, yet the impathed emotions exceeded any of the t-path sensations he knew. He'd become used to looking at people to sense their emotions. This time, he impathed the feelings of every person involved in the entire battle. Determination and hate from General Comfors. Concentration from the planning soldiers in the room. Dismay and fear from the Rathas and Tileus soldiers in the city below. Panic from the citizens cowering in their homes. His empathic senses spread farther and wider. He picked up concern from his secretary over the mountains in Praise, worry from the lead proctor in Glorify, even individual dismay from Governor Welton Moller in Thad City, eight hundred kilometers away. The breadth of Beltaret's impath matched the scope of his ambition for Rathas. The collected feelings screamed at his senses like the shrieking of a frightened mob.

Over it all threaded the all-knowing, all-powerful love of Elláh as Beltaret had never grasped it before. He thought he knew his God, but never like this. Overwhelmed and stunned, he fell to his knees and raised his hands in sorrowful prayer for what he had done.

⁂

Hardly aware of what happened, Fenet clung to Tenpos' and Lorefim's hands like lifelines on a sinking ship. The entire world had gone crazy. Red swirls buffeted the group with hurricane winds. Gusts threw Fenet left and right, fore and back. The noise deafened him. Silver-bright sparks emanated from the t-path units, flying up to create silver bands in the carmine swirl. Dirt lifted from the ground, swept up into the tornado. The dust peppered his hands and face like stinging salt from a hurricane sea.

Fenet had done many miracles, but none like this. Elláh exceeded Fenet's capacity to understand, as the power flowed through and beyond him. His body shook violently with each wave of miracle feeding the tornado above him. Was this the end of his life? The finality of being Elláh's tool for good in the world? His mind overwhelmed by the intense sights, sounds, and sensations, he gave in to the experience. He chose to trust in Elláh.

In the grand resort lobby, Jake watched Randy stride away. The change in the man had been stunning. Where Randy had always before been bristly, difficult to talk with—though brilliant in his work—he had just demonstrated a vast amount of humility.

Jake shook his head in wonder. He reached out and touched Zofia.

"Is he gone?" Zofia whirled to face Jake. Her eyes darted to find Randy across the room, walking away.

"Yes." Jake sighed and opened his arms, inviting her in. "He's changed."

She relaxed her stiff shoulders, flipped her hair back, and settled into his embrace. "Maybe. But we'll never be able to trust him."

"You're right at that." Sharing a hug with Zofia always soothed Jake's soul. They had become so close through all their troubles, often joined in some deep spiritual way. He tightened the hug and moved one hand down to cradle the small of her back, pressing her against him.

The earth moved.

"What?" Zofia exclaimed.

Wait, the earth really *was* moving. Jake's eyes opened wide. The two braced each other, staggering in the quake. The immense picture window beside them wavered, emitting a piercing treble keen. Jake spread his legs for balance. The screech from the window intensified.

"Should we get out of here?" Zofia's voice sounded loud in his ear.

Before he could answer, the window shattered. Glass shards flew around them and outward onto the wide patio below. Jake and Zofia cowered in each other's arms.

"Great stars," Jake shouted. "Are you hurt?"

The rain of glass had ended, yet the floor still swayed. Tottering, they released the hug and held hands for balance while they checked each other. Zofia had glass in her hair. Sparkling fragments fell from her shoulders when the two staggered. Jake wanted to pick the glass off her, but the unstable ground still moved.

"I'm not hurt." Her eyes darted over him. "But you've got cuts on your arms and glass on your head."

Her statement seemed absurd. "'Not hurt'? You've got cuts, too." They clung to each other's hands against the wild motion.

He impathed her love for him, then realized their emotional connection to be deeper than he'd ever known it. He gasped.

She did the same. "What's going on, Jake?" Her eyes went wide.

The depth of emotion astonished him.

The quake stopped as suddenly as it started. She released his hands and turned to look down into the city. "Damn, I'm impathing emotions from all over."

"Same here. I feel anguish and regret and pain from people throughout the city. They're aghast at what they're doing. Soldiers are rejecting their training, turning their backs on war."

"Look!" Zofia pointed toward the city. "The explosions have stopped. The aircars are turning away from the battle."

Jake wrapped an arm around her. "Zofia, it's our dream. The t-path can do it."

She looked up at him. "But it's not the t-path. We never designed anything like this. How can we be impathing emotions from so many people, so far away?"

"I never designed anything like this, either." Randy stepped up beside them, his voice filled with awe. "I don't know what this is, if not a miracle."

Zofia started at Randy's voice. She turned toward him. Her shoulders tightened.

Jake impathed Zofia's quick anger, ready to lash out. Before she did, however, he felt her reaction to seeing inside Randy: a sudden release of her anger.

She relaxed. "A miracle indeed, Randy."

❧ ✳ ☙

The battleground had gone silent. Morat's weapon lay on the ground. He hung his head, putting his forehead against the cold hard plascrete of the ditch they'd been defending.

"Corp, whadda we do now?" Gutstrong sounded lost and afraid.

Morat shook his head. He didn't have the emotional strength to give guidance. "I don't know. I can't fight anymore, and these emotions I get from the enemy say they can't either."

He looked up. Gutstrong and Windo watched him, their eyes filled with dismay and their emotions ringing of uncertainty. Windo still held his rifle. The burden of leadership laid heavy on Morat.

"Put the weapon down, Windo. You're not going to use it." Morat took a deep breath. Across the damaged parkland, movement showed the Tileus forces still holding their position halfway up the battlefield. However, their emotions told him no resistance existed to anything he might do.

He came to a decision. "Let's go meet them, boys."

Morat rose to his feet, leaving his weapon where it lay. He climbed the last meter of the ditch, spread his hands wide to show himself unarmed. and walked across the field. Gutstrong and Windo followed him. Morat glanced to the other Rathas forces to his right and left and caught the wonder in his compatriots' emotions.

A couple of Tileus soldiers left their line and came forward. Like Morat, they carried no weapons. The two small groups met in the middle of the grassy park over which they'd been fighting.

Morat looked back and forth at the two Tileus men. They didn't look any different from Rathas men, only in a dark green uniform instead of his grey. The emotions he impathed from the two matched his own: dismay, wonder, a bit of shame.

"We're not going to fight anymore," he said. "What about you?"

"Can't do it." The Tileus soldier reached out his hand.

❧ ✳ ☙

On the mountain overlook, the scarlet and silver tornado wound down, withdrawing its tendrils from the faraway places it had reached. The many fingers returned to the central swirl. The tower of wind then raced downward toward the mountain bluff where Fenet and the Khadam stood.

Fenet's hands still clamped with the others, as if fused together. He had no idea whether this miracle had lasted minutes or hours.

The gusts buffeted him, yet he did not feel them. Lost in the immense sense of power, his ears ringing with the scream of the wind, Fenet's mind reached distant horizons without him.

Exhausted, he blocked the ineffable images, sounds, and scents of the miraculous whirlwind, feelings more powerful than any he'd known. Fenet barely felt the hands of Tenpos and Lorefim. His head whirled like the wind.

When the tempest collapsed down to them on the overlook, it exploded in a wave of vermilion blast. The seven t-paths shattered. Plastic and electronic parts scattered around them. The trees around the overlook blew outward in reaction, then stood tall and still again.

Shouts from the novim faded into the blackness of oblivion. Fenet collapsed.

44 – Empathy Ascendant

Lightning and thunder are the heralds of a silver lining.

—*Sayings of Reb Fenet* by Ellen Thranadil, Tileus
Press 448 A.T.

How did this happen?" With a sense of awe, Jake stood in front of the shattered window.

Zofia slid her arm around his waist. The two held each other without speaking. A breeze blew into the hotel lobby, carrying the faint acridity of the turbulent smoke from the city far below.

She cocked her head. "We're going to have to find out, Bucko."

"I'd like to know, too." Randy stayed a pace away from the couple, his contrition evident in pathed emotion, tone and action. "Whatever did this is greater than anything we've come up with."

Jake sighed. He used his free hand to brush the larger pieces of glass off Zofia's head. "You sparkle, love," he said with a chuckle.

She smiled and looked up at him. "You do, too. Wait, don't cut yourself. I've got a comb."

She let go of his hand and retrieved the comb from her purse, then reached up to comb his hair. The shards tinkled when they dropped to the floor. When done, she handed him the comb.

Crunching glass under their shoes, the colony team joined them. Coordinator Serban's normal outgoing voice sounded subdued. "Be you having any explanation for this event, friend Jake? It feels like your transpath, but much more."

Jake finished one last careful pass with the comb through Zofia's hair. "We have none, Coordinator. Our equipment could do nothing like this. And yet ..." He paused in thought.

Zofia spoke up. "We may not know yet how this happened, Coordinator, but we recognize the result. Since last year and the events in Verdant Prime, Jake and I have shared a dream about the t-path." She waved a hand toward the city and the diminishing pillars of smoke. "This dream."

Jake nodded. "The genius who invented the t-path, Yitzak Goren, passed on his vision to us, that the empathy provided by our devices would foster understanding among people. If t-paths spread and emotional perception became both common and strong ... perhaps wars would cease."

"We are amazed, Coordinator," said Zofia, "because what happened this morning is exactly our dream. The fighting has stopped."

"But we didn't do it." Jake gave a smiling shrug "We'd like to know who did."

"And how they did it," added Randy.

Serban looked out over the city. "We be wanting to know, also. Maybe we can be starting a new world without the human propensity for differences."

Behind them, the door to the conference room opened with a crash against the wall. Minister Leaderlist stalked out with storm clouds on his face. He glanced at the assemblage of colonists and technologists, gave a dismissive snort, then strode through the lobby and out the hotel door, radiating extreme anger.

Inside the conference room, the soldiers appeared to be packing up.

Minister Dominact followed Leaderlist out of the room at a more measured pace. The man's face was grim but satisfied. He came over to the group.

Dominact glanced at Jake and Zofia, then addressed Serban. "Coordinator, it appears we will no longer need your services to arbitrate."

Serban's eyebrows rose. "Have you then made an unfortunate decision, sir?"

"No, not unfortunate at all. We are ending our Holy War and will return our Khubar f'Elláh forces to our own country."

Jake suppressed a cheer. Zofia squeezed his hand.

"This be a good decision." The coordinator nodded. "We had been hoping that might be the case. May we then proceed to schedule colony presentations in your Rathas cities?"

Dominact seemed surprised at the question. He put a hand in his pocket. "Well, sir. Our thoughts have been rather full, and I had forgotten your request." He paused, then smiled. "However, that does make eminent sense. Much more sense than what we have all experienced this morning. For instance, I have a lingering taste of the empathy that overwhelmed us, and I feel your sincerity. We will be pleased to work with your people."

"I also be still feeling your emotions, Minister, at a level greater than the t-path device has shown so far."

Dominact waved a hand at the country around them. "Do we have any idea what caused this … miracle? I hesitate to call it such, but so far that's the best word. Mr. Palatin, was this your doing?"

Jake had been marveling at the harmony in this group despite the disparity in their positions. A national minister, a colony leader, and a couple of technologists. "We were just discussing that, Minister. No, TechEmpath had nothing to do with such widespread empathy. Our devices are limited to individuals."

Zofia raised her hand holding a small device. "I might have a clue. The jammer detector I carried into your conference room is still active. It's pointing toward some strong activity in the mountains to the west."

Serban cocked his head. "Be you thinking your device might lead us to the source?"

"It might, sir. We just need to play 'follow the needle.'" The twinkle in Zofia's eyes coupled with her smile.

Jake gave an amused snort. Zofia's playfulness swelled his heart with joy. With all the problems—Randy's theft, the fire in the lab, a sudden war—there'd been far too many days recently when nothing triggered that impishness.

"Then let us try," said the coordinator. "There be sufficient room in our airvan for all of us. Minister, Jake, Zofia, let us see if we can be finding out."

Scanat stepped up to quiet leadership when their teacher collapsed. He knelt at Fenet's side and checked for life signs. The reb's respiration barely registered, infrequent and shallow. Scanat held a finger to Fenet's carotid, feeling a faint pulse. He saw no physical damage. Nothing had struck Fenet, and he'd not hit his head.

Scanat suggested, "Tenpos, let's move Reb Fenet over to the comfortable grass."

Durnadat and Penilos stepped up to help. The four of them made for an easy, careful lift. Lorefim retrieved one of the backpacks for a head rest.

Reb Eregim seemed to be in mental trauma. He fluttered his hands toward his friend of twenty-five years as if it would help. "Does anyone know enough triage or first aid to help Fenet?" His voice quavered.

Everyone around the group shook their heads.

Scanat didn't know what to do about Reb Fenet. He had no practical medical knowledge. He stood up, feeling helpless. Looking over the group with some dismay, he thought about what to do next.

The obvious solution came to him. "Durnadat, please use your imp to call for an ambulance?"

While Durnadat made the call, Scanat noticed the t-path units. Every one showed black scorching. Puzzled, Scanat removed his own from his belt. The control wheel would not move; the unit appeared dead.

When he looked again at the other novim, however, his sense of empathic connection stayed strong. "Huh. We still have the t-path power, though our units are fried."

Tenpos showed surprise, then nodded. "You're right. Has Elláh given us this gift?"

What Scanat impathed from the others surprised and fulfilled him. Despite his large transgressions over the last three weeks, they showed feelings of trust for him. Even Beneim had given in. A vast sense of relief about his own situation flooded Scanat.

Durnadat raised a finger. "We have a problem, Scanat. Uptown emergency services are overloaded with war casualties. They say they can't get an ambulance up here in less than three hours."

"Three hours?" Scanat swallowed hard.

"There's worse," Durnadat said, "I also called over to Praise. They can't send any vehicles here, across the border, because of the war."

Scanat looked down at Fenet again. Stymied, he had no other solutions. Could they carry Fenet back down the mountain to Pincely's bus? They'd need some type of stretcher.

"Look!" Penilos shouted. "There's an aircar coming."

Tenpos turned to face it. "Is it the Heresy Angels returning?"

Beneim shook his head. "No, this is a larger vehicle. And it's coming from Uptown."

The group stood around the disabled teacher awaiting this arrival. Maybe the arrivals would help Reb Fenet. Or perhaps this vehicle portended a new challenge from Elláh.

With nothing to do but wait, Scanat brooded again on his own future. Once they'd finished, what would *he* do? He still faced the same decision that had driven his actions: should he remain in the Khadam and seek a life of ministry, or should he return to tertiary school? What would Reb Fenet advise him to do? He had no idea whether Captain Forsfear's contract with him still held, but it was a written contract with the state of Rathas. Scanat had fulfilled his part.

The airvan rose from the valley below and flew over their heads.

Pincely broke the group silence. "Man, wish I had one of them. Can't carry as many as my hoverbus, but I could charge more for flying trips."

The van settled onto the grass crushed earlier by Forsfear's vehicle. A dozen people stepped out, many of them dressed in the most outlandish bright clothes Scanat had ever seen. Foreigners for sure, but not from any culture Scanat knew. Were they off-worlders?

Scanat's eyebrows went up when he recognized the robes and collar of a Rathas national Service Minister among the remaining few. The others had more ordinary attire. A very mixed group.

Reb Eregim still crouched beside Fenet. He kept checking the teacher's body, straightening Fenet's clothes, lost in grief over his friend.

None of the novim made any move to meet the new arrivals, who looked important. Scanat didn't believe himself to be the appropriate person to greet them. Without Eregim, however, the responsibility fell on him. He hoped this assemblage threatened less than the Heresy Angels.

He took a step forward. "May I help you?"

The eldest of the bright-clothed party answered him in a strange accent. "We be hoping so. I see by your robes most of you be in the ministry. We be wondering what your purpose be, here on this mountain?"

How could Scanat answer that question after what had happened? He glanced at Tenpos, who shrugged. Honesty would be in order, yet the full honest answer would be unbelievable. He opened his mouth, then closed it again, still uncertain what to say.

"Wait a second, Coordinator." One of the two men in ordinary attire stepped forward beside the foreign leader. He looked at Scanat. "I remember you. You're the young man who took a bunch of t-paths from us in Glorify, aren't you?"

Scanat looked again at the man and memory flooded back. "Yes, sir. You're ... uh ... Jake Palatin, right?"

The man nodded.

"I'm Scanat, sir. It's good to meet you again. Your t-paths have been very useful to us since then."

Durnadat broke into a merry laugh and gave Scanat a friendly push. "That might be the understatement of the century, Scanat, after all we've been through."

Scanat waved the nov back. "Enough, Durnadat. This is too serious for your hijinks."

While this interchange happened, the leader with the strange accent glanced at Jake and waved a hand forward, encouraging Jake to continue.

Jake's eyes narrowed. "Scanat. You stood out to me at that meeting. Not many people came forward for the free transpaths we offered, and you wanted ... what was it, seven of them?"

"Yes, sir. And we've used them." Scanat unclipped and held up his own blackened unit. "I'm afraid they're destroyed now."

Jake took the t-path and puzzled over it. "What did this? Are they all like this?"

Two of the other novim held up theirs, likewise scorched. Scanat gestured to the plastic and electronic shards on the ground, all that remained of the others.

Still holding the unit, Jake reached for the others. "Do you mind if we take them back to our lab for testing? We can replace them for you."

"Not at all, sir." Scanat flashed his eyes to Tenpos with a small smile. "But I think we're not going to need them anymore."

Jake paused in thought. "Back at that presentation, you also said something that startled me. You said you and your group performed miracles." He glanced at the other novim.

Scanat looked down at Reb Fenet. Scanat didn't see himself as the right person to talk about the miracles. Yet the Khadam all watched him. "Yes, sir, I did. And we do." New pride in the miracles emboldened his voice.

Several of the novim straightened at the statement.

The foreign leader put his hand on Jake's shoulder. "Miracles? We did certainly see a miracle this morning. Young man ... Scanat ... I be Coordinator Deniz Serban from the planet Brightness. We be here to organize a colony ship to the new planet Bluewater. What we did witness this morning did amaze us. An active war did stop in its tracks by empathy exceeding anything Jake's devices be capable of doing." The coordinator paused. "Did you and your people make this happen?"

Scanat's face flushed with embarrassment. "We were part of it, sir. It stretched much bigger than anything we'd ever done before." He waved a hand at their incapacitated teacher. "But Reb Fenet led it and used Elláh's power to make it happen. And now he's in deep trouble."

Everyone looked toward the comatose Fenet.

Reb Eregim looked up at the sudden attention with dismay. He wrung his hands and stood up. With a deep breath, he regained his composure. "He needs help. Is there anything you can do?"

Durnadat said, "We've called for an ambulance, but they're all busy with war injuries."

The Rathas minister raised a finger for attention. "Reb Fenet? Is that Reb Fenet Powrfaith?"

Scanat cocked his head. "Yes, Minister. You've heard of him?"

"We have indeed, son. I'm Pronas Dominact, Minister of Trade. The Service Ministry has heard of Reb Fenet several times recently, about his trip from Glorify. Mostly bad, I'm afraid. We have reports saying he's been guilty of heresy and flouting the Church—"

Scanat cut him off, raising his voice. "He's done nothing but good, Minister. The Heresy Angels have been making all sorts of false accusations. The powers Fenet has taught us to use come from Elláh. Through us, Elláh healed people all the way from Glorify to Praise. He transported us great distances, made us comfortable in adverse weather. Elláh stopped and reversed a huge earthquake outside of Praise. He rescued us from the dungeon under Church Center One—"

Dominact held up his hands. "Whoa, son, whoa. Too fast. An earthquake? I don't remember—"

"No one remembers, sir. Part of Elláh's miracle made everyone forget about it but us."

A slight wash of vermilion waved from Scanat to Dominact.

The minister took a step back. Eyes wide, he said, "I remember now. An earthquake. There really was one. Yet I didn't remember anything about it until now. How could that be?" His eyebrows lowered and he stepped forward again, pointing a finger. "You said something about a dungeon?"

"Yes, sir. We've been hounded by proctors and by the Heresy Angels throughout our trip." Scanat's ire tinged his entire being. "They've accused us of heresy over and over. Captain Forsfear arrested us. Twice. He threatened us and had us beaten. And he threw the Khadam in your terrible prison, living in their own waste, right in the basement of—"

"Church Center One, yes. I get it." Dominact raised his palm, his eyes on fire. His jaw clamped, vision going far away as if looking elsewhere. "I've known nothing of such a dungeon." He paused. "Leaderlist!" He spit out the name like a bitter taste.

Scanat rode his anger back down, taming it like a wild hawk. Surprise. Intrigues within the Service Ministry went on all the time. Now, he had direct contact with one. This level of national interaction exhilarated him. He actually talked one-on-one with a member of the Service Ministry. And the other novim accepted his role as leader. Scanat stood taller.

Dominact went on, thinking out loud. "So, there have been three such huge miracles in the last few days? An earthquake repaired, your prison breakout ... and now this incredible instance of empathic connectivity."

The entire group became silent in the awe of what Elláh had done.

In the pause, Reb Eregim spoke again. "Can we *please* get help for Fenet? He's the one central to all of these."

Dominact stepped over to the comatose figure, then turned to Durnadat. "You say the ambulances aren't available?"

"That's right, sir," said Durnadat.

"Then we'll have one of our military vehicles drop by here and take him to a hospital in Praise."

With the decision made, help on the way, Scanat turned back to the rest of the Khadam. They watched him with smiles; pathing acceptance and pride in his leadership. A sense of wonder burst into him; he'd never known this level of acceptance.

45 – Peace Ascendant

When Elláh gives us storm clouds, we can dance in the fog.

—*Sayings of Reb Fenet* by Ellen Thranadil, Tileus
Press 448 A.T.

So, why were you fighting?" asked Morat Vengeact. He stood on the shattered parkland with the Tileus corporal. Sunlight broke through the fading clouds of smoke. Other small groups of soldiers from both sides stood around sharing the residual empathy. So far, Morat had learned the man's first name, Terence, and impathed his deep sorrow about the battle they'd been fighting.

Terence answered, "I've been in the Army for a year. When your lot declared war, we mobilized. Called up a lot of reserves, too."

"I was a quick recruit. Only joined the Khubar f'Elláh two weeks ago."

"Two weeks, and you're already a corporal?"

Morat shrugged. "We needed fireteam leaders, and I sort of stood out during training. I was angry. Wanted to punish Tileus, and I guess it showed. Besides, I became famous in a small way. My girlfriend Faï was the one kidnapped and left to die in the mountains. The girl that became the excuse for us to declare war."

Terence looked shocked and ashamed. "I'm sorry for that. We shouldn't have done it."

"We?"

"Yeah." Terence paused. "I knew of it. I've been part of The Freethinkers for six months, trying to stop religion in Tileus."

A part of Morat wanted to be angry all over again. Then he impathed Terence's shame and contrition, and let go of the anger. "You knew of it? Did you take part?"

"Not in the kidnapping, no. But I was on the streets in the protests against that last group of missionaries."

The statement stunned Morat. He knew his emotions showed his shock, because Terence's eyes got wide. "Uh … I was there, too. One of the missionaries in that last group."

Terence snorted a bitter laugh. He pathed a wry sense of amazement. "So, we've already met once."

"Yeah. I was the one on the ground, trying not to get stepped on." Morat also laughed, dry and bitter at the coincidence.

A shout came from behind him. "Corporal Vengeact! Gather your team and assemble at the jump-vee. We're moving out."

"Right away, Sarge," Morat shouted back. He turned back to the Tileus corporal. "Maybe we'll meet a third time, Terence, under better circumstances."

Half an hour later, Morat and his team were back inside the jump-vee with a mere half of the soldiers of yesterday, growling their way over the mountains. The vehicle radiated the emotions of the platoon, and sorrow blanketed most of those emotions like a heavy cloud. Morat glanced at Gutstrong and Windo and remembered Privates Grinhand and Manmove. He hung his head, wishing everything had been different since his disastrous missionary trip to Uptown.

The metal monster tilted to descend. Puzzling; there hadn't been enough time to get over the mountains yet.

The new staff sergeant spoke through the platoon imps. "Making an unscheduled stop here in the mountains, men. We're picking up a special casualty. The word is this is the guy responsible for the miracle that stopped the war. Corporal Vengeact, get your fireteam to bring him aboard. There's a stretcher by the door."

Morat lifted his head. "Okay, Sarge." A miracle man? And Morat and his team would help him? That must have been some doing, to spread those feelings across the entire war. The more he thought about it, the more awed he became.

The jump-vee grounded and the loading gate dropped open.

Morat gave commands to his team. "Gutstrong, Windo, leave your weapons and gear here. Grab the stretcher. Let's go."

The three stepped out the loading gate into a mountain clearing overlooking a long valley. Smoke rose from the city of Uptown in the distance. Morat's two remaining privates carried the stretcher. A couple of robed clerics helped to load the casualty. The man didn't look like a miracle worker, just a frail older man dressed in country clothes. Gutstrong and Windo lifted the man back into the jump-vee, settling him onto an empty bench.

A group of novim in robes followed them into the vehicle. Morat started to object, but the staff sergeant waved his hand in permission. The novim, no older than Morat, settled themselves on benches. An older cleric joined them, wearing the tan collar of a local minister. He sat beside the miracle man to tend him, obviously a good friend.

The last of the young men turned back to speak to another man wearing a boxy uniform hat. "Will you be okay, Pincely?"

"You bet, Scanat. These here Brightness people say they can take me to my bus."

The Scanat fellow turned in when the loading gate lifted to a close. He caught Morat's eyes.

Morat gasped as he sensed Elláh's power in the emotions of this man, just a couple of years older than him. Morat looked more closely at the other novim and had the same sense of spiritual potency. He gazed again in awe at the older man on the stretcher. If these young men filled with such might were his disciples, what would this man be like? Any doubt Morat had about the identity of the miracle worker disappeared.

Miracles from Elláh? Huh. Morat had felt them. He'd have to change his powername back to Intelact.

46 – Censure

When you have done wrong, the best approach is humility. It can open doors that otherwise would slam shut.

—A Practical Guide to Sensitive Negotiation by Ellen Thranadil, 426 A.T.

Two days later, Beltaret Leaderlist left his office on the top floor of Church Center One for the Service Ministry conference room. It would likely be the last time. In the midst of the miracle, they'd voted him out of the leadership chair. He'd been pondering his role in the last month's events since storming out of the war center, and he had no good answers yet. Except he'd lost the confidence of the Service Ministry. Dominact had taken charge in his place.

Captain Forsfear strode beside him, as military in bearing as Beltaret himself. "What do you expect, Minister?"

"Some level of condemnation, Captain. Hopefully, we'll be able to make right the wrongs we've done."

Their shoes clicked in unison on the hard floor. Beltaret impathed the man's distasteful emotions. While the miraculous empathy effect had faded in these two days for everyone else, Beltaret's remained as strong as during the event. He'd always viewed himself as a godly man, doing his best to protect the Church and its country. Seeing into other's emotions now played a strong role in Beltaret's considerations. He perceived how others viewed him, and it called into question his definitions of best.

What he perceived in Forsfear made Beltaret wonder why he had ever trusted and selected the man. The captain evidenced no remorse for the evil things he'd done. Forsfear pathed a twisted eagerness tinged with sadistic glee. Why had Beltaret not seen this in the man before?

The captain broke the silence. "We can correct the wrongs, sir, and do it better. With more force, less wavering."

"Perhaps," said Beltaret. He would wait to hear what the Ministry had to say.

The two entered the Seat of Elláh conference chamber to find the rest of the Service Ministry already assembled. Dominact had the head of the table, the seat Beltaret had occupied for the past six years. Bishop Menos Evangel, Brevet Curiorat and the five other national ministers had their usual places. Support staff sat around the walls. No chairs remained. Beltaret and Forsfear would have to stand before the Ministry.

Beltaret took a position two meters away from Forsfear, wanting to separate himself from the captain. He scanned the room, impathing variations on sadness, annoyance, disappointment, even disgust. The emotions might have been aimed at Forsfear, himself, or both.

"Thank you for coming at our behest." Minister Dominact took charge. "As you know, Beltaret, the Ministry voted in the midst of the miracle to rescind our declaration of war and to elect me to the leadership in your stead."

Beltaret acknowledged the statement with a curt nod.

Dominact tapped the table. "We've been considering what to do about the new situation ever since. First and foremost is the recognition of the godly miracles done by Reb Fenet Powrfaith. The minister is still in a coma, so we've been unable to talk to him. Like a rocket in the sky, he's become famous, and his novim are still performing miracles. Crowds surround the hospital, praying for Powrfaith. These facts change our perception of what the Church teaches. We must accept miracles as part of our doctrine." He paused. "One of our decisions concerns you, Captain Forsfear."

The captain raised a defiant chin.

"We've made a preliminary investigation of your activities, and we are frankly appalled. We have testimony of your heavy-handed persecution of anyone you personally deemed a heretic. Such actions are not in keeping with the love of Elláh. They smack of religious oppression." Dominact's voice elevated in anger. "Even more, we have toured your torture chamber in the basement of this very building—the center of our Church—and are struck with horror at what you've done. Reb Powrfaith's escape from your dungeon left a hole in the wall as a permanent testament to your evil.

"Frinat Forsfear, by the power vested in this Ministry, we hereby strip you of your position and disband your so-called Heresy Angels. We also banish you from the roll of Church proctors.

"Furthermore," Dominact said, "we have preferred charges against you for torture, misuse of authority ... and heresy." The minister spat the last word like a dagger.

The door opened behind Beltaret. Four proctors came in to surround Forsfear. Beltaret turned his head just enough to watch, and he impathed the captain's disdain for the proceedings. Two proctors gripped the man's arms while a third pulled his hands behind him into tanglecuffs. Forsfear barely held his anger in check, and he pathed a sense of determination. Perhaps the man already plotted revenge. The last proctor used a laserknife to slice off the insignias from Forsfear's shoulders, lapels, and cuffs, throwing them to the floor. Then he removed the captain's cap, dropped it onto the pile, and ground it under his heel.

"You are dismissed," Dominact snapped. "Proctors, get this man out of my sight."

Forsfear pathed such anger Beltaret feared the man would do violence. The ex-captain frothed at the mouth while he ranted last words. "I only did what the rest of you were too weak to do. My work kept Rathas pure from—"

The doors shut on his diatribe, leaving the room in silence. A staffer got up from his chair to clean up the scattered emblems of misused authority from the floor.

Dominact took a deep breath. He smoothed a palm across the table, then looked at Bishop Evangel. The two traded a look of mutual support before Dominact turned again to Leaderlist.

"Beltaret," he said. "That is, Minister Leaderlist ... your situation is more problematic for us. We've been friends and colleagues for many years. The ministry discussions about you have been difficult. We know your motives have always been godly, with the best interests of Rathas at heart. And of course, you have led this Ministry well for six years."

Beltaret stood more at ease. "That has been my goal in everything I've done."

Dominact and several others nodded. "We know. Yet … your recent handling of security affairs has led to a national embarrassment. We wrongly declared war on Tileus and were only stopped from further wrong by Elláh's strong hand through this unknown minister. In addition, we find two recent wrongs that call your judgment into question. First was your violation of your own prohibition against the transpath—"

"—which we changed yesterday," Bishop Evangel inserted. "Church doctrine now affirms the transpath to be a godly device to help the faithful."

"Yes," Dominact confirmed, "we made that change. Elláh has shown us the error of our way. And second was your hiring, promotion, and encouragement of Captain Forsfear. You funded his development of that chamber in the basement." He nodded. "Yes, we have looked at the financial records. You also authorized the creation of his misguided corps of Heresy Angels."

Beltaret impathed the sorrow and concern with which his colleagues viewed his actions. He lowered his eyes. "You're right. I did both of those, overriding my own better judgment. My conscience—Elláh's voice—spoke to me against them, but I thought I knew better."

"A common failing, my friend, thinking we know better than Elláh." Dominact drew himself up. "In any case, we believe it inappropriate for you to continue in the role of Minister of Security. We must ask you to step down."

Beltaret recognized the request as an ultimatum. Looking around the table, he impathed firm determination from all. "Thank you for your kind words, Pronas. You're right; my ways have strayed recently. I expected this action."

He straightened. "I hereby volunteer my resignation as Minister of Security. I'm sure you will find a capable replacement."

Dominact looked around the table to nods from the others. "Your resignation is accepted, Beltaret. Thank you."

The ministers relaxed. Beltaret impathed the tension they'd felt as it released.

Dominact tilted his head. "We've been friends a long time, Beltaret. We wish you Elláh's blessing and hope you'll find something worth your while. Have you considered what you will do next?"

Beltaret's gaze went out the window to the mountains beyond the city. "Unlike the rest of you, Elláh has granted me a continuation of His miracle of interpersonal empathy. Others will require the transpath devices. For some reason, He's chosen to give me that permanent gift. There's a monastery in the Gortooths somewhat north of Praise. I believe I'll retire to a meditative life to sort out why. I'll renew myself with Elláh, and let Him guide me to what I may do afterward."

Jake and Zofia exited the autocar and strode into the Eluxor hotel. Down the block, two groups waved signs at each other across the street. Who knew what issue they were asserting? "Do you think Randy will accept the challenge?" Jake asked.

"He'd better," she spit out. "He'll never get a more promising opportunity." Her voice softened. "He really is a brilliant engineer. If we appeal to his desire for glory, it ought to suffice."

Randy jumped up from a lobby chair when they approached. He ran his palms down his pants. "Hi. Thanks for asking me to meet you. I'm still willing to do whatever I can to make things better between us." He paused, pathing embarrassment. "And thanks for calling off Detective Moller and the police."

Jake stepped in and shook hands. "We think we've found a way to solve our problems, Randy."

"Reluctantly," said Zofia, though with a slight smile.

"What is it? And why are we here at this hotel?"

"Let's go together." Jake gestured toward the lift tubes. "We need to meet with Coordinator Serban before his entourage leaves for their tour of Rathas."

When they reached the executive floor, Jake said, "We have an offer for you, Randy, that's related to this meeting."

Serban greeted them all in cordial fashion. With t-paths all around, the shared emotions eased any possible conflict. "Be welcome, friends Jake and Zofia. Welcome, new friend Randy. What may I do for you today?"

Jake went right to the point. "Coordinator, you asked us to go with you to Bluewater to further develop the transpath for your new world."

"Yes. We would be overjoyed to have you do so."

"However, we told you then—and still maintain—we cannot leave our business here in Tileus. The enterprise is still growing and is the basis for our dream of the t-path changing humanity." Jake glanced at Randy and impathed the man's growing interest. "We now have a replacement candidate for you. Someone who has already demonstrated the necessary deep technical knowledge and also has the desire to advance. We believe he'll do well for you while rising to greatness."

Jake turned to Randy. "I know we're springing this on you, Randy. But Zofia and I believe this may be the most excellent opportunity you can ever seek. How would you like to be our independent agent to a new world?"

47 – Different Kind of Fame

Every day is a new gift from Elláh.

—*Sayings of Reb Fenet* by Ellen Thranadil, Tileus
Press 448 A.T.

Scanat sat beside Reb Fenet in the antiseptic cleanliness of the hospital room. Quiet noises intruded from the nurse's station in the hall. In this room, the only sound was Scanat's own breathing and the regular beep of a monitor. Fenet breathed once every ten seconds, shallow and weak. His heart worked, but he lay as still as stone. The nurses had just given Fenet an alcohol sponge bath and the scent still hung in the air. The tubes keeping the reb nourished did little to ease Scanat's worry.

He spent the time thinking of his recent actions. Everything he'd done seemed right at the time. In hindsight, he recognized his self-centeredness, his willful disregard of Elláh's wishes. Scanat wished he'd learned his lessons earlier. Fenet certainly warned him about his own self-sufficiency many times.

Yet Elláh had brought things to good. The t-paths became crucial to that final miracle. He'd become the acknowledged leader of the Khadam. The cost along the way had been brutal.

A week had passed since the miracle, yet the crowds outside the hospital had not diminished. If anything, they'd grown. The news media filled everyone's imps with widespread stories of Fenet's miracle, in the war zone and out. Everyone had felt *something*. Worshippers created a memorial of piled flowers in the park opposite. Some kept vigil there day and night, waiting for the famous Reb Fenet Powrfaith to wake up.

"Keep healing anyone who needs it," Scanat had told the Khadam. Doing so kept the miracles alive for the people. It also allowed Scanat to be alone with Fenet.

The Khadam, including Scanat, retained the miraculous empathic ability given to them on that morning in the mountains. Transpaths were making their way into Rathas, so others discovered the amazement of true mutual understanding. With Elláh's power showing in Scanat, the Khadam had accepted him back. He could stay and become the minister he'd wanted to be.

And yet, he thought.

To Scanat's amazement, the national Minister of Education, Brevet Curiorat, had called him three days ago. Rathas would honor the contract forced on Scanat by Captain Forsfear. He could return to tertiary school in particle physics. Jake Palatin had also offered Scanat a place in the TechEmpath company if he completed school. As much as he had once wanted to be a minister like Fenet, the events had pointed out to him how self-driven he could be. Such an attitude detracted from the path of ministry, but would enhance his growth in engineering.

Scanat still faced this difficult decision: intellect or faith, ministry or science. He knew now his intelligence had long stood in his way of getting miracles, and how to set it aside to let faith work. However, he did not know where his artha lay, and Elláh had not yet given him any sign.

Fenet stirred. His breathing changed, became agitated.

"Nurse!" Scanat jumped to his feet and reached for the call button.

Reb Fenet's hands moved, plucking at the covers over his chest. His back arched, eyes clenched tight. He cried out an agonizing sound that struck Scanat to his core.

"Nurse!" Scanat shouted louder.

Three of them, dressed in starched whites with peaked hats, charged into the room, pushing Scanat aside. Two ran to either side of Fenet's bed, the third moved to the monitor holo. Fenet thrashed on the bed, the covers tangling in disarray.

Scanat stood back, eyes wide, impathing the alarm from the nurses. For the first time in the last week, he also impathed emotions from Fenet: anguish, pain, terror.

"Respiridone," urged the nurse by the monitor. "Calm him down."

"Got it," said the second nurse while she grabbed the doser and pushed a few buttons. She reached for Fenet's writhing arm.

He pulled his arm out of her grasp. All three nurses stepped in to hold him down, yet he clawed at his chest as if trying to tear his heart out. Scanat stepped in to help, pressing down on Fenet's forearm while the nurse pressed the doser against his skin. After the injection, it took all four to hold him until he quieted.

He quieted too far.

Scanat stood in shock watching his teacher sink into the sheets, Fenet's breathing becoming incredibly slow. Would Fenet even take the next? Each breath brought an agonizing wait. The pathed emotions fell to nothing again.

"Is he ... dying?" Scanat asked with a tremor, stepping back. His mouth fell open, gasping for air to put into Fenet's lungs, to keep him going.

Fenet opened his eyes. Drenched in sweat, he lay on his back in a strange white room. He looked at the ceiling and took a deep breath. Three nurses in white leaned over him with hands on his arms. A hospital, then. While he became aware, they released him. One stroked his arm in a kind, gentle gesture. All three broke into smiles.

"Oh, thank Elláh!" came a cry from elsewhere in the room. A voice Fenet knew.

He rolled his eyes toward the voice. Scanat stood with hands clasped and raised to the ceiling. The strength of the nov's joy pathed into Fenet like a wave of fresh air. He tried to lift his head to see Scanat, but it hurt his neck. He laid his head back down. His mouth felt dry and caked with sticky saliva.

One breath after another. He took stock of himself.

The last thing he remembered was the dark red, sparking tornado on the mountain bluff. He furrowed his eyebrows, trying to remember what came after, but recalled nothing.

"Where ..." His dry mouth prevented talk.

One of the nurses leaned over him. "Welcome back, Fenet Powrfaith. We've been waiting for you." She ladled a few ice chips between his cracked lips.

Sweet relief! Thank you, Elláh. The ice melted around his tongue. He wetted his lips. The sweat on his body cooled.

"You're in Blessed Health hospital in Praise, Fenet." The nurse gave him another few chips. "We've been giving you care for a week. Everyone wants you to get well."

"Everyone, Reb Fenet!" Scanat stepped beside the bed. "I'm so glad you're awake. We've been very worried about you."

Fenet suddenly pushed himself up with his arms. He whispered, "The war! We've got to stop the war. Elláh said so." His unused muscles screamed in pain, and he fell back.

Scanat patted his shoulder, grinning. "It's stopped, Reb. You already did it, there on the mountain." Then Scanat pathed deep concern. "Don't you remember your miracle? The red tornado?"

Fenet nodded and relaxed. More ice chips eased his throat. His voice cleared. "Yes, I remember." He laid still. "So … the war stopped?"

"Yes, Reb," Scanat said. "Empathy spread so far and wide none of the soldiers could fight each other. They couldn't kill someone they understood so well. The fighters just dropped their weapons and started talking instead of shooting. Rathas has already taken back their declaration of war, and the Khubar f'Elláh came home."

Fenet impathed Scanat's excitement. Empathy still? Puzzling. Looking at the nurses, he felt their delight. "I can still feel peoples' emotions."

Scanat nodded, enthusiasm flowing from him. "We all can. The whole Khadam. Reb Eregim, too. Even Pincely. Everyone who took part in your miracle, Reb. It's faded for everyone else, but we still have the miraculous power."

"Help me up, please. I feel stiff and sore." He tried to sit again.

Scanat lifted his shoulder to help him.

One of the nurses stopped them. "We can elevate the bed." Her eyes unfocussed as she imped a control. The upper part of the bed did a slow lift.

Once Fenet was sitting, Scanat and the nurse helped him swing his legs over the edge of the bed. She tended the IV line to keep it from tangling.

Fenet's head whirled like the tornado. He had to sit still, supported by Scanat's hands, until it cleared. His back itched all over. A nurse gently rubbed it. After a few breaths, he took in his surroundings. His clothes hung on a hook, cleaned. His broad-brimmed floppy hat sat on the nightstand. While he watched, the brown and wilted *astradell* perked up, stood up straight again, and

334

resumed its bright yellow. The flower reminded him of the entire path he'd been on, how Elláh purified him from the very beginning. Each step, all the way from his home north of Glorify, had been part of Elláh's plan to forge them all anew.

"Don't get up yet, Reb," said one of the nurses. "Let's remove the IV first." A few deft motions later, the cool of an alcohol swab replaced the irritation of the needle.

Fenet slid onto his feet with Scanat's help. He wobbled a bit, but straightened his back while holding onto the bed rail. "This feels good."

"You know you're famous now?" The nurse bound the IV nick with a bandage pad.

"Famous?" Fenet puzzled.

Scanat laughed. "All the times you talked about it back in Glorify, Reb. How you dreamed your miracles would be so well-known your name would be as recognizable as the Zikri? Well, it's happened. Thousands of people wait outside this hospital for you to wake up."

"What?" Fenet's eyes went wide. "I've got to see this." He held onto the bed rail and took a few tentative steps toward the window. Each step strengthened him, until he could walk on his own.

Four stories below, in the plaza in front of the hospital, a massive throng milled about an enormous collection of flowers. Some people sat on the grass and pavement. Others stood talking with each other. People packed so close as to have difficulty moving. Farther away, more kept arriving.

"They've been here for days." Scanat stood beside him looking down.

Just below them, close to the building, knots of people formed half a dozen queues. At the head of each queue stood a robed figure with the yellow collar of a nov. The waiting people moved forward by ones and groups. Red light flashed along the line of figures.

"Are those ... the Khadam?" Fenet asked.

"They're healing people, Reb. Elláh's healing power still works in all of us." The young man paused, pathing awe. "Me, too. The people can't wait for you to show yourself. They all want to thank you. They all want your touch."

Fenet had never pictured a scene like this for recognition. So many people! Pushing forward, clamoring for attention, waiting for service. So much responsibility, all dependent on him? He thought he'd wanted fame. Now, the idea of going out there in front of thousands made him take a step back from the window. He realized himself to be just a simple country preacher, helping people one by one. He'd like to be known, but didn't want to face so many.

In a moment, his dream had changed. Proctors. Heresy Angels. Politics. War. Fame was not as comfortable as his old flower-topped floppy hat. Elláh had brought him full circle.

"Is there a back way out, Scanat? Can we just slip away and return to the country north of Glorify?"

Scanat smiled. "I'll call Pincely and see what we can do."

48 – Graduation Day

The greatest joy is helping someone else achieve their goal.

—*Sayings of Reb Fenet* by Ellen Thranadil, Tileus
Press 448 A.T.

As much as he wanted to, Fenet could not slide away unnoticed. The adoring crowds demanded his presence.

In the hospital room, Eregim joined Scanat to convince Fenet. "You need to show yourself, Fenet. This trip has taught me much, and I'll go back to my flock with far more confidence in Elláh. Use that confidence yourself, my friend."

Eregim held out Fenet's clothes with a smile. When Fenet nodded acquiescence, his friend helped him dress, then walked him to the hospital entrance in a wheelchair.

Fenet rolled out onto the raised veranda like a new actor with stage fright. The crowd screamed its approval. Being in front of so many people gave Fenet shudders. He got through it by focusing just on the few people in front of him, limiting the ones he could see and feel.

The new empathy power within him made it worse. The combined emotions of thousands of people proved overwhelming. Even with his gaze on a few, peripheral vision forced on him the feelings of many others. Now he had another reason to dislike crowds. The emotions rewarded him with affirmation. People adored him, revered him, loved him. Yet that endorsement remained insufficient to compensate for being engulfed.

At least he didn't have to make a speech. Eregim rolled him down the steps. He shook some hands, patted some shoulders, and healed one teenage girl of a love heartache.

By the time Pincely got the hoverbus through the crowds, the Khadam had gathered around Fenet. The bus gave blessed relief in its comparative quiet.

∾ ✳ ∿

A week later, Fanwell Hall in Glorify served as a celebration venue. Reb Fenet fidgeted in his chair on stage while the Bishop of Glorify made introductory remarks in ringing tones. Fenet's six novim sat in a row behind him,

The bishop's glowing words smacked of hypocrisy. The man praised Fenet for the very deeds he had earlier claimed as an excuse to send chiding proctors to him. The speech displayed another example of the frequent unreal nature of the Church. People often obstructed and perverted Elláh's way. However, people filled the Church. Fenet had made his own mistakes, too.

Crowds mobbed the hall, standing three deep around the walls. Fenet's fame brought them in to see the miracle worker. The throng made him nervous, but he would do this for the novim. They deserved it. As for Fenet, he couldn't wait to return to his home and mother north of Glorify to resume his lifelong ministry.

The bishop brought his overlong introduction to an end. "Without further ado, folks, I present to you our own miracle man: Reb Fenet Powrfaith." The bishop stepped aside and gestured for Fenet to take the podium.

Fenet stood. At his first step, his feet tangled in the unaccustomed robes. He had to stop and move one foot to free the hem. He put up with wearing them for an hour to honor the graduates. Yet he still wore his hat, complete with the same *astradell* he'd picked on the way to Praise four weeks ago.

Fenet took the podium and activated his imp as a microphone to connect with the speaker system. From his chair, the auditorium had looked full. Now, standing at the lectern, the crowd seemed insurmountable. *There must be fifteen hundred people in here.* He opened his mouth, then closed it again. Swallowed a hard lump.

Finally, words came out. "Welcome, friends. I know the bishop wants to acknowledge the great events of two weeks ago. However, today is not about me. Today is a celebration for these six young men behind me, who are advancing to the rank of ministers of the One Church. Each of them has trained with me for as many as four years. They've learned the tenets of Elláh and how to help others in

His name. They've proven their worth by taking part in Elláh's miraculous events. And—wonder of wonders—each of them retains the connection to our God that allows them to perform miracles."

The last statement brought enthusiastic applause. Fenet waited it out with a smile.

"So, I ask each of these novim: please come forward and form a line beside me when I call your names: Nov Penilos Humildef..."

Penilos stood with a shy smile and joined Fenet at center stage, "Nov Durnadat Jovamaze ..."

Rotund Durnadat jumped up and spun once, to the laughter of the audience.

Fenet continued with each name, introducing Tenpos, Beneim, Lorefim, and Scanat. The audience followed each name with clapping. Six young men in grey robes, still wearing the yellow collars of novim, formed a beaming line of broad smiles.

When the exuberance died down, Fenet said. "With the power vested in me by the One Church, I hereby advance each of you to the position of minister." To the sound of further crowd approval, he walked down the line to present each man with the pale blue collar of a local sub-leader minister.

At the end of the line, Fenet stopped to face the audience while resting his hand on Scanat's shoulder. When the auditorium quieted again, he spoke. "I want to offer a special recognition to my friend Scanat. He has been with me the longest. He came to me from secondary school in physical sciences, where he had led his class. He's had a most difficult time learning to surrender his own intellect and follow Elláh by faith—yet he has done so."

Scanat blushed, pathing deep embarrassment at the extra attention.

"This young man is special. He is now a minister, but he will also continue as a student. Despite four years away, Scanat has been accepted to return into tertiary to study the challenging field of particle physics."

Applause rang out again.

When it eased, Fenet smiled and made one last statement. "So, my friend Scanat has chosen a most formidable path—to marry his love of science with his calling as a minister. We wish him all success, with Elláh's grace," Fenet stepped to one side and waved a hand at the line, "as we do each of these new ministers."

❧ ❊ ❧

The next couple of hours brought more crowd discomfort for Fenet. People clamored for miraculous healing, which he referred to the Khadam. Many only shook his hand. Others simply wanted to talk with the famous miracle worker. Children cavorted around him. Through all this, he wilted inside the uncomfortable, unfamiliar robes.

Finally, he found an opportunity to relish the blessed quiet in a back room of Fanwell Hall. He shed the robes, leaving them in a heap, exposing his usual loose-legged pants and tunic underneath. Donning his floppy hat and picking up his walking staff, he checked to make sure *The Holiest* rested in its accustomed place in his back pocket. He opened a back door and checked for a clear escape path. Unnoticed, he took to the small streets and alleys to leave the city.

When he cleared the city buildings and moved into familiar farmland, the tension in his body eased. He stopped and felt Elláh's muse come on him, intoning verse to himself in a quiet voice.

> *Roadways long and cities broad*
> *   I sought to find the Lord*
> *Yet everywhere these old bones trod*
> *   They found instead the horde.*
> *People try and people fail*
> *   Conflict fills the soul*
> *I find the truth at end of tale*
> *   The Lord's in cup and bowl.*

Footsteps came up behind him. "Still speaking doggerel, my friend?" said Eregim, his teasing voice filled with warmth.

Fenet answered with his own smile. "It can't be doggerel if it comes from Elláh." He glanced back. "Are you following me, Eregim?"

"I've got someone for you, Fenet. Please meet Waltos. He hasn't yet chosen his powername."

A teenager bounced on his toes in excitement. The boy jerked a quick bow, tousling his brown hair. His eyes sparkled. "I'm honored, Reb Fenet. Truly honored. I can't believe I'm meeting you."

Fenet raised an eyebrow at Eregim, who smile and cocked his head.

Waltos rattled on. "I want to learn from you, Reb Fenet. Will you take me on as a nov?"

Raising his eyes to heaven, Fenet laughed. This kind of task gave him much greater joy than being famous. "I'm willing to try, Waltos. What are you willing to do to join me? Will you walk in my shoes?"

The End

For the Esteemed Reader

If you enjoyed *Verdant Divided*, please tell your friends.

Also help other sci-fi fans discover Doc Honour by writing a review on Amazon. Even just giving it a star rating helps!

Your efforts are especially appreciated. Thank you!

Find out more at DocHonourBooks.com

Subscribe to my newsletter also at the website for:
- Special discounts and giveaways
- Reading new stories before publication
- Upcoming books
- Everyday life of an author

Books by Doc Honour

Empathic Humanity series
Tales of Verdant
Not Like Us
Verdant Divided

Discover the other Doc Honour books on the next pages.

Discover the prequel to the Empathic Humanity series, in short stories that introduce the world of Verdant.

How do you live on a world about to destroy itself? Individual lives are impacted by impending disaster, yet people can find hope and joy even in the worst situations. Fourteen stories from the four countries of Verdant tell a larger tale in the flow from first to last.

Verdant Prime: Alba Castilan searches for peace in a country of totalitarian control, while trying to get a fish processing plant to work. Her search leads her to worse conflicts than she could imagine.

Rathas: In a theocracy, Thoret Speakeach preaches against the rigid One Church from the pulpit of an esteemed congregation. How much leeway will the Church give him?

Tileus: Lisa Westhof is a diplomat trying to stop a war knocking at her door. Her husband Chris wants to join a colony ship to a new planet. She cannot succeed in both; which will she choose?

Winter: Marta Bloom finds a friend in the strange teacher who came from Tileus teaching principles opposed to their tribal life. But her friend sparks a conflict that nearly destroys the village.

Includes the award-winning story "Fishing Hands," first place Gold, 2022 Royal Palm Literary Awards.

Find it on Amazon at _Tales of Verdant_.: Hardcover, Paperback, or Kindle.

The first novel of the Empathic Humanity series, a thrilling escape from authority to develop the technology that can save humanity from itself.

Winner, Best Science Fiction Novel, 2023 Royal Palm Literary Awards

How do you escape totalitarian control? Jake Palatin is forced to develop an antimatter bomb on the planet Verdant, where global war using his technology is terrifyingly close. Zofia, a woman with a secret, tempts him to resist. She also has a solution, a new technology for empathic connection that might save humanity.

Fleeing in desperation, they confront a powerful foe who holds everything in totalitarian control. They must learn to trust each other while facing oppressive police, devious leaders, and a war that could break out at any instant. Danger looms at every step, while love threatens to derail all their plans.

Success is crucial. One mistake, and Verdant will go the way of a dozen other worlds, including old Earth: dead to everything.

Humanity destroys every world it touches, because those other people are "Not Like Us." Jake and Zofia discover the key.

Find it on Amazon at *Not Like Us*.: Hardcover, Paperback, or Kindle.

Acknowledgements

Once again, as with my previous books, I cannot take single credit for this novel. I envisioned it; I laid out the plot line and the characters; my fingers typed it; but much of what is between these covers has been shaped and modified by others who influenced me.

Every chapter went through a two-stage review by my local group, the Advanced Writers' Workshop. In a single week, the chapter got written critiques (and changes) from all members. Then, after revision, I'd read the chapter aloud while they marked up hard copies with further critiques (and changes). The process not only improved the book immensely, but had a great positive impact on my writing as a whole. The members included Keith Abbott (*The Spill*), Kate Bathon, Susan DeLay, Diane Dean, Rich Friedman, Bill Jansen (*When the Owl Speaks, Shadows of the Khyber*), Shelley Jones (*Music, Men, and Madness*), Linda Keenan (*With Love from Poland, The Journal*), Jack O'Brien (*The Roundabout Way, The Last U-Boat*), Jennifer Perkins (*The Ball at the Circus*), Barbara Rein (*Tales of the Eerie Canal*) and Carey Winters. I thank each and every one of them for their many insights. I give special credit to the esteemed Phil Walker, who founded the group and passed away during the writing of this book.

Of those members, I want to single out Jack O'Brien, whose suggestion about combining the transpath and the miracles re-shaped the powerful climax of this book.

In the last year, I've been making great strides in writing technique by being part of "The WulfPack" of acclaimed author and writing coach Wulf Moon (*How to Write a Howling Good Story*). Have to give the man a long howl of thanks!

A heartfelt thanks goes to Detective David Clarkson of the Wildwood, Florida, Police Department, who graciously sat with me to talk about actual detective procedures. Soren Moller appreciates that knowledge, too. And another to my nephew Lt. Scott Honour of the Seminole County, Florida, Fire Department for his help on fire procedures. I used both of their knowledge sets in this book.

With a smile, I note that the character Randy Princeton has a real-life namesake in my friend Randy Purinton, who bought the first copy of each of my books, including this one.

But of course, my greatest gratitude of all goes to my wife Beth, who supported me and put up with all those hours when I was buried in the computer.

Doc Honour
January 2025

About the Author

Iconoclast, polymath, and award-winning author, Doc Honour has been a US Navy pilot, an international leader in systems engineering, and a successful entrepreneur. He holds a PhD from the University of South Australia in systems engineering. Doc has led teams of up to 50 people to build complex systems. He taught nearly 500 short courses to help others learn to do what he has done. Doc Honour's short story "Fishing Hands" won Gold in the 2022 Royal Palm Literary Awards, and his first novel *Not Like Us* took Gold in same contest in 2023. Born on Guam, he's lived in 34 different places. These days, he lives in Florida with his wife, a long-arm quilting machine, and a set of golf clubs.

www.ingramcontent.com/pod-product-compliance
Lightning Source LLC
Chambersburg PA
CBHW020235010826
48973CB00006B/1519